"Kathy Herman's latest series is off to a flying start with *Ever Present Danger.* Be prepared to stay up late as you get to know the people of Phantom Hollow—a place you'll want to visit again and again."

CAROL COX, author of *Ticket to Tomorrow* and *Fair Game*

"*Ever Present Danger* has all the tightly woven drama, excellent characterization, and suspense Kathy Herman's readers have come to love. This newest series digs even more deeply into the heart, leaving a powerful impression of God's forgiveness and His loving direction in each of our lives."

HANNAH ALEXANDER, author of *Grave Risk* and *Death Benefits*

"Kathy Herman writes stories that draw us into the lives of characters that we grow to care more and more about. *Ever Present Danger* is one of Kathy Herman's 'usual' surprising and excellent mysteries."

LYN COTE, author of The Women of Ivy Manor series

"Another wonderful book from Kathy Herman. *Ever Present Danger* is an exciting, breath-holding adventure as only Kathy can write. Tops in this category."

LOIS GLADYS LEPPARD, author of the Mandie books

"*Ever Present Danger* will take you on a wonderful journey from regrets and heartache through unexpected twists and turns of storytelling to a deeply satisfying conclusion filled with redemption and forgiveness. As usual, Kathy Herman mixes sympathetic and admirable characters and unexpected story events to create an engrossing tale. This is a great beginning for what is sure to be a terrific series."

JANELLE CLARE SCHNEIDER, author of "A Distant Love," in the anthology *Christmas Duty*

"Kathy Herman is a master at weaving heart-racing mystery and biblical precept into unforgettable narrative. Not only will the twists and turns in *Ever Present Danger* keep the pages turning, her newest characters will inhabit the soul."

DEIDRE POOL, author of *Loving Jesus Anyway*

"In Kathy Herman's *Ever Present Danger,* a long-concealed murder has deadly consequences and hidden sins must finally be brought to light. The action never stops!"

DEANNA JULIE DODSON, author of *In Honor Bound,* *By Love Redeemed,* and *To Grace Surrendered*

PHANTOM HOLLOW
BOOK ONE

EVER PRESENT
DANGER

KATHY
HERMAN

Multnomah Books

EVER PRESENT DANGER
published by Multnomah Books
a division of Random House, Inc.

Published in association with the literary agency of
Alive Communications, Inc.,
7680 Goddard Street, Suite 200
Colorado Springs, CO 80920
www.alivecommunications.com

© 2007 by Kathy Herman
International Standard Book Number: 1-59052-921-9

Cover design by The DesignWorks Group, Inc.
Cover photos by Getty Images
Interior design and typeset by Pamela McGrew

All scripture quotations are from *The Holy Bible,* New International Version®. NIV®.
Copyright ©1973, 1978, 1984 by International Bible Society.
Used by permission of Zondervan. All rights reserved.

Multnomah is a trademark of Multnomah Publishers, and is registered in the U.S. Patent and Trademark Office. The colophon is a trademark of Multnomah Publishers.

Printed in the United States of America

For information:
MULTNOMAH BOOKS
12265 Oracle Boulevard, Suite 200,
Colorado Springs, CO 80921

Library of Congress Cataloging-in-Publication Data
Herman, Kathy.
Ever present danger / Kathy Herman.
    p. cm. — (Phantom hollow ; bk. 1)
  ISBN 1-59052-921-9
  I. Title.
PS3608.E762E94 2007
813'.6—dc22

                                              2006039126

07 08 09 10 11 12 13 14 — 10 9 8 7 6 5 4 3 2 1

To Him who is both the Giver and the Gift.

ACKNOWLEDGMENTS

THOUGH PHANTOM HOLLOW exists only in my imagination, the rugged, heart-stopping beauty of the San Juan Mountains is reality at its best and offers the perfect backdrop for this series. In the writing of this story, I drew from several resource people, each of whom shared generously from his or her storehouse of knowledge and experience. I did my best to integrate the facts, as I understood them. If accuracy was compromised in any way, it was unintentional and strictly of my own doing.

I'd like to acknowledge my dear friends Danny and Deanna Tyler of Montrose, Colorado, who refreshed my memory about the lifestyle on the western slope, and my friend Allen Burt for suggesting (with a twinkle in his eye) that my husband and I might find it worthwhile to take the scenic drive from Ridgeway to Telluride as part of the "research" for this series. I'm sure we got a glimpse of what heaven will be like.

I owe a special word of thanks to Paul David Houston, former assistant district attorney, Nacogdoches County, Texas, for his valuable input regarding criminal charges and legal issues and for taking the time to read pertinent chapters. Paul, I always thought that someday we'd finally catch up to each other, but I never dreamed I'd also get to meet Nicki and have the chance to hold baby Ben. What a blessing!

A warm thank-you to my friend Will Ray, professional investigator, state of Oregon, for taking time to give his input on forensic evidence, crime scene investigations, autopsies, and background checks. Will, when you ordered the very first copies of *Tested by Fire* from my husband's store, I had no idea what great friends we'd become or how much I would come to appreciate and rely on your various levels of expertise. Thanks for being so willing to take the time to answer my many questions.

I wish to extend my heartfelt thanks to my sister and zealous prayer warrior, Pat Phillips, and my online prayer team—Joanne Lambert; Carolyn Walker; Jackie Jeffries; Sondra Watson; Judith Depontes; my mother, Nora Phillips; and my uncle, Chuck Allenbrand—for your amazing support. How God is using you!

Thanks also to Travis and Rebecca May for a very timely prayer at my kitchen table. And to Susie Killough, Judi Wieghat, Mark and Donna Skorheim, Pearl Anderson, my friends at LifeWay Christian Store in Tyler, Texas, and Donna Ridenour and the ladies in my Bible study class for your many prayers for my writing ministry. It means so much.

To those who read my books and those who sell them, thanks for encouraging me with e-mails and cards and personal testimonies about how God has used my words. He uses you to bless me more often than you know.

To my novelist friends in ChiLibris, thanks for sharing so generously from your collective storehouse of knowledge and experience. It's an honor to be counted among you.

To the staff at Multnomah Publishers, whose commitment to honor God through the power of story has never wavered, it's been a joy linking arms with such dedicated professionals.

To my editor and friend, Rod Morris, I'm so grateful to have been a beneficiary of your decades of experience. Each of my stories has made a deeper, more lasting impression because of the suggestions you made. How I'll miss working with you! There's no doubt in my mind you're going to shine in your new job, but don't ever forget the legacy you've left at Multnomah. I know I won't.

To my husband Paul, who comes home from work eager to hear me read whatever I've written on any given day, how blessed I am that we're partners in this venture—and that your unwavering enthusiasm never lets me forget why I do what I do.

And to my Father in heaven, how I thank You for allowing me the privilege of writing stories that challenge and bless Your people. I pray that the truth of Your Word woven into this story will come to life in the heart of every reader.

PROLOGUE

"Do not be misled: 'Bad company corrupts good character.'"

1 CORINTHIANS 15:33

IVY GRIFFITH STOOD beside her pink and silver snow-mobile, her breath turning to vapor in the late afternoon chill, her gaze set on the giant cottonwood tree that marked the secret grave like a towering headstone. She knew that even after the spring runoff came rushing down the mountain and the Phantom River became like a torrent of baptismal white water lifting the impurities and washing them away, the horrible deed that was done here would not be cleansed. Not then. Not ever.

She blinked to clear her eyes and willed away the emotion, the same unanswerable question running through her mind: What if Joe Hadley wasn't dead when they buried him? What if his heart was still beating and they couldn't hear it—or didn't want to? Never being allowed to know the answer seemed a fitting punishment for a spectator guilty of gross indifference.

She moved closer to the giant cottonwood, the snow crunching under her boots, the ears of her memory alive with the sound of flesh hitting flesh and then Joe struggling to breathe. She wasn't sure why she hadn't tried to stop Pete from choking him, only that she'd been smoking pot spiked with angel dust and nothing seemed real.

Sometimes she obsessed about how horrible it must be for Mr. and Mrs. Hadley to speculate about the ways their son might have died—or if he was still alive and suffering at the hands of some pervert. She had thought about typing a letter and sending it to them anonymously, telling them that Joe was dead and hadn't suffered long. But the fear of what would happen if the letter were traced back to her was greater than her desire to ease their anguish.

Her heart felt blacker than the blackest night, as if the light inside her had gone out. If only she had never met Pete Barton! It was bad enough that she had given away her virginity and had experimented with drugs, but it felt as though she had sold her soul when she made a pact with Pete and the others never to speak of Joe's demise.

That agreement stood between her and God, but it was the only thing keeping her and Pete together. He kept reminding her over and over that she was an accessory to the killing and that telling the police would ruin not only her life and his, but also her parents'. Then she'd have no one, except the inmates at some dank and dreary women's prison.

A noise broke the stillness, and Ivy realized a car was coming. She turned around, her pulse racing, and saw a white Jeep Cherokee outfitted with chains moving in her direction on the snow-packed road. She forced a friendly smile and waved at the driver, relieved when he nodded and drove past. She stood frozen until the Jeep's taillights disappeared over the hill and the only sound was the wind whistling through the bare aspens.

Why was she so skittish? It's not as though her being seen out here would raise suspicion. As far as anyone was concerned, she was just Elam and Carolyn's daughter out for a ride on her snowmobile.

She turned back around, her eyes drawn like a magnet to the secret grave, and wondered for the umpteenth time how different things might have been had she simply shouted at the boys to stop hitting Joe before it went too far.

Ivy breathed in slowly and then let it out. In a few months, she and Pete and the others would be parting ways and going off to college, beginning a new chapter in their lives and leaving that gray January afternoon on the pages of the past.

She walked back to the snowmobile, her burden heavier than when she came, thinking Joe Hadley was the lucky one. At least his suffering was over.

1

BRANDON JONES STOOD at the scenic overlook on
Tanner's Ridge, his gloved hands wrapped around a cup of hot
coffee, his eyes drinking in the jagged San Juan Mountains that
rose high above the valley floor and surrounded Phantom Hollow
like a pure white fortress.

Directly below he spotted the log buildings at Three Peaks
Christian Camp and Conference Center. "Honey, look. There's
our house. To the right of the dining hall. See it?"

Kelsey Jones nodded. "Looks small from up here."

"It still hasn't hit me that I'm camp director and actually get
paid to do what I love doing—*plus* have access to all this natural
beauty. There's no way we'd be here if you hadn't gone to college
with Jake Compton."

"It never hurts to have a connection, but Jake hired you
because you're exactly what he was looking for in spite of the fact
that he considered *me* a ball and chain."

"Oh, come on, Kel. He never said that."

"No, but Jake never thought I would adjust to the idiosyn-
crasies of a small town. I don't deny that moving here was a culture
shock after Raleigh, but now I *love* living in Jacob's Ear…What are
you grinning about?"

"Jacob's Ear sounds more like an ailment than a town."
Brandon rested his elbows on the railing and looked out beyond

the camp at the mining town-turned-tourist attraction that still bore the distinctive character of the gold rush days. "Too bad they didn't give it a name like Gold Town or Jacob's Mine."

"Oh, I think Jacob's Ear is much more intriguing. Besides, the tourists get a kick out of the legend."

"Which the chamber of commerce is more than happy to capitalize on."

"And why not? Maybe the widow Thompson really did find Jacob Tanner's ear on the back porch—not that I believe some nineteenth-century Bigfoot came out of the woods and devoured him. But a little folklore is more intriguing than saying a bear got him."

Brandon nudged her with his elbow. "And you don't think naming a town after a body part is weird?"

"They didn't exactly *name* it that. It just sort of…stuck." Kelsey smiled and then burst into laughter. "Okay, it's weird. Unique, but definitely weird."

"And hard to say with a straight face."

"At least we'll be smiling a lot."

Brandon put his arm around her and pulled her close. "I've already got plenty to smile about, Mrs. Jones. The four months since we got married have been the happiest of my life. And living here in Colorado…well, it's just a blessing on top of a blessing."

"It's wonderful seeing you excited about your job, and I'm hooked on the mountains. I could spend all day up here."

"Me, too, but not if I'm going to get started on those changes to the Three Peaks website. Since you're not scheduled to work today, why don't you meet me for lunch at the dining hall?"

"I'd love to, but I doubt I'll be back from town in time."

Brandon put his hand on his heart. "I'm crushed. What could be more important than a romantic buffet lunch with your husband and seventy-five conference attendees?"

Kelsey laughed. "How about if I make us a romantic dinner for two? I need to run errands and get the grocery shopping done before we get all that spring snow they're predicting tonight. And if I'm going to be snowbound, I want to have everything I need to do some baking."

"I have a feeling I'm not going to get all these homemade goodies when summer rolls around."

Kelsey poked his chest with her finger. "According to Jake, you're going to be too busy to care. I'd better spoil you now while I have the chance."

Carolyn Griffith put the last of the breakfast dishes in the dishwasher and turned it on just as the phone rang.

"Hello."

"Mom, don't faint…it's me."

Carolyn gripped the phone with one hand and groped behind her for the kitchen chair and eased into it.

"Is this is a bad time?" Ivy Griffith said.

"No, I—I just wasn't expecting it to be you." *I don't even recognize your voice. You sound so grown-up.* "How are you?"

"Okay. How's Rusty? Did he ever marry Jacqueline?"

"Yes, they're living in Albuquerque and have two little girls. Tia's three and Josie's two. Rusty just started his own veterinary practice."

"That's really great. How are you and Dad?"

Feeling much older than we are. "We miss you, Ivy."

There was a long, agonizing stretch of dead air. Carolyn wondered why, after all the years of longing to talk to her daughter, she couldn't think of anything to say.

"I miss you, too…" Ivy's voice cracked, and she paused for several seconds. "Do you think maybe I could…come home?"

"You mean to *stay?*"

"If you don't want to see me, just say so. I'll understand."

"No, it's okay! We definitely want to see you. Just give me a minute to let my heart catch up. This is so unexpected."

"I know, and I'm sorry for calling out of the blue like this, but I just lost another roommate. Denver's too expensive. I need to live someplace where I don't have to rely on another person for half the rent."

Carolyn wondered if the roommate Ivy had lost was her boyfriend but decided not to ask.

"Actually, Mom, it's more than that. I just need to be with family. I can't make up for all the years I stayed away, but I want to make things right."

"When do you want to come?"

"I have friends who're going skiing at Purgatory day after tomorrow. We can hitch a ride with them."

We? Carolyn felt the muscles tighten in her shoulders. "Someone's coming with you?"

"Would it be okay? Just till I find a job and get my own place?"

"Ivy, your father and I would welcome your coming home. But we need you to be up-front with us about what's going on. No more secrets. No more game playing."

"I'll be bringing a very nice lady named Lucia. And a little boy named Montana."

"Are they hiding from someone?"

"No. They're the only family I've had for a long time."

"I see. Is Lucia your partner? Are you…?"

"Mom, she's seventy years old. It's not like that. I just want you to meet her."

"Is the little boy her grandson?"

"Not exactly."

Carolyn sighed. "Ivy, please. For once in your life, just say what you mean."

"Montana's mine…he's my son."

Brandon Jones brushed the snow off his down jacket and stomped his feet on the mat, then went inside the dining hall of Three Peaks Christian Camp and Conference Center and spotted Jake Compton at a table by the windows.

"Thanks for meeting me for lunch," Jake said. "How're the website changes coming?"

"Great. I should be done before the weekend." Brandon laid his coat across the back of a chair and sat at the table. "So what's up?"

"Ivy Griffith is coming home Saturday."

Brandon stared at Jake for a few moments and let the words sink in. "How do you know?"

"Carolyn stopped by the administrative office this morning and told me. She asked me to fill everyone in."

Brandon threw back his head and felt a smile stretch his cheeks. "Praise God! We shouldn't be surprised. That's what the staff's been praying for."

"Well, there's another huge surprise: Ivy's got a seven-year-old son."

"Whoa. Carolyn and Elam never mentioned him."

Jake's eyes grew wide. "Because they didn't know. They're not sure what to expect either. Ivy's been in and out of drug rehab, but swears she was clean during the pregnancy. She says a lady named Lucia has helped her with the boy all these years. Apparently Lucia's coming, too."

Brandon looked out the window and spotted the Griffiths' log house at the base of the mountain covered in a blanket of new snow. "So Ivy, her son, and this woman are all going to stay at Carolyn and Elam's?"

"I got that impression. They've got a ton of room."

"Is Ivy moving here?"

"Carolyn says Ivy rarely gives her a straight answer but mentioned she wants to find her own place."

"So is Ivy supporting her son and this woman?"

"I guess so. Carolyn won't say it, but she has to be afraid that she and Elam will end up supporting all three of them. Most jobs in Jacob's Ear are seasonal."

"I doubt money's an issue, Jake. Elam's made more dollars on his real estate investments than there are people in the state."

"That's true. I suppose if Ivy started to infringe on their space, he and Carolyn could buy her a house of her own."

Brandon glanced out the window again at the Griffiths' house and noticed smoke snaking out of the chimney. "Maybe all she really wants is to come home to the familiar—you know, find her roots again."

"Then she's going to be sorely disappointed."

"Why do you say that?"

"For one thing, Three Peaks is sitting on the open range where she and her brother used to ride horses. This land was the Griffiths' homestead, and ten years ago their house was the only thing out here."

"I didn't know that. So the camp property belonged to them?"

Jake nodded. "Still does. This and half of Tanner County. After their son Rusty was out on his own, they decided to invest money in a camp and conference center and had it built just a couple hundred yards from their house. The Griffiths wanted a sense of community and liked the ministry aspect. But they never had the desire to be involved in the day-to-day operation, which is why they hired me to be the administrator. Ivy doesn't know any of this."

"Maybe it won't matter that much to her. At least the house is still there. Do you know if Elam and Carolyn ever heard from her during the years she was gone?"

"A few times. I know that when she dropped out of college they arranged for her to go through drug rehab—and then again several years ago. But she's never been back to Jacob's Ear since she left for college."

Brandon turned his eyes on the embers in the huge rock fireplace that made up one wall of the dining hall. "Can you imagine dropping out of your family at eighteen and showing up again at twenty-eight?"

"Not really. But I've seen firsthand how deeply Ivy's absence has affected Elam and Carolyn. I'm sure they're glad she's coming home. But they've also stuffed a lot of hurt and anger over the years. At some point, all that's going to have to be dealt with."

"Well, I know one thing: They can count on the support of the staff here."

"Definitely." Jake pushed back his chair. "Okay, you're up to speed. Let's go get in that buffet line while the food's still hot."

2

CAROLYN GRIFFITH WALKED into the family room and set a mug of hot tea on the coffee table, aware that her husband had been staring out the picture window for over an hour.

"We're supposed to get another four inches of snow before midnight," she said. "But it's supposed to be sunny tomorrow and there's no more snow in the forecast, so the roads should be clear on Saturday when Ivy arrives."

"Ah, yes, with her *family*." Elam Griffith picked up the mug and took a sip of tea.

Carolyn sat on the sofa, her arm linked in his, her gaze set on the row of icicles along the eaves.

"Why don't I feel excited to see my own daughter?" Elam said.

"You're probably as terrified as I am. We don't really know Ivy anymore. I'm not even sure what to talk about."

"I wonder if she's even told Montana he's coming here to see his grandparents."

"I'm sure she has. Ivy knows we'd never go along with keeping it from him. It's hard to believe the child's lived in Denver all his life and has never been up in the mountains. Coming here should be quite an adventure."

"I'll ask Brandon to take him snowmobiling and sledding and maybe cross-country skiing. It's been a long time since I've entertained a kid."

Carolyn squeezed his arm. "Or we could just take him ice skating in the park and let him meet some of the local kids. I don't think Ivy's expecting us to entertain him."

"Good, I've got a lot going on. We're ready to bulldoze the south end of Collier Ranch and get it ready for the condominium project."

"With a foot of snow on the ground?"

"The snow won't last long. The sun's supposed to shine every day next week. We need to push hard if we want phase one completed before summer."

Carolyn glanced over at Elam and then out the window at the whirling mass of white. "You know Ivy isn't going to find a job in Jacob's Ear that will pay her enough to support herself, let alone Montana and Lucia. We need to decide before they get here what we're willing to do and not do."

Elam set the mug on the coffee table. "One thing I'm not willing to do is be manipulated. The only reason she's coming back is she can't make ends meet. If she'd finished college instead of shooting up, maybe she'd have some options."

"It's not just about Ivy anymore. We have a grandson to consider."

"She'll just use him to get what she wants."

"But why now? Why not seven years ago?" Carolyn spotted Ivy's Student Bible in the bookshelf next to the fireplace. "We prayed she'd come home, Elam. We need to trust the Lord's timing."

"I always thought she'd change first."

"Maybe she has. We haven't even eyeballed the poor girl and already you've decided what's in her heart."

Elam sighed and looked over at Carolyn. "Ivy's been consistently disappointing for ten years. I don't trust her to be straightforward about anything."

"This has nothing to do with her being straightforward. We know the job situation here, and she can't make enough to live on."

"There's nothing I can do about that."

"Yes, there is." Carolyn lifted her eyebrows. "You could *create* a job for Ivy and make sure she draws enough to cover her expenses. That way she could make it on her own and preserve her dignity."

"You think she's worried about dignity? This is the same girl who sold herself to support a drug habit."

"I'm well aware of what she did!" Carolyn jumped up off the sofa and stood facing the fire. Finally she spun around, her hands moving faster than her mouth. "Elam Griffith, you listen to me! We have to treat this situation with Ivy like a whole new day and leave the past behind us. The worst thing we can do is guilt that girl over mistakes she can't do a thing about now! She wants to come home. She's taken the first step. The least we can do is meet her halfway without dooming her to failure."

Ivy Griffith walked out of Elmer's Market holding a sack containing a can of tuna, three potatoes, and a can of cream of celery soup.

"I'll carry that, Mom." Montana Griffith took the sack from her hands and tucked it under his arm.

"Does this mean you forgive me for making you move again?" Ivy said.

"I guess so. Are your parents happy we're coming to their house?"

Ivy nodded. "And a little nervous, I'm sure."

"Gramma Lu's coming, too, right?"

"Of course."

Montana looked up at her and smiled, his lips cracked and starting to bleed again.

Ivy handed him the tube of lip balm she had slipped into her pocket while the checker rang up her purchase. "Use it sparingly. It has to last us awhile."

She reached over and pulled Montana's neck scarf up around his ears, a brisk north wind stinging her hands.

"Are we having that tuna stuff on potatoes for dinner again?" Montana asked.

"Yes, but when we get to Jacob's Ear, my mother will fix us delicious meals. She's a wonderful cook."

"And they have lots of money, right?"

"A lot more than we have."

"Do I have to call them Grandmother and Grandfather?"

"Why don't we wait and see what feels right, okay? The most important thing is that you remember to be polite." Ivy brushed his cheek with the back of her hand.

"What if they don't like me?"

"They will."

"Maybe not. They didn't like *you.*"

"Nobody liked me when I was high."

Montana slipped his hand in hers. "Gramma Lu did."

Ivy blinked quickly to keep her eyes from clouding over. "Gramma Lu is special."

"Why does she have to leave us?"

"She doesn't want to leave, sweetie. She doesn't have a choice. But she'll be with us for a while yet."

"Where is she going?"

"A long, long way from Denver."

"Farther than Pike's Peak?"

"Yes."

"Farther than the ocean?"

"Uh-huh."

Montana looked up at her, his dark eyes wide, his expression guileless. "Farther than...the *moon?*"

"Much."

"Man! How many days will it take Gramma Lu to get there?"

As many days as she has left. Ivy walked a little faster. "How about for now we just concentrate on getting to Jacob's Ear?"

3

On Saturday morning, Brandon Jones held open the door of Jewel's Café and waited for Kelsey to squeeze past him. He stomped the snow off his hiking boots and stepped inside on the creaky wood floor, the distinct aromas of fried bacon and freshly brewed coffee wafting under his nose.

"Well, if it isn't the Carolina kids," Jewel Sadler announced. "So what do you think of spring on the western slope?"

Brandon smiled and slid his arm around Kelsey. "Suits us just fine. The sky's bluer than blue, the snow's dazzling, and the mountain air's invigorating. What more could we ask for—except a cup of hot coffee and the Hungry Man Special?"

"Cheese blintzes would do it for me," Kelsey said.

Jewel laughed and wiped her hands on her apron, her white hair flat under her hairnet. "I knew that. Comin' right up. Your friends are over there." She motioned toward Buzz and Maggie Easton, who sat at the table closest to the mounted moose head. "I just put a fresh pot of coffee on the table."

Kelsey walked up to the Eastons, who were already eating. "Sorry we're late, but we—"

"Hey, sugar, no explanation needed. You're newlyweds." Buzz stuffed the last bite of a biscuit into his smug grin and moved his eyebrows up and down. "We all know how it is. First things first, right?"

Brandon was sure Maggie kicked Buzz under the table and

could almost feel the heat emanating from Kelsey's face as several other customers turned and looked at them.

"Actually, we got an important phone call just as we were walking out the door," Brandon said.

"Sure you did." Buzz flashed Brandon a toothy grin and winked.

"I'm serious. Kelsey and I are not in the habit of keeping friends waiting. But my brother and his wife called to say they've started the process to adopt a little girl in China, and they were so pumped we didn't have the heart to cut the conversation short. We tried to call Jewel's to tell you we were on the way, but the signal kept cutting out."

"If you say so," Buzz said, louder than he needed to, "but why are your faces redder than my Tabasco sauce?"

Maggie pushed her shoulder against Buzz's. "You'll have to excuse my husband. I guess prolonged exposure to the altitude has rendered him completely tactless. We went ahead and ordered because we thought we'd gotten our wires crossed."

"Well, don't let your breakfast get cold," Brandon said. "We'll just have coffee till ours gets here." He sat at the table and filled Kelsey's cup and then his own, sensing her annoyance and eager to change the subject. "So, Buzz. How much longer will you be working as a ski instructor?"

"At least through April, depending on the snowfall. Then I'll get my white-water rafting business ready. Of course once it's in full swing, it'll mean working sunup to sundown seven days a week, and I'll hardly see Maggie until September."

"Even God rested on the seventh day." Brandon blew on his coffee. "You're liable to burn out if you don't recharge your batteries."

"Well, I haven't yet and I've been doing this a long time."

"It really works out fine," Maggie said. "Summer's huge here in the real estate business, and there are hardly enough hours in a day. I'll earn 90 percent of my commissions in June, July, and August."

"Are you able to slow down in the off months?" Kelsey said.

"I am. But Buzz works a second job during ski season so he

puts in long hours year round. We're willing to make sacrifices to live in this part of the state."

Brandon wondered what was so great about living here if they never got to see each other.

"So how's it going at the camp?" Buzz took a bite of what appeared to be a Spanish omelet.

"We just finished recruiting counselors and are gearing up for a busy summer. I'm pretty pumped."

Maggie looked at Kelsey. "What're you going to do?"

"I've got plenty to do at home," Kelsey said. "And don't forget I work at the administrative office two days a week."

"But how do you deal with all that downtime? I'd go nuts."

"I wouldn't exactly call it *down*time. I enjoy cooking, baking, and quilting. I do my own housework. I handle the bills. I'm in a ladies' Bible study. I volunteer in the nursery at church. And I love to sew."

"Yeah, and you should see the stuff she sews," Brandon said. "Curtains. Drapes. Pillows. You name it. The log house we're living in is one of the perks they give the camp director, and Kelsey's added all the right touches that make it feel like ours." Brandon smiled. "Plus she makes quilts and sells them."

"I envy her," Maggie said. "I get really bored staying home."

Brandon was aware that Carolyn and Elam Griffith had come in and sat at the table near the front window.

"I heard their daughter's coming home today," Buzz said.

"Did you know Ivy?" Kelsey asked.

"Not in the biblical sense, though I was certainly open to it." Buzz laughed when Maggie poked him with her elbow. "Actually, I did odd jobs for her folks way back when and used to see her around. Drop-dead gorgeous. Too bad she turned out to be a crackhead."

"Where'd you hear that?" Kelsey asked.

Maggie spoke softly. "Everyone knows Ivy dropped out of college and was in and out of drug rehab. It's hard to keep a secret in this town."

———

Carolyn Griffith picked at her French toast and wondered why she had suggested to Elam they go out for breakfast. She heard familiar voices and looked up and saw Brandon and Kelsey paying their bill at the register and talking to Jewel Sadler.

"Elam, the Joneses will be coming this way any second. Will you at least try to appear positive?"

"This place is Grand Central Station," he mumbled. "We should've just stayed home."

"Hi, you two!" Kelsey came over to the table, Brandon on her heels, and hugged Carolyn and then Elam. "We're so excited for you. What time are Ivy and Montana supposed to get here?"

"They were planning to leave Denver at six this morning," Carolyn said. "We figure they could be here as early as two, depending on how many stops they make."

"We can hardly wait to meet them," Brandon said.

Elam nodded and didn't say anything.

"As soon as the dust settles," Carolyn said, "we'll have you and the Comptons over for dinner. Might take awhile for our emotions to catch up with everything."

Brandon put one hand on Elam's shoulder and the other on Carolyn's. "Well, if you guys need some time with Ivy, Montana's welcome to hang out with us. There's plenty to do here at the camp, and I'm not recruiting this week so I'll be around."

"Thanks," Elam said. "Just might take you up on your offer."

Carolyn watched Brandon and Kelsey walk out of Jewel's Café just as Pete Barton walked in. She looked down to avoid eye contact, but a few seconds later he was standing at their table.

"I saw your Suburban parked out front," Pete said. "Did I hear right: Is Ivy coming home today?"

"You heard right." Carolyn decided not to offer Pete details and suddenly wished he'd stayed in Alaska instead of coming home to run the family deli after his father died.

"Is she visiting or actually moving back?" Pete said.

Elam stared at his coffee mug. "You mean the gossip mill didn't know?"

"I don't mean to pry, Mr. Griffith. I just don't want to miss seeing her. I've thought about her a lot in the past ten years."

"Ivy's exploring options," Carolyn said. "We'll be sure to tell her you were asking about her. Say hello to your mother."

"Thanks. I will."

Carolyn was aware of Elam's foot tapping as she watched Pete leave the café and walk across the street toward Barton's Deli.

"I don't want him around Ivy," Elam said. "The whole time they were going together she was depressed. I know he talked her into sleeping with him and smoking pot and heaven knows what else."

"Ivy wasn't the first young girl to compromise her values in order to hang on to her boyfriend. She wasn't an innocent bystander, Elam. She had a choice."

"But he corrupted her. He caused her to turn away from God—and everything good and decent we raised her to believe. I'll never forgive him for that. And I'm not going to sit back and let him smooth talk her again. Ivy's easily swayed and the last thing she needs is to get involved with a freewheeling playboy who spends his leisure adding notches to his bedpost and playing blackjack at the Indian reservation."

"I agree we should discourage her from pursuing any kind of relationship with him. But we also have to start trusting the Lord and stop blaming Pete Barton for everything that's wrong with her."

Elam gulped the last of the coffee, pushed back his chair, and picked up the check. "Well, I'll tell you one thing: It feels a lot better than blaming myself."

Ivy Griffith sat in the middle seat of her friend's Ford Expedition, wondering if the handful of dry Cheerios she'd just eaten was going to stay down.

"How much longer?" Montana Griffith said.

Ivy smiled. "What time does my watch say?"

"Fifteen after eleven."

"When it's one o'clock, ask me again." Ivy turned to Lucia Ramirez and noticed her eyes were closed. "Lu, are you asleep or resting your eyes?"

"Just resting my eyes. And thinking I must be loco for letting you talk me into this. You should have left me in Denver. My grandson would have come for me."

Not unless he smelled money. "And if he didn't? What would you have done then?"

Lu patted Ivy's hand and didn't say anything.

"Gramma Lu, you have to stay with us," Montana said. "What if Grandmother Griffith doesn't know how to make tortillas and frijoles?"

"Then maybe you would get a better diet, no?"

Montana leaned forward and turned toward Lu, a grin on his face. "I *love* frijoles. Mom says we'll have beef and chicken a lot now, too. I hope we have fried chicken and mashed potatoes. I could eat that every single day. I would never *ever* get tired of it. And I could have *seconds* of grilled cheese sandwiches, and apples any time I want, and orange juice and chocolate milk…"

Ivy smiled at the sound of Montana verbalizing his food cravings and tried not to let her guilt ruin the moment.

Despite what her parents might think of her, she couldn't imagine they wouldn't grow to love this little boy who looked enough like her brother Rusty that they might forget he was illegitimate. Yet the thought of missing part of Montana's life was almost more pain than she could bear. Would he ever understand that the only way she could ever feel alive again was to step back into the past and allow the truth to be uncovered—even if it meant going to prison? She was suddenly aware that Lu's gaze was fixed on her.

"Are you getting cold feet, Ivy girl?"

Ivy managed a weak smile. "I've always had cold feet. I was just thinking that this would be much easier if my heart were cold, too."

4

CAROLYN GRIFFITH STOOD at her bedroom window, her hands tucked in her sweater pockets, her eyes feasting on the jagged peaks of the San Juan Mountains that appeared almost ghostly under a thick blanket of spring snow. Just beyond the split rail fence, the afternoon sun spotlighted the red tail of a hawk as it swooped down on the open range and then flew into the woods, its prey clutched in its talons. The Westminster chimes of the grandfather clock announced it was half past two.

Lord, be with us in the midst of our fears and our hurts and all the unresolved issues. Help us just to love Ivy—and Montana.

Elam's voice resonated from the bottom of the stairs and startled her. "A car just turned off Three Peaks Road and is headed this way."

It took Carolyn only a second to spot a white SUV coming up the steep, snowplowed drive.

She ran downstairs and out to the front porch and stood next to Elam, feeling as though her heart would pound out of her chest. She waved even though she didn't recognize the two people in the front seat and couldn't see through the tinted windows on the side.

The Ford Expedition pulled up in the circle drive and stopped. For several agonizing seconds nothing happened, and then the passenger door opened. A skinny little boy climbed out, his auburn hair thick and straight, his smile tentative.

Montana! Carolyn felt an unexpected twinge of affection.

The boy turned and reached for a woman's hand and helped her out. She was short and thickset, hair dark as coal and streaked with white.

So that's Lucia.

As Carolyn hurried down the porch steps, Elam on her heels, her gaze set on the third passenger climbing out of the backseat.

"Ivy?" Carolyn stopped, unsure if she had said the name or merely breathed it.

Her daughter looked two decades older and thirty pounds thinner. Her face was pale and gaunt, her lips cracked. Her hair, which once fell past her shoulders in shiny blond tresses, had been cropped and appeared as dull and lifeless as broom bristles. Carolyn was thinking that if she had run into this person on the street, she wouldn't have known it was her daughter.

Ivy's gray eyes had the look of a frightened animal and moved from Carolyn to Elam and then back to Carolyn, as if to ask whether she was still welcome or if they'd had second thoughts.

Carolyn opened her arms, and Ivy ambled into her mother's embrace, neither of them saying anything. In the next second, Elam's hands were caressing Ivy's back, and he seemed as unable to talk as they were. Carolyn wasn't sure how much time passed before she realized a young man was talking.

"Hey, I'm done unloading your bags," he said. "Unless you need me to do something else, we're gonna head on to Purgatory, okay?"

Carolyn let go of Ivy and noticed a young man in a red ski jacket standing next to the driver's door.

"Thanks, Rocco," Ivy said. "I can't thank you enough for everything you've done."

"No problem. Be happy, okay?" He nodded at Carolyn and Elam, then got in the car and drove to the end of the circle drive and back down the driveway.

Carolyn didn't ask why Ivy hadn't introduced them. She felt a tug on the bottom of her sweater and looked down into a pair of puppy eyes that looked remarkably like Rusty's.

"You must be Montana."

The boy nodded and flashed an elfin smile, minus a few teeth. "Yes, ma'am. And this is my Gramma Lu."

The woman extended her hand. "I'm Lucia Ramirez. I go by Lu."

Ivy shook her head and apologized for being so absentminded and finally made the introductions.

"What should I call you?" Montana said to his grandparents.

Carolyn brushed the hair out of his eyes. "What would you like to call us?"

"Well, since—"

"I'd better get the suitcases into the house." Elam walked over and picked up two tattered duffle bags and headed for the porch steps.

"I can help," Montana said.

"Suit yourself." Elam went up the steps and into the house.

Carolyn hoped her face didn't give away her irritation. "Montana, why don't you get a couple of the smaller bags and follow me."

"I'm *very* strong," he said. "Mom lets me carry the groceries all the time."

Carolyn heard barking and looked up and saw Sasha racing full throttle up the snowy slope, her tail wagging, a cloud of white powder kicking up behind her. "Oh, no. I hope you like dogs."

Two seconds later, the Siberian Husky's front paws collided with Montana's shoulders and knocked him on his behind, the dog's tongue swiping his face.

"Don't be afraid, sweetie—she doesn't bite!" Carolyn exclaimed. "Sasha, back! Get back!"

The dog ran in circles, then sat in the snow and yelped, her eyes on Montana, her body posed to pounce.

"She's rambunctious but she just wants to play," Carolyn said. "You're not hurt, are you?"

"Nope." Montana sprang to his feet and brushed the snow off his jeans, then clapped his hands. "Come here, girl. Come here."

Sasha bounded forward and then backwards, barking all the while, her tail swishing from side to side.

Montana laughed. "I think she likes me."

"I thought you were bringing in those bags, boy." Elam stood in the doorway, his arms folded.

"Oh, yeah." Montana picked up the two largest bags and walked penguin-like over to the steps and up on the porch and went inside.

Ivy picked up the last bag and two sacks of clothes. "You go first, Lu. I'm right behind you."

Carolyn followed them up on the porch and glared at Elam as she squeezed past him.

"What was that for?" he said.

Carolyn didn't say anything, certain that Elam already knew the answer.

Brandon Jones walked in the living room and saw Kelsey curled up on the couch, reading a novel. "You've been pouting all day. Are you still mad about Buzz's comment at breakfast?"

"What do you think?" Kelsey Jones turned the page.

"I think it was inappropriate, but that's just Buzz. He didn't mean anything by it."

"Yes, he did. And everyone who overheard his tacky comment knew *exactly* what he was getting at. There's no excuse for him embarrassing us that way."

"No one takes Buzz seriously."

Kelsey sighed. "That's beside the point. Why didn't you just tell him to knock it off?"

"I thought it was more important to explain the real reason we were late, especially with so many ears around."

"Well, after Buzz's smarty remark about our faces being as red as the Tabasco sauce, I'm sure everyone thinks you made up the whole story about getting a phone call on our way out the door."

Brandon flopped on the couch next to her. "Sorry. I didn't think it was that big a deal."

"Maybe it wouldn't have been if it were just a one-time comment, but Buzz deliberately makes me blush every time we're around him. And that off-color remark he made about Ivy was uncalled for. I just wanted to slap him. I've never appreciated his innuendos or his off-color jokes or the way he tries to make me feel like a prude because I don't laugh at his locker-room humor. I put up with it only because he and Maggie were so nice to us when we first moved here. But I've had it. His comment today was just too personal and too public."

"Come on, Kel, you're overreacting."

"I don't want to be around Buzz anymore." She turned the page on her book and didn't look at him.

"You'd seriously drop the Eastons just because Buzz is a big tease?"

"No, because Buzz is a big jerk."

Brandon reached over and took the book from Kelsey's hand. "Okay, honey. We don't have to hang out with the Eastons as a couple. Buzz and I can do our own thing."

"I just don't get why you put up with him."

"You kidding? He's my free ticket to shooting the rapids. I've always thrived on adventure. You know that."

"There's plenty to do right here at the camp. How much adventure do you need?"

Brandon tugged playfully at her sleeve. "Oh, I don't know. I still haven't jumped out of an airplane, gone hang gliding, or tried to climb Mt. Everest. I haven't been scuba diving or bungee jumping. I've never hunted for bear. Raced the Indy 500 or the Iditarod. I've never applied for a job as a stuntman or gone out for rugby, or—"

"Okay, okay, I get the point." Kelsey smiled and leaned her head on the back of the couch, then turned to him, her sleek, dark hair draping her shoulders. "I suppose I should be glad you have a guy friend to do the rough stuff with since I'm never going to enjoy it."

"But there're plenty of things you and I do together that are great fun. I love being with you. And for those occasional times when I need an outlet for this wild and crazy streak of mine, there's Buzz."

"Well, at least he's good for something."

Brandon moved over next to Kelsey and put his arm around her. "What do you say we go take a ride on the snowmobiles?"

"Now?"

"Yeah. I thought we could ride up to the Griffiths' house and see if Ivy and Montana made it in."

Ivy Griffith sat at the kitchen table, her hands wrapped around a mug of hot cocoa, keenly aware that her father seemed to have disappeared after depositing their suitcases outside the guest rooms in the upstairs hallway.

"Montana and Sasha are getting along famously," Carolyn said, nodding toward the window.

Ivy looked outside, hit with a sense of déjà vu as she saw her son riding a sled down the same steep hill she and Rusty had favored when they were kids, Sasha romping alongside, yelping playfully.

"Mom, whatever happened to Zeke?"

"That old pooch lived to be sixteen, and then one morning his heart just stopped. Nearly killed Rusty when he couldn't rouse him."

"Montana's never had a dog. None of the places we lived would allow pets without a huge deposit." *Plus I couldn't afford another mouth to feed.*

"Well, Sasha has more energy than your father and I ever imagined when we bought her. She loves to roam but never stays gone long. She seems to need a lot of company and affection. Montana will be good for her. How's the hot cocoa?"

Ivy nodded. "Good. Thanks."

"Does it seem strange being back in your old bedroom?"

"Yeah, kind of. But I like the room yellow, and the patchwork quilt you have on the bed really looks nice."

"Thanks. I bought it from Kelsey Jones. She's about your age and married to our camp director. I'll introduce you."

Ivy looked out at the log buildings nestled among the trees a couple hundred yards down the hill. "It never occurred to me you and Dad would sell off the property."

"We didn't. We own the land *and* the facilities," Carolyn said. "But after Rusty left home, we felt pretty isolated out here. So your dad got the idea to invest in building a camp and conference center. It's been a wonderful way for us to stay plugged in somewhere without having to be involved in the day-to-day operation. Plus it's been a real boost to the town's economy, and we've met some of the most interesting people from all over the world."

"Don't you ever miss looking out and seeing only land and mountains?"

"The camp doesn't obstruct our view of the mountains in the slightest, and we have enough privacy. I can't wait to show you what a beautiful facility it is."

Ivy didn't care if it looked like the Taj Mahal. Its presence was intrusive—and a stumbling block to preserving the memories of her childhood.

"You look upset," Carolyn said.

"Not really. It was pretty dumb of me to think nothing had changed in ten years."

"A lot has changed in Tanner County, and especially Jacob's Ear. You're going to be amazed at the volume of tourists."

"Is Jewel's Café still in business?"

"Uh-huh. Your father and I ate breakfast there just this morning. Jewel Sadler still runs it. She's getting old, but I don't think the café has changed at all since you left."

Ivy smiled. "Is that dreadful moose head still hanging on the wall?"

"Unfortunately." Carolyn took a sip of cocoa. "Honey, do you think you should go check on Lu? If she sleeps much longer she may not sleep tonight."

"Don't worry. Lu can always sleep."

Carolyn moved her spoon slowly back and forth in her cup. "You haven't told me much about her."

"Lu lived in the apartment next to mine and knew I was spaced out on drugs and half the time didn't even know Montana was there. She'd come get him and take care of him at her place. We've been through a lot together. Would it be okay if we don't get into that right now?"

"All right."

"So why is Dad avoiding me?"

"Avoiding is a strong word. I think he's cautious about opening his heart too quickly. Your absence has been devastating to him."

"I get that. But he was abrupt with Montana, don't you think?"

"I do. But again, he's cautious about getting hurt again. Give him time."

"Maybe it was a mistake coming home."

Carolyn glanced up, her gaze colliding with Ivy's. "Not if you're serious about wanting to make things right. We love you. And there's nothing we want more than to see you happy."

"I know. I don't think until I had Montana that I understood how much parents love their kids."

"It's pretty amazing, all right."

Ivy glanced at the calendar that was stuck to the refrigerator with a magnet. "I guess I'll need to get Montana enrolled in school Monday."

"Not next week," Carolyn said. "It's spring break."

The doorbell rang.

A few seconds later Elam appeared in the kitchen doorway. "Brandon and Kelsey are here. They already met Montana outside and wondered if they could say hello to Ivy. They can only stay a minute."

5

On Monday morning, Ivy Griffith sat at the breakfast table with Montana, Lu, and her parents. Her father had hardly spoken to her, and his indifference hurt almost as much as the reason for it.

"Would anybody like another waffle?" Carolyn Griffith said.

"Yes, please." Montana held up his plate and flashed a charming grin. "Do you have more strawberries?"

"Just waiting for you. I love a young man with a hearty appetite." Carolyn got up and walked over to the griddle.

"So, Ivy...where are you planning to apply for a job?" Elam said.

Ivy tried not to squirm, determined not to let the intensity of her father's gaze bore a hole in her defenses. "I think I'll start by asking Jewel Sadler if she needs a waitress."

"Pays minimum wage plus tips. Is that enough?"

"I can work two jobs." Ivy took a sip of orange juice.

"That'll leave you time to sleep. What about the boy?"

If you call him "the boy" one more time I'm going to scream! "Montana will be fine. I've always found time for him." Ivy stole a glance at Lu, sobered by the reality that Lu would not be there to help her this time. She fluttered her eyelashes until she could focus clearly. "I'll go talk to Jewel after the breakfast rush dies down."

The phone rang.

Elam reached behind him and snatched the receiver off the wall phone. "Hello…You're kidding…Are you absolutely sure it's human? All right, don't touch anything and call the sheriff. I'm on my way." He hung up the phone and looked at Carolyn. "That was the construction foreman on the time-share project. They're out there with the bulldozers clearing trees and uncovered a human skull, of all things—and some bones."

"How awful," Carolyn said. "Where?"

"At the south end of the old Collier ranch. Probably been out there since the gold rush days."

Ivy started to choke on her food and picked up her glass of orange juice and took a few gulps.

"You okay, Ivy girl?" Lu said, giving her a couple whacks on the back.

Ivy nodded. "Went down…the…wrong pipe."

Elam drank the last of his coffee, wiped his mustache with a napkin, and stood. "I'll call and let you know what's going on. I hope this doesn't delay construction. It's already a push getting the model finished by July for the Getaway Homes Show."

Ivy watched her father leave the kitchen and avoided making eye contact with her mother.

"Goodness," Carolyn said. "I wonder who the person is and how they died?"

Montana cut off a big piece of waffle and stuffed it into his mouth. "On *CSI* they could tell from a guy's skull that he died 'cause someone hit him in the head."

"Where did you see *CSI*?" Ivy said.

Montana smiled sheepishly. "At Josh's sleepover. Are you mad?"

"Well, I'm not thrilled. You don't need to be filling your head with that stuff."

Carolyn got up and started clearing dishes off the table. "How about if I drive you into town? And while you're talking to Jewel, Lu and I can take Montana over to the ice rink. Should be a lot of kids there since it's spring break."

Ivy walked into Jewel's Café at ten o'clock and smiled when she saw the dreadful moose head hanging on the wall opposite the windows. She noticed only a few customers, none that she recognized, and was aware that someone had come out of the kitchen.

"Well, will you look at this: Ivy Griffith in the flesh." Jewel Sadler put her arms around Ivy before she could protest, then stood back and seemed to study her. "You've grown up."

"Can you believe I'll be twenty-nine next month?"

"That's nothing, doll. I've got dust bunnies older than that." Jewel Sadler threw back her head and laughed. "Sit down over here and have a cup of coffee with me. Or would you like something else?"

"No, coffee's fine." Ivy sat at the table closest to the kitchen and waited while Jewel set two mugs on the table and filled them with coffee.

"Cream and sugar are there on the table," Jewel said. "So what do I have to do to get you to come to work for me?"

Ivy suppressed a smile, tickled all over again at how funny Jewel looked wearing a hairnet. "Which of my parents bribed you?"

"They just gave me a heads-up that you might come in looking for a job. And with tourist season just around the corner, I just happen to have a position for someone reliable."

"I'm reliable," Ivy said. "I have a seven-year-old son to support."

"Right. Montana. Carolyn told me. Says he's the spitting image of your brother."

Ivy nodded. "Right down to the auburn hair."

"Have you ever waited tables?"

"Lots of times," Ivy said. "I'm good at it, too."

Jewel looked at her hands and lowered her voice. "Carolyn also mentioned you got into some trouble. What was that all about?"

Ivy felt the color heat her face. "I was messed up on drugs a long time ago, but I'm clean now. I work hard and I'm honest. I've got references if you need them." *Please don't make me tell you I was arrested for soliciting and ended up in drug rehab.*

"I can pay six dollars an hour and let you keep your own tips. Doesn't seem like enough for a single mom."

"I'm surprisingly frugal."

Jewel's eyes narrowed. "Tell you what, doll. I can give you thirty-two hours to start: Tuesday, Thursday, Saturday, and Sunday. Then when tourist season hits, I'll give you as many hours as you want. How's that sound?"

Ivy nodded and forced back the emotion. "When can I start?"

"Be here at six tomorrow morning and plan to work till two."

"Will my hours vary?"

"Not that I can see. I need someone to cover breakfast and lunch."

"This is so great. With those hours, I'll even be able to pick up Montana from school."

Jewel reached over and patted Ivy's hand. "Good. Let me go get the papers you'll need to fill out tonight and bring back in the morning."

Jewel left the dining area through the swinging doors.

Ivy took a sip of lukewarm coffee, aware of the front door opening and closing. She turned and looked up into a pair of clear blue eyes she would have recognized anywhere.

"Hello, Pete."

Pete Barton stared at her blankly for a few seconds, and then a look of recognition lit his face. "Ivy!" He came over and stood next to the table, decidedly older but handsome as ever. "I wasn't expecting to see you. I saw your mother's Jeep parked outside and came in to ask her if you'd arrived okay. So are you moving back?"

"I already have." Ivy was thinking Pete did a lousy job of masking his shock at how much she'd changed. "I start working for Jewel tomorrow."

"You're going to be a *waitress?*"

"You know of anything in this town that pays better?"

"I guess not. Well, how are you?"

"Fine. I have a son now. Montana. He's seven."

"I hadn't heard that. So you're divorced?"

"More or less." Ivy glanced around the room and lowered her voice. "Listen, something came up this morning. We need to talk…but not here."

Pete's gaze was probing. "Okay. When you're done here, walk over to the deli. We can talk in my office. Is something wrong?"

"I'll see you in a few minutes."

Pete left the café, and Ivy watched him through the window, thinking he still looked great and she was more likely to pass for his mother than his former girlfriend.

"Here you go." Jewel handed Ivy some papers. "Be sure to bring them back with you in the morning."

"Thanks. I'm excited to get started."

Ivy gave Jewel a hug and then left the café and put the papers in the Jeep.

She walked across the street to the deli, questioning the wisdom of her being seen with Pete right now. On the other hand, it would be less risky if things appeared normal. And certainly her seeing Pete Barton was something most people here would anticipate.

Ivy followed Pete into his office and pulled the door shut behind her. She sat in a blue vinyl chair facing him, thinking how ghastly she must look under the fluorescent lights.

"Okay, what's up?" Pete said.

"My dad got a call this morning from a construction foreman bulldozing trees on the south end of Collier Ranch." Ivy looked into his eyes and saw her own fear staring back at her. "They discovered a human skull and some bones."

The color left Pete's face. "It was bound to happen sooner or later. Not to worry. We just stick to the pact, right?" Pete cocked his head and looked at her questioningly. "*Right?*"

Ivy felt herself nod. "Is Flint Carter still sheriff?"

"Yeah, and you can bet he's already jumped on it. He's been trying for ten years to figure out what happened to Joe. You know your dad and Flint are good friends now?"

"No, I didn't. But you know he's going to want to talk to us again."

"That's why we *have* to stick together on this, Ivy. It was a stupid mistake, but we were kids. Our going to jail won't bring Joe back. And it's not as though we're a threat to society."

"Are Reg and Denny living here?"

"No. Reg owns a ski shop in Telluride, and Denny's an architect in Durango."

"Are you in touch with them?"

"Every now and then. They're both committed to keeping the pact. They've never breathed a word of it to anyone, not even their wives."

"What if the autopsy reveals something incriminating?"

Pete rolled his eyes. "Like what?"

"I don't know. It seems like medical examiners find evidence in incredible ways these days."

"On TV, maybe. But after all this time, Joe's clothes have rotted. His flesh is gone. There's no DNA and no way anyone can ever trace this to us. We sure didn't touch his bones."

"*I* never touched Joe at all."

"You were there." Pete's voice spiked with irritation. "You're just as guilty as we are."

"You don't have to remind me. I spent a huge chunk of the past decade snorting cocaine, hoping I *could* forget. It didn't work."

"Yeah, I heard. I'm sorry about that. I forced myself to stay away from drugs."

"Don't you ever struggle with guilt?" Ivy said.

Pete shrugged. "Not anymore. It's not like we set out to kill Joe. Things just got out of hand. And don't forget he was going to rat us out."

"Maybe we'd be better off if he had. At least it would be over."

"Not for me. I would've been thrown off the basketball team, and Dad would've disowned me. It would've ruined my life."

"And killing Joe didn't?"

"I don't think about it, okay?" Pete sighed. "I wouldn't even have left Alaska if Dad hadn't died. Mom couldn't handle the deli by herself. She needs me. That's the only reason I'm living here."

"What were you doing in Alaska?"

"Running a tour agency in Anchorage. I forgot all about Joe Hadley while I was there."

"Lucky you. I never could."

Pete looked her up and down. "I can see you've had it bad. Truthfully, I wouldn't have recognized you at Jewel's if you hadn't spoken first."

Ivy rose to her feet, crushed that this man who had talked her out of her virginity now found her repulsive. "I should go find Montana. He's at the ice rink with Mom."

"So you're keeping the pact, right?"

"I don't have any other choice." *Yet.*

Ivy found a parking space at Spruce Park and put a dime in the meter. She walked past the bandstand toward the ice rink, glad that the snow was quickly evaporating and patches of ground were already visible.

She stopped for a moment and looked out at the colorful collage of skaters on the ice, and was flooded with memories of her childhood that suddenly didn't seem all that long ago. She spotted her mother and Lu sitting on a bench and went over to them.

"Hi, honey," Carolyn said. "How'd your interview go with Jewel?"

"Great. She hired me to work four days a week, starting tomorrow."

"Mom!"

Ivy turned toward her son's voice and spotted him skating next to a boy in a green stocking cap who was about his size. She waved.

"Montana's having a ball," Carolyn said. "He and Ian Carter seem to have hit it off. Ian is Flint Carter's son. You do remember Sheriff Carter?"

"Yeah, but I wouldn't have thought he'd have a kid that young. Doesn't he have some that are practically grown?"

Carolyn smiled. "Two in college. I'm guessing Ian was a big surprise. Flint is still sheriff, by the way. He and your dad have become good friends."

Ivy watched the boys skate around the bend, laughing happily and holding each other up. She couldn't get over the irony that, of all the kids in Jacob's Ear, Montana would connect first with the one boy she would've preferred he avoid.

It bothered Ivy that Lu was so quiet. She glanced over at her and thought she looked drawn and listless. "We need to get you home so you can rest."

Carolyn gave Lu a double take. "Goodness, I didn't realize we wore you out. Ivy, why don't you drive Lu back to the house, and I'll stay here with Montana? He's getting along so well with Ian that I hate to cut it short."

"How will you get home?"

"Why don't you come back and pick us up at the deli at one? When the boys get hungry, I'll ask if Ian can join us for lunch. If not, I'll just enjoy the time with my grandson."

With my grandson. Her mother's words penetrated her deepest fear like a healing balm. "Okay, Mom. Call if you need me to come sooner."

Ivy sat on the side of the guest room bed and pulled up the covers and tucked them around Lu. "I know the doctor said it would be a matter of weeks, but I kept hoping he was wrong."

"So did I," Lu Ramirez said. "I've been trying really hard. I thought I could keep pushing myself until you got settled, but I just can't anymore."

Ivy sighed and felt her own strength waning. "I'm going to have to tell my parents about your leukemia so we can break the news to Montana. He's going to be so sad."

Lu looked up at her. Her dark eyes welled, and a tear trickled down the side of her face. "I'm sorry, Ivy girl. I wanted to see him grow up. I wanted to be here to help you face the past."

"You've helped me more than you'll ever know. Now it's my turn." Ivy wiped the tears off her cheeks. "Do you want to tell Montana, or do you want me to?"

"I'll tell him. But I'd like you to be there."

"Okay."

Lu held her gaze a long time, and then said, "I think it's time for you to move me into hospice. I can't help you with Montana anymore. And you don't need to be worrying about me right now."

"You don't have to move. You can rest right here. Mom will help with Montana."

"But *I* need help. You can't take care of me. Your parents aren't prepared to have a stranger die in their home, and I could never ask it of them. We've already been over this. You agreed to let me decide when it was time."

"No! I'm not ready to let you go!"

"But God's ready for me, Ivy girl." Lu gently stroked her hair. "I'm not afraid. Really."

Ivy clutched Lu's arm, unable to verbalize the agony she felt—or the impending abandonment she feared.

"I know it's hard. But if you won't accept it, how can you expect Montana to?"

Ivy knew the answer, but the choice wasn't fair. Life wasn't fair. Death wasn't fair. God wasn't fair!

6

SHERIFF FLINT CARTER went into his office in the Tanner County Courthouse, pulled the blinds on the afternoon sun, and flopped in a chair. "I've been waiting ten years for a break like this!"

Lieutenant Bobby Knolls blew a pink bubble and then sucked it into his mouth and sat in the chair next to the sheriff. "It's really gonna be somethin' if our John Doe's dental records match Joe Hadley's."

"I'm betting they will. How else could Joe's class ring have gotten buried out there?" Flint leaned back in his chair, his weight balancing on the balls of his feet. "I suppose the ring could've fallen off Joe's hand if he were the one who buried the victim. But he's the only one reported missing."

"Maybe we'll get a bonus and the ME can tell us the cause of death."

"Well, we know there was foul play. The kid didn't bury himself." Flint heard his administrative assistant's voice on the intercom.

"Sheriff, Mr. Griffith has arrived."

"Okay, Tammy, send him back." Flint turned to Bobby. "I'll handle Elam. Why don't you go pull together everything we have on the Hadley case. If we reopen it, I want you handling the investigation."

"All right." Bobby got up and left the office.

A minute later, Flint heard a gentle knock on the door. "Come in."

Elam Griffith came in and shut the door behind him and sat in the chair Bobby had just vacated. "How long are you planning to keep my building site restricted?"

"As long as it takes," Flint said. "We need to sift through a lot of dirt and snow, but I'm thinking we'll be out of there in a week or ten days."

Elam shook his head. "Come on, Flint, you're killing me. I have to have the model home ready for the Getaway Homes Show in July. I'm stretched as it is."

"Sorry, bud, but I can't do you a favor on this one. I promise I'll pull out as soon as I can."

Elam stroked his mustache and seemed to be looking at nothing. "There's talk that the bones belong to Joe Hadley. What do you think?"

"I think it should be easy for the medical examiner to compare dental records."

"Have the Hadleys been told about the discovery?"

"Oh, yeah. Right off the bat this morning. They want nothing more than to find closure on this."

"Think they will?"

Flint smirked. "Nice try, but I'm not commenting till we know something. Did Ivy get in okay?"

"Yeah, on Saturday."

Flint patted Elam on the shoulder. "You and Carolyn must be thrilled after all this time."

"It's awkward, but I suppose it will be for a while. She's not pretty anymore, Flint—hard as nails and looks much older than she is. I didn't even recognize her."

"Sorry. Drugs can really do a number on a person. What about her son?"

"Yeah, he's with her."

"I figured that. Does he have a name?"

"Montana." Elam rolled his eyes. "She couldn't have picked a normal name like Jason or Scott or Mike?"

"Call me weird, but I kinda like the name." Flint decided not to ask about the boy's father. "Listen, be sure to fill her in on what's going on. If the bones turn out to be Joe Hadley's, I'll need to turn back the clock ten years and do some more digging—no pun intended."

Ivy Griffith sat at the kitchen table, waiting for her mother to react to the news about Lu's failing health.

"I don't know what you expect me to say." Carolyn Griffith took a sip of decaf and seemed to grip the mug tighter than was necessary. "I'm very sorry about Lu, but equally upset that you concealed her illness from us."

Ivy brushed a tear off her cheek. "I'm sorry. I was afraid if I told you, you wouldn't let me bring her here, and there was no way I was going to leave her to die alone."

"I'm surprised you didn't get her into hospice when you were in Denver and just stay there until it was over."

"I wanted to, but I didn't have anyone to stay with Montana. Lu always did that."

"How did Montana react when you told him?"

"I haven't yet."

Carolyn's jaw dropped. "Ivy, what are you thinking? That child dearly loves her. He's going to be hurt and angry if he hasn't had time to say good-bye."

"I know. I was in shock when the doctor told us Lu's leukemia was acute and she didn't have long—maybe only weeks. I didn't want Montana worrying about it the whole time."

"You don't think he suspects something?"

"He knows Lu's been really sick but thinks it's the flu hanging on. That's what we all thought. I told him that after we got to Jacob's Ear, Lu would have to leave us and go someplace far away, but he doesn't know she's dying. I thought I'd wait and explain it to him when Lu started to look sicker. I guess it's happening sooner than I thought."

"Then that's the only reason you came here?"

"No! I really wanted to come home. Lu and I have talked about it for a long time, and she's encouraged me to come back and make things right. I wanted to try to save some money first. But when we got the bad news, I realized that without Lu's Social Security, I wouldn't be able afford the rent in Denver. And I needed a safer neighborhood if Montana was going to stay by himself after school till I got home." Ivy sighed. "I had hoped to be settled here before Lu got really bad. After I get my first paycheck, I'll rent a room in town and have hospice bring what she needs so she can stay with me and Montana."

"How're you going to handle that when you work?"

Ivy's chin quivered. "I don't know what I'm going to do. But I know what I'm *not* going to do. I'm not going to make Lu feel like a burden. She's always been there for me and Montana, and we wouldn't even be alive if it hadn't been for her…" Ivy's voice cracked. "She deserves to die in a peaceful place surrounded by people who love her. I won't let her die with strangers. I just won't!"

Ivy put her face in her hands and sobbed. She heard her mother get up and come around to the other side of the table, and felt a hand caressing her back.

"How long has it been since Lu was diagnosed?" Carolyn said.

"Five weeks, but she seems to be going downhill all of a sudden."

"Let me talk to your father about this. Maybe we can arrange for hospice to get her set up here at the house."

Ivy wiped her eyes and looked at her mother. "You would do that?"

"Lu has her own room, and I don't see why it couldn't work. Besides, the nearest hospice in-patient facility is probably in Durango. That would make it tough for you to work and drive back and forth to visit Lu."

"What if Dad doesn't want to do it?"

"Your father has a tender heart, Ivy. I can't imagine he would say no. At least if you're all staying here, I could watch after Lu the mornings you work, and you could spend as much of the rest of the time with her as you want."

Ivy fluttered her eyelashes, but tears escaped down her cheeks anyway. She turned and buried her head in her mother's breast, wondering how she was going to break the news to Montana.

Carolyn Griffith set the platter of roast beef and potatoes and carrots on the table and then sat down and bowed her head as Elam said the blessing.

"Too bad your friend's not feeling well," Elam said after he finished praying. "Maybe she'll feel like eating later."

Montana shook his head. "Gramma Lu's never hungry since she got the flu. I miss her tortillas and frijoles. Maybe she could show Grandmother Griffith how to make it. It's *real* good."

Carolyn smiled. "I'll ask her. Elam, tell us the latest on the discovery at the site."

"Everybody I talked to thinks the bones are Joe Hadley's. Of course, Flint won't say what he thinks, just that he's going to tie up my construction site for a week to ten days."

"I would guess they'll check dental records?"

Elam nodded. "We'll just have to wait for the preliminary autopsy report. Wouldn't it be something if it turns out to be Joe after all this time?" Elam glanced up at Ivy. "You ever wonder about him?"

Like every day of my life. "Of course. He was a good friend of Pete's. None of us were the same after he died. How are his parents doing?"

"Never did get over it," Elam said. "Probably because there was always a possibility that he was still alive."

"If this will bring them closure, I hope it turns out to be Joe," Carolyn said. "I just hope it doesn't present a whole new set of unanswered questions that makes their grief worse."

Elam took a sip of water. "Surely we can find something more appropriate to talk about over dinner. So Ivy, when are you working for Jewel?"

"Tuesday, Thursday, Saturday, and Sunday from 6:00 a.m. till 2:00. My afternoons will be free, and I'll have three weekdays off. That'll give me lots of time with Montana."

"Whatever happened to working two jobs?"

Carolyn reached over and touched Elam's hand. "We can discuss that later. Did you know that Montana made a friend at the ice rink? Ian Carter. I told him you and Ian's dad are good friends. The boys are going to be in the same class at school."

"You don't say?"

Montana bobbed his head. "The teacher's name is Mrs. Leopard."

"Shepard," Ivy said. "Mrs. Shepard."

Montana flashed her a smile framed with a milk mustache. "Yeah. Can I buy lunch at my new school? Ian says they have really good spasketti and meatballs!"

Carolyn saw Ivy wince and figured she was already worrying about the money and embarrassed by Montana's seemingly obsessive references to food. "I'm sure we can arrange for a boy with a healthy appetite like yours to buy lunch at school." Carolyn brushed the hair out of his eyes.

Elam shot Carolyn an I-told-you-so look and stuffed a big bite of roast beef into his mouth.

After dinner Ivy helped her mother with the dishes, then went upstairs to check on Lu and found Montana sitting on her bed, recounting every detail Ian Carter had told him about the new school and the teacher.

Ivy stood in the doorway and memorized the moment, thinking it might be the last normal interaction between Montana and his Gramma Lu. She swallowed the wad of emotion that rose in her throat, then pushed a chair to the foot of the bed and sat. Even Lu's brown skin couldn't hide the dark circles under her eyes.

"You and your mother are going to like it here," Lu said. "This was a good move for you."

Montana took her hand in his. "You like it, too. Right, Gramma Lu?"

Lu held his gaze, and then said softly, "This is not where I'm going to live, Montana. It's time for me to go to heaven, and I can't take you with me."

Montana let go of her hand and looked over his shoulder at Ivy, his expression like that of a helpless puppy, then turned back to Lu. "Why not?"

Lu gently pulled him down next to her and cradled him in her arms. "Because you haven't lived your life yet. Don't worry about me. Heaven is a wonderful place. I'll be very happy there."

"I don't want you to leave."

Lu nodded. "I know."

"What is heaven, anyway?"

"It's a faraway kingdom where God lives. And it's the happiest place you could ever imagine—better than Casa Bonita or Six Flags or even Disney World. Only you never have to go home because heaven is your *forever* home."

"Will I ever see you again?"

Lu looked up, her eyes colliding with Ivy's, her hand stroking Montana's hair. "Ask your mom to tell you about Jesus. He's God's Son, and He knows the way to heaven. You just need to follow Him."

Ivy was surprised and a little annoyed that Lu had put her on the spot like that, knowing it would force Ivy to confront her spiritual roots that seemed to have long ago withered and died. How many years had it been since Ivy had even said the name of Jesus, much less felt loved by Him? And God's stealing Lu away so tragically certainly didn't make her want to trust Him again.

"When are you going?" Montana said, his voice sounding shaky.

Lu pressed her lips to his cheek. "Sometime soon I'll close my eyes and go from here to heaven, just like that."

"Will you disappear?"

"No, my body will be buried. But my spirit—the special part of me you can't see with your eyes—will be alive in heaven with God. And someday He'll bring my body back to life and change it into a much better one that won't get old or feel sick or sad."

"Like Wonder Woman!" Montana said.

"Oh, even better." Lu tilted Montana's chin and looked into his eyes. "I don't know how many days I'll be here, but there's something I need you to remember always."

"What?"

Lu placed her hand on his heart. "Even after I'm gone, a part of me will be in your heart. And you'll remember things I've said and happy times we had. Those are yours. No one can take them away."

Montana's chin quivered. "I don't want to *remember*. I want you to stay here."

"I know you do, but I need you to be the bravest you've ever been. It's a little sad and scary when someone you love is dying. But remember I'll see you again. I'll be waiting for you in the heavenly kingdom."

Ivy dabbed her eyes and got up quietly and slipped out of the room, thinking this conversation should belong only to them.

"I don't know what else we can do, Elam." Carolyn Griffith stared at the flames in the fireplace. "It's a horrible situation. But I'm grateful that Ivy brought Lu to us instead of trying to deal with this in Denver by herself. Can you even imagine what would have—"

"Settle down, Carolyn, I agree with you," Elam said. "It's just that everything this girl does involves a drama of some kind. When does it end?"

"I don't know. Obviously not today."

"Are they up there telling the boy right now?"

"I think so." Carolyn sighed. "Maybe Montana would seem more like your grandson if you stopped calling him *the boy*."

"I'm not about to get attached to him till I know Ivy isn't going to take him away from us. I don't trust her to do anything she says. She's manipulating us, just like I said she would."

"Well, don't punish Montana for Ivy's mistakes. He needs a male figure in his life, and right now you're it."

"What if I don't want to be it?"

Carolyn heard footsteps on the stairs and seconds later saw Ivy standing in the doorway. "Come in and sit by the fire, honey. Did you tell him?"

Ivy nodded but couldn't seem to get any words out. She sat on the couch across from her parents, then wiped her eyes with a tissue and blew her nose. "Lu told him."

Ivy recounted the conversation in short, emotional sentences.

"Then Lu's a believer?" Carolyn said.

"Yes, but she never pushed the envelope till today. I can't believe she put me on the spot like that in front of Montana."

"Has the boy ever been to church?" Elam said.

Ivy shook her head. "I haven't been since I left home."

"Well, after Lu's remark about Jesus, the boy's bound to have questions. So I take it you lied yesterday morning when you said you were exhausted and couldn't go to church with us?"

"Don't be mad. I didn't know how to tell you I don't know what I believe right now."

"Why don't you try leveling with us?" Elam said. "You've got to stop the game playing if we're ever going to put this family back together."

"I'm sorry, Dad. I wasn't sure you would understand that I need to get my head on straight before I try to be any kind of spiritual example."

Elam rolled his eyes. "Trust me, I get it."

7

THE BLENDED AROMAS of freshly brewed coffee and warm fruit muffins permeated Jewel's Café at six o'clock on Tuesday morning as Ivy Griffith pinned her name tag to her uniform shirt and prepared to start her shift.

"Don't be nervous, doll." Jewel Sadler put her hands on Ivy's shoulders and looked her in the eye. "And don't expect not to make mistakes on your first day, okay?"

Ivy nodded, aware of the front door opening behind her.

"There's your first customer," Jewel said. "I'm sure you remember Sheriff Carter."

Ivy turned and watched Flint Carter walk over and sit at the table closest to the moose head, thinking the age difference between them didn't seem as huge as it once had. His sideburns were graying and his waist was thicker. But he looked good. And less intimidating.

She walked over and handed him the menu. "Good morning, Sheriff."

"Good morning."

"You don't recognize me, do you?"

Flint studied her, a blank look on his face. "Can't say that I do. Have we met?"

"It's me, Ivy. Elam's daughter."

His face turned pinker than the grapefruit half pictured on the menu. "Good grief, Ivy, I…uh…ten years is a long time. You're all grown up."

"Don't feel bad. Nobody recognizes me."

"Actually, I knew you were back because my son told me all about meeting Montana at the ice rink yesterday. I guess the boys are going to be in the same class at school."

"It was so sweet of Ian to make Montana feel welcome. Moving here from Denver is a huge change."

"I'll bet. So, you ready to take my order?"

"Sure, what can I get you?"

"A ham-and-cheese omelet with rye toast, a side of hash browns, a small orange juice, and a black coffee."

Ivy jotted as fast as her pencil would move, hoping the cook would be able to read her writing. "Anything else?"

"No, that's it."

"Okay, I'll get your coffee right out to you."

Ivy walked through the swinging doors to the kitchen and slid the first order of the day onto the peg. "Order!"

Jewel smiled and winked at her. "Atta girl."

Ivy went back out to the dining area and waited on several more customers, aware that Sheriff Carter was on his cell phone. She eased her way over to a nearby table and pretended to be arranging condiments.

"Are you absolutely sure?" Flint said. "Because I can't afford to raise false hopes…So you're saying that the dental impressions on the Joe Doe are a perfect match to Joe Hadley's dental records?…No chance you could be wrong?…Okay, then. That's good enough for me. Let's consider the case officially reopened."

Ivy's heart pounded so hard she was sure her name tag must be moving. What if investigators found Pete's DNA at the site? Or Reg and Denny's? What if the boys decided to tell police that she had gone along with concealing the truth about Joe's disappearance?

Ivy held the back of a chair and let a wave of nausea pass. She couldn't go to jail now—not when Lu was dying. Not before Montana was bonded to his grandparents.

"You doing okay, doll?"

Ivy looked up into Jewel's face and forced a smile. "Yeah, I'm fine. I'm starting to get the hang of it. I just need a few more customers."

The door opened and two ancient-looking men came in and shuffled over to the first table by the window.

"Recognize those old coots?" Jewel said.

"Deke and Roscoe? I can't believe they're still alive. They were old when I was a kid."

Jewel chuckled. "Shoot, they were old when *I* was kid. Roscoe's nearly deaf as a door yet seems to know everything that goes on in this town. Just take their orders and tell them you'll put it on their tabs. But you can tear up the tickets. I'm not about to collect anything. It's just a game we play. Their tab's been running for twenty years."

Brandon Jones blew on his coffee and looked out the window of the Three Peaks dining hall and saw Elam Griffith getting into his Suburban.

"That was a bummer of an update," Jake Compton said.

"Well, at least we know what we need to be praying about," Brandon said. "I can't imagine the pressure of adding a dying woman to the mix. It was already hard enough for them to deal with Ivy coming home—and a surprise grandson."

"Elam and Carolyn are strong in their faith. We just need to pray they have wisdom."

Brandon pinched off a piece of a glazed doughnut and popped it into his mouth. "Jake, have you and Suzanne met Ivy yet?"

"No, I thought we might drop by the Griffiths' late this afternoon after Ivy gets home from work. What'd you and Kelsey think of her?"

"She was nice. Her son Montana is a kick in the pants." Brandon smiled. "I had a blast playing in the snow with him and Sasha. I told Elam I'd get him on a snowmobile this week. This might be his last chance now that April's got her foot in the door."

"You're really just a kid trapped in a thirty-one-year-old body, you know that? You gonna work on the website today?"

"Yeah, till three. I told Buzz Easton I'd ride down to Durango with him."

"I didn't realize you were hanging out with Buzz."

"He wanted to show me the ticket office and gift shop he's building for his rafting operation. Is that a problem?"

Jake scratched his ear. "Just be careful, okay?"

"What does that mean?"

"Just don't let him rub off on you."

Brandon took a sip of coffee. "Could you be a little more specific, Jake?"

"I don't like bad-mouthing people. Just don't lose sight of the fact that your values and his are at odds."

Brandon grinned. "What—you think I'm going to start swearing, telling locker-room jokes, and drinking tequila?"

"I hope not."

"Don't worry. I blow off two-thirds of what Buzz says and does. But I *really* want to get on the white water, and he's the man. Besides, how is he going to get saved if he's never exposed to the Word?"

"So you're sharing your faith?"

"I will one of these days. But first I think it's important to build a relationship. He's not going to listen to me unless he knows I care about him. You know that."

Jake held up his palms. "Hey, you're a big boy. Just be sure you're praying about it and not jumping in blindly, thinking you can handle whatever Buzz throws your way."

"Why do I get the feeling this is personal?"

Jake pushed his glasses to the bridge of his nose. "It's really not. Forget I said anything."

Ivy walked in the front door of her parents' home and found her son sitting in a chair, staring out the window, his arms folded across his chest.

"Hi, sweetie." Ivy went over and sat on the arm of the chair and kissed the top of his head. "What'd you do today?"

"Nothing," Montana Griffith said.

"Didn't you go sledding?"

"No."

Ivy put her arm around him. "Are you mad at me for going to work and leaving you here?"

"No."

"Where's your grandmother?"

Montana shrugged.

Carolyn Griffith came out of the kitchen and shot Ivy a knowing look. "Well, as you can tell, it's been a *quiet* day around here. How was your first day at Jewel's?"

"Good. Montana, would you believe my very first customer was Sheriff Carter? That's Ian's father."

"Duh."

Ivy had never seen her son act this way and decided to ignore his behavior. "We had a busy couple hours right off the bat, and then again from eleven to one. I think I did really well. I was surprised how many people I knew. Of course, none of them recognized me till I told them who I was—except for Deke and Roscoe. I can't believe they're still around."

Carolyn smiled. "Roscoe supposedly can't hear worth a hoot, but he somehow manages to hear everything in the gossip mill. So it was somewhat enjoyable as first days go?"

Ivy nodded. "Yeah, not bad." *Thanks,* Ivy mouthed to her mother, gesturing toward Montana. "So why's everybody so quiet?"

"I think we're having a mental health day," Carolyn said.

"Did Lu come downstairs?"

"Actually she did for both breakfast and lunch. I was going to have Montana bring her a tray, but she insisted on coming down. She watched a little TV before lunch and then crashed afterwards. I checked in on her a few minutes ago, and she's out."

Ivy combed her hands through Montana's hair. "Did you spend some time with Gramma Lu?"

"Everybody acts like she's not even gonna die!" He jumped up and stomped up the staircase. A few seconds later a door slammed.

Ivy winced, then turned to her mother. "Has he been like this all day?"

"Pretty much. Nothing I say seems to help. I think he just needs to feel the grief. And we need to help him through it."

"I'm really sorry, Mom. I had no idea he would be a problem for you. I've never seen him behave this way."

"Well, he's never had to face losing someone he loves before."

Ivy waited fifteen minutes and then went upstairs to Montana's room and knocked on the door. "Sweetie, it's Mom. I'm coming in."

Ivy slowly opened the door, surprised to see Lu sitting in the rocking chair, holding Montana in her lap.

"We're having a little quiet time." Lu's eyes looked tired and sallow. "How was your first day?"

"Good." Ivy went over and sat on the side of the bed, her hands folded in her lap. "Montana, I know you're hurting, but that doesn't mean it's okay to treat Mom and Grandmother Griffith rudely."

Montana sniffled and wouldn't look at her.

"Tomorrow will be a better day," Lu said. "I think maybe Montana and I will just sit here together for a while."

Ivy observed the calming effect Lu had on Montana and felt as if the wounds of her own inadequacies had been reopened. She had no one but herself to blame that Montana would allow Lu and not his own mother to comfort him. Wasn't it Lu who had cared for him when Ivy was too high even to realize that she was neglecting him? Wasn't it Lu who had picked him up from school? Fixed his meals? Held him when he was sick? Tucked him in at night?

Lu began to hum softly, and seconds later she and Montana seemed to be lost in a world of their own. Ivy got up and left the room, wondering if her hurting little boy would ever accept Lu's death—or the fact that no one, not even his own mother, could take her place.

Ivy went downstairs to the living room and saw her mother sitting on the couch, soaking in the afternoon sun streaming in through the windows.

"How is he?" Carolyn said.

"He'll be okay now. Lu always knows what to do."

"You sound like you resent it."

Ivy shook her head. "I just wish I were more like her, that's all."

"The two of them have been very close, haven't they?" Carolyn said.

Ivy was distracted by the sound of the kitchen door opening from the garage. Seconds later, Elam walked in the living room, kissed Carolyn's cheek, then sat next to her on the couch.

"How'd it go down at Jewel's?" he said to Ivy.

"Good. Nothing much to tell, other than Sheriff Carter was my first customer."

"Yeah, that's what he said."

"So you did talk to him," Carolyn said. "Has he heard any more about the bones they found?"

"They're definitely Joe Hadley's. Not only did the dental records match, but also the DNA. There's absolutely no doubt. The investigation's been reopened."

"Wow," Ivy said, trying to act surprised. "What exactly are they investigating?"

"Right now, they're walking around my construction site with metal detectors, looking for a weapon."

"They really think someone murdered Joe?" Ivy said.

"Flint won't say what he thinks, but that's what I think. He's not commenting till he gets the preliminary autopsy report."

Ivy breathed in slowly and let it out, wondering if Pete Barton had heard the news.

Brandon Jones pushed open the front door of his home and was hit with the delicious aroma of something spicy.

"Good timing." Kelsey Jones met him at the door and put her arms around his neck and kissed him. "I hope you're hungry. I made enough Cajun meatloaf to feed a family of six."

Brandon grinned. "Sounds about right."

"So what'd you think of Buzz's white-water operation?"

Brandon followed her out to the kitchen and sat at the table. "It's so slick. If I could actually make a living at it, I'd be tempted to work for him. I can't imagine shooting the rapids every day and getting paid to boot."

"That's what you said about working at the camp."

"I know, honey. I love what I'm doing. But it's fun thinking about the adventure aspect of that kind of operation. I can see why Buzz is excited about it."

"Too bad he's not as nuts about Maggie."

"Oh, they're okay. Not everyone is as in love as we are. So how'd your afternoon go?"

Kelsey opened the oven door and removed a loaf-size Pyrex pan of meatloaf. "Suzanne Compton stopped by for tea. She told me that the bones they found yesterday at Elam's building site for sure belong to a boy that went missing ten years ago—a classmate of Ivy's."

"Really? I didn't hear that. Do they know how he died?"

"No, but the bones had been buried. That's not a good sign."

Brandon ran his finger along the rim of his dinner plate. "This is really not Elam's week. He had breakfast this morning with Jake and me and told us that the lady friend Ivy brought home with her has acute leukemia and is dying—like anytime. They're going to get hospice involved and see if she can stay there at the house."

Kelsey put a lid on the pan of rice and turned around. "Ivy didn't tell her parents before she came?"

"No. She's just full of surprises."

8

IVY GRIFFITH WENT OUT to the garage and put Wednesday's edition of the *Tri-County Courier* on the stack of newspapers to be recycled, painfully aware of Joe Hadley's high school yearbook picture on the front page.

She heard the phone ring and rushed back inside, hoping hospice was calling back. "Hello."

"Ivy, it's Pete."

"I guess you heard the bones were Joe's."

"Yeah, I did. So…we're all on the same page with this, right? I called Reg and Denny, and they agreed we need to stick with the pact."

"I already told you I would." Ivy glanced in the living room and didn't see anyone within earshot.

"I have another reason for calling. Did you get the reminder in the mail about our ten-year class reunion?"

"No, the school lost track of me a long time ago. When is it?"

"The twenty-second of this month. In the Aspen Room at the Phantom Hollow Lodge."

"Well, have fun. I'm not going."

"Not so fast. This isn't just about you. The four of us are in this together, and I think it's important we all show up and give the impression that everything's normal with us. You know the sheriff's going to shift his focus now and look at everyone who knew Joe as a potential suspect. If you aren't at the reunion, he may ask himself why. I don't think you want that."

"But I've never been to any of the class reunions. Why would anyone give it a second thought if I miss another one?"

"Because you're back in town. Look, everyone in our class is under a microscope. If we show up at the reunion and act completely natural, we won't end up on the suspect list. That's my point."

"And just how am I supposed to act natural when everyone starts asking me what I've been doing since graduation? It's not like I'm proud of it."

There was a long moment of dead air and she could hear Pete breathing.

Finally he said, "You can hang out with me, just like old times, and I'll control the conversation. All you have to do is smile and act like things are normal. Come on, Ivy, this is important. I'll even RSVP for you."

"I'm sure it's not free, and I don't have any money right now."

"It's sixty-five bucks a head, and I'll pay for it."

Don't let him manipulate you. Stand up to him! "I…I'd like to think about it."

"Okay, I'll go ahead and put your name in. You can always back out."

"Pete, I don't—"

"Someone just walked in. I've gotta go. Talk to you soon." *Click.*

Ivy hung up the phone, her heart pounding, and let out a loud sigh. She walked over to the mirror in the hallway and stared at her reflection. Her face was thin and bony, her gray eyes hollow and void of life. Even her hair had lost its luster.

Could her classmates find even the slightest resemblance to the bubbly, high-spirited beauty that had once worn Pete Barton's ring? Was she willing to turn her conspiracy with Pete, Reg, and Denny into an entire evening of public playacting? Did she really have a choice?

Ivy looked into her eyes staring back at her, pierced by the sadness she saw there. As ready as she was to clear her conscience and tell the sheriff the truth about Joe Hadley's death, her need to be there for Lu and Montana took precedence. She couldn't leave either of them right now.

Lu Ramirez's reflection appeared next to hers in the mirror, the circles under her eyes deep purple. "You look lost, Ivy girl."

Ivy linked arms with Lu and led her to the kitchen table. "Sit. I don't want you wearing yourself out."

"It's good for me to get up sometimes. I've been reading stories to Montana."

"Where is he now?"

"Upstairs playing checkers with your mother."

"He's not handling your illness well."

"I doubt if he will till he has to. But it's good we have time to prepare him." Lu folded her arms on the table and looked almost too weak to sit up. "I'm just as worried about you."

"I'm fine."

Lu's thick eyebrows seemed to settle on her eyelids. "Is that so?"

"I can't think about me right now."

"Why not? Sit down and tell me what you're thinking."

Ivy sat at the table and looked into Lu's probing eyes and lowered her voice. "Pete called. Our ten-year high school reunion is in a few weeks, and he thinks the four of us who made the pact should go so the sheriff won't get suspicious."

"And what do *you* think?"

"Well, I'm certainly not ready to go to the sheriff with what I know, and I don't want him getting suspicious before I'm ready to talk. I guess it can't hurt just to be seen there. It's not like I'm going to tell any more lies."

"You're not letting Pete talk you out of confessing, are you?"

"No, absolutely not. But I need to be sure Montana…" Ivy's voice cracked. "He needs to be able to live without both of us, Lu. I just don't know if he's strong enough. It seems so overwhelming for a seven-year-old."

Lu reached across the table and patted Ivy's hand. "Trust God with it. He will help you figure it out."

"I'm sure God gave up on me a long time ago."

"You know better than that."

Do I? "I wish you hadn't told Montana to ask me about Jesus."

"If not you, then who? You know what you believe, whether you'll admit it to yourself or not."

Ivy got up and poured herself a glass of water. "I called hospice this morning, and I'm waiting for a call back. I got the impression that with the letter from your doctor explaining your condition, they can get you set up here."

"Your parents are generous to allow a stranger to die in their home."

Lu's words seemed to squeeze her heart like a vice. In a matter of weeks or perhaps days, Lu—her anchor, her best friend, her one constant source of love and security—would be gone. And there wasn't a thing she could do to stop it.

Sheriff Flint Carter sat at his desk looking through the preliminary autopsy report, aware that Lieutenant Bobby Knolls had walked into his office, set a can of Pepsi on the coaster, then flopped in a chair.

Flint took off his reading glasses. "Here, take a look at this. We got a bigger break than we thought."

Bobby perused the report, then turned the page. "Well, whad-dya know, a broken hyoid bone. I guess we can stop lookin' for a murder weapon and start lookin' for whoever had his hands around the kid's throat—beginning with the good ol' boys that were workin' at Collier Ranch at the time."

"I want you to go over the crime scene with a fine-tooth comb."

"Don't worry," Bobby said. "If there're any clues within a hun-dred yards of that scene, we'll find them. I'm guessin' the shovel used to bury him is out there somewhere."

"It's really weird. I'd pretty much come to the conclusion someone had abducted him and taken him somewhere else. I never expected him to be found right here in Jacob's Ear."

"It could still be a serial killin', Sheriff."

"I know. We need to find out as much as we can so his parents can find closure."

Bobby pursed his lips. "Closure might not be all that comforting."

"It can't be any harder than what they've already imagined. Listen, I've requested assistance from a couple other sheriff's departments. I promised Elam we wouldn't tie up his building site any longer than we had to. Think you can wrap this up in ten days?"

"Oh, yeah. No problem. If we can't find anything in ten days, it's not out there. You gonna bring the feds back in on this?"

"I don't see the point in complicating the investigation. They didn't find out anything last time. And since Joe's body was found in our backyard, I'm thinking maybe the killer will be, too."

Carolyn Griffith stood at the front door with Ivy and Sonya Roe from hospice.

"The medication I left should get Lu through the next twenty-four hours," Sonya said. "I'll be back tomorrow afternoon around three, right after Ivy gets off work, and we can go over what to expect and what options we can implement in the days ahead. Our primary objective is to keep Lu as comfortable and pain-free as possible, and as I explained, we've been given a great deal of leeway to do precisely that. I don't want you to worry about a thing." Sonya put her hand on Ivy's arm. "I've been working with hospice for a very long time, and it's one of the most compassionate, effective organizations you'll ever find. You did the right thing by calling."

"Thanks," Ivy said. "I really want to be with Lu till the very end, and I know she wants that, too."

Sonya gave a nod. "Then that's our goal."

"We really appreciate your responding so quickly." Carolyn held open the door.

"You're very welcome." Sonya squeezed past her and went down the steps and out to a red SUV.

"Is that lady gone?"

Carolyn turned and saw Montana sitting at the bottom of the staircase. "Yes, she just left."

"Why do strangers have to be here?" Montana folded his arms across his chest, a scowl on his face.

Carolyn went over and sat on the step beside him. "I'd like to think of them as new friends and not strangers. She's a very nice hospice nurse that will be coming here often to make Lu as comfortable as she can be."

"I hate leukemia!"

Carolyn put her arm around Montana and felt him stiffen. "We all do, sweetie. But hospice is going to help us to help Lu. So we need to be glad when the nurse comes."

"I'm not glad," he mumbled. "I wanna go back to Denver. I hate it here."

"Hey." Ivy came over and stood next to him. "That's no way to talk. Grandmother Griffith has been very nice to us."

"I don't care! I want Gramma Lu!" Montana wiggled out from under Carolyn's arm, then turned and ran up the stairs.

Ivy started to go after him, and Carolyn gently took her arm. "Let him go, honey. You're not going to get a seven-year-old to change his mind about hating what's happening. We all hate it."

A door slammed, and Ivy sighed. "I won't stand for him treating you like the enemy."

"Well, maybe he perceives me to be the enemy right now. He's about to lose the only grandmother he's ever known, and it probably feels as though we're all expecting me to take her place."

"That's not true."

Carolyn's eyes widened. "It is to a scared little boy."

Ivy finished putting the dinner dishes in the dishwasher when the doorbell rang. A few seconds later, her father stood in the doorway, his mouth forming a straight line of disgust.

"Pete Barton is here," Elam Griffith said. "What do you want me to tell him?"

Ivy didn't say what she was thinking. "I'll come talk to him."

Elam mumbled something under his breath and went upstairs.

Ivy went to the front door and saw Pete standing on the porch, a Denver Broncos stocking cap pulled down over his ears. She went outside and closed the door behind her.

"What're you doing here?"

"Is that any way to greet your high school sweetheart?" Pete flashed his trademark smile that would have melted her a decade ago.

"If you came to tell me the sheriff knows Joe was strangled, my dad already told me."

"I figured." He took a card out of his ski jacket pocket and handed it to her. "Actually, I wanted to give you the invitation to the class reunion. I called and made reservations for the four of us."

Ivy glared at him. "I told you I wanted to think about it."

"Okay. But now you're all set if you decide to go."

"I already told you I'm ashamed of my past and don't really want to face everybody. Besides, I know I look awful. The last thing I want is everyone's pity."

Pete rolled his eyes. "Then do something about it! Have your hair styled. Wear something that at least makes you *look* like you have a figure. And put some color on your face."

"Is that your idea of a pep talk?"

"What'd you expect me to say: You haven't changed a bit? I'm not blind."

Ivy hated that she was blushing. She struggled to find her voice and finally said, "I don't have to go if I don't want to."

Pete leaned down until he was nose to nose with her, his breath turning to vapor. "Why don't you cut the whiny kid routine? This is no joke. You know what's at risk, so I suggest you start thinking about your loyalty to the other three people involved in the pact."

"Or what?"

The look in Pete's eyes sent a chill up her spine. Or was it the cold air?

"Do you really need me to spell it out again?" he whispered. "What happened to Joe happened a long time ago. I never meant to kill him, and I'm not going to prison for it. Period. Do you understand what I'm saying?"

"Are you threatening me?"

His face softened and he brushed her cheek with his hand.

"Why would I do that? Look, all I'm saying is there's nothing to be gained by getting caught now. Rotting in prison won't bring Joe back. You and Denny have kids to raise. Reg's wife is pregnant. My mom needs me to run the deli. Just honor the pact. That's all I ask. We've come too far to blow it now."

The front door opened.

"Everything all right?" Elam said.

"I'm fine, Dad. I'll just be a minute."

"You need to come in out of the cold."

"I was just leaving, Mr. Griffith." Pete's gaze caught hers. "Think about it. Everyone would love to see you." Pete nodded at Elam, then turned and went down the steps and out to his shiny green truck.

"What'd he want, anyway?" Elam said.

"Our high school class is having its tenth reunion on the twenty-second. Pete thinks I should go."

"Is he trying to date you again?"

"No, nothing like that. Besides, I have no interest whatsoever in Pete Barton." *If anything, he scares me.*

Elam drew her inside and put his sweater around her shoulders. "Good. I should've discouraged you from dating him the last time. He made you miserable. And just so you know, Pete's got a reputation with the ladies. He drinks too much, and he's gambling over at the Indian reservation."

"I couldn't care less what he does."

"So are you going to the reunion?"

"I don't know. With Lu's situation, I'm reluctant to plan ahead. But it might be good for me. I probably will."

Her father looked into her eyes and it was hard to look back. "Ivy, you've lied so much over the years it's going to take time for me to trust you again. But I love you. Always have. Always will. As long as you're under my roof, don't expect me to sit back and watch you go down the wrong path without speaking my mind."

"I just want to get my life together. Honest. It won't be easy without Lu, and I don't have time to go down any path, much less a wrong path." *At least not a new one.*

9

ON THURSDAY MORNING, Ivy Griffith put on her name tag and looked out beyond the green and white checked curtains of Jewel's Café to Barton's Deli across the street. She wondered if she had the courage to tell Pete Barton she had decided not to go to the class reunion and wasn't going to be pressured into it.

"Doll, would you turn on that Open sign?" Jewel Sadler hollered from the kitchen.

Ivy bent down and plugged in the sign, then stood and turned just as Flint Carter came through the front door. "Good morning, Sheriff."

Flint tipped the rim of his hat. "Good morning, yourself. So do you think you're finally getting settled in Jacob's Ear?"

"Yes, but I'm sure my dad told you my friend Lu's very sick."

"Yeah, sorry to hear it." Flint went over and sat at the table closest to the moose head. "I don't need a menu. I'll have my usual: a—"

"Ham-and-cheese omelet with rye toast, a side of hash browns, a small orange juice, and a black coffee, right?"

Flint smiled. "You're good."

"Thanks, I'm working on it."

"Interesting about Joe Hadley, eh?" Flint said. "All those years of wondering what had happened to him, and he was here all the time."

"Well, I was shocked." Ivy felt a shiver as Flint's gaze caught hers, and she hoped he hadn't noticed. "Do you have any leads?"

"I've got some theories I'm kicking around. Nothing I can talk about yet."

"Why would anyone hurt Joe Hadley? He was such a nice guy."

"I don't know, Ivy. But I promise you I'm going to find out. I've waited a decade to get a break, and now that I've got it, no way am I letting this case get away from me again."

"I'll be right back with your coffee." Ivy went over to the coffeemaker and picked up the full pot and a mug and went back to the sheriff's table.

"By the way, I hear your class reunion is coming up," the sheriff said. "I want to use the opportunity to talk to Joe's classmates. Any idea what kind of turnout you're expecting?"

"Not really. I just found out about it myself."

"You going?"

Ivy nodded without intending to. "Sure. It'll be nice seeing everyone after all this time." *So much for not being pressured.*

Brandon Jones sat at his desk in the administrative offices of Three Peaks Christian Camp. He saw an e-mail come in from Buzz Easton and opened it.

Brandon,
   Thanks for riding down to Durango with me the other day and taking a look at my white-water operation. I thought you might enjoy taking a look at some highlights of my other favorite interest.
   Buzz

Brandon clicked on to the link, and pornographic images popped up on the screen. He quickly backed out of the site and deleted the e-mail, wondering what would've possessed Buzz to think he would find something like that amusing.

He reached over and picked up the phone and dialed Buzz's cell number, wondering if he should wait till he wasn't mad.

"This is Buzz."

"I didn't appreciate the link to your *other* favorite interest," Brandon said.

Buzz laughed. "Why is your nose out of joint? It was just a joke. I'm sure you've seen naked bodies before."

"I just don't happen to believe sex is a spectator sport, all right? Plus I work at a Christian camp, and having stuff like this on my computer could threaten my job."

"I said all right, but it's not like it's illegal." There was laughter in Buzz's tone. "Just hit the delete button. It won't tarnish your halo."

"You really think this is funny?"

"Truthfully? Yeah. I mean, you're a grown man, and you're reacting like my mother."

"I don't need that stuff in my life, Buzz. I'm serious. Don't send me anything like this again."

"Suit yourself. I just don't get what you're so afraid of."

"I just don't want it, is that clear?"

"Yeah, sure. Whatever."

A few moments of awkward silence separated them, and then Buzz said, "So are you or aren't you going to help me paint the inside of the gift shop?"

"Of course I am. But I need to be sure you and I are on the same page with this because I—"

"Okay, bud. I got the message. I'm going to head down to Durango again tomorrow. Can you take off?"

"Sure. I can pretty much set my own schedule for the next few weeks now that we're finished hiring for summer camp."

"How about I pick you up at your house at seven and we can make a day of it? With two of us painting we might be able to finish in one day."

"All right, sounds good." Brandon hung up the phone just as Kelsey walked in his office. "Hi, honey. How's your morning going?"

"Busy," she said. "I'm on my way to the break room to get coffee and wondered if you'd like some."

"Sure. That was Buzz on the phone. He wants me to help him paint the inside of his new gift shop tomorrow. I said I would since I know you're going to be taking your quilts to that shop in Silverton."

Kelsey nodded. "They're taking everything I've made on consignment."

He pulled her onto his lap. "You're starting to get a reputation as the quilt queen of Jacob's Ear."

Kelsey laughed. "Now *that's* a title for you."

"I love you, you know that?"

She put her arms around his neck. "I love you, too. And just to prove it, I'm making you beef stroganoff for dinner tonight."

"Mmm, my favorite."

Kelsey smiled. "Everything I fix is your favorite."

"You're right."

"I'd better go get the coffee before Jake wonders what happened to me." Kelsey eased out of his lap. "We're in the process of laying out the new promotional brochure, and Elam's coming by this afternoon to approve it."

Brandon watched her leave his office, thinking she was all the woman he would ever need and wondering why Buzz Easton was too dense to understand that.

Ivy took the spray bottle of Clorox water and began wiping down tables in preparation for lunch customers. She heard the door open and looked up into Pete Barton's trademark smile.

"What are you doing here?" she said.

He glanced around the nearly empty café. "Can we talk for a minute—outside?"

"Hold on." Ivy poked her head in the kitchen where Jewel was making a batch of her famous chicken salad. "Would it be okay if I step outside for five minutes? The only ones out here are Deke and Roscoe, and they've been served."

"Sure, doll," Jewel said. "I'll keep an eye on things."

Ivy followed Pete outside and stood with her arms folded. "What is it?"

"Look, I know I hurt your feelings last night. It's just that I hate to see you let yourself go when—"

"You made that crystal clear. I need to get back to work." She started to go inside, and Pete put his hands on her shoulders.

"Wait. Some investigator from the sheriff's department called. He wants to talk to me this afternoon, and I'm sure you can guess what about."

Ivy turned around and spoke just above a whisper. "So? Just stick to the pact and tell him what we agreed on."

"You're right. Guess I'm a little paranoid. I know Sheriff Carter comes in here for breakfast every morning. Has he been pumping you for information?"

"No, but I haven't ignored the subject either. I don't want him to think I'm avoiding talking about it. I have more to lose than you do."

There was that threatening look again. "Yeah, I guess you do at that."

Ivy stood at the window and stared at nothing as Sonya Roe got into her car and drove off. She turned to Lu and studied her face, thinking how surreal it was preparing for her death.

"Sonya's nice," Ivy said. "And seems caring. So why do I resent her being here?"

Lu Ramirez held out her hand, and Ivy went over and sat on the side of the bed.

"Maybe what you resent is the intrusion of someone you don't know helping to care for me." Lu picked up Ivy's hand. "But that resentment will go away if you let Sonya be your friend."

Ivy closed her eyes and shook her head from side to side. "How am I going to go on without you, Lu?"

"You will. You're stronger than you think."

"I hate that there's nothing I can do to stop you from dying."

"So let's enjoy each other while we have time. We have much to be thankful for. Just look how far you've come. No drugs for three years."

Ivy sighed. "Yeah, but it's still a choice every single day."

"So keep choosing. You can do it."

"I know. But it would be less of a struggle if I could unload all this guilt about Joe's death. But I can't do that without going to jail, which is out of the question until Montana's secure with my parents. And who knows how long that'll take? He's going to have such a hard time without you. We both are." Ivy put her face in her hands.

"Make peace with God, Ivy girl. He wants to help you."

I sincerely doubt that. "Did I tell you Pete was here last night and came by the café this morning? He's still trying to pressure me into going to our class reunion."

"Maybe he wants to go out with you."

Ivy sneered. "Hardly. The man finds me repulsive. And frankly, he scares me."

"Why?"

"I'm not sure how to describe the look he gets in his eyes sometimes, but I feel threatened, like if he thought I was going to cross him, he could just as easily strangle me as he did Joe."

"I wish you'd stay away from him."

"I'm trying. But he's the one who keeps showing up on my doorstep. It feels as though he's trying to keep me on a short leash."

Ivy heard footsteps on the stairs and what sounded like the rattling of a dog collar. Seconds later, Sasha charged into Lu's room and ran in circles, then sat at the foot of the bed and barked.

Montana came in after the dog and grabbed her by the collar. "Bad girl! You have to be quiet in here. Sorry, Gramma Lu."

"Maybe Sasha just needs a little girl talk." Lu reached over and scratched the dog's chin. "Is that it?"

Montana smiled, seemingly pleased that Lu was in good spirits. "Did that hospice nurse leave?"

"Yes, Sonya's gone. She'll be back tomorrow afternoon."

"I don't like it when she's here."

"The medicine she gave me made me feel better," Lu said. "Why don't you go get your favorite books, and let's read awhile?"

Montana flashed a jack-o-lantern smile. "Okay. But *I* get to read *Green Eggs and Ham*."

He ran into his room and came back with several books, including the threadbare copy of Dr. Seuss's *Green Eggs and Ham* that Lu had bought at Goodwill years ago. He crawled into Lu's bed and sat with a pillow propped behind him and started reading in a typical first-grader monotone.

"Are you sure you're up to this?" Ivy said.

Lu looked over at Ivy, her eyes starting to look glassy from the painkiller Sonya had given her. "Every second of it."

Ivy memorized the moment, then left Lu's room and went into her own and shut the door. She put her face in her hands and wept quietly.

10

LATE SATURDAY MORNING, Brandon Jones followed Kelsey into Jewel's Diner, his eyes peeled for Buzz and Maggie Easton.

"I'm sure they've already come and gone," Brandon said. "Man, this place is packed out. Looks like there's one table open over there by the window."

Ivy Griffith came over with menus in hand. "Hi, you two. Right this way." She led them to the empty table. "Today's special is meatloaf and whipped potatoes. But I'm sure you know we serve breakfast anytime."

"I'll have the Hungry Man Special," Brandon said. "Orange juice and coffee."

Kelsey smiled. "Cheese blintzes for me. Heavy on the strawberry topping. And coffee."

"Okay, coming right up. By the way, Montana's really excited about you taking him out snowmobiling this afternoon. That's all he talked about all last night."

"We're looking forward to it," Brandon said. "Elam said we could borrow the Suburban and trailer the snowmobiles up to the state park where the snow's still deep. There's a ton of powder up there and plenty of room to play."

"I'm grateful for Montana to have something fun to do. It's getting intense at home with Lu's situation, and I don't want him worrying too much about it."

Brandon nodded. "We'll do what we can to keep him entertained. Maybe we'll take Sasha with us. He seems attached to her."

"Thanks. You guys are too much. I'll be right back with your coffee."

Brandon put his hand on Kelsey's. "You're a good sport to give up part of your Saturday to entertain Montana."

"He's a sweet little boy whose world's turning upside down. It's the least we can do."

Ivy brought two mugs and a plastic pitcher of coffee and set them on the table. "There you go. Your breakfast will be out in a few minutes."

Brandon waited until Ivy was out of earshot, and then said, "If you didn't know, how old would you guess her to be?"

"I don't know—somewhere between thirty-five and forty. Certainly not twenty-eight."

"I would never have recognized her from the picture on the bookshelf at the Griffiths' house."

Kelsey blew on her coffee and took a sip. "She can't help looking older than she is, but you'd think she'd wear makeup or style her hair or something." Kelsey set down her mug and looked at Brandon. "Sorry, that sounded really petty. I'm just surprised she doesn't try to look her best. She's never going to attract a husband looking that drab."

"Maybe she doesn't want a husband."

"Then she'd better go to trade school because she's not going to make it on her own waiting tables."

Brandon noticed two young men come in the door and walk over to Ivy, who was busy brewing a fresh pot of coffee.

"Ivy?"

Ivy Griffith turned and saw two men about her age standing there. "Yes?"

"It's me: Reg Morrison," the tallest one said. "Don't look so surprised. I haven't changed *that* much, have I?"

Ivy couldn't find her voice and turned her eyes on the

redheaded man next to him and heard herself say, "Denny?"

"That's me," Denny Richards said. "It's great to see you, gal."

Ivy hugged both of them, surprised that she was actually glad to see them.

"We were in town for the weekend and thought we'd say hello. Pete told us you were working here."

I'll bet he did. "I'm curious how you both just happened to be here for the weekend. Pete said he hadn't seen you in ages."

"Actually, we came to see you," Reg said. "Pete called and told us you were back, and we thought it'd be fun to get together like old times. How about meeting us for coffee at Grinder's when you get off?"

"Sorry, I can't. There's something I have to do this afternoon." Ivy saw a man, woman, and two kids walk in the door. "I really need to take care of those customers."

Reg gently held her arm. "Surely you can make time to have coffee with old friends?"

"Not this afternoon."

"What about tonight then? Or tomorrow?"

A party of six got up from a table in the back and ambled toward the register. "Guys, I can't talk about this now. Excuse me." Ivy picked up four menus and walked over to the family waiting at the front door. "Welcome to Jewel's. We'll have that empty table cleaned off in just a minute. Would you like booster seats for the little ones?"

Reg and Denny shuffled past her with the party of six, smiles on their faces, and Ivy knew she hadn't seen the last of them.

Ivy zipped up Montana's coat and pulled his stocking cap down over his ears.

"Mom, you're obsessing again," Montana said.

Ivy stifled a grin and handed him his gloves. "Where'd you learn a big word like that?"

"Watching Dr. Phil. I'm seven now. You don't have to dress me like I'm a baby or something."

Ivy tilted his chin and looked into those brown puppy eyes. "You're right. Sorry." She resisted the urge to take the tube of ChapStick out of her pocket and apply it to his cracked lips.

Sasha barked playfully outside, and Montana ran to the window and pulled back the curtain. "Brandon and Kelsey are here!" He pulled open the front door and went out on the porch.

"Hey there, big guy," Brandon said. "You ready to rock and roll?"

"Yeah. Can I drive the snowmobile?"

"If you pass your driver's test. We need to have a lesson first."

Kelsey came up on the porch and hugged Ivy. "Don't worry about a thing. Brandon's great with kids, and he won't take any chances."

"Here's a tube of ChapStick," Ivy said. "Don't tell Montana I gave it to you or he won't use it."

"I'll never tell." Kelsey slipped it in her pocket and looked at Brandon and Montana, tussling with Sasha. "Looks like it's going to be me, *two* boys, and a dog. Why don't you go do something this afternoon and get your mind off Lu?"

"That's an excellent idea." Carolyn Griffith came outside and stood next to Ivy. "Lu's asleep, and I plan to be here all afternoon." She handed Ivy a piece of paper. "Reg Morrison just called. He and Denny Richards are in town and wanted to know if you could meet them at Grinder's. Why don't you call them back? It would do you good to see old friends."

"Mom, I can't dump my responsibility on you, especially after you spent the entire morning watching Montana."

"We made cookies. It was fun. Your dad's gone till supper, and I'm going to curl up on the couch and read my new issue of *Woman's Day*. Why don't you go meet your friends?"

Ivy sat in the car in front of Grinder's Coffee House and moved the rearview mirror until she saw her reflection. She applied the lipstick she had shoplifted from the drugstore, and then wondered why she had bothered. It did nothing to change the fact that she looked thin and pale and dried-up. She ran a comb through her limp hair and wished she had the money to have it shaped and styled. Why did she care what Reg and Denny thought, anyhow?

Ivy got out of her mother's Jeep, went in Grinder's, and spotted Reg and Denny sitting in a booth.

"Hey, girl," Denny said. "Glad you decided to fit us into your schedule." He moved over and patted the empty seat. "Sit down. I'm buying."

"It's great to see you guys," Ivy said, realizing she actually meant it. She took off her ski jacket and slid in the booth. "I think the last time we did this was the week before we all left for college."

"Man, does that seem like forever ago." Reg's hearty laugh hadn't changed.

The waitress came over to the table. "What can I get for the lady?"

"I'd love a chocolate latte." Ivy decided this was her chance to finally try one, and she'd pretend to like it even if it tasted horrible.

"Anything to go with it?"

"No thanks."

"Oh, come on, Ivy. Have one of those giant cookies or something gooey," Denny said. "You obviously don't need to worry about calories."

"I'm still pretty full from lunch."

"Bring her a chocolate-chip cookie," Denny said. "If she doesn't eat it, I will."

The waitress nodded. "I'll be right back."

Denny grinned and nudged Ivy with his elbow. "My wife's thirty pounds overweight and has to fight it all the time. You're lucky you don't."

Ivy stared at her hands. "Look, guys, I know how different I look. We don't have to tiptoe around it, okay?"

No one said anything for a long time.

Finally Reg said, "We heard you had a drug problem, but Pete told us you kicked it."

"I did."

"Well, good for you." Denny patted her hand. "So what're you up to now?"

"I have a seven-year-old son, Montana. No husband. And not much else to tell. I'd rather hear about you."

Reg and Denny didn't hesitate, and Ivy became absorbed in listening to them talk about what they'd been doing for the past decade. She glanced at her watch and realized that forty-five minutes had gone by.

"So when's your wife due?" she said to Reg.

"June eighth. I still need to paint the nursery blue, but I've already bought cigars. Zack Winfield Morrison. Sounds like a jock, eh?"

Ivy smiled. "It's a great name. Congratulations."

The door opened and Ivy saw a flash of light and then Pete Barton walking toward the booth.

I should've known Pete-the-control-freak wouldn't be able to resist being here, Ivy thought.

Pete slid into the booth next to Reg. "Hail, hail, the gang's all here."

"Gee, what a surprise," Ivy said, wondering if anyone picked up on the sarcasm in her tone.

"Hey, it's a momentous occasion having the fab four together again." Pete lowered his voice, and Ivy could barely hear him above the drone. "Plus I didn't want to pass up the opportunity to fill you all in on my conversation with the sheriff's investigator. I'm happy to report he doesn't suspect a thing."

"What kinds of questions did he ask?" Denny said.

"A lot of the same stuff the sheriff asked everyone on the team right after Joe disappeared. You know, was Joe having trouble with anyone? Was he depressed? When was the last time you saw him? How did he seem? But this time he asked me what I was doing the afternoon Joe disappeared and if anyone could confirm that. And I just stuck with the pact. Piece of cake. If we all say the same thing, we're home free."

Reg leaned forward, his arms folded on the table. "What if he checks out our story and finds out no one down at Louie's remembers seeing us?"

"How can anyone prove we weren't there? And who remembers details that far back anyhow? I think we're fine as long as our stories mesh."

The waitress brought Ivy's latte and a chocolate-chip cookie the size of a salad plate. "Anything else?"

"Pete, you want coffee?" Denny said.

"No, I've got to get back to the deli."

The waitress left, and a few seconds later a young man with wavy dark hair and navy coveralls got up from a table and walked over to the booth, a toothy grin connecting his ears. "I thought I recognized you guys!"

Pete held his gaze. "Do I know you?"

"It's me, Bill Ziwicki."

"Who?"

"Bill Ziwicki. I hung out with you guys in high school."

"Sorry, I don't remember."

Bill rolled his eyes. "Yeah, right."

"You think I'm kidding?"

"Come on, Pete. We had a business arrangement. I used to make some *really* good buys for you guys."

"You must have us mixed up with someone else." Pete glanced around the booth, an eyebrow raised, the corners of his mouth twitching. "You guys know him?"

Reg and Denny shook their heads.

Bill put his palms flat on the table, leaned forward, and lowered his voice. "I used to buy you guys weed and angel dust. I put my neck on the line for you. There's no way you don't remember me."

Pete folded his arms across his chest. "We just said we didn't."

"But they do," Ivy said. "We all do."

Bill's face suddenly looked pinker than Ivy's sweater. "I knew it! You let me sit with you at lunch a few times. You said I was your friend."

"We lied," Pete said. "We told every guy who bought us drugs that he was our friend."

"But there wasn't anybody else. I was your main man."

"Okay, live with that illusion. Now maybe you could let us get back to our conversation?"

Bill backed away from the booth, his bushy eyebrows scrunched. "Yeah, you do that." He went over to his table and sat, his jaw set, his hands wrapped around a Styrofoam cup.

Pete snickered. "Man, what a loser. Wait…" He put his hands to his forehead and closed his eyes. "It's all coming back to me now…Icky Ziwicki, the walking zit."

Reg and Denny chortled.

"Will you guys knock it off? He can hear you." Ivy looked over at Bill and then at Pete. "Would it have killed you to be nice to him?"

"Why, because he bought us drugs? Come on, Ivy, the guy sucked up to us because he was a nobody who wanted to be a somebody. That's the only reason he'd do something that demeaning."

Yeah, well. He wasn't the only one. Ivy slid out of the booth. "I hate to be a party pooper, but I need to get home. Thanks for the latte, boys."

"It was really good seeing you," Denny said.

Reg nodded. "Yeah, it was fun catching up. See you at the class reunion?"

"Oh, she'll be there," Pete said. "I've already signed her up."

Ivy manufactured a smile and slipped on her ski jacket. "Well, there you have it. The mighty Pete Barton has spoken."

She caught a glimpse of Bill Ziwicki's face as she walked to the exit and decided it was a good thing that Sheriff Carter wasn't around on Saturday. At that moment, she'd gladly spill everything she knew about what had happened to Joe Hadley.

11

SHERIFF FLINT CARTER sat in his office perusing Monday's issue of the *Tri-County Courier* and sipping the to-go coffee he'd brought with him from Jewel's.

"Mornin', Sheriff." Lieutenant Bobby Knolls came in and sat in the chair next to the desk. "How was your weekend?"

"Not bad. Hard to put the case out of my mind. So what'd the lab say?"

"The keys we found were Joe Hadley's, all right—house and the family Impala. Probably were in his pocket when he was buried." Bobby blew a pink bubble, then sucked it into his mouth and popped it. "We've covered a lot of ground near the scene, but everything we've found relates only to Joe Hadley: bones, class ring, keys. Whoever buried that kid sure didn't leave any evidence behind."

"Are you done looking?" Flint said.

"Give me another day or two. But my gut tells me we've found everything we're gonna find."

"How many people have you questioned so far?"

"About twenty, give or take." Bobby looked up and shook his head. "Sheriff, this case is as cold as it was ten years ago. There's no motive. It just doesn't seem like Joe Hadley had any enemies. Everyone loved the kid."

"Somebody didn't."

"I don't think we can discount the possibility this *was* a serial killing."

Flint looked out the window at the snowcapped San Juans on the other side of Phantom Hollow and took a sip of coffee. "I'm not. But the chance that a stranger could slip in and out of a town of five hundred—in the off-season, no less—without anyone noticing seems pretty remote."

"Maybe there's a serial killer livin' here."

"Then why hasn't someone else gone missing?"

"Wish I knew the answer."

Flint set his Styrofoam cup on the desk. "Me too, Bobby. But I'm going to get answers or die trying. I can't spend another ten years addicted to this case."

Ivy Griffith stood outside Rita Shepard's first-grade classroom at Tanner County Elementary School and looked through the window in the door. Ian Carter was introducing Montana to the other kids as if he were a new toy.

Rita walked over to the door and stepped out into the hallway next to Ivy. "I think Montana's going to be just fine."

Ivy nodded. "Seems like it. I really want school to be a positive experience, especially with all the pressure he has at home."

"I understand. I'll do everything I can to make school fun. And from what I've seen so far, he won't have any problem socially. How old is Montana?"

"He just turned seven last month."

"He's younger than about half these kids, but his vocabulary and social skills seem above average. Is there anything else I should know?"

Ivy hesitated and then said. "Yes. I'm a recovering drug addict. I've been clean for three years, and my friend Lu—Montana calls her Gramma Lu—was there for him when I wasn't. He has a very special attachment to her. Also, there's never been a father in the picture."

"Thanks for being candid," Rita said. "Knowing that will help me be sensitive to Montana, especially while Lu is so ill."

Ivy looked through the window again and saw Montana and two other boys working on what appeared to be a jigsaw puzzle.

"Don't worry about him." Rita reached for her hand and squeezed it, almost as a handshake. "I have a feeling he's going to have a really good first day."

Ivy smiled. "You're probably right."

She glanced in the classroom one last time, then walked down the long corridor and out of the building to her mother's Jeep.

She drove several miles back to Three Peaks Camp and pulled up the long, steep driveway and parked out in front of her parents' log home. She went inside and found her mother in the kitchen, pouring batter into the bread maker.

"So how'd it go?" Carolyn Griffith asked.

"Good. The other kids were practically fighting over who got to play with Montana next. I like his teacher a lot."

"What a relief, eh?"

"Yeah, really. I want him to have a good experience this spring so he won't balk at going back to school in the fall. I'm going to go check on Lu, okay?"

Ivy went upstairs and peeked in Lu's room. She was sitting up in bed, her Bible open in her lap.

"Come in."

"Don't let me interrupt. I was just checking on you."

Lu took off her reading glasses. "Come tell me about Montana's first day at school."

Ivy went over and sat on the side of the bed. "So far so good. His teacher's a doll, and he seemed to fit right in with the other kids. He was so busy when I left he didn't even look up. I have a feeling he's going to love it there."

"That's so good. I prayed it would go well." Lu seemed to be pondering something for a few moments, and then caught Ivy's gaze and held it. "There's something I need you to do for me. Your parents had a talk with their pastor, and he's offered me a burial plot at Woodlands Community Church cemetery. I need you to go pick out a casket. I'm not fussy—the least expensive one you can find. There should be enough in my account to cover the cost."

"I can't—" Ivy put her fist to her mouth, surprised at the surge of emotion that had stolen her words.

Lu combed through Ivy's hair with her fingers. "The cemetery will be a comforting place to come when you feel the need to talk to me—or when Montana does. It's important to me that you're comfortable with it."

"What about a headstone?"

"A simple wooden cross will do fine."

Because you don't have any more money, Ivy thought.

"As soon as everything's arranged, I'd like to ride out there and see it with you."

"I hate talking about this!"

"I know, but we have to. I'm getting worse. I need your help to get these details finalized while I still feel up to it. The more we talk about it, the easier it will be. I've already talked to Pastor Myers about the graveside service."

Ivy put her hands over her ears. "Lu, I can't handle this."

Seconds passed, then Lu gently took her arm and pulled it down. "Pastor Myers says it's a beautiful spot. Either your parents are big tithers, or the pastor is a very compassionate soul. I'm guessing a little of both."

"It's not like he's handing you the moon. It's just a plot in his churchyard cemetery."

"Pretty nice since I'm not a member. And you'd be surprised what a plot would cost if we had to go looking. This is a gift."

Ivy sighed. "You deserve better than a wooden cross to mark your grave."

"It's enough. If it bothers you, plant some flowers—maybe some alyssum. They're easy."

"I'm not going to handle this well."

"Yes, you are. You're braver than you think."

"You keep saying that. I'm not."

Lu's deep brown eyes grew wide. "You kicked a cocaine habit, no? And you came back here to make peace with the past, which

will probably mean going to jail and being separated from your
son for a while. And now you're preparing to bury your closest
friend. If that doesn't take courage, I don't what does."

Ivy wiped away a tear trickling down her cheek. "You always
see something in me I can't find. How do you do that?"

"It's easy. When I look at you, I see light under the door."

"What does *that* mean?"

Lu just smiled.

"You're not going to tell me?"

"No. But you'll feel me smiling in heaven when you figure it
out."

Brandon Jones walked down the main hall of the administrative
offices of Three Peaks Christian Camp and Conference Center
and knocked on Jake Compton's open door.

"Come in," Jake said.

Brandon went in and sat in the blue cushy chair he had threatened to take home with him because it was so comfortable. "Did
you and Suzanne have a nice weekend?"

Jake nodded, his eyes fixed on the newspaper. "Yeah, we did.
Have you been following the murder investigation? The *Courier* is
usually pretty folksy, but this discovery of the kid's bones is big
news."

"Yeah, I guess the dead kid was in Ivy Griffith's graduating
class."

"That's what Elam said." Jake folded the newspaper and
pushed it aside, then got up and closed the door and sat in the
chair next to Brandon. "I came in Saturday to tie up a few loose
ends. My computer was messing up so I used yours. Hope you
don't mind."

"Not at all."

Jake linked his fingers together. "Is there anything you want to
tell me?"

"About what?"

"You still hanging around Buzz Easton?"

"I rode down to Durango with him on Friday and helped him paint the inside of his new souvenir shop. Is that a problem?"

"I don't know. You tell me."

Brandon studied Jake's face and decided he looked angry. "Is this about my being with Buzz? Because I was under the impression that what I did in my free time was my business."

"There's pornography on your computer, Brandon. That makes it my business."

Brandon felt his face get hot and the words seemed to be stuck in his throat. Finally he said, "What specifically are you talking about?"

"I accidentally deleted an e-mail message I meant to forward to myself. And when I got into your delete box to retrieve it, I saw an e-mail from Buzz. I opened it and saw the porn link."

"You opened my e-mail?" Brandon said. "For crying out loud, Jake!"

"Look, I know a lot more about Buzz than you do. I tried to warn you to stay away from him."

"Just what is it you know that I'm in the dark about?"

Jake folded his arms across his chest. "I'm not at liberty to say."

"Is he wanted by the law or something?"

"No, nothing like that."

"All this talking in circles doesn't help me!" Brandon sat for a few moments until he could talk without sounding mad. "I don't know what's going through your mind, Jake. But the second I got that e-mail from Buzz, I called him and told him never to send me anything like that again, and that having stuff like that on my computer could threaten my job."

"Has it happened before?"

"Absolutely not. Look, if I had anything to hide, don't you think I would've made sure that e-mail was deleted from the delete box?"

Jake exhaled. He got up and leaned against his desk, his hands in his pockets. "I'm not questioning your integrity, Brandon. I think you're a great guy. I'd like to see you stay that way. It's Buzz I don't trust."

"Okay. But do you think this is the first time in my life someone who likes porn has tried to get me interested? It's not like I can't say no."

"Did you tell Kelsey?"

"She doesn't like Buzz. I didn't see the point in upsetting her."

"I wish you'd tell her."

"Why?"

"Just as a safeguard—a way to be accountable."

"Accountable for what? I haven't done anything."

Jake turned and held his gaze. "Bad company corrupts good character, Brandon. Buzz is a bad apple."

"He just needs the Lord. How is he going to hear the Good News if Christian guys aren't willing to befriend him? So he's rough around the edges…I'm a big boy. It's not like I'm going to let him take me down a wrong path."

"All right," Jake said. "Have it your way. But you'd better be darned sure it's the Lord prodding you to spend time with Buzz and not just your passion for white-water rafting."

Ivy walked across the churchyard of Woodlands Community Church and past the wrought-iron gate. Only a few patches of snow remained, and the cemetery looked exactly as she had remembered it. She spotted the angel monument that marked baby Amy's grave. She walked over and stood next to it, flooded with the memory of Rusty holding her hand, their mother weeping, and their father steely silent as Pastor Myers prayed for God to receive the spirit of this stillborn child.

Ivy reached up and traced the smooth features of the marble angel and wondered what her sister would have been like and if she knew she had a family—and that Ivy had disgraced it.

She turned and trudged toward the back of the cemetery, her heart heavy with the grim reality that soon she would have to leave Lu there.

When she'd gone beyond the reddish headstone marked "Weaver" to the open area just inside the fence, she turned around and looked out at the snowcapped mountains in the distance. The words of Isaiah came to her almost audibly. *"Though the mountains be shaken and the hills be removed, yet my unfailing love for you will not be shaken."*

Where had that come from? She hadn't opened a Bible since the day Joe died. Not that she believed it anymore.

Ivy moved her eyes slowly across the quaint old cemetery and the breathtaking landscape beyond and tried to imagine a simple wooden cross on the spot where she stood. It seemed perfect, better than she had envisioned. A shadow crossed over her, and she looked up and saw a bald eagle—the first in a very long time—and wondered if it was a sign.

Pastor Rick Myers came out the back door of the church, his graying hair tossed about by the April breeze, and met her halfway across the churchyard. "What'd you think?"

"It's a pretty spot. I'm sure Lu will be pleased." Ivy studied his face and sensed in him no condemnation of her past. "Can I ask you a personal question?"

"All right."

"Did my parents pay you for this?"

Pastor Myers smiled with his eyes. "Ivy, your parents donated this land to the church when you were a baby. We're happy to accommodate them and you any way we can." The pastor put his hand on her shoulder and walked her to her mother's Jeep. "Is someone going with you to pick out a casket? If not, I'd be glad to go with you."

"Thanks, but I think I'll be okay now."

12

CAROLYN GRIFFITH POURED Elam a cup of coffee and then sat at the kitchen table. She looked out the window just as a doe and her fawn ambled into view just this side of the split rail fence.

"I'll bet you're glad investigators are through at the construction site," Carolyn said. "Now you can get back to the condominium project."

Elam Griffith nodded. "Yeah, but we'll be lucky to get the model ready in time for the Getaway Home Show. And after tying up my building site for ten days, all Flint found was a set of keys that belonged to Joe Hadley."

"You wouldn't think much of Flint if he hadn't done a thorough job."

"Let's just hope he solves the case." Elam took a sip of coffee. "Is Ivy at work?"

"No, she's not scheduled on Wednesdays. She drove Lu out to the church to take a look at the cemetery plot."

"What's Ivy thinking? The poor thing is so weak she can hardly walk."

"Lu insisted," Carolyn said. "They took the wheelchair with them. Truthfully, I think it's good for them to face this together. It might help Ivy get through the grief later."

"It's obvious she's real fond of Lu."

"I think it goes beyond *fond*. Lu's a mother figure—for both Ivy and Montana. We owe a lot to that woman. Who knows what would've happened to Ivy and Montana if it hadn't been for her?"

Elam added a little more cream to his coffee and stirred. "Don't you think it's odd Lu doesn't have any family? Seventy's not that old."

"I didn't ask questions."

"What're we going to do about a headstone? We can't just stick a wooden cross in the ground. Doesn't the cemetery have some kind of rule about that?"

"Yes, but Lu doesn't know that. It might help her hold on to her dignity if we let her think she's got her own expenses covered."

"What kind of casket did Ivy pick out for her?"

"The least expensive, but I think it wiped out Lu's account. I'd like to talk to Ivy about our buying a vault, but we don't need to say anything to Lu about it."

Elam shook his head. "What would they have done if they'd stayed in Denver?"

"Lu planned to be cremated, but Ivy wouldn't hear of it."

"Well, at least it's settled now. We just need to get Ivy and the boy past this so they can start living like normal people. Ivy needs to learn how to be the mother. She can't spend the rest of her life depending on someone else to do it for her."

Flint Carter sat at his desk, perusing the list of names and addresses of the kids who were in Joe Hadley's graduating class at Tanner County High School—one hundred sixteen in all.

"It's amazing how many of these kids don't live in the area anymore." Flint handed the list back to Bobby Knolls. "Any idea how many aren't coming to the class reunion?"

"Nineteen that we know of."

"Is there anybody who's been absent from all previous reunions?"

"Yeah, four guys and two gals. But all of them are registered to come this time except Adam Mills."

"Know anything about him?"

Bobby nodded. "Yeah, artsy type. Well liked. Travels with some highfalutin dance company in London. He played the lead role in the school play junior and senior years. If there was bad blood between him and Joe Hadley, nobody's alluded to it."

"What about the basketball teammates?"

"We've already questioned the ones who still live in the state. Their alibis checked out, and they were more than happy to cooperate. I'll wait to approach the others till they're in town for the reunion and I can eyeball them. But none of the players we've talked to had a beef with Joe or could remember anyone who did. Coach confirmed it. I think this is a dead end."

"I never suspected his teammates anyway. What about teachers?"

"The kid was an honor student. Never gave anybody trouble. As far as we can tell, he didn't smoke, drink, or drug. Didn't even have a steady girlfriend."

"Any chance he was involved with a lady teacher—maybe someone whose husband got jealous?"

"Nothing leads me to think that."

"What about the ranch hands?"

Bobby blew a bubble with his gum. "We grilled every person who was workin' on Collier Ranch at the time. No red flags there."

"Have you gone back and talked to Joe's family?"

"Yeah, the ones who were livin' in Jacob's Ear at the time he disappeared: parents, maternal grandparents, and two sisters. They were extremely cooperative. The father's the only one who would've had the strength to break the hyoid bone, and I'd bet my firstborn that he didn't do it."

"I agree. So we're back to square one."

"Yeah, it looks that way."

Ivy Griffith pulled into the parking lot at Woodlands Community Church just as the bells chimed ten. She parked the car and looked over at Lu, who seemed too drained even to open the door.

"I brought Mom's digital camera," Ivy said. "Why don't I go take some pictures of the grave site so you don't have to get out?"

"No, I want to see it for myself," Lu said. "Just help me get in the wheelchair."

Ivy opened the back door of her mother's Jeep and unloaded the lightweight wheelchair that hospice had brought to the house. She rolled it around to the passenger door and helped Lu get into it, wondering if she'd be able to push her stocky frame through the dried grass in the cemetery.

"Okay, I'm ready," Lu said.

Ivy pushed the wheelchair across the parking lot, then out into the churchyard and beyond the wrought-iron gate, surprised and pleased that the wheels were moving.

"Sorry it's so bumpy, Lu."

Ivy pushed Lu past Amy's grave to the empty plot behind the reddish headstone marked "Weaver," and turned the chair around. "Here were are."

Lu didn't say anything for the longest time, her eyes seeming to take it all in. Finally she said, "Thank You, Jesus."

"Does that mean you like it?"

"It's wonderful. Just wonderful." Lu reached back for Ivy's hand. "Thanks for bringing me here. I really wanted to see it."

"Don't you think this is just a little morbid?"

"Not at all. It's peaceful."

"If you say so. At least it's pretty." Ivy put her hands on Lu's thick shoulders and gently massaged. "Aren't you even a little scared?"

"Not of death. I'd like to skip the *dying* part, but I try to think about heaven and seeing my Jesus for the first time."

Ivy exhaled. "I wish I had your faith. All I think about is how much Montana and I will miss you, and how unfair it is that you have to die this way. I can't believe you're not even angry."

"I don't want to spend what little time I have left being angry. Come around here where I can see your face."

Ivy went around to the front of the wheelchair and squatted facing Lu.

"God brought us together for a reason." Lu tilted Ivy's chin and seemed to look deep into her eyes. "And He's allowing us to part ways for a reason. You mustn't let anger eat you up."

Ivy felt the emotion tighten her throat, and she forced out the words. "I'm more scared than angry! I know you're going to heaven, and I'm not. I turned my back on God when I chose to cover up Joe Hadley's death, and I made it worse by snorting blow and turning tricks to pay for my habit. I've been a rotten mother and an even worse daughter. I lie. I steal. I can't even support myself, let alone my son. There's no way I'm going to heaven. And I'm terrified that once you're gone, I won't ever see you again."

Lu took her thumb and wiped the tears off Ivy's cheeks. "I don't know why you won't ask God to forgive you. He wants to."

"I know you believe that, Lu. I wish I did."

Brandon Jones sat at his computer finishing up the last of the changes to the camp website when he heard a knock on his open door.

"Okay if I empty your trash?" Bill Ziwicki said.

"Sure. I'll be out of your way in just a second."

"I can clean another office and come back."

"No, I'm done." Brandon shut down his computer and waited for it to go off as Bill picked up the trash can and dumped the contents into his rolling trash receptacle.

"I'm surprised to see you here this late," Bill said.

"I just wanted the satisfaction of finishing this project. Feels good to have closure on something."

Bill laughed. "I can't imagine what that'd be like. I no sooner get done cleanin' than I'm back doin' the same thing all over again. Gotta look at it as job security."

"Do you own this cleaning service?"

"Yeah, three years now. I'm doin' real well, too. I like bein' my own boss. The guy I was workin' for treated me like a moron—till I became his competitor." Bill grinned. "I'm smarter than I look."

"Well, I appreciate your keeping the offices clean. Without

you, this place would look like a junk heap."

"Thanks. People pretty much take me for granted."

"Not me. Maybe it's because I remember what a slob I was when I was a bachelor."

"How long've you been married?"

"Just since Thanksgiving."

Bill gave a slight nod. "Hope it works out. I was married once. Lasted eighteen months, and then my wife left me. Said I'd never amount to a hill o' beans. Guess I showed her when I started my own business."

"Any chance you'll get back together?"

"Nah, she's remarried and has three kids."

"Well, I hope you meet the right woman someday." Brandon locked the drawer on his desk and walked toward the door. "Good night, Bill. Have a good one."

"Yeah, you too."

Brandon walked out of the administration building and down the street toward his living quarters, amazed that all the snow had disappeared. Out to the west, the jagged peaks of the San Juans were silhouetted against the orangey sky and looked surprisingly like the phony-looking velvet paintings he had seen in tourist shops.

He waved at Suzanne Compton as she passed him in her SUV, then walked up the front steps of his log house. He pushed open the door and was hit by the aroma of corned beef and cabbage, and suddenly realized he was famished.

Seconds later, Kelsey came into the living room and put her arms around his neck and kissed him. "Did you get the website updates finished?"

"Finally. Hope you didn't mind me working late, but it feels great having it behind me. So how was your day?"

"Busy. I did the banking, ran some errands, got caught up on the laundry. *And* I got a call from the shop in Silverton. They sold one of my quilts to a cross-country skier from Nebraska."

"That's great, honey. Looks like you've found a money-making outlet for your creativity."

"Yes, but what if they sell the other three before I can get replacements made?"

Brandon smiled. "Then you can take special orders."

Kelsey took his hand and led him out to the kitchen where the table was set for dinner. "I've got bad news. Lu's worse. Carolyn just called and said Ivy drove her out to the church this morning to look at a cemetery plot. By the time they got home, Lu was so weak they almost couldn't get her up the stairs. Carolyn said the bottoms of Lu's feet are starting to turn bluish, and the hospice nurse thinks maybe her organs are starting to shut down. The end may be really close."

"Sorry to hear that. But I guess it's a blessing, all things considered."

Kelsey pulled a pan of corn muffins out of the oven. "Well, no one wants Lu to live like this."

"I wonder how Montana's handling it? It was good seeing him totally relaxed when we took him home Saturday night."

"Carolyn said he's so quiet it bothers her. She wonders what's going on in that little mind of his."

"Maybe Elam needs to have a man-to-man with him. A boy his age may be afraid of what he's feeling, especially if he's never lost someone he loves before."

"I got the impression Elam and Montana haven't really clicked yet," Kelsey said. "It's beyond me, though. Montana is such a sweetheart. You'd think Elam would be thrilled to have a grandson."

13

BY LATE THE FOLLOWING AFTERNOON, Lu had slipped into a coma and was no longer responsive.

Ivy Griffith sat in the rocker in Lu's room, alone with her thoughts and aware of the *tick tick tick* of the clock on the nightstand. Montana's voice startled her.

"Gramma Lu's not gonna wake up, is she?" he said.

Ivy pulled her son into her lap. "I don't think so, sweetie."

"She told me she was gonna close her eyes and go from here to heaven, just like that." Montana tried to snap his fingers the way Lu had.

"I know, but she hasn't gone yet. She's still breathing."

"Will she hear me if I tell her something?"

"I bet she will."

Montana got out of Ivy's lap and walked over and stood next to the bed. "Gramma Lu, it's me. I'm doing what you said. I'm trying to be brave." He leaned over, his face close to hers. "I'm not scared now, and I'm glad you won't be sick anymore when you get to heaven." He stood up straight and picked up her hand. "I might be really big next time I see you, but don't worry if you don't recognize me because I won't forget what you look like."

Ivy blinked several times, trying to clear her eyes, but tears streamed down her face. It felt as though a part of her heart were being ripped away.

"Mom?"

"What, sweetie?"

"Listen…Gramma Lu isn't breathing anymore. Has she gone to heaven now?"

Ivy got up and took Lu's pulse. Nothing. She leaned down and put her ear against Lu's chest. Not even a faint heartbeat. She shuddered at the realization that Lu might already be in the presence of God—and forever beyond her reach.

"Is she gone?"

"I think so." Ivy brushed the hair away from Lu's eyes and blinked the stinging from her own.

"I hope Gramma Lu heard what I said."

"Of course she did." Ivy pulled Montana into her arms and held him tightly, more for her benefit than his. She choked back the emotion, thinking the best thing she could do for him was stay calm.

Carolyn Griffith walked into the room and stopped, her eyes moving from Ivy to Lu and then back to Ivy.

"She's gone," Ivy said softly. "Just a minute ago."

"Oh, honey. I'm so sorry." Carolyn put her arms around Ivy and Montana and held them without saying another word for a long time, and then said, "I guess we should call Sonya first and then the funeral home."

Brandon Jones sat in his office, working on cabin assignments for the counselors he had hired for summer camp. He was aware of footsteps and then saw Jake Compton standing in the doorway.

"Hey, Jake. What's up?"

Jake came in and stood next to Brandon's desk. "Elam just called. Lu Ramirez just died. He said it was peaceful. Apparently Ivy and Montana were with her."

"I'm sorry. But at least she's at peace. Is there going to be a funeral?"

Jake shook his head. "Just a private graveside service at Woodland Community on Monday. Apparently, Lu has a son and grandson in Pueblo, and Ivy feels obligated to try to get a hold of them and give them the option to come. But she doesn't think they will."

"That's so lame. What kind of son doesn't come to his own mother's burial?"

"Yeah, that's pretty sad. Anyhow, I knew you'd want to know." Jake started to leave, and then turned around. "Brandon, I hope there are no hard feelings over our disagreement about Buzz."

"Kind of hard to disagree when you didn't tell me anything specific."

"You know what I mean."

"I don't have hard feelings, Jake. I'm just confused, that's all."

"Yeah, I know. I probably overstepped even bringing it up the other day. I just know that it's easier to get sucked into the darkness than to walk in the light, and I worry about you having a foot in both worlds."

"You're worrying for nothing."

"All right. I won't bring it up again."

After Jake left, Brandon glanced at the clock and was surprised that it was almost five. He picked up the phone and dialed home.

"Hello."

"Hi, honey. Did you hear about Lu?"

"Yeah, Carolyn just called. She sounded exhausted."

"Did she say how Ivy and Montana were handling it?"

"They're both pretty stunned. Carolyn said Montana had a good visit with Lu last night while she was still alert, and he seems to be dealing with it much better than she thought he would."

"Well, that's good. Elam told Jake that Ivy's not inviting anyone to the graveside service. Think we ought to send flowers to the house?"

"That'd be nice. I wish Ivy would let people reach out to her. I have a feeling she's hurting a lot more than she lets on."

14

AT THE CRACK OF DAWN the next morning, Ivy Griffith plugged in the Open sign at Jewel's Café, feeling as though the gloomy gray clouds that hid the tops of the mountains had also settled over her.

"You shouldn't be working today," Jewel Sadler said. "I can call and get someone else to take your shift. I really think you're pushing too hard. You know what Saturdays are like."

Ivy put on the most pleasant expression she could muster. "I'll be fine. It's good for me to stay busy and get my mind off Lu's burial. I'd go nuts having today and tomorrow to think about it." *Please don't send me home. I need the money.*

"Okay, doll. But if it gets to be too much, you come tell me and I'll call my niece or ask one of the other girls to come in early."

By midmorning, the place was packed out, and Ivy felt as if she were just going through the motions. Was it grief, she wondered, that was causing her to feel so detached—and would it pass quickly or mess with her mind for a long time to come?

A steady flow of customers came and went, including Brandon and Kelsey Jones, whose tender words of sympathy caused her to get teary-eyed and hide out in the bathroom until she regained her composure.

Finally two o'clock came, and Ivy went into the back room and leaned against the wall for a moment, relieved that she had muddled through her shift without messing up any orders. All she wanted now was to go home and comfort her son.

"Why don't you take off tomorrow and Tuesday?" Jewel's voice startled her. "That'll give you a day before and after the burial."

"Thanks, but I'd really prefer to work."

Jewel put her hand on Ivy's shoulder and gently squeezed. "I'm sorry about your friend. I know you were real close. If you change your mind and want to take time off, you call me."

Ivy looked into Jewel's kind eyes until her own clouded over, then walked out the back door and around the side of the building. Pete Barton was standing next to her mother's Jeep.

"Hi," he said. "I thought I remembered you got off at two."

Ivy pushed out the words, "What do you want?"

"Bite my head off, why don't you?"

"A close friend died. I'm not in the mood for chitchat."

"I didn't know. When'd it happen?"

"Yesterday. Her burial's Monday." *Not that you care.* "So what do you want?"

"Nothing in particular. I haven't seen you in a week and just wondered how you were. And if you're going to let me pick you up for the class reunion next Saturday."

"I'm kind of out of it at the moment. I need to get Lu's burial behind me."

"Please tell me you're not thinking of skipping the reunion."

"I'm not *thinking* at all, Pete. That's what I'm trying to tell you. I feel like I have mush for brains."

Pete's face softened. "Yeah, I remember feeling like that when my dad died. Sorry, I didn't mean to push."

Ivy sighed. "I'll talk to you when we get closer to the weekend. Right now, I can't handle any more pressure."

Ivy walked in her parents' house and saw Montana sitting with her mother on the couch. "Hi, sweetie."

Montana looked up at her with his droopy eyes but didn't say anything.

"How's he been?" Ivy said.

Carolyn Griffith brushed the hair off Montana's forehead. "He slept till almost noon. I fixed him a grilled cheese sandwich, and since then we've been talking about all the happy things we remember about Lu. How were things at Jewel's?"

"Busy. I think she was surprised I rode out my shift. Thinks I should take a couple days off."

"She's right."

Ivy shook her head. "Skipping work won't make me feel any better. I'm much better off to stay busy."

"Well, you're not the only one I'm concerned about," Carolyn said.

Ivy locked gazes with her mother—and then moved her eyes to her son. "Fresh air might do us both good. Would you like to take a walk and show me that hiking trail you found?"

Montana shrugged. "Not really."

"Well, it's much too pretty an afternoon to just mope around. Isn't there something we could do—just the two of us? You'll feel better if you get up and move. Maybe we could take a drive and—"

"Take me where they're gonna bury Gramma Lu," Montana said.

Ivy breathed in slowly and exhaled. "You'll see it Monday when we all go out there to say good-bye."

"But I wanna see it now. So I'll know what it looks like."

Ivy looked at her mother. "Is that wise?"

"Considering the circumstances," Carolyn said, "I think it might be good to ease his mind."

"So you'll take me?" Montana's eyes were round and wide.

"All right. Get your coat."

Thirty minutes later, Ivy and Montana stood in the cemetery behind the reddish headstone marked "Weaver."

"When are they gonna dig the hole?" Montana said.

"I don't know, sweetie. Before Monday."

Montana reached down and picked up a leaf and twirled it

between his thumb and forefinger. "Why did Gramma Lu like it here?"

"She thought it was peaceful."

"Why did she care since she's gonna be in heaven?"

Ivy put her hand on Montana's shoulder, wishing he would run out of questions. "Gramma Lu wanted her grave to be at a nice place for you and me to come visit."

"Why come visit if she's not really here?"

"Her body will be here. Remember what she told you about her spirit?"

Montana nodded. "It's a special part of her I can't see with my eyes that will be alive in heaven."

"And someday God will bring her body back to life and change it into a much better one that won't get old or feel sick or sad."

"Will she look the same?"

"I don't know, sweetie."

Montana picked up a thick twig and moved it through the air like a toy airplane. "What if I can't recognize her anymore?"

"People who love each other will always recognize each other."

"How do you know?"

"I just do."

"But what if you're wrong?"

Ivy exhaled loudly, and then wished she hadn't. She paused for a moment, struggling to think of an answer, and then placed her hand on Montana's heart. "You won't need your eyes to recognize Gramma Lu because you'll know her with your heart. There's no one else like her."

Montana looked up at her, his head tilted, and seemed to be processing. Seconds later, a smile stretched his cheeks. "That's pretty cool."

"Yes, it is." She combed his hair with her fingers. "You ready to go now?"

"Okay."

Ivy held his hand and strolled past Amy's grave toward the parking lot. Under the overhang in front of the church, she saw a white van with red letters painted on the side: Bill's Cleaning Service. A man got out of the van and looked over at her and smiled.

Oh, no. "Montana, get in the Jeep," she said. "I don't want to get stuck talking to that guy."

"Hey, Ivy! Wait up!" Bill Ziwicki came running over to her before she could even get her door open. "Fancy runnin' into you twice in one week. I couldn't believe it when I saw you with Pete, Reg, and Denny the other day. Then I heard you were livin' here again."

"I'm staying with my parents for a while."

"But you're back for good, right?"

"I haven't decided. What are you doing at the church?"

"I clean it on Saturdays. I've got my own business." Bill gestured toward his van. "Guess I'll need to adjust my work schedule next weekend for the class reunion. I'm lookin' forward to it now that I know you're gonna be there. I've never been to one before."

"I might have to work."

"But I heard Pete say—"

"Pete doesn't know everything."

Bill snickered. "Yeah, well, don't say that to him or his stuck-up jock pals."

Ivy glanced through the window at Montana buckling his seat belt. "Listen, Bill…I'm really sorry about the way the guys treated you at Grinder's the other day."

"Pretty lame, all right. Why'd they blow me off like that?"

Ivy shrugged. "I don't know."

"They had a lot of nerve dissin' me. I put my neck on the line to get you all the drugs you wanted. That should count for somethin'."

"Well, don't expect me to pat you on the back. I went from killer weed to blow and meth and spent the past ten years in and out of rehab." *I can't believe I just spilled my guts to Bill Ziwicki!*

"Yeah, I heard about that." Bill looked down at the ground, his hands in the pockets of his coveralls. "I never bought drugs again after we graduated. I only did it for you guys."

"Yeah, right." *Keep telling yourself that.* She put her hand on the door handle.

"Ivy, wait! For what it's worth, I'm really sorry about the drugs. I was young and stupid and just wanted you guys to like me. I never thought I was hurting anyone."

Ivy turned around and looked into his eyes and saw her own insecurity staring back at her. "It was my choice. I don't blame you. I'd just as soon forget it, okay?"

"Yeah, me too." Bill looked beyond her and seemed to be thinking. Finally he said, "I'll never be able to make it up to you, but is there any chance we could go out sometime—maybe drive down to Durango and have dinner and see a movie?"

"Thanks for the offer. But right now I'm trying to deal with a death in the family and decide what I want to do with my life."

Bill shrugged. "Yeah, okay. I didn't figure a classy lady like you'd go out with me anyway. You seein' Pete?"

"No, I'm not seeing anyone. Like I said, I'm just trying to cope."

"So you're not brushing me off?"

"It's not personal, Bill. I'm just not dating right now."

"All right." He opened the door and held it. "Hope I see you at the reunion."

Ivy started the Jeep, made a U-turn, and pulled out of the parking lot onto Three Peaks Road. She glanced at Bill Ziwicki in her rearview mirror and wondered why he was willing to go to the reunion and subject himself to more of Pete, Denny, and Reg's cruelty—and if he actually thought of her as a classy lady.

15

JUST AFTER ONE on Monday afternoon, Ivy Griffith stood between Montana and her parents, trying to focus her attention on Pastor Rick Myers's words as he prayed over Lu's coffin, which was draped with a magnificent arrangement of spring flowers that Ivy's parents had insisted on buying.

Lu's good-for-nothing son and grandson hadn't shown up—not that Ivy expected them to. She wondered if Lu knew, and if she was looking down from heaven at this very moment.

Pastor Myers's sudden change in volume brought her back to the moment.

"And so, Father, we commit to You the spirit of Lucia Guadalupe Maria Ramirez and rest in the assurance that because she trusted Your Son Jesus Christ for her salvation, she is forever at peace in Your presence. We pray that the light Lu left behind will continue to shine in the hearts of those she loved until that great and glorious day when all believers will be united with You in Your eternal kingdom. In Jesus' precious and holy name we pray. Amen."

Ivy put her hand to her mouth and choked back a sob, then put her arm around Montana and pulled him close. When she finally regained her composure, she realized her parents had huddled around them.

"Is there anything else I can do for you?" Pastor Myers asked.

Ivy shook her head. "Thank you for doing this. It was just what Lu wanted."

He patted her shoulder and shook her father's hand, then walked toward the church.

Montana glanced over at the coffin and then at Ivy. "Will Gramma Lu be lonesome if we leave?"

"No. People in heaven never feel lonesome."

"Gramma Lu said to ask you about Jesus, that He knows the way to heaven. I wanna know how to get there."

Ivy caught her father's eye and felt at the same time shame and regret and fear. "Why don't we talk about this on a day when Mommy's not feeling sad, okay?"

Ivy reached for the two red roses in a vase near the coffin and handed one to Montana, then took his hand and walked over to Lu's coffin. "Remember what I told you about saying our private good-byes. I'll go first."

Ivy stood staring at the flowers that probably cost more than she cleared in a week. *I love you, Lu. I always will. Thank you for not judging me…and for loving Montana and me as if we were your own. I'm not going to say good-bye. I just can't.*

Ivy laid the rose on Lu's coffin, then turned to Montana and said softly. "Your turn."

Montana stood for a moment, his eyes closed and seemingly lost in thought. Finally, he kissed the rose in his hand and placed it on the coffin next to his mother's.

Ivy fluttered her eyelashes to clear her eyes and hoped she'd make it home without losing it.

After the burial, the Griffiths went back to the house, and well-wishers dropped by, bringing warm embraces and words of comfort. Many brought food. Some brought flowers. Ivy recognized several people who had been members of Woodlands Community Church when she was going there. Others were from the camp.

She mingled for a while, and then sat on the couch next to Montana, who was hugging a couch pillow.

"How're you doing, sweetie?" she said.

"I don't want all these people here."

"They came to make us feel better about Gramma Lu."

Montana pushed out his bottom lip and clutched the pillow tighter. "It's not working."

"Well, be polite because they think they're helping."

Brandon Jones came out of the kitchen carrying two plates of food. "Here you go." He handed one to Ivy and one to Montana.

"Hey, where'd you find the hot dog?" Montana smiled with his eyes. "I didn't see those out there."

Brandon sat on the couch next to him and lowered his voice. "I didn't figure a seven-year-old would get excited about a tuna log or broccoli casserole or that carrot-raisin salad. So I went by my house and picked up a package of hot dogs and some potato chips. You want mustard or ketchup on it?"

Montana shook his head. "I like it plain."

Ivy reached over and squeezed Brandon's hand. "Thanks. That was thoughtful. I appreciate how sweet you and Kelsey have been to Montana."

"It's easy. He's a great kid. What can I get you to drink?"

"Iced tea, if there's any out there."

"I'll have Coke." Montana glanced up at Ivy and quickly added, "I'll drink milk at dinner. Please?"

"Oh, all right."

"I'll be right back." Brandon turned and went in the kitchen.

Ivy heard the doorbell ring and wondered if the steady stream of comforters was ever going to stop. Seconds later her mother came over to the couch, holding a big vase of cut flowers.

"These just came for you," Carolyn said. "Why don't you take the card and I'll put them in the dining room with the others."

Ivy plucked the tiny yellow envelope from the vase and read the sentiment on the enclosure card. *Thinking of you today and sharing your grief. Your friend, Bill Ziwicki.*

"Who're they from?" Montana said, his mouth chock-full of hot dog.

"Oh, that guy we saw at the church the other day. He just wants me to know he's sorry about Gramma Lu."

"He likes you."

"Not really. He's just someone I knew in high school."

Montana popped a pickle into his mouth and licked his fingers. "Maybe he *would* like you if you liked him."

"Well, I don't."

"Why not? He seemed nice."

"How would you know?"

Montana shrugged. "I can just tell."

Ivy reread the card, surprised and touched by Bill's sensitivity.

"Who were the flowers from?"

Ivy looked up and saw her mother standing there. "A guy I went to high school with. Montana and I ran into him when we were out at the cemetery the other day."

"Well, it was awfully sweet of him to send flowers."

After dinner, Ivy lay on her bed, her hands behind her head, relieved that Montana had fallen asleep early and half expecting Lu to come walking through the door. How long had it been since she felt this vulnerable? Lu had been her anchor since Montana was a baby. Now she felt as if she were adrift at sea.

She heard footsteps on the stairs, and then saw her mother in the doorway, the cordless phone in her hand. "Bill Ziwicki's on the phone. You want to take it in here?"

"Okay."

Ivy took the phone from her mother and waited until she left the room, then put the receiver to her ear. "Hello, Bill."

"Hi. Hope you don't mind me callin', but I wanted to be sure the flowers got there."

"Yes, they're beautiful. I really appreciate the thought."

"You're welcome. You mentioned a death in the family but

never did say who it was. I didn't recognize any of the names in the obituaries."

Ivy sighed. "Actually it was my best friend, a lady who took care of my son and me when I was messed up on drugs. She was like a second mother to both of us. We buried her this afternoon, and I'm feeling pretty lost."

"Yeah, I hear it in your voice. Wish there was somethin' I could do to help."

"You already have. The flowers meant a lot to me—more than you know."

"Good. Well, I won't keep you. I'm sure it's been a hard day."

Ivy suddenly realized she was bone tired. "Yeah, it has."

"By the way, I'd be glad to give you a ride to the class reunion."

"Thanks, but I'm not even sure I'm going."

"I really wish you would."

"Well, if I do, I'll drive myself. Pete asked me first, and I really don't want to go with him. It's best if I just come alone."

There was an uncomfortable moment of dead air.

"Why do you care what he thinks? You're not his girl anymore. You're a grown woman."

"I guess I don't, really."

"Good, because he's been back in town less than a year and has a reputation for gamblin' and sleepin' around. You deserve better."

"And you don't need to worry about me. I can take care of myself."

Bill exhaled into the receiver. "Yeah, okay. It's none of my business."

"Thanks again for the beautiful flowers."

"I'm glad you liked them. I hope I see you at the reunion. But if not, maybe I'll see you around sometime. Good night."

"Good night, Bill."

Carolyn Griffith sat on the couch knitting a sweater for Montana, her eyelids heavy, her ability to focus quickly fading.

"I'd better head for bed while I can still make it up the steps," she said. "By the way, I finished reading this month's *National Geographic* and left it there on the coffee table for you."

Elam Griffith poked the logs on the fire, then placed the screen in front of the fireplace. "I'm not much in the mood for reading."

"What's wrong? You hardly said a word at dinner."

"I'm worried about Ivy. What's she going to do now that Lu's gone? She has no earning power. She's not going to come close to making it on what Jewel's paying her."

"I know. I worry about that, too."

"If she works several jobs, she'll have no time with her boy and will either have to pay someone to watch him or saddle you with taking care of him. And that's not right."

"I don't look at spending time with Montana as a ball and chain. But I do think it would be good for Ivy to be independent."

Elam flopped on the couch next to Carolyn. "So what do we do? How far can we trust her with money?"

"She's clean, Elam. She hasn't done drugs in three years."

"Grief does funny things to people. What if she can't cope without Lu? Having money in her pocket might open the door to more temptation than she can resist."

"Well, before we decide what she is or isn't capable of, it might be wise to discuss our concerns with her." Carolyn noticed the lines on his forehead. "Something else is bothering you."

"Harriett Barclay down at the drugstore saw Ivy slip a tube of lipstick into her purse."

"When?"

"Last week. Didn't confront her, though. I'm sure it was because she didn't want to get on my bad side. Her lease is coming up for renewal."

Carolyn's heart sank. "I can't believe Ivy would steal."

"Ivy's done a lot of things I had a hard time believing she was capable of."

"Are you going to ask her about this?"

"Not right now, but I'm not going to let it go long. I won't have a thief living in my house."

Ivy threw off the covers and sat on the side of the bed, exhausted and wide-eyed, her heart pounding. She looked at the clock: 3:10 a.m.

She raked her hands through her damp hair, her mind racing with images of Lu and of impending financial disaster—and the irrational fear of facing her classmates at the reunion. Everything in her wanted to flee—to just get in the car and keep driving. She remembered that Lu used to say anxiety attacks were the result of feeling trapped.

Ivy considered her situation for a few minutes and decided she couldn't do anything about missing Lu or fixing her finances, but she could start facing her fears about the reunion.

It's just one night, for heaven's sake. I can do this.

She went out in the hallway and tiptoed up the steps to the attic and pulled the chain on the light. She found the cedar chest and opened it, then dug down until she found her high school yearbooks. She put them under her arm and carried them to her room and closed the door.

She picked up her senior yearbook and began reading the comments classmates had written on the inside cover.

Too bad Pete found you first. We would've been dynamite together—Oooh la la! Reg

When you're ready to get rid of your pink cashmere sweater, can I have it? Oh, and Pete Barton, too? Luv ya, Aimee R.

Ivy, you're drop-dead gorgeous, but I'm attracted to your mind. Ha! Ha! Friends forever, Denny

Thanks for being a totally awesome distraction in third-period calculus. Mike Anderson

I should hate you for being every guy's fantasy—but actually I'm just glad we're going to different colleges! Hugs, Kendra Miller

Ivy read remark after remark and wondered how these same classmates would react when they saw how different she looked. She doubted anyone would instantly figure out who she was, and there would be a lot of whispering going on. Could she handle them feeling sorry for her? She decided she could endure it for one night—especially if it meant getting Pete off her back and keeping the sheriff at arm's length.

She read through several more comments and came across what Bill Ziwicki had written.

Ivy, thanks for never calling me "Icky Ziwicki." I've always <u>hated</u> it but never had the guts to say so. Your friend, Bill

Ivy could almost feel the pain Bill must've felt when he wrote those words. How could Pete, Reg, and Denny and so many others have been so cruel? And was Ivy any less guilty for having kept silent when she was in a position to speak up and express her disapproval? In spite of her good looks and acceptance by her peers, she'd been as insecure as Bill. She wondered how shocked he would be to know she'd compromised far more than he had.

Ivy sighed. She turned to the pages of senior class photographs and found Joe Hadley's picture. She studied his face, her mind replaying the sound of flesh hitting flesh, and then Joe gasping for air.

She closed the yearbook and laid it on top of the others, then turned off the lamp and fell back on the bed. She buried her face in her pillow and started to sob, and then sob harder and harder until it seemed as though a dam had broken somewhere deep inside her and there was no stopping it.

How was she supposed to face tomorrow, much less her wretched past, without Lu's wisdom and gentle prodding? What if she never found the courage to tell the truth about Joe Hadley's death? What if the pressure got to be too much and she turned to drugs again? What if she couldn't be the mother Montana wanted or needed? What if life never got any better than it was at this moment?

Oh, Lu. What am I going to do without you? I feel so lost.

Ivy wept until she had no tears left, then slid out of bed and knelt on the cold wood floor. She couldn't make herself say anything to God. But she knew He was watching. He seemed so close she could almost feel His breath.

She knelt in the dark a long time, just resting in the quiet. Finally, she climbed back into bed and fell asleep almost the instant her head touched the pillow.

16

TUESDAY, WEDNESDAY, and Thursday seemed to run together, but by Friday morning, Ivy Griffith was feeling more like herself and anxious to get tomorrow's reunion over with. She dropped Montana off at school, then came home and studied her pitiful wardrobe and tried to decide what to wear.

Carolyn Griffith came into Ivy's room and sat on the side of the bed. "So what's the verdict?"

"Everything I have makes me look anorexic. It's depressing enough looking older than I am, but I don't even have a figure anymore."

"Is the reunion dressy or casual?"

"Somewhere in between. I guess I could wear my black stirrup pants and a sweater. I don't really have anything else."

"Then let's go shopping."

"Mom, I can't afford to spend money on clothes right now. I'm saving for a deposit on an apartment."

"So let me help out. You're going to need clothes for work, too."

Ivy looked at her mother and sighed. "I don't expect you to buy me things. I can make it till I save some money."

Carolyn got up and put her arm around Ivy's shoulder. "I'm thrilled to have my daughter back. I've missed the girl stuff. It'll be fun."

"I'm not sure anything would seem fun the way I'm feeling these days."

"I know, honey. It'll take time for the grief to pass. But wouldn't it be nice to feel good about yourself when you go to the reunion tomorrow night?"

"That'd take a miracle."

"Or maybe just a new outfit, a good haircut, and a facial. A manicure might be nice, too."

"It's exhausting just thinking about all that."

"I have a feeling you'll feel energized once you see how good you can look. You're still attractive, honey. You just haven't done the maintenance for a while."

Sheriff Flint Carter pulled into a parking space at the Phantom Hollow Lodge and got out of the Ford Explorer the county had provided as his official squad car.

He went inside and spotted Charlie and Robin Becket, owners of the lodge, behind the front desk, studying a computer screen.

Charlie gave him a double take and flashed a boyish grin, then put his hands in the air. "Don't shoot. I'm innocent."

"We both know that's a lie." Flint laughed. "Please tell me there isn't a long wait for lunch. I've been craving Robin's chicken potpie all morning."

"We can get you in and out pretty quickly today. Tomorrow'll be another story."

"How many are you expecting at the reunion?"

"At last count one hundred and fifty-nine, which includes some spouses and companions. Should be great. They're already starting to arrive."

"Yeah, Bobby arranged to talk to some of Joe Hadley's teammates this afternoon and during the day tomorrow."

"Any leads on the case?"

"Nothing I can talk about."

Flint followed Charlie out to the restaurant and sat next to the wall of glass that overlooked Phantom Creek.

"I still love the sound of rushing water," Flint said.

"Me, too. Smartest thing my granddad ever did was build this place next to that creek. If the charm doesn't draw them back, the sound will. If I could bottle it, I'd be rich man."

"So are you ready for tourist season?"

Charlie smiled sheepishly. "You kidding? The back deck still needs to be stained, and the pool needs paint. I got caught up in the dirt bike races, and the cold weather snuck up on me before I could get to it. But I'm proud to say I did make a dozen new pine rockers for the deck. And six more to sell. Gotta do something to keep me out of trouble."

Flint chuckled. For a moment he was a kid again, daring Charlie Becket to cross the rapids using the big boulders as stepping-stones. The two of them had gotten into plenty of trouble together. How they had managed to survive their foolhardy boyhood adventures seemed nothing short of miraculous.

"I'll get that potpie right out to you," Charlie said. "Small salad with blue cheese on the side and black coffee?"

"Yeah, one of these days I may shock you and try something different. Listen, Betty and I want to have you and Robin over for Sunday dinner before you get buried in tourists."

"Sounds great. Just tell us when." Charlie turned and walked toward the kitchen.

Flint glanced around the restaurant and noticed it was about half filled with guests. He placed a napkin on his lap and looked out at the rushing water and the bare trees that lined the creek bank, thinking it wouldn't be long until all of Phantom Hollow was green and lush and dotted with wildflowers.

"I *thought* that was your squad car outside."

Flint looked up and saw Elam Griffith standing there. "You here for lunch?"

"Yeah, Carolyn's out shopping with Ivy, and I wasn't in the mood to make a sandwich."

"Why don't you join me?"

"All right. Thanks." Elam pulled out a chair and sat across from Flint. "So, the Hadley investigation keeping you busy?"

"The final autopsy report came this morning. Didn't tell us anything new. We know Joe was strangled, but that's about it."

"So what now?"

"We've pretty much eliminated the ranch hands as suspects. They were mending snow fences on the north side of the ranch that day—miles from the scene. Bobby Knolls has set up a time to talk to the basketball players that are coming in town for the reunion. But truthfully, I don't think it's going to lead anywhere. Joe Hadley didn't seem to have any enemies. Never got into trouble. Never bad-mouthed anybody. Far as I can tell, the kid was a real straight arrow."

"Remind me if he was dating someone," Elam said.

"No one steady. He'd gone out with a girl named Amanda Talbot the weekend before he disappeared, but she didn't know anything."

The waitress came over to the table and filled two mugs with coffee. "Your potpie will be out in a minute, Sheriff. What can I get for you, Mr. Griffith?"

"Potpie sounds great. Throw in a green salad with ranch dressing."

"Coming right up."

"So back to the Talbot girl," Flint said. "She ran into Joe at school the day he went missing and thought he seemed preoccupied. But that could mean anything, even that Joe had decided he wasn't interested in her. Everyone else we questioned said his behavior seemed normal."

"So how in the world did he end up murdered?"

Flint shook his head. "I've wracked my brain trying to think what motive anyone would've had for killing him. After ten years, I'm still drawing a blank. All we're really sure of is that Joe Hadley never got on the school bus the afternoon of January 18. We don't know where or even when the strangulation took place, just that his body was buried on Collier Ranch."

"Must be frustrating," Elam said. "So close and yet not close at all."

"Yeah, it's become an obsession again. The only thing that

makes sense is that Joe either left willingly with someone after school—or he was abducted."

Ivy stood in front of the full-length mirror on the back of her bedroom door and admired the young woman staring back at her.

"What do you think?" Carolyn said.

"I think it's a miracle. The print on the dress adds at least ten pounds. The blond highlighting brought my hair back to life, and the bob made it look thick."

"Your eyes are gorgeous," Carolyn said. "I knew a little makeup would bring out the best in you."

Ivy went over and put her arms around her mother. "Thanks. At least now I don't have to feel like the ugly duckling. I was really dreading that."

"You've never said, but since Pete's called several times this week, I assume you're going to the reunion together?"

"Actually, we're not. If you don't mind me borrowing your car, I'd like to drive myself."

"You've seemed put out with Pete lately."

"Yeah, well, we've both changed a lot." Ivy paused to choose her words. "Plus he made some jerky comments about my appearance, and I really don't care to spend time with him."

"You won't get an argument from me and your dad. Pete's a little on the wild side these days. But don't be surprised if he's suddenly attentive when he sees how nice you look tomorrow night."

Ivy shrugged. "Doesn't matter. I'm not interested in him."

"You ready to go downstairs and show off your new self? Montana's been chomping at the bit since I picked him up from school."

"I hope he doesn't faint."

"Come on," Carolyn said. "This'll be fun."

Ivy followed her mother down the steps and into the living room where Montana was coloring a picture, Sasha lying on the floor next to him. Her father was reading the newspaper.

"Ta da!" Ivy waited until they looked up, and then slowly turned three hundred and sixty degrees. "What do you think?"

"Wow!" Montana got up and came over to her, wearing a wide grin. "You look really pretty, Mom! Your hair's more blonder."

Elam Griffith smiled warmly, the way he had the night she went to her first dance. "You look terrific, honey."

"Thanks." Ivy caught her mother's gaze. "For everything."

Ivy carried a platter of baked chicken and new potatoes to the table and took her place next to Montana. Elam said the blessing, and within seconds Montana had stuffed his mouth with a huge bite of a Parker House roll.

"While you girls were out shopping today," Elam said, "I had lunch at the Phantom Hollow Lodge with Flint. He's really working hard to solve the Joe Hadley case. He's talked to everyone from the hired hands at Collier Ranch to a girl Joe was dating to the basketball team. Still no solid leads."

Carolyn passed the platter to Ivy. "I just can't understand why anyone would hurt a nice boy like Joe Hadley."

"Maybe Joe was kidnapped," Ivy said. "The sheriff always said that was a possibility."

"Maybe," Elam said. "But it's not likely that a kid his size would be forced off the school premises. It's more likely he left willingly, which implies it was with someone he knew."

"But nobody saw him leave, Dad."

"Maybe they did. Maybe they didn't. It's hard to say what somebody might own up to now that it's a full-blown murder investigation. Flint's not going to leave any stone unturned, I'll tell you that. The one thing he feels sure of is that whoever killed Joe was at the school that day."

17

IVY GRIFFITH DROVE past Jewel's Café and noted that it was already packed out in Saturday-night fashion. How she wished she were waiting tables instead of attending a class reunion she had no interest in. At least by the time her head hit the pillow tonight, the event would be history—and she could distance herself from Pete, Reg, and Denny until she got Montana settled with her parents and could come forward with the truth about Joe Hadley's death.

Ivy drove a mile beyond the city limits and pulled into the guest parking lot at the Phantom Hollow Lodge and found a parking space in the back row. As she walked toward the entrance, her heartbeat seemed almost as audible as the thumping of the bass coming from the rock band performing inside the lodge. She fought the temptation to turn around and forget the whole thing.

She pulled open the heavy wood door and walked into the lobby. A big poster set on an easel indicated the class reunion was being held in the Aspen Room on the second floor. She pushed the button on the elevator just as a deep voice behind her caused her to jump.

"Ivy! Wait!"

She turned around and saw Bill Ziwicki walking briskly toward her and looking nice in khakis and a brown leather jacket and brown loafers.

"Guess we're on the same wavelength," Bill said. "I must've

pulled in right behind you. Wow, do you look nice! Pretty hair-cut."

"Thanks." Ivy wondered what he'd think of her new dress when she finally took off the coat she had borrowed from her mother.

"I'm glad you decided to come. So…you're by yourself, right?"

"Yes, but I'm meeting Pete and Reg and Denny."

"Oh."

The elevator opened and Ivy stepped inside, Bill on her heels. She pushed the button, and they rode up to the second floor in awkward silence. In the hallway just outside the elevator, a gal about her age sat behind a table, name tags laid out in front of her.

"Welcome, I'm Kendra Miller Clawson." The just-a-little-too-heavy redhead looked at Ivy and then at Bill. "You're Bob Ziwicki. I remember you."

"Actually, it's Bill. Do I just pick up my name tag and—"

Kendra turned her eyes on Ivy and smiled. "I give up. Who are you?"

"Ivy Griffith."

Kendra shrieked. "I'm going to faint! It's really you!" She came around the table waving her arms and gave Ivy a hug. "You weren't at the five-year reunion, and I've wondered about you a lot. You look terrific with your hair that length. I'm jealous you're so skinny. I've gained twenty-five pounds since I had my kids."

Ivy suspected Kendra's compliment was just her way of being polite, but it was nice having someone welcome her with such gusto.

"Pete Barton's already here." Kendra smiled. "He said to tell you he wants the first dance. Last time I saw him, he was with Reg Morrison and Denny Richards at table six. Oh, don't forget your name tag. Notice the JH at the bottom right corner to commemorate Joe Hadley. Good to see you, Ivy."

"Thanks. It's nice being here." *Not really, but it's looking up.*

Ivy turned to say something to Bill and realized he was gone. She hated that he was probably feeling slighted.

Ivy checked her coat and then walked into a large room tightly packed with people. She was able to identify a number of class-mates, more from name tags than actual recognition. She spotted Pete Barton making his way over to her.

"You look great," he said. "Whatever you did, it works for me."

"I didn't do it for you, but I'll take that as a compliment. You said you were going to do all the talking. I'm just here for the ride."

"That's right. Let's go sit at the table with Reg and Denny and see if you can figure out who the others are."

Ivy saw Bill Ziwicki standing by himself next to the bar, a mug of beer in his hand. "I'll be right back." She worked her way through the crowd and over to Bill. "I didn't mean to ignore you. Kendra's welcome was a little dramatic. She hasn't changed a bit."

"Doesn't seem like anything's changed," he said.

"Please don't take it personally that I'm sitting with Pete and the guys. I agreed to this weeks ago."

Bill took a sip of beer. "Do what you want. But why'd you tell me you wanted to go by yourself when you planned to be with Pete all along?"

"I told you I didn't want to *go* with Pete. I never said I wasn't sitting with him. I wanted to drive myself so I could come and go when I want."

"Guess I misunderstood. Oh well, I hope you have a great time seein' everyone."

Ivy didn't miss the emptiness in Bill's voice or the impatience in Pete's as he called out to her from across the room, his hands waving in the air.

"You'd better go." Bill pushed his free hand deep into his pants pocket. "I'll catch you later."

Carolyn Griffith heard the Westminster chimes strike nine o'clock. She put her knitting aside and went upstairs to check on Montana. She looked in his room and his bed was empty. She went in Ivy's room and the bathrooms, and she finally found him sitting in the rocker in the room that had been Lu's.

Carolyn went in and sat on the side of the bed, her hands folded in her lap. "It's really hard missing someone you love, isn't it?"

Montana shrugged.

"I have an idea how you feel. My mother and grandmother were killed in a car wreck when I was eight, and I remember feeling empty and sad and angry. I thought life would never ever be okay again. Or that anyone understood."

Montana glanced up at her and then stared at nothing, his arms folded tightly across his chest.

"Your Gramma Lu came here with you because she knew you'd be safe with us, and that your mother would find a job. And she knew that once the sadness went away, life would be good again."

"But it won't," Montana said. "Not without Gramma Lu."

"Well, you'll always love her. And no one can ever take her place. But that doesn't mean that life has to be awful from now on. Sadness really does go away after a while. It's supposed to. Sadness is our way of missing someone. But happiness is our way of remembering how much we loved someone. I think Lu would want you to remember her with happy thoughts."

Montana let out a sob and in the next instant seemed to inhale it. "I can't. My happy thoughts are all gone."

Carolyn got up and knelt beside the rocker and took his hand. "Sweetie, they aren't gone. The sadness just feels bigger right now."

She pulled Montana close and held him, his sobs evoking tears of her own. She had never expected to love this child as much as she did.

"What's the problem?" Elam Griffith said.

Carolyn turned and saw Elam's silhouette in the doorway. "Montana is just missing Lu tonight."

"What time's Ivy coming home?"

"I don't know. Late."

Elam stood there a moment and then she heard his footsteps on the stairs.

"Grandfather Griffith doesn't like me," Montana said.

"That's not true."

"Then why is he always grouchy?"

"Well, it's not your fault. How about you and I have some hot cocoa before you go back to bed?"

Ivy looked around the room, thinking it had been a more enjoyable evening than she had anticipated, but the conversation at the table had been going steadily downhill for the past hour.

"Sure you don't you want to add a little rum to your beverage of choice?" Reg laughed so hard he almost fell over in his chair. "The rest of us are feeling mighty good. Yes, indeed. Mighty good."

"I'm fine," Ivy said

"How can you be fine when you're still sober?" Denny's words were slurred. "How can it hurt to have an itsy bitsy teenie weenie splash of rum in your Coke?"

"Because I'm driving myself home." *And all I need is to get addicted to something again.*

Reg moved over and slid his arm around her, then put his lips to her ear and said loudly. "Why don't you come upstairs with me and Denny and we can have a sleepover?" He guffawed and knocked over his glass, the drink spilling across the table.

Ivy peeled his arm off her and grabbed a handful of napkins and laid them on top of the spill, then looked at Pete, her eyes pleading. "These guys are wasted. Why don't you take them to their room and let them sleep it off? The party's over."

"For them, maybe. Not for me. Promise you won't leave? I'll be right back."

"Oh, all right."

"Come on, guys. Time to go beddy bye." Pete linked arms with Reg and Denny, and they bid a boisterous farewell before heading down the hall to the elevator, singing the school alma mater way off-key.

Ivy looked around the room, her feet jiggling nervously, and noticed Bill standing at the bar—and Kendra Clawson making a beeline for the table.

"I haven't had a chance to visit with you yet." Kendra sat next to Ivy, her arms folded on the table. "So have you had fun?"

"Yeah, it's been good seeing everybody."

"Somehow I pictured you married to a plastic surgeon and living in a mansion with five kids and a nanny, chunking down bonbons all day without losing your perfect figure."

Ivy manufactured a smile. "Instead, I'm a grossly underweight single mom with a seven-year-old son and absolutely nothing exciting to talk about. I'd much rather hear what you've been doing for the past ten years."

Ivy pretended to be interested as Kendra rattled off the details of all three pregnancies and the admirable traits of her children, and then talked about her real estate business, her husband, her nitpicky mother-in-law, and the new house they had just moved into. Ivy glanced at her watch and realized Pete had been gone twenty-five minutes. So much for him carrying the conversation.

"Now that we're living in Phoenix," Kendra said, "I'm just not used to the cold weather anymore, and—"

"My turn." Bill Ziwicki dropped in the chair next to Ivy. "I don't mean to be rude, but I haven't had a chance to talk to Ivy all night."

Kendra seemed embarrassed by the abrupt intrusion and rose to her feet. "I guess I should move on so I can get around to everyone. Nice talking with you, Ivy."

Bill watched Kendra bounce over to the next table. "You don't mind if I sit here, now that Pete's gone?"

"No, but he's coming back any minute. I don't want him to start in on you. He's bad enough when he hasn't been drinking. By the way, you look very nice. I meant to tell you earlier. I don't know how you can stand to wear that leather jacket in here, though. It's so stuffy."

"Well, for one thing, I haven't been out there dancin' and workin' up a sweat like the rest of you."

"But you had a good time, didn't you?" Ivy asked.

"Not really. I got stuck listenin' to Ronnie what's-his-face dump on me about his divorce."

"Ronnie Unger?"

"Yeah. Talk about bitter. Said his old lady was cheatin' on him. I thought the guy'd never shut up, and I finally started minglin' just to get away from him."

Ivy saw the sadness in Bill's eyes. "Sorry. Every time I spotted you, you were talking to someone different, and I thought you were enjoying yourself."

"Not really. Most of these people only spoke to me to ease their conscience for treatin' me like dirt." Bill put down his glass, his dark eyes holding her gaze. "But there is one thing that'd make up for the whole evening. Would you dance this last dance with me, Ivy? I've wanted to ask you that since the day I met you."

Ivy glanced at her watch. Where was Pete? Did she really care what he or any of these people thought? She decided she didn't. "You know what, Bill? I'd be honored."

She offered Bill her hand, and he led her out to the dance floor and pulled her closer than she would have chosen, his cheek next to hers. Ivy was aware of heads turning and people whispering, but for some reason, she felt better about herself than she had in a long, long time.

When the music stopped, the leader of the band thanked everyone and bid the gathering good night. Ivy went back to the table, and Bill sat next to her, his face beaming.

"Thanks. You'll never know what that meant to me."

"I enjoyed it, too. It was a nice way to end the evening." She took a sip of her Coke. "Pete must be passed out somewhere. He said he was coming right back, and that was forty minutes ago."

"Want me to help you look for him?"

Ivy sighed. "Okay. No one's going to hang around here now that the band's packing up, and I really hate to leave without saying something. I guess I could start by calling Reg and Denny's room. He might've just crashed there."

"Okay. Do you know the room number?"

"No. We can ask at the front desk."

Ivy rode down the elevator with Bill and went over to the young man standing behind the registration desk.

"Excuse me," she said. "Could you give me the room number for Reg Morrison and Denny Richards?"

"Sorry, miss. We don't give out room numbers."

"Not even to a friend? We were together all evening until they got smashed and went back to their room to sleep it off. I just want to be sure they made it before I go home."

The young man glanced at her name badge. "Are you the Ivy Griffith that used to date Pete Barton?"

"Yeah, how'd you know that?"

"I graduated two years behind you guys. Everybody knew who you were." He keyed something into his computer. "Your friends are in 312. Just don't tell anybody I told you."

"Thanks."

Ivy picked up the house phone and dialed and let it ring six times. "They're not answering," she said to Bill. "Probably out cold. Let's go see if Pete's there."

She went to the elevator, Bill on her heels, and went up to the third floor and walked to the end of the hall.

Ivy made a fist and pounded on the door. "Reg? Denny? You guys awake?"

She listened carefully, but didn't hear anything.

"Guys, it's Ivy. Open the door."

She turned the handle and was surprised when the door opened. "Why don't you peek in and see if Pete's with them?" she said to Bill.

"You sure it's okay?"

"Well, I can't just walk in. What if they're not dressed?"

"All right." Bill pushed open the door and saw the light was on. "Guys, it's Bill Ziwicki. Anyone here?" He walked through the narrow entryway past the bathroom and stopped for several seconds, then stumbled backwards and almost tripped over Ivy, his face drained of color.

"What's wrong?"

"Somethin' horrible's happened! Th—there's blood all over the wall—all over them!"

Ivy started to go inside, and Bill grabbed her arm. "Ivy, don't. Let's call 911!"

She pulled her arm free and went inside, her eyes darting from one blood-soaked body to the next, her mind trying to assimilate the carnage. She went over to where Pete lay, his eyes open and void of life, and saw the gaping hole in his forehead and the shower of red on the wall. A wave of nausea swept over her. She held her hand over her mouth and ran into the bathroom and retched. Seconds later, she realized Bill was standing behind her.

"You okay?" he said.

Ivy shook her head, wondering if she ever would be.

"All three of them are dead. I checked. Come on, let's go out in the hallway, away from all this."

He took Ivy by the arm and led her out of the room, then took his cell phone out of his pocket and keyed in three numbers.

"Hello, I'm callin' from the third floor of the Phantom Hollow Lodge. Three men have been shot in one of the guest rooms, and I'm pretty sure they're dead...No, I'm attendin' a class reunion...What?..." Bill turned and looked at the door. "Room 312...Yeah, my name's Bill Ziwicki: Z-i-w-i-c-k-i...I don't know if their wallets are missin'. I didn't think to check...No, I'm not goin' anywhere...Look, I'm not thinkin' straight. Please just send help!"

Bill folded his phone and put it in his jacket pocket. "None of this seems real."

Ivy leaned against the wall and then slid down into a sitting position. "Who would just kill them in cold blood like that?"

"I can't imagine."

Minutes passed and then Ivy heard the elevator bell. A man who appeared to be a hotel security guard ran down the hall toward them.

"I need to seal off 312," the security guard said. "Sheriff's orders."

Bill moved over and sat next to Ivy. "Don't worry, we're not goin' back in there."

"Are you the one who called 911?"

Bill nodded. "The victims are friends of ours from the class reunion. They got a little drunk, and we came up to check on them. The door was unlocked."

The security guard went in the room and came out half a minute later, his face a peculiar shade of gray. He picked up his walkie-talkie and put it to his lips. "Artie, this is Seth. Do you read me? Over...I've checked out the damage in 312. Three dead males. All shot at close range. A real bloodbath. The couple that discovered them is still here. Over...Copy that. I'll secure the room till the sheriff arrives. Out."

A door opened and a male guest poked his head out in the hallway. "The party's over. Think you could tone it down? We're trying to sleep in here."

"Sorry for the noise," the security guard said. "Go back to bed. We've just had a little mishap here."

Mishap? Ivy put her face in hands and tried to will away the bloody images that kept popping into her mind, hoping she would wake to find it was all a bad dream.

18

CAROLYN GRIFFITH HEARD a ringing noise and groped the nightstand till she found the telephone. "Hello," she said sleepily.

"Carolyn, it's Flint. I need to talk with Elam."

Carolyn squinted until she could make out the digital numbers on the alarm clock: 4:15. "What's wrong?"

"Just let me talk to Elam."

"All right, Flint. Hang on." She reached over and gently shook the body on the other side of the bed. "Wake up. The phone's for you."

"Yeah, I heard." Elam Griffith turned over and took the receiver from her hand. "What's up?"

"Three of Ivy's classmates were murdered at the Phantom Hollow Lodge sometime during the reunion: Pete Barton. Reg Morrison. Denny Richards. All shot in the head with a Glock .45."

"Lord have mercy." Elam reached over and took Carolyn's hand.

"Ivy and another classmate, a guy named Bill Ziwicki, found them. They're down here at the sheriff's department, answering questions."

"Good grief. You don't think Ivy had anything to do with it?"

"Not at all. She's been very helpful. She's really shaken, though. I was at the scene. It wasn't pretty."

"You want me to come down there?"

"No. We need to finish getting her statement, but she's going to need plenty of TLC when she gets home. I wanted to give you a heads-up. KTNR is running the story on *Daybreak*, if you're interested in knowing the details."

"Okay, Flint. Thanks. Be gentle with my girl."

"Will do."

Elam handed the receiver back to Carolyn. "I can hardly believe this: Pete, Reg, and Denny were—"

"Yeah, I could hear every word." Carolyn lay stunned, her hand clutching Elam's, her mind trying to comprehend the magnitude of the situation. "I hate it that Ivy's alone. We should be with her."

"You heard what Flint said. He doesn't want us down there right now."

"Well, *Ivy* might. I can't imagine how shaken she must be."

Sheriff Flint Carter stood on the other side of the two-way mirror and listened to Investigator Buck Lowry's questioning of Ivy Griffith.

"I know I've asked this already," Buck said, "but I need to hear you tell me again. Who sat at your table at the reunion?"

Ivy rested her elbows on the table, her chin on her palms. "Me. Pete Barton. Reg Morrison. Denny Richards. Jason Arnold and his wife Caitlin. Chart Severson and his wife Morgan. That's it."

"So the eight of you were together all evening?"

"Yes and no. We got up to dance and mingle, but we always came back to the table."

"Who left the dance first?"

"Caitlin had a headache, so she and Jason went back to their room around twelve-thirty. Chart and Morgan left later. I didn't pay attention to the time. I know they were staying with Chart's parents and wanted to get home in time for Morgan to nurse the baby. Pete, Reg, and Denny left after that."

Buck wrote something on the yellow pad in front of him. "Tell me again what time they left."

"Around 1:20. Reg and Denny were smashed and getting really obnoxious. I suggested Pete take them back to their room. He left with them and said he'd be right back."

"Did you see anyone else leave right after they did?"

"Sure. People were coming and going all the time. The restrooms are right there in the hallway."

"Do you know where Bill Ziwicki was when the guys left?"

"I saw him at the bar."

"Can anyone else confirm that?"

"I don't know. Why?"

"Just covering all bases."

"So now you were all by yourself at the table?"

"Actually, Kendra Miller came over and started talking. I forget her married name: Clements or something like that. She talked my ear off for twenty-five minutes. I remember because I kept looking at my watch wondering what was taking Pete so long."

"So at this point, Pete had been gone twenty-five minutes?"

Ivy nodded. "Yes."

"And that's when Bill Ziwicki asked you to dance?"

"Right. And after that, the band packed up. I didn't want to leave without saying something to Pete, so I found out Reg and Denny's room number and went looking for him. Bill went with me. That's when we discovered them shot."

"So it was your idea to go find Pete?"

"Yes."

"When you saw the guys had been shot, did you make any attempt to revive them?"

Ivy shook her head, her chin quivering. "I just remember feeling sick and running into the bathroom. Bill came in right after that and said he checked, and they were all dead. At that moment, I just wanted to die..." Ivy's voice failed.

Flint moved away from the two-way mirror and over to the coffeepot and stood next to Lieutenant Bobby Knolls. "I'm satisfied that Ivy and Bill's stories are consistent."

Bobby filled Flint's cup with coffee, and then his own. "So where's the connection between these murders and Joe Hadley's?

There has to be one. All four victims were basketball jocks. All in the same graduatin' class. All popular. Seems a little too coincidental."

"Then again, if it was the same killer, why did he wait ten years to take out these three?"

"Maybe he was waiting till they were together. Class reunion was the perfect chance."

Flint took a sip of coffee. "But it's not the first time the victims attended a class reunion. And it was totally unplanned that all three victims went up to Room 312. I'm not convinced that whoever did this planned to kill all three of them."

"So you think the shooter might've had a personal grudge against one of the three, and the other two guys got in the way?"

"It's possible. I'll tell you what I know for a fact: This isn't the time to get territorial. The ATF's already here, and I need to bring in the FBI. We're going to need all the help we can get to flesh out the facts, and we've got more than a hundred fifty classmates and spouses to question."

Bobby glanced over at the other interrogation room and set his coffee cup on the table. "Looks like it's my turn to play bad cop with Ziwicki."

Carolyn Griffith sat on the living room couch, an afghan wrapped around her, her eyes fixed on nothing. She wondered how her already-fragile daughter was handling the horror she had witnessed.

"The news is coming on." Elam took the remote off mute.

"Good morning, Southwest Colorado. This is Jillian Parker."

"And I'm Watson Smyth. Welcome to *Daybreak*. The small community of Jacob's Ear was shaken early this morning by a triple homicide at the renowned Phantom Hollow Lodge. A 911 operator in Tanner County received a call at 2:13 a.m. from a male caller at the lodge, who reported three men had been found shot to death in one of the guest rooms.

"The caller, twenty-eight-year-old William Ziwicki of Jacob's Ear, was at the lodge attending his tenth high school reunion when he and another classmate, Ivy Griffith, also of Jacob's Ear, made the gruesome discovery.

"According to a spokesperson from the sheriff's department, the victims were classmates of Ziwicki and Griffith and were also there for the reunion. Their names have not been released, pending notification of next of kin. But according to Griffith, who shared a table with the victims prior to their leaving the dance, all three left intoxicated and—"

"Watson, let me interrupt here. We just learned the identity of the victims, and I'd like to pass that information along to our viewers. The victims were: Peter Justin Barton, twenty-eight, of Jacob's Ear; Reginald Zachary Morrison, twenty-seven, of Telluride; and Dennis Patrick Richards, twenty-eight, of Durango. All pronounced dead at the scene from a gunshot wound to the head."

"What a tragedy, Jillian. Do we know if the sheriff's department has established a motive for the murders? Or if there are any suspects?"

"They're not commenting on that at this time. But we do know that the ATF and FBI are involved in the investigation, and that all the attendees at the reunion have been detained for questioning. And don't forget that earlier this month, the bones of another classmate, Joseph Ryan Hadley, were uncovered at a construction site on the south end of what used to be Collier Ranch. Hadley disappeared ten years ago, and the recent autopsy revealed that he died of strangulation. Authorities have no leads in that case and won't say whether they think last night's murders are in any way linked to Hadley's. Needless to say, we'll be following this story carefully and will interrupt our regular programming with any breaking news that might develop."

"Thanks, Jillian. Our hearts really go out to the families of these victims. In other news this morning, a fire broke out overnight and destroyed a warehouse in Durango..."

Elam turned off the TV, and the two of them sat in silence.

Finally Carolyn said, "What are we going to tell Montana?"

"The truth. Might have to clean it up a bit. No point in putting those images in the boy's head."

"I really hate this—especially so soon after Lu's death. I really wanted Ivy and Montana to get settled here. Who knows how long it'll take now."

"Well, I've got to talk to Ivy about Harriett Barclay's accusation that she stole a tube of lipstick. I've already put it off longer than I should've."

"Ivy's already got a lot to deal with. Can't it wait?"

Elam brushed his mustache with his fingers. "If I'm going to stand by our daughter, I've got to be sure she's leveling with us."

"You don't think she had anything to do with the shootings?"

"No, of course not. But if she's desperate enough to steal, we need to address the issue of finances now before she really does get into trouble."

Flint Carter stood at the two-way mirror, a cup of cold coffee in his hand, and listened intently as Bobby Knolls continued to push Bill Ziwicki as far as he could.

"So you didn't really like Pete Barton and Reg Morrison and Denny Richards?"

Bill shook his head. "I never said that. I said they didn't really like *me*. I'm used to it. And it's not like I'm not the only one. I've never been part of the in crowd. But I thought they were cool. Everybody did."

"Must've made you mad that they didn't speak to you."

"Not really. I doubt they even knew I was at the reunion."

"So how'd you feel about them?"

"I told you, I thought they were cool."

Bobby folded his arms across his chest and balanced his weight on the balls of his feet. "You own a handgun?"

"No. I own several huntin' rifles, though. I love to hunt."

"Ever fired a handgun?"

"No. Never been interested in them."

"You a good shot?"

Bill nodded. "Yeah, I bag my limit every season."

"You have any problem with us testing your hands for gun-powder residue?"

"No. But I resent the implication. I didn't shoot those guys. I'm the one who called 911, remember?"

"Convenient, don't you think?"

"What?"

"Who's to say you didn't leave the reunion, slip into Room 312, and catch those three guys off guard: Bam. Bam. Bam."

"Come on, I never left the Aspen Room except to go to the bathroom!"

"Can you prove that?"

Bill rubbed the stubble on his face. "I guess not."

"What's your relationship with Ivy Griffith?"

"We went to high school together. She recently moved back to Jacob's Ear, and we've become friends. I sent her flowers when a friend died the other day."

"Have you ever seen her socially?"

"No. But I'd like to." Bill smiled. "I've always had a thing for her."

"She used to date Pete Barton, right?"

"In high school."

"Must've made you jealous."

Bill folded his hands on the table. "Not the way you're thinkin'. Everybody knew no one besides Pete was ever gonna get to first base with Ivy Griffith. She was *every* guy's fantasy. Ask around."

"I intend to. So'd you fantasize about her?"

"I lusted. What can I say?"

"Do you still?"

"Sure. Is that a crime? I told you I'd like to go out with her. I asked her, in fact. She said she's not datin' anyone right now. She's tryin' to get over losin' her friend."

"It seems odd to me that if you find her so attractive, you didn't sit with her at the reunion."

Bill shifted in his chair. "She'd made arrangements ahead of time to sit with someone else."

"That would be Pete, Reg, and Denny, right? The fab four. Isn't that what everyone called them?"

"Yeah. I suppose they just wanted to relive the good old days. Isn't that what reunions are all about?"

Bobby leaned forward, his elbows on the table. "What about you? What'd you go there to relive: Rejection? Name callin'? Pain? Look, Bill. I know Pete nicknamed you Icky Ziwicki. Everyone knows. I have to ask myself why you'd want to go back and face that—unless you wanted to get even with Pete. Maybe even kill him."

"No way! He made me feel lousy, all right? I got over it."

"Who ever gets over being laughed at?"

"When you're not a jock or anything special, you get called stuff. You can either let it make you tough or let it get to you. I chose to get tough."

"You just let it roll off your back?"

"That's right." Bill looked intently at Bobby. "Look, I'm not a kid anymore. I know who I am. I have my own business. I own my home. I'm certainly not dependent on what Pete Barton thinks of me to make my day."

"Really? Then what does make your day?"

Bill's face turned red and he suddenly seemed at a loss for words. Finally he said, "I guess the hope of settlin' down someday with a woman who loves me. Havin' kids. Doin' all the normal stuff."

"And maybe having a crack at Ivy Griffith now that Pete's out of the picture?"

"Stop twistin' my words! I like Ivy. I'd like to date her. Do you really think if I'd killed those guys, I would mess with her mind by lettin' her walk in there with all that blood? Do you really think she's ever gonna get over what she saw? I'd be cuttin' off my nose to spite my face. I may be lonely, but I'm not stupid."

"Pete thought you were stupid."

"He never said that."

"That's the way he treated you."

"And that's the way you're treatin' me! You think I don't know what you're tryin' to pull?" Bill sat back in his chair, his chin quivering. "What do you want from me? I already told you everything I know."

Bobby smirked. "Sure you did. You think *I'm* stupid?"

The door flung open, and Buck Lowry entered the room. "Hey, Bobby, how about giving the guy a break? Why don't you take a walk around the block or something?"

Bobby pushed back his chair and rose to his feet. "Whatever. I'm done talkin' to this clown."

"Bill, I'm Investigator Lowry. Can I get you something to drink? Or maybe a breakfast biscuit?"

Bobby came out of the interrogation room, shaking his head. "I don't know what to think. I actually feel sorry for the guy. Doesn't seem like he's hidin' anything."

"I hate making victims of the wrong people," Flint said. "Let's move on to another classmate. At the rate we're going, we're not going to get any sleep tonight either."

19

ON SUNDAY EVENING, Ivy Griffith sat at the kitchen table with her parents, staring at the floral print on the tablecloth and wondering why her father had seemed so solemn when he asked her to come talk to them.

"This has been one incredible day," Elam Griffith said.

Ivy put her elbows on the table and rested her chin on her palms. "I still can't believe they're dead."

"I hate having to bring this up right now," Elam said, "but I don't anticipate there being a better time in the near future, and I think it's crucial that we're all on the same page about a few things."

"Like what?"

"Your financial struggles, for starters. And what you're doing to get a handle on it."

"I've been up-front about that. I'm saving the money I'm making at the café, and when I have enough for the deposit, I'll get an apartment. I'm not planning for us to stay here long, if that's what you mean."

Elam stroked his mustache and seemed to be lost in thought. Finally he said, "There's no easy way to ask this, so I'm just going to say it outright: Did you steal a tube of lipstick from the drugstore? Yes or no? I suggest you think carefully before answering."

Ivy felt her face get hot. "I was going to go back and pay for it."

"Really? And when were you planning to do that?"

"As soon as I got paid. But then Lu died and I got distracted. You think I'm in the habit of taking things that don't belong to me?"

Elam's gaze seemed to bore a hole in her conscience. "How would I know what you're in the habit of? First you drop out of sight for a third of your life, and then waltz back in here without telling us about Lu's situation. I find out from Harriett Barclay that you're stealing. And now you're in the middle of a triple homicide investigation. I'm not sure I even know you anymore."

Ivy blinked the stinging from her eyes, but a runaway tear trickled down her cheek. "You *can't* believe I was involved in the shooting!"

"I didn't say I did. But your mother and I need to know who it is that's living in our house. I can't stand by you if I don't trust you. I'm not going to put up with lying and stealing."

"I already told Mom why I didn't tell you about Lu. I was afraid you wouldn't let her come here, and I couldn't leave her to die alone. I couldn't afford the rent by myself." She got up and tore off a paper towel and wiped her eyes, then sat at the table again. "I took the lipstick when I went to meet Reg and Denny because I felt ugly, and I thought it might help. I didn't have eight dollars to buy it then. I'm sorry I took it. I'll go back and tell Mrs. Barclay what I did and give her the money."

"ASAP, I trust?"

Ivy nodded. "I'm sorry, Dad. I'm really trying to change." Ivy swallowed the emotion and hated that her lip was quivering. "It's surprising what you learn to justify when you're used to being desperate."

"Well, you're not desperate as long as you're in this house. There's no cause ever to steal, you hear me? I won't have it. And don't lie to me again."

"I won't. I promise."

"Does the boy steal, too?"

"No!" Ivy shook her head. "Montana doesn't know anything about it. I've always taught him to be honest. You can't tell him about the lipstick. You just can't!"

"I'm not planning to tell him anything. This is between you, me, and your mother."

"I've made a lot of mistakes, but I'd *never* encourage Montana to do anything wrong."

"He's a well-behaved little boy," Carolyn Griffith said. "It's easy to tell he's been loved and cared for."

Elam glanced over at Carolyn, and his face softened. "I want to think the best about you, Ivy. I truly do. But I won't settle for less than complete honesty. Are we straight on that?"

"Yes."

"I'm shocked and sorry about what happened to your friends. There's no doubt in my mind that Flint's going to catch whoever killed them. In the meantime, he thinks we need to consider that you might be in danger."

"Me?"

"The four of you were pretty tight. Maybe you ticked somebody off way back when."

Or someone figured out who killed Joe and took the law into his own hands! Ivy's heart raced so fast she felt light-headed.

"Honey, you look exhausted," Carolyn said. "Why don't you go on to bed? I'll take Montana to school in the morning, and you can sleep in. At least you're not scheduled to work tomorrow. It's just as well."

The only thing heavier than Ivy's eyelids was her heart. "I can't get their faces out of my mind—and all that blood. I wish I had never gone looking for Pete."

"Well, until the sheriff figures out what's going on," Elam said, "I don't think you should be alone. Just as a precaution."

"Dad, I work. I need to take Montana to and from school. I have a life. I can't just put everything on hold till Sheriff Carter catches whoever did this."

"No, but your mom and I can be available to drive you."

"You can't put your lives on hold either."

Elam lifted his eyebrows. "We can do whatever it takes to keep you safe."

Sheriff Flint Carter sat in his office with FBI Special Agent Nick Sanchez, Lieutenant Bobby Knolls, and Investigator Buck Lowry, exhausted but satisfied with the progress they had made since involving the FBI in the investigation.

"Nick, thanks for everything you've brought to the table," Flint said. "And especially for acting so quickly and efficiently. There's no way this department could've mustered enough manpower to investigate the murder scene and interview all the reunion attendees."

"Not *quite* all," Nick said. "A guy named Ronnie Unger was at the reunion, but we haven't been able to locate him. He must've left before the shooting. He's not at his apartment in Mt. Byron, and his estranged wife doesn't know where he is. Neither do his parents or his brother."

"You have reason to suspect him?"

Nick shrugged. "Don't know enough about him yet to have an opinion. But if we can't catch him at his apartment tonight, we'll be on his employer's doorstep first thing in the morning."

Nick reached for a small stack of papers and handed one to each of the others. "Okay, people, here's what our profiler worked up on the perp: Male. Introverted. Experienced with firearms. Highly skilled at concealing his emotions, especially anger. Had a personal ax to grind with at least one of the victims and regarded the shooting as a public service. He lives in his own fantasy world where he can turn off the emotional pain, perhaps in response to being rejected or abused by a parent or caregiver early in life. He lacks the social skills to form healthy relationships and probably has a trail of broken relationships. He's neat and methodical and deliberate in his approach to life. He's smarter than everyone thinks he is—and he knows it."

Flint perused the profile and then said, "How do we begin to identify someone like this?"

Nick sat back in his chair, his arms folded across his chest. "Process of elimination. We know the evidence points to just one shooter, and none of the classmates tested positive for gunpowder residue or blood spatter, which certainly lowers the probability that our shooter was present at the reunion. Of course, Unger is still a question mark."

Bobby blew a pink bubble and sucked it into his mouth. "The shooter could've worn gloves and changed his clothes."

"I'll keep that in mind, Lieutenant," Nick said. "Also, we matched the bullets that passed through the victims and lodged in the walls to a Glock .45 used in a convenience store robbery two years ago in Fort Collins. At that time, it was registered to a doctor who had reported it stolen the month before. It's never been recovered."

"So the murder weapon was hot," Bobby said.

Nick smirked. "No big surprise. The shooter was careful not to leave fingerprints or DNA at the scene, and it stands to reason he's not going to let us trace the murder weapon back to him."

"So where do we start?" Flint said.

"We narrow down the list of classmates to the ones who fit any part of the profile and then start digging deeper. And we locate Unger ASAP."

Ivy lay in the dark, staring at the moonlit ceiling, and was struck with a bold new thought. Did it even matter if she confessed the truth about Joe's death now that his killers were dead? It's not as though she could prove what really happened.

"The truth will set you free, Ivy girl," Lu had said. *"Just confess it to God and accept His forgiveness. He'll be with you when you tell the sheriff. You can never go wrong doing the right thing."*

Something rattled the window, and Ivy froze, her heart galloping, her body feeling as though it were plastered to the bed. Was someone out there?

She sucked in a breath and couldn't seem to exhale, then heard what sounded like a gust of wind slam into the window. She rolled over on her side and looked out at the swaying silver spruce trees and remembered that a cool front was supposed to move through overnight.

Ivy pulled the blankets up to her eyes and listened to the wind howl. It was a long time before her pulse quieted down. Finally, she slid out of bed and went over to the window and made sure it was locked. She moved her eyes across the moonlit grounds and didn't hear Sasha barking. She checked the window locks again and pulled the blinds, wondering how feasible it was for someone to climb up to the second story and break in.

Ivy grabbed the blue and beige afghan off the old wooden trunk, wrapped it around herself, and sat in the rocking chair.

Brandon Jones woke up at 3:30 a.m. and realized the other side of the bed was empty. He got up and found Kelsey sitting on the couch, her Bible in her lap.

"What're you doing up?" Brandon said.

Kelsey Jones put her hand over her mouth and captured a yawn. "Praying like nuts for Ivy Griffith. I can't get her off my mind."

"Well, after what she's been through, it's not hard to understand why. I can't even imagine what it would be like to find your friends shot to death like that."

"And on top of losing someone who's been like a mother to you. Though I'm not feeling nudged to pray so much about her grief as her fear."

"Fear of what?"

Kelsey shrugged. "I don't know. But I sense there's some sort of spiritual battle going on. Maybe I should make an effort to get to know Ivy. She really doesn't have anyone her age to talk to."

"What would you have in common, Kel? She's been a drug addict most of her adult life."

"I know it's a stretch, but with Lu gone, who has Ivy got? Carolyn said Ivy doesn't really talk to her, and we women need to talk in order to process our feelings."

"Maybe she'll turn to her mother now."

"I hope so. But it won't happen overnight. Besides, most gals don't communicate with their mothers the same way they do with close girlfriends. Believe it or not, girl talk is often a prelude to meaningful conversation."

"I'll take your word for it." Brandon sat next to her on the couch, the corners of his mouth twitching. "Meaningful conversation with the guys can be a lot of hootin' and hollerin' when our team scores a touchdown. Or grunting and groaning while we're backpacking or climbing or shooting the rapids."

"That surprises me since you're such a good conversationalist."

"With you. Not with the guys. We don't need conversation to process our feelings. Thinking things through seems to work better."

"Don't you and Buzz talk when you guys go places?"

"Yeah, but not about anything meaningful."

Kelsey smirked. "As if Buzz were capable of it."

"If I want meaningful guy talk, I go to Jake. If I want adventure, I hang out with Buzz. Most of the time I just work things out on my own. Or talk to you."

"Well, I'm convinced Ivy needs a friend, if nothing else. I know she doesn't work Wednesdays, and I'm usually off that day, too. Maybe I'll see if she wants to come over here for coffee and cookies or something."

20

Ivy Griffith spent Monday in a fog, but when Tuesday morning came around, she dressed for work and made the choice not to let Lu's death or the murders of her friends rule her thinking. Life had been too sad for too long. She knew she had to find something to look forward to if she stood any hope of staying off drugs. A knock on the door startled her.

"Come in."

The door opened and her father poked his head in the room. "You about ready?" Elam Griffith said. "I'm your taxi this morning."

"It just seems like a lot of trouble for you to drive me into town when you've got other places to be."

"No problem. I decided to meet Flint for breakfast."

Great. Then I'll have two of you breathing down my neck.

"Don't look so grim. It's really no trouble. I have an early meeting with my stockbroker, and your mother will be chauffeuring the boy back and forth to school."

Ivy wondered if her father persisted in calling Montana *the boy* just to irritate her. She grabbed her coat and her purse. "I want to kiss Montana good-bye before I leave. I'll be right down."

Ivy went into Montana's room, stood over his bed, and listened to his deep breathing. She wondered if she had ever fallen asleep last night and if she would be a zombie at work today.

She bent down and whispered, "I'm leaving for work now. I'll see you after school. Be good for Grandmother Griffith. I love you so much."

She pressed her lips to his warm cheek, then hurried downstairs to the front door, where her father was waiting.

"We'll be lucky to get there by six," Elam said. "Should've been on the road ten minutes ago."

"I always leave at twenty till six." Ivy tried to keep her voice sounding pleasant. "I haven't been late yet."

"Then you were driving too fast."

Ivy resisted the impulse to remind her father that she wasn't a high school kid anymore and didn't need him telling her how to get to work on time. She followed him out to the Suburban and climbed in the passenger seat, aware of the brightness of the moon and a crisper feel to the air.

"The wind really whipped through here last night," Elam said. "Did you hear it?"

"Yeah, scared me a little at first. Then I remembered we were supposed to get a cold front." Ivy glanced up at the second story windows and didn't see how anyone could reach them without a ladder.

"Did you sleep okay?"

"No, I was pretty restless."

Ivy half listened to her father talking about some projects he had in the works, but didn't say anything else until they arrived at Jewel's and she pointed to her watch. "See? It's five minutes till six. I've got plenty of time. All I need to do is time in and plug in the coffeepot. The night crew sets the tables."

"Whatever happened to giving yourself an extra five minutes?" Elam said as he followed her in the back door of Jewel's Café.

"There you are, doll!" Jewel hurried over to Ivy and hugged her. "That turned out to be *some* class reunion. You sure you're ready to come back to work?"

"I am *so* ready," Ivy said. "I need to get my mind on something else."

"Well, that shooting's the biggest thing to happen here since the widow Thompson found Jacob Tanner's ear on the back porch. You're going to hear customers talking about it. Some might even be tacky enough to ask you about it. Think you can handle that?"

Ivy nodded. "I'll just tell them it happened exactly the way they heard about it on the news. But it's usually too busy in here for me to stand around and talk anyway."

"Hope you don't mind me sneaking in the back door with her," Elam said. "But I'm meeting Flint for breakfast right at six."

"Heavens no. You go right out there and sit wherever you like. We'll have this place open in nothing flat."

The café was packed with customers, and Ivy hardly had a chance to slow down until ten o'clock. No one besides Flint Carter had even mentioned the shooting to her directly, though she heard several people talking about it.

When the breakfast traffic thinned out, she began wiping down tables with Clorox water. Her thoughts turned to Montana, and she hoped he was able to forget his grief over Lu while he was at school and just be a kid. She was glad he didn't know the graphic details about the shooting and hoped he wasn't hearing things at school he didn't need to know.

Ivy started to put silverware on the tables when Bill Ziwicki walked in the door.

"Hey, Ivy!"

"Bill...what a surprise. Are you here to eat?"

"Yeah. And to see you. Just seat me anywhere. I really don't care."

Ivy smiled. "Well, since you're the only customer at the moment, why don't you choose?"

"Okay. How about there by the window?"

Bill sat at the second table by the window and handed the menu back to her. "Just bring me a couple of Jewel's homemade cranberry muffins and a cup of coffee, and I'll be in hog heaven."

"I've never seen you in here before."

"I used to come in pretty often. It's been awhile. Guess I got tired of eatin' alone. Now that you're here, I have an incentive." Bill held her gaze. "So how're you doin' after the weekend?"

"Not all that well," Ivy said. "I'm really jumpy and can't get the murder scene out of my head."

"Yeah, I hear that. I sure haven't been sleepin' through the night. Were the sheriff's investigators nice to you?"

"I guess so. But they wore me out asking the same questions over and over."

Bill nodded. "I noticed that, too. They must've asked me a hundred times if I left the Aspen Room—which I didn't, except to go to the men's room. They came at me really hard. Like *I* know anything. Asked me all kinds of gun questions and even tested my hands for gunpowder residue. Kinda ticked me off, but they were just doin' their job I guess. I think they always suspect whoever's first on the scene."

"Well, I've wracked my brain and can't think of anybody in our class who would've killed those guys."

"Me either. But I sure never expected to be treated like a suspect when all I was doin' is tryin' to help."

"Well, you certainly did help, and I told the investigators that. You're the one who stayed rational and took control of the situation." Ivy smiled. "Why are you blushing?"

"I don't know. I'm not used to people sayin' nice things about me."

"Well, they should." Ivy patted his arm and wrote something on her green pad. "Let me bring your coffee and get a couple of cranberry muffins warmed up for you."

Ivy left Jewel's at two and started walking down the block to the drugstore, prepared to make amends for the stolen tube of lipstick before her mother came to pick her up. She spotted Evelyn Barton coming out of Barton's Deli, looking older than she had the week before.

Ivy crossed the street and walked over to her as she was unlocking her car.

"Mrs. Barton?"

Evelyn turned around, wearing a puzzled look, and then one of recognition.

"I just wanted to say how sorry I am about Pete." Ivy's chin quivered with unexpected emotion.

Evelyn put her hand on Ivy's shoulder and squeezed. "I know, honey. It must've been horrifying for you. I'm not sure I would have survived seeing—" Her voice caught in her throat.

Ivy couldn't think of any comforting words to say. "I know Sheriff Carter is going to figure out who did it."

"I hope so. But after ten years, we still don't know what happened to Joe Hadley."

Thank heavens you don't.

"I've been talking to Reg and Denny's parents, and we want to hold a memorial service here in Jacob's Ear for our sons—and for Joe. We're still working out the details with the Hadleys, but it'll probably be on Friday at the civic theatre. We've all been through the loss of our sons and need to draw strength from one another."

Ivy stared at Pete's clueless, grieving mother and thought the whole thing was just too bizarre.

"I'm so sorry, Mrs. Barton," Ivy heard herself say. "I can't imagine how awful you must feel."

"Thanks, honey. My Pete was no angel, but he didn't deserve this."

"Of course he didn't. If there's anything I can do, please call me."

Ivy held the car door for Evelyn, then crossed the street and hurried down to the drugstore. She spotted Harriett Barclay rearranging some hair care products on an end cap. She took a slow, deep breath, thinking she'd rather be doing almost anything else.

"Mrs. Barclay?"

Harriett turned around and held her gaze. "Yes, Ivy. What is it?"

Ivy reached in her purse and handed Harriett a ten-dollar bill. "I came to pay for the lipstick I took. I don't know what made me do such a thing. I guess I was too proud to ask my folks for money until I got paid. I'm really sorry. It'll never happen again."

Harriett went over to the cash register. "Would you show me the lipstick so I can match the numbers when I ring it in?"

"Sure." Ivy reached in her purse and handed the lipstick to Harriett.

"I hated telling your father about it. But this is a small business, and it's not as though we can just write off these losses and never feel the impact."

"I'm really not in the habit of doing this," Ivy said.

"I sure hope not, young lady. Not everyone would be willing to let you pay for the stolen merchandise and not report it to the authorities."

"I appreciate that. Like I said, it'll never happen again."

Harriett keyed in the numbers and rang up the purchase, then handed Ivy the change. "Next time you come in here, I trust it will be to *buy* something."

"Definitely. Thank you." Ivy put the change in her purse, aware that her face was hot and probably red, and pushed open the exit door.

She walked down the street feeling as if a huge weight had been lifted and stood on the sidewalk in front of Jewel's Café, waiting for her mother. The north wind was nippy, and she put her hands in her pockets to warm them and felt a piece of paper. She took out an envelope that had her name on it and tore it open. Inside was an index card with words formed from letters that had been cut from a magazine.

I KNOW WHAT HAPPENED TO JOE HADLEY.

Ivy stared at the words, her heart pounding, her skin feeling like gooseflesh. She looked up, feeling light-headed and slightly nauseated, and wondered if whoever left the note was watching her.

Ivy went inside the café and walked to the back room where she found Jewel sitting at her desk.

"Forget something, doll?"

"No, but do you know who put this envelope in my coat pocket?"

Jewel shook her head. "No, what is it?"

"A sympathy card. They forgot to sign it."

"Well, I left the back door open for the UPS driver. Maybe someone slipped in and left the card for you."

"How would they know it was my coat?"

"Probably was someone who knows you. You seem upset."

Ivy forced a smile. "No. I just hate not knowing who was thoughtful enough to leave this. See you Thursday."

Ivy walked out the back door and around to the front of the building. Her mother was just pulling into a parking space.

"Sorry I'm late," Carolyn Griffith said when Ivy got into the car. "I took the car in to be serviced, and they were running behind."

"That's okay. I haven't been waiting long."

"So how'd it go with Harriett Barclay?"

"It was humiliating. But she was very nice, and I paid her for the lipstick."

"I'm glad. How'd your day go at Jewel's? Were people wanting to talk about the murders?"

"Yeah, but not to me." *At least not the murder you're talking about.* Ivy looked up and down the street as they drove off, wondering if she'd just been threatened.

Flint Carter sat at his desk, mulling over the facts of the case when Nick Sanchez waltzed in and flopped in a chair. "You still mad about Unger?" Flint said.

"Yeah. What kind of guy goes on vacation and doesn't tell anybody where he's going—not even his boss?"

"One who's in the middle of an ugly divorce and wants to disappear for a while and be incommunicado."

Nick smirked. "Or wants to lay low long enough to destroy all the evidence. I put out an APB on this clown. I'm not waiting to talk to him till *next* Monday when he gets back."

"You know something you're not telling me?"

"No, but it's convenient no one knows how to reach him. Plus we're drawing a blank everywhere else, and he's the only one we haven't caught up with. I hate loose ends I can't tie up."

Ivy put a small portion of mixed vegetables on Montana's dinner plate, and then a more generous portion on her own.

"You're awfully quiet," Elam said.

Ivy avoided eye contact with her dad and wished he'd just let her eat in silence. "Montana, why don't you tell your grandparents how many ribbons you've earned in the Do's-and-Don'ts club."

Montana smiled. "Mrs. Shepard says I'm the bestest one in the class since spring break. I already have nine ribbons."

Ivy listened as Montana told what each ribbon was for, glad to see her son smiling and her mother listening intently. Her dad seemed far away, as though he had a wall around him—the same as every other time Montana had tried to communicate with him.

"That's fabulous," Carolyn said. "We're so proud of you, aren't we, Elam?"

Elam gave a slight nod and looked at Ivy. "By the way, Rusty called me this morning. Just wondering how you and the boy are getting along. He was sorry to hear about Lu and about Pete and the others. Said to tell you he wants to come visit soon and bring his family. Maybe in June."

"That'd be nice." Ivy wondered if she'd even know what to say to her big brother after all this time. It was hard to picture him married with children. And with his own veterinary practice.

The phone rang, and Carolyn reached over and picked it up. "Hello…Oh, hello Bill…We just sat down to dinner. Could she call you back?…Oh, that's quite all right. We're usually finished before now." Carolyn jotted something on a phone pad. "Okay, I'll tell her. How are you holding up?…Yes, it certainly was. Well, you take care. I'll have Ivy call you. Good-bye."

Carolyn hung up the phone and sat back in her chair. "Bill Ziwicki wants you to call him. I wrote down his number in case you don't have it."

Ivy sighed quietly. Did she even have the energy? "All right, thanks."

"You two seeing each other?" Elam asked.

"Not really. We just keep bumping into each other. Bill's been very nice to me."

Montana put his hand over his mouth and stifled a giggle. "My mom has a boyfriend."

"He's just a friend who happens to be male," Ivy said. *But he's treated me more like a lady than any guy has in a long, long time.*

Ivy read Montana two bedtime stories, then tucked him in and went downstairs to the kitchen and called Bill Ziwicki's number.

"Hello."

"It's Ivy. What's up?"

"I was just checkin' in to see how you're feelin' tonight."

"So-so. I didn't say anything to you earlier, but my dad and the sheriff think I should be careful, that whoever killed Pete, Reg, and Denny might be after me, too, since we used to be pretty tight. Dad insists that I don't go anywhere by myself, and he or my mom have to drive me everywhere. It's so oppressive. I feel like I'm fourteen again."

"I never even thought about the killer bein' after *you*. Are you worried about it?"

"I guess it can't hurt to be cautious."

"I'll be glad to drive you anywhere you need to go. Might be better than havin' your folks haulin' you all over town."

"Thanks for the offer, but my hours would make it hard. I have to leave for work around five-thirty in the morning and get off at two. I couldn't ask you to be available at such odd times."

"I have a lot of flexibility. I have my own business, remember?"

"It's really sweet of you to offer. If I have to do this very long, I may take you up on it."

"I hope so. You sound really bummed."

Ivy was tempted to tell him about the index card she'd found in her pocket, but how could she without having to turn it over to the sheriff? It was baffling to her that anybody could know what happened that afternoon on Collier Ranch. She was sure no one had followed them out there. And the guys all swore they had never breathed a word of it to anyone.

"Ivy...you there?"

"Uh, yeah. Sorry. I'm just not myself right now."

"Listen, I know you've got a lot on your plate with losin' your friend and all—and now the shooting—but maybe we could have coffee sometime, talk things out. I know it would do my heart good to unload a little. This is the worst thing that's ever happened to me."

"I'd like to have coffee with you, but I need to be home in the evenings. It's the only time I have with my son."

"You said you had Monday, Wednesday, and Friday off."

"Yes, but you don't."

"I could pick you up any of those days and take you to lunch—anywhere but Barton's Deli. I don't know if I could handle bein' there right now."

"Actually, I ran into Mrs. Barton when I was leaving work. She looked devastated and told me that the memorial service will probably be Friday at the civic theatre—for Pete, Reg, Denny...and Joe Hadley."

"That's a cool idea. I never really thought about it before, but I guess Joe never really had a funeral."

Ivy sighed. "Can you imagine what it must've been like for his parents, wondering all those years if their son was alive and then finding out he was murdered?"

"At least now they can put it behind them, other than they're probably thinking the same thing I am: that the four deaths must be related. I mean, how weird is it that four basketball players from the same class were murdered?"

"Yeah, but ten years apart and in different ways. Nothing about the murders is the same."

"Wanna bet the sheriff's not thinkin' that way?"

Ivy put on her pajamas and took an Excedrin PM, then sat in the rocker in her bedroom, her eyes fixed on the index card, her mind running through all the implications of someone actually knowing what had happened to Joe Hadley.

If the person who left the note was telling the truth, then he knew that Ivy was involved in the cover-up and not the murder. He would be just as guilty as she for not having gone to authorities with the truth. Which probably meant he wasn't planning to tell the authorities anything.

Ivy felt a chill crawl up her spine. So what was the note meant to convey? Was he trying to tell her he killed Pete, Reg, and Denny to avenge Joe's death? Or was it intended to be a threat?

21

FLINT CARTER PUSHED Wednesday's newspaper off to the side of his desk and got up and stood at the window, wishing he were outside in the spring sunshine instead of buried under the weight of a triple homicide.

He heard footsteps and turned around to see Lieutenant Bobby Knolls come into his office, a file in his hand.

"We just got another dozen background checks," Bobby said. "There's nothin' here either."

"Have you gotten the report on Bill Ziwicki?"

"Uh, yeah. Hold on. It's in this batch." Bobby laid the file on the desk and thumbed through the stack. "Here we are. William Arnold Ziwicki, Jr. Divorced. No children. Has his own cleaning business. Owns his home. Credit record is squeaky clean. Very little debt. No criminal record. No arrests. Not even a traffic ticket. Absolutely nothin' here to make me suspect him."

"How many reports have you gotten in so far?"

"I don't know the exact count, but there're sixteen outstandin'. We should have this part wrapped up by Friday."

Flint hung his thumbs on his belt buckle. "We have to suspect everyone who was at that reunion and doesn't have someone who can verify they were in the Aspen Room between 1:20 and 2:10 a.m. How many fit that description?"

"Probably half the people there. Quite a few had left to go to the restroom. One went out to the car to get somethin'. Another was off playin' Romeo with his old sweetheart. The wife didn't know where he was, and Juliet finally admitted he'd been in her room. Quite a few were stayin' with relatives and had already left the lodge before 1:20. So far all the stories check out."

"What about Ivy Griffith?" Flint said. "Do we know for sure she was in the Aspen Room at the time of the murders?"

"Yeah. A lady classmate verified she'd pulled up a chair after the victims left and talked to Griffith for quite a while, and then Ziwicki interrupted and asked Griffith to dance. That's a solid alibi, no matter how you cut it. I *was* shocked at some of the drug-related charges on her arrest record. Never been convicted of anything, though."

Flint nodded. "I know about all that. Okay, keep at it. Don't get sloppy."

"I won't. Just keep Special Agent Sanchez out of my way."

"You and Nick starting to grate on each other?"

"Let's just say if he talks down to me one more time, I'm gonna tell him what I think of him."

Ivy Griffith was making her bed when she heard the phone ring. She raced down the stairs and picked up the phone in the kitchen. "Hello."

"Ivy, it's Bill. Listen, I need to see you. Somethin's come up. Can I pick you up for lunch?"

"You sound upset."

"More like confused. This is really important and not somethin' we should talk about over the phone. When's a good time for you?"

Ivy wondered if Bill was too shy just to ask her to lunch out-right. "Montana's in school until three."

"How about eleven-thirty? We can get sandwiches at the sub place and sit in the park. The sun should make it warm enough if we stay out of the wind. I'd like to talk to you without a lot of ears around."

"All right. But can't you give me a hint?"

"Not till I see you. I'll just honk when I pull up out front, okay?"

"Sure. I'll watch for you."

"See you then."

Ivy hung up the phone and went back upstairs, her mind racing with questions. She straightened her room and then went into Montana's and smiled at what a good job he had done making his bed and putting his clothes away. Her eyes filled with tears. Her sweet, disciplined little boy was the product of Lu's nurturing and selfless giving—not Ivy's.

There's so much I want to tell you, Lu. I just don't know where to turn. I'm scared. I'm sad. Ivy heaved a sigh. *I feel so incredibly lost.*

Ivy went into the bathroom and straightened the countertop, wondering what Lu would think of Bill Ziwicki. Of all the males in her graduating class, Bill was the last one she would have ever thought she'd be drawn to. And yet she was. Could it be because he seemed to genuinely like her and found her attractive? She decided it was more than that. His thoughtfulness appealed to her—and the tender way he had held her when they danced. Tenderness is something that had been sorely absent in all her relationships with men.

In the year she had dated Pete, he had never seemed content just to *be* with her. Their relationship had been one of unbridled passion and experimentation with drugs. Pete always called the shots. It was his way or no way. It didn't take her long to figure out that he was attracted to her because she was pretty and complied with his every desire.

And years later when she was desperate for drug money, the guys who paid her for sexual favors were crude and demanding, and she avoided looking at their faces. That phase of her life was a blur—a huge regret. Especially that she had no idea who Montana's father was.

Maybe part of the reason she was drawn to Bill was because he wasn't judgmental and had never pressured her about her past—or the dramatic change in her appearance. He seemed attracted to her in spite of it, yet had never made an improper advance or even a comment with sexual overtones. The thought that he might actually enjoy her company was flattering.

Ivy gathered up the dirty towels and put them in the laundry hamper, then put fresh ones on the racks and went downstairs, wondering what had Bill so confused that he had to see her to talk about it.

The phone rang and she picked it up. "Hello."

"Ivy, it's Kelsey Jones. I hope I'm not calling a bad time."

"No, not at all."

"I'm so sorry about what happened to your friends. I can't imagine what you must be feeling. I wanted you to know that Brandon and I have been praying for you."

"Thanks. That's very sweet of you." *Wasted, but sweet.*

"Listen, when you get through the memorial service and things settle down, I'd really like to have you over. I've got the recipe for a chocolate cream cheese Bundt cake that'll knock your socks off. I thought we could take some time to get to know each other. I don't know many gals my age around here."

"Uh, well, sure. I have Mondays, Wednesdays, and Fridays off. And I don't have to pick Montana up from school until three. But I'm not very good company right now."

"Understandably. But sometime soon when you feel up to it, let's get together, okay?"

"Okay. Thanks, Kelsey. I can't remember the last time I went to anybody's house just to visit."

Ivy sat in the passenger seat of Bill Ziwicki's van as he turned into Spruce Park and pulled into a parking space in front of the bandstand. There was only one other vehicle in the parking lot, and Ivy noticed a young woman strolling a baby on the sidewalk, a toddler in tow.

Bill got out and opened her door. "There you go. Watch your step."

Ivy hopped out and looked across the park that encompassed two square blocks in the middle of town. "How about that picnic table on the other side of the bandstand? It's in the sun and I doubt we'll feel the wind."

Bill nodded. "I'll follow you."

Ivy walked over to the table and sat on the bench, deciding it would do nicely.

"The sun feels great, doesn't it?" Bill sat across from her, then set the sack from Subs and Suds on the table and handed Ivy a wrapped sandwich and a tall cup of root beer. "I'm glad you agreed to meet me. I'm goin' out of my mind about this." He reached in his pocket and handed Ivy an envelope like the one she found in her coat pocket on Monday. "Go ahead. Read it."

Ivy took out an index card with pasted-on letters.

IVY GRIFFITH KNOWS WHAT HAPPENED TO JOE HADLEY.

Ivy's heart raced so fast she was sure her hand was shaking when she handed the card back to Bill. "Where'd you get this?"

"Under a brick on my front porch. Someone must've put it there last night. It's totally insane, right?"

"If I knew something, why wouldn't I have told the sheriff?"

Bill shrugged. "Exactly. What makes it even weirder is that somebody would tell *me* that you knew. Like I'm gonna turn you in."

Ivy felt as though her head would explode. She wanted to confess everything to Bill and trust him not to say anything, but how could she?

"Sorry to ruin your day," he said. "I don't blame you for being mad."

"I'm more scared than mad. What if you're not the only one who got a card like this? What if someone goes to the sheriff with it? It's going to look really suspicious that I'm being accused of withholding information about Joe Hadley's death right after having discovered Pete, Reg, and Denny shot to death."

Bill's eyebrows furrowed. "Why? You didn't shoot anybody. And they're not even sure the deaths were connected."

Shut up, Ivy. You're digging yourself a deeper hole.

"What's wrong?" Bill said. "You can tell me."

I wish. "It's just that I have a lot of history I don't talk about. I did some things when I was shooting up that I'm not proud of. If it wasn't for some hotshot lawyer my dad paid to help me, and a very intense rehab program, I'd be in jail. The last thing I need is to get accused of something I can't defend. My record won't work in my favor."

Bill ran his finger around the rim of his root beer. "The way I figure it, you wouldn't have held back information about Joe's death unless you had a darned good reason."

"I never said I did that."

Bill lifted his eyes. "You never said you didn't."

Ivy felt the color scald her cheeks and knew he had noticed. She stared at Bill's questioning face, her heart hammering—past, present, and future seeming to converge into one defining moment.

Brandon Jones sat in Buzz Easton's Chevy truck, enjoying the beauty of the mountains as they drove into the Durango city limits.

"Thanks for riding down here with me," Buzz said. "I appreciate your willingness to help me get my operation ready for the season."

"I'm glad to help," Brandon said. "Can hardly wait to get on the white water. Gets my heart pumping just thinking about it."

"Well, if you can stand the cold, we can take a trial run this afternoon."

Brandon laughed. "I won't even notice the temperature. When I'm shooting the rapids, I'm in another world."

Buzz pulled off the main highway into a private drive leading to the Crystal Creek Condominiums. He pulled up behind a green Subaru Forester and turned off the motor. "I need to take care of something. I might be a few minutes. Help yourself to some of those doughnuts. CDs are in the case."

"Do what you need to," Brandon said. "I'll just sit here and enjoy the sights and sounds."

Buzz got out and walked up the steps to the front door and knocked. A dark-haired woman opened the door and let him in.

Brandon ejected the country western CD that had been playing since they left Jacob's Ear, deciding that he and Buzz had very different tastes in music. He reached in the sack and pulled out a chocolate frosted doughnut and ate it in three bites, then did the same with a glazed doughnut. He chased it with the last of his lukewarm coffee and looked up at a patch of white on the foothills, wondering if they'd seen the last of the snowfall for the season.

As the sun heated up the car, Brandon became increasingly drowsy. He closed his eyes and relished how much he loved living in Colorado and having access to the outdoor beauty and every sporting opportunity that it afforded him.

He thought back on his struggle of the previous year and how lost he had felt until he decided being in an office all day wasn't for him. Working at a Christian camp was a totally different experience from being a vice president of a women's apparel company. Less money. Less prestige. Fewer benefits. Yet it gave him the freedom to be more of what God made him to be and to bring people closer to Christ. And then marrying Kelsey, who shared his passion for both the Creator and His creation, was the ultimate reward.

Brandon gave in to the drowsiness, and then woke with a start. He glanced at his watch, and noted that Buzz had been gone forty minutes.

What're you doing in there, Buzz, negotiating a peace treaty?

Brandon stifled a yawn and grabbed another doughnut out of the sack just as the front door opened. Buzz came down the steps, turned around and said something to the woman, then walked over to the truck, a smile stretching his cheeks.

"Thanks for waiting. That was *well* worth the stop. Always is."

"So'd you get your business taken care of?"

Buzz snickered. "Oh, yeah."

"What is this place?"

There was a long pause.

"My girlfriend's condo. What'd you think it was?"

"You had me wait in the car while you had sex with your girlfriend?"

"Don't act so shocked. We're consenting adults."

"For crying out loud, man. Does Maggie know?"

"Why does she need to know? I've been doing this for years, and it's never hurt anyone."

Brandon shook his head. "Are you nuts? How would you feel if she were cheating on you?"

"Shocked. She's not all that interested in sex. Why do you care what I do?"

"Because I don't appreciate being a party to your deception, that's why."

"Maybe if you'd climb out of that Christian box you're hiding in, you'd discover that having sex with someone besides your wife is actually good for your marriage."

Brandon exhaled loudly. "That's baloney. Kelsey's enough for me. And I happen to believe in keeping the vows I made to her."

Buzz rolled his eyes. "Yeah, well, you're newlyweds. It'll be interesting to see where you stand a year from now. Take it from a guy who's been married eight years—a little forbidden fruit will make you a better lover."

"More like a sleaze. No thanks."

Buzz shot him a look. "How about keeping your self-righteous religious garbage to yourself and stop judging me? I'm not hurting anybody."

"Look, man. I can't tell you what to do. Just don't expect me to be a party to your fooling around on Maggie."

"You gonna tell her?"

"No, but don't put me in this position again. I don't want to know anything about it."

Ivy looked at Bill, instantly regretting having said the words.

"*Pete* killed Joe Hadley?" Bill repeated. "How do you know?"

Ivy fixed her eyes on the magpie that had just landed on a lower branch of a nearby tree. "Because I was there. Reg and Denny were involved too."

"I can't believe this! What happened?"

Ivy felt as if her mouth were stuffed with cotton. Finally she said, "I...I sat in Pete's car after school, waiting for him. I was upset that I failed my calculus test, so I rolled up a killer joint and smoked it. Then Pete got in the car with Reg, Denny, and Joe Hadley. Pete said we were going to take a ride, that there was something the guys wanted Joe to see.

"Pete drove as far as Collier Ranch and then stopped the car. He and the guys got out and started arguing. Somehow Joe had spotted a bag of weed in Pete's locker and threatened to tell the coach. So Pete went to Reg and Denny, and they agreed to help him convince Joe not to say anything.

"But Joe was furious when he realized why the guys drove him out there, and he said he wasn't going to cover for Pete. He turned on his heel and started walking back to town. I guess the guys were scared that if Pete got caught, we all would, so they grabbed Joe to stop him, and the next thing I knew they were punching him…" Ivy started to cry, and then stifled her sobs. "They just kept hitting him and hitting him. Finally Pete put his hands around Joe's throat and squeezed until he stopped fighting."

Ivy wiped her cheeks. "Reg and Denny finally pulled Pete off him, but Joe wasn't breathing. Things got even crazier after that. The guys dragged Joe's body down by the river, and then we drove to Reg's house and got shovels out of the garage. We went back, and they dug a hole under a big cottonwood tree and buried Joe.

"I've never forgiven myself…" Ivy stopped and choked back the emotion, "for not doing anything to stop them. The guys were beating Joe, and I just let it happen."

"You really think one female could break up a fight between four basketball players?"

"But if I hadn't been high, I might've screamed at them to stop. Maybe they would've realized they were out of control. Maybe Joe would still be alive. Maybe they all would."

Bill heaved a sigh. "I feel awful. I'm the one who got you the drugs."

"It's not your fault."

"Now that I know what happened, I'd say there's no doubt the murders are connected. Don't you think so?"

"That's just it, Bill. How? There was no one else around when it happened. I'm sure of it. The four of us made a pact never to breathe a word of it. The only one I ever told was Lu, but she didn't tell anyone. The guys swore they never told a soul—not even their wives. So who else knows?"

"Maybe Pete got tanked and shot off his mouth. He'd been hittin' the bottle pretty hard since he came back from Alaska."

"I can't believe this is happening to me! If I go to the sheriff, I have no way of proving what really happened. And what if he thinks I know something about the shooting, too?" Ivy's eyes brimmed with tears. "I can't go to jail, Bill. Not right now. My son just lost the only stabilizing force in his life, and it might scar him forever if he lost me, too."

Bill seemed to be deep in thought, and then turned to her. "I say we go on as if we never got the notes. You had nothin' to do with killin' Joe. And you shouldn't be forced to take the heat for it."

"Then you won't turn me in?"

Bill shook his head. "Never. Your secret's safe with me."

"But what if the person who shot the guys is leaving the notes? What if he's planning to kill me, too?"

Bill took a gulp of root beer and wiped his mouth on his sleeve. "I don't think that's on his agenda or he'd have already done it."

"Then what does he want?"

"Well, judging from the messages he pasted on the index cards, he seems sure of two things: that *you* know how Joe died. And that once he made me aware of it, I'd pressure you into going to the sheriff."

"But if he already got his revenge, why would he care?"

"I'm only guessin', but if he admits what he knows about Joe's death, he'll automatically be a suspect in the shooting. And that's what he doesn't want."

Ivy threw up her hands. "So what does he want from me?"

"Well, since you're the only livin' eyewitness, he probably wants you to make it public that Pete, Reg, and Denny killed Joe."

"But I can't do that without risking going to jail."

"Don't worry. We're not going to let that happen."

22

BRANDON JONES WALKED in the front door and laid his ski jacket over the back of the couch. He heard the TV on in the kitchen and headed that way. Kelsey stood at the stove with her back to him.

"Perfect timing," Kelsey Jones said. "Dinner's almost ready."

Brandon walked up behind her and put his arms around her, his cheek next to hers, and caught a whiff of her perfume. "How's my favorite girl?"

"I'd better be your *only* girl." Kelsey turned around in his arms and pressed her lips to his. "I had a great day. How was your afternoon with Buzz?"

"Super. We took a short rafting trip. Really got me pumped for a day on the white water."

"Were you able to get the dock stained?"

"Yeah. The sun was warm. It was a perfect day for it."

Kelsey turned around and unplugged the vegetable steamer. "So are you done now?"

"Not quite. We have to move fixtures around in the gift shop and put product out, but we're getting there. Looks great."

"When does he open for business?"

"Officially, June 1. But he's got a few enthusiasts who don't mind the colder temperatures and have signed up early." Brandon smiled. "Like me. We're going out this Sunday."

Come on, honey, say something, Brandon thought.

Kelsey turned around, her eyes like searchlights moving across his conscience. "What about church?"

"I didn't think it could hurt to skip it, just this once. Buzz wants to get going early."

"Can't you go Saturday?"

"No, he's got other plans." Brandon could almost feel the ice forming around Kelsey's heart as she walked over to the oven and took out a loaf of sourdough bread.

"I thought we agreed when we moved here that you weren't going to let your weekend recreation interfere with church anymore."

"Oh, come on, honey. I haven't missed a single Sunday. This is an exception. I'm going to be completely immersed in camp before long and won't have many chances to go rafting. Besides, I don't have to go to church to connect with God. I can do it outdoors."

Kelsey lifted her eyes. "How many people who say that actually do it? It's just a big fat excuse."

"That's a cheap shot. You know I've *always* felt closer to God in nature than I do in church."

"That's not the point! You promised you weren't going to do this!"

Brandon threw up his hands. "For crying out loud, honey. It's one lousy Sunday. Why are you going off about this?"

"Maybe it's because I can't stand Buzz Easton and don't trust him any farther than I can throw him! Why can't you find someone else to hang out with?" Kelsey turned off the burner under the cheese sauce and glared at him. "I don't think white-water rafting is a valid excuse to miss church, especially when you've got all day Saturday to play. Buzz isn't going to be sensitive to that. So why don't you find a guy at the camp you can do things with?"

Brandon went over and put his hands on her shoulders and waited until he got her to look up at him. "I'm not going to make a habit of missing church, Kel. I think you could cut me a little slack just this once. I've waited months to go rafting. I have to grab the opportunities that are offered to me. Don't forget Buzz isn't charging me."

"Well, you've been working to help him. It's not as though you haven't earned it."

"Fair enough. And I have a chance to start collecting on Sunday. Can't you just be happy for me?"

Kelsey breathed in and exhaled. "I doubt if I'll ever be happy about you spending time with Buzz. But it's not going to do me any good to hound you about church."

Ivy Griffith sat in the moonlight flooding the front steps, wrapped in a wool blanket, and wondering how she was going to deal with the stress of not knowing who it was that knew the truth about Joe Hadley's death.

It had felt good telling Bill the truth. He was sweet not to make her feel guilty for having done nothing to stop the fight. Why she decided to trust him, she wasn't sure. But Bill seemed like a friend who would keep confidences. She couldn't get over how ironic it was that "Icky Ziwicki" was now her sole confidant, and the one man she found attractive. He was nothing like Pete Barton, inside or out.

Bill wasn't muscular or particularly masculine or handsome. Not someone who would stand out in a crowd. But he had a gentleness about him that seemed to pull her in and not let go. Was it just because she so desperately wanted someone to care about her that she found him attractive? Or was she seeing something in him that had matured over the years? She felt almost guilty at how satisfying it had been, dancing with him at the reunion and creating a stir. Too bad Pete didn't know. It would have been fun to see his ego put in its place. It felt odd that she wasn't sad about not seeing Pete again. Certainly she was horrified by the way he had died, but it was also a huge relief not having to deal with the pact anymore.

Sasha nudged Ivy's hand with her cold, wet nose.

"You're spoiled, you know that?"

Ivy stroked the fur under Sasha's chin, thinking Bill was right—that if whoever had shot the guys planned to kill her, he would have done it by now. She simply couldn't allow herself to be intimidated into going to the sheriff and taking the fall for Joe's death. Why should she be the one to carry the shame? The one who ended up in jail? With no one to corroborate her story, she'd be taking a huge risk.

Trust God with it, Ivy girl. You can never go wrong doing what's right.

Ivy wrapped the blanket more tightly around her, Lu's words seeming almost audible. How could she be sure what was right anymore? Telling the truth about Joe might give his parents closure, but it couldn't take away their grief. And it would surely add to hers on several levels.

A low growl emanated from Sasha, her gaze set on something Ivy couldn't see.

"What is it, girl?"

Sasha stood up on all fours and let out a long, rolling growl, then barked several times and walked in a circle and barked again.

Ivy peered out into the moonlit landscape, her skin covered in goose bumps, and thought she saw a dark form duck behind a tree just as Sasha sprang from the porch and ran barking toward the open meadow.

Ivy jumped to her feet and ran up on the porch, her hand on the doorknob, and listened intently. Sasha's barking stopped almost as abruptly as it had started, and half a minute later she sauntered back up on the porch, seeming as content as if she had just wandered back to the house from one of her roaming adventures.

Ivy pushed open the front door and followed the dog inside, convinced she was being paranoid and wondering how she would ever find peace with all the uncertainty hanging over her.

Carolyn Griffith sat in the kitchen, dressed in her quilted bathrobe and sipping a mug of warm milk. "Montana, you need to finish your milk, sweetie. It's past your bedtime."

Montana Griffith lifted his eyes, a white mustache framing his smile. "I'm bigger now. Can't I stay up till nine? Ian gets to."

"Well, maybe Ian gets up in the morning when he's called."

"Lu always called me three times and let me stay under the covers awhile. She said I woke up happy that way."

"Is that back talk I'm hearing?" Elam Griffith stood in the doorway.

Montana shook his head, his eyes fixed on his mug. "No, sir. I'm just finishing my milk. It's kind of hot to drink fast."

Carolyn hated that Elam's presence seemed to intimidate Montana and shut him down. "I think I'll buy you a snooze alarm and show you how to use it. Then you could wake up slowly all by yourself. Would you like that?"

Montana bobbed his head. "Cool."

"Seems like coddling to me," Elam said. "If the boy would get to bed on time, he'd be ready to get up."

"I never like getting up." Montana glanced up at Elam and then at his mug. "Not even on Saturdays or in the summer."

"A healthy kid like you? That doesn't make sense."

"Lu says I'm not a morning person."

"Well, life doesn't cater to you just because you're not." Elam went over and poured himself a glass of water. "The sooner you learn to discipline yourself around other people's schedules, the better."

Carolyn cleared her throat to signal her annoyance. "If you'll recall, Rusty was the worst at getting up and getting ready for school. And he's doing just fine with his veterinary practice. Besides, if Montana learns to use a snooze alarm to get himself up on time, that's certainly a form of self-discipline."

Elam said something under his breath and left the kitchen, a bag of corn chips in his hand.

There was a long pause, and then Montana said, "Grandfather Griffith doesn't like me."

"Sweetie, he doesn't *know* you yet. Give him time. He seems like a grouch, but he's really a big softy."

"Mom said he didn't like her either."

Carolyn's heart sank. "That's not true. He loves your mother."

"Mom said nobody loved her when she was on drugs—except Gramma Lu." Montana's expression was suddenly somber, and he looked at her with those brown puppy eyes. "Grandmother Griffith...how long is *someday*?"

"I'm not sure what you mean, sweetie."

"Gramma Lu said *someday* I would see her again in heaven."

Carolyn folded her hands on the table. "Well, it's hard to say how long someday is because it's never the same. It can come quickly. Or it can take a very long time."

"Like someday I'll grow up and be a man, and that's a long time? And someday I'll get a snooze alarm, and that's a short time?"

Carolyn touched the end of his nose with her finger. "Exactly. You know what? I think we should think of an easier name than Grandmother Griffith. Can you think of something else?"

"Maybeeeee...just Grandma?"

"That sounds nice."

Montana took a sip of warm milk and wiped his mouth with the back of his hand. "I never had a *real* one before. Gramma Lu was my pretend grandma."

"But you loved her just as if she were your real grandmother. And you always will. That's very special."

Montana pushed his mug aside. "I'm feeling sleepy now. Would you read me a story?"

"Of course I will."

Ivy sat in the living room, thumbing through the newspaper and distracted by the sound of her father crunching corn chips.

"So are you and Bill Ziwicki seeing each other now?" Elam said.

"We're getting to know each other, Dad. There's no romance, if that's what you mean."

"I was just curious. I saw the two of you having a picnic at the park today."

Ivy sighed under her breath. "Are you following me now?"

"No, I was driving by and happened to spot Bill's van and saw you sitting with him, that's all."

"We had sub sandwiches and root beer. Not exactly a candle-light dinner. Both of us are distraught about the shootings. It's nice to be able to talk to someone who can empathize."

"Yeah, I'll bet. By the way, you ever going to tell me what happened with Harriett Barclay yesterday?"

"I apologized and paid her for the lipstick. She gave me a short lecture on how lucky I was she was willing to take the money and not report me to the police, and then I left."

"She's right, you know." Elam wadded up the corn chip bag and set it on the end table. "The last thing you need is another charge on your arrest record."

"No one knows that more than I do." Ivy folded the newspaper and laid it on the coffee table. "It won't happen again."

A few moments of awkward silence passed, and then Elam said, "We need to do something to take the pressure off your financial situation. You and I both know you're never going to be able to support the boy on what you're making."

"Then I'll get another job. I have to figure out how to make it work."

"Your mother and I have been talking about it. We'd like to buy you a car. That would give you a lot of freedom, and it's one less expense for you to worry about."

"You don't have to do that. I just need time to get on my feet."

Elam came over and sat next to her on the couch, his hands folded between his knees. "But this is a big step. You've never tried to support the boy on your own before, and we don't want the financial pressure to discourage you."

Or cause me to shoot up again. "I can't believe you'd do that for me."

The corners of his mouth twitched. "I've already had my eye on a nifty little Jeep Liberty I want you to take a look at. Seems about the right size. I'm pretty sure they'd sell it to me for a couple hundred over dealer's cost."

"So I can start going places by myself again?"

"Not just yet. It concerns me that whoever shot Pete and the guys might have a beef with you, too."

Ivy shook her head. "I don't think the shooting had anything at all to do with me."

"Honey, an irrational person could be mad at you merely by association. You can't discount that possibility."

Suddenly Ivy was flooded again with doubt—and fear. Did whoever knew about Joe Hadley's death hold her as responsible as Pete, Reg, and Denny? Is that what the cryptic messages were meant to convey?

"Look, Flint might wrap this up really quickly," Elam said. "I just think it's wise for you not to go out alone until we know more. But that doesn't mean we can't start looking at cars."

"I haven't had a car since college. When I lived in Denver, I took the bus or walked everywhere. Montana won't know how to act."

"You and the boy can stay here till you save enough money to find your own place. Your mother enjoys babysitting, so that'll save on expenses. Better for the boy not to be with a stranger."

Ivy studied her father's face and saw genuine concern. "Dad, I know I've been a big disappointment. I'm sorry for all the trouble I've put you through."

"Well, the best way to prove it is to stay clean—and to stay out of trouble."

Ivy nodded. "I will. I promise."

23

BRANDON JONES LEANED against the bedroom window, a mug of coffee in his hand, and admired the majestic peaks that looked as if someone had painted them on the pale canvas of Thursday morning sky. He stifled a yawn, bemoaning that he had tossed and turned all night.

Was it wrong not to tell Maggie Easton that Buzz was cheating on her? After all these years, she must've seen and heard clues that either she chose to ignore or were too painful to consider. It's not as though Buzz were subtle or possessed even a smidgen of tact. Somewhere along the line he was bound to have slipped up and given Maggie a reason to suspect he'd been unfaithful. Was she even aware that Buzz was into pornography?

Brandon took a sip of coffee, wondering if Jake Compton had been trying to warn him about Buzz's indiscretions and help him avoid getting caught in the middle. Too late for that. But it wasn't as though Brandon had never been in such a delicate position before. During the seven years he worked at the clothing company in Raleigh, he had known colleagues who were addicted to pornography and sex. Others who had affairs. He had never really considered he had the right or responsibility to express his opinion about their behavior—not that they would have welcomed his two cents anyway. He figured people knew right from wrong and didn't need anyone to point a finger. So wasn't it wise just to forget that

Buzz was cheating on Maggie and let them work it out?

He was suddenly aware that the room was warm and damp and permeated with the scent of herbal shampoo.

"The shower's all yours." Kelsey Jones walked over and took a sip of his coffee, her hair wet and draping down the back of her yellow terrycloth bathrobe. "You were sure restless last night."

"Yeah, sorry. I probably should've slept in the guest room so I wouldn't bother you."

"Were you upset because we argued?"

Brandon studied her flawless complexion that looked prettier to him without makeup. "Yeah, I really hate it when we have disagreements."

"Me, too. Why don't we start this day off right?" She slipped her arms around his neck and let her warm lips melt into his.

Brandon yielded himself to the tender urgency of Kelsey's kiss and was suddenly aware of every inch of her—and the fact that he had a staff meeting in twenty minutes.

"Wow, you make it tough for a guy to think about getting ready for work."

Kelsey rested her head on his shoulder. "I know you have to leave in a few minutes. I just wanted to be sure that things between us are okay."

Brandon's mind replayed the smug look that had been on Buzz's face when he had emerged from his girlfriend's place. How could any guy be happy deceiving his wife day after day?

"Are we okay or not?" she said.

Brandon pushed back so he could see her face, then brushed the wet hair from her eyes. "Better than okay. I was just thinking how blessed we are."

"Then let's decide right here that today we're going to act like it."

Sheriff Flint Carter sat at the table in Bobby Knoll's office and looked at scores of photographs that had been turned over to authorities by class reunion attendees.

"Just a bunch of old friends having fun," Flint said. "Who

would've guessed this thing would turn deadly?"

Bobby unwrapped a piece of bubble gum and popped it into his mouth. "Want some?"

"No thanks. So did the pictures reveal anything helpful?"

"Yeah, I've got Lowry workin' with a couple feds, and it's surprisin' how many photos have that clock in the background. Helped us nail down a number of alibis. I just wish Unger's employer knew where he went on vacation so we could get his statement before Monday. The APB hasn't yielded anything. We can't find him in any of the photos after 11:30 p.m. Several classmates remembered talkin' to him. Said he seemed angry about his upcomin' divorce."

"What did his wife say when you questioned her, Bobby? Is he prone to violence?"

"She says he's got a short fuse but has never hurt her."

"Did she shed any light on why they're getting divorced?"

"Says Ronnie's married to his TV remote. It was obvious this isn't an amiable split, if you get my drift. She was cooperative enough, but kept lookin' away when she talked to me, like she was embarrassed to be in the middle of this."

"I can sure understand that." Flint picked up a wide-angle shot of the room and recognized Ivy Griffith sitting at a table near the band, talking to Bill Ziwicki. "The clock shows 1:45 when this was taken."

Bobby looked over Flint's shoulder. "The clock in several of the photos confirms Griffith was in the Aspen Room durin' the entire time in question. That's the only photo we have of Ziwicki that shows the time. We have only Griffith's word for it that he was at the bar when the victims left the room at 1:20. But we can't find any inconsistencies in what he told us. The leader of the band remembers Ziwicki leavin' with Griffith right after the band quit around 2:00. The front desk clerk remembers them askin' for Richards and Morrison's room number around 2:05. Ziwicki made the 911 call at 2:13. It's not airtight, but I don't see any red flags either."

"What about the other basketball players? Have you confirmed where they were between 1:20 and 2:10?"

"Yeah, they're all accounted for."

"And nobody else in the class had a bone to pick with the victims?"

"Not that we can tell."

"Did you ask Unger's wife?"

"Yeah, she doesn't remember him ever mentionin' the names of our three victims."

Flint tossed the pictures on the table and looked up at Bobby. "So where does that leave us?"

"You mean other than empty?"

"I'm serious."

"So am I. Only four classmates have registered handguns—all accounted for. Not even fired recently. Unger's wife said he has a hunting rifle but no handgun."

"Well, somebody at that reunion knows how to shoot and got his hands on a Glock .45!"

"Believe me, sheriff, I'm as frustrated as you are. That arrogant FBI special agent is leanin' on us. But we can't pull a murder weapon out of a hat. And we can't track a shooter who didn't leave a trail. We've got no fingerprints. No weapon. No DNA. No motive."

Flint groaned. "I can't believe this. I've got a ten-year-old murder I can't solve, and now a triple homicide with more than a hundred and fifty potential suspects—and we can't come up with any suspects?"

Bobby blew a pink bubble and sucked it into his mouth. "Yep. Not today, anyway."

"Well, if we can't solve this one, I might as well clean out my desk."

After the breakfast crowd had left Jewel's Café, Ivy Griffith started cleaning tabletops and listened to the conversation between Deke and Roscoe, who seemed to be in no hurry to leave.

"I'm tellin' ya, that shootin' is a payback for somethin'," Roscoe said. "Sheriff hasn't figured out squat, but I see the writin' on the wall."

"Aw, you don't know nothin'." Deke dismissed him with a wave of his hand. "Think yer smarter than the FBI, ATF, and ever body else?"

Roscoe lifted his faded brown eyes, his grin revealing a row of stained teeth. "Well, I'm a darned sight smarter than I look."

"I sure hope so." Deke guffawed and slapped his knee.

"Listen, you ol' coot. I've been followin' the news real close, and I'm thinkin' them young men was executed—maybe even by the mob. That Pete Barton was always gamblin' over at the Indian reservation and sweet-talkin' the women folk." Roscoe scrunched his wiry gray eyebrows. "Who knows what else he was doin'? Coulda been involved with gangsters or drug traffickin' or smugglin' illegals into the country. There's a lotta that goin' on, I hear."

"You can't hardly hear nothin'," Deke hollered. "You're almost as deaf as that chair yer sittin' on, so where'd you come up with all that?"

Roscoe folded his arms across his chest, a smirk on his face. "I've got close captionin' on my TV set. You'd be surprised whatcha can learn on cable."

Ivy was relieved no other customers were being subjected to the high-decibel dialogue between these two old guys. It had never occurred to her that Pete might have been involved in the mob or some illegal activity and that the shooting might have had nothing at all to do with Joe Hadley.

She looked up just as the front door opened and Bill Ziwicki walked in and flashed her a big smile.

"What're you doing here?" she said.

"Thought I'd grab an early lunch." Bill winked. "What's the special?"

"Baked ham and cheesy mashed potatoes," Ivy said. "But I can't serve you lunch for another forty minutes."

"Then bring me a couple of Jewel's cranberry muffins and a cup of coffee, and I'll be happy as a lark."

Roscoe ever so slowly rose to his feet, then looked over at Ivy. "Put everything on my tab, will ya please?"

"No, it's my turn to pay," Deke said. "Put it on my tab."

Ivy stifled a grin. "How about if I split it and put half on each bill?"

Roscoe smiled. "Yep, that'll do 'er."

"Thank ya kindly," Deke said.

The two men shuffled past her and out the door.

Ivy finally gave in to the laughter and turned to Bill. "How old do you think they are?"

"Not sure about Deke, but Roscoe's a hundred and one."

"I believe it. Okay, sit wherever you want. I'll be right back."

Ivy went in the kitchen and put two still-warm cranberry muffins on a saucer, grabbed a mug, filled a plastic pot with coffee, and carried them to Bill's table. "Here you go."

"So how're you feelin' today?"

Ivy glanced over the top of the swinging doors that led to the kitchen and didn't see anyone. "I'm okay. Listen, Deke and Roscoe were discussing the possibility that Pete might've been involved in the mob or drugs or something illegal. That maybe his death was an execution. What do you think?"

Bill spoke barely above a whisper. "It'd be great if people would start believin' that. But you and I know it had to be revenge for Joe Hadley's death. How else can you explain the messages we got?"

"Yeah, you're right. I guess I keep hoping I'm off the hook. I'm so tired of living in fear. I just want to relax. Live my life. Put the past behind me."

Bill took her hand, and she didn't resist. "It's gonna be okay, Ivy. I'm not lettin' anything happen to you."

"If someone wanted to get to me, you couldn't stop it."

"But whoever killed Pete, Reg, and Denny already got his revenge. He's not out to hurt you. He's just tryin' to scare you into tellin' the sheriff that Pete killed Joe because he can't do it without lookin' suspicious."

Ivy rolled her eyes. "You don't know that."

"It's the only thing that makes sense. You really don't know whether Pete shot off his mouth—or if Reg or Denny did, for that matter. Just because they told you they didn't doesn't make it true."

"I think they were very serious about not having told anyone."

"Well, somebody found out." Bill lowered his voice to a whisper. "I'm thinkin' it was Mr. Hadley."

"Joe's dad?"

"Just think about it. After all those years of hopin' Joe was alive, he finds out that he was murdered right here. Wanna bet he went lookin' for answers on his own? I would've."

"But if he had reason to believe Pete and the guys killed Joe, why wouldn't he just go to the sheriff?"

Bill snickered. "With what—hearsay? Investigators didn't find any DNA evidence. Mr. Hadley knew Joe's killers weren't goin' down unless he took them down. And the way he decided to do it made the authorities think one of his classmates did it. Pretty smart."

Ivy sank into the chair across from him. "My head's spinning. It makes total sense! This was the perfect crime, and if he actually did it, Mr. Hadley's going to get away with it. How'd you figure it out?"

"I couldn't stop thinkin' about it, and the pieces started fallin' into place. Sometimes I think I would've made a good cop."

"So you don't think Mr. Hadley wants to hurt me?"

"Nah, I'd stake my life that he's only tryin' to intimidate you into tellin' the sheriff so everyone knows Pete killed Joe. When he realizes you're not gonna do it, I think it'll all go away."

There was a long pause, and Ivy realized Bill was still holding her hand.

"So you wanna go to a movie tomorrow night?" he said. "We're both gonna need a stress breaker after goin' to the memorial service."

"Okay."

"You want me to come pick you up for the service? You can bet the media's gonna be all over us."

"Thanks, but my parents are expecting me to go with them." Ivy shook her head slowly back and forth. "It's gonna be so weird watching all those clueless people paying their respects to Joe, never even knowing the other guys killed him."

"Well, pay special attention to Mr. Hadley and remember what I told you."

24

By noon on Friday, the traffic had begun streaming into Jacob's Ear for the two o'clock memorial service, and Jewel's Café was packed with lunch customers.

Ivy Griffith sat with her parents at a table by the window, thinking how odd it felt staying seated while customers were coming in the door. She pulled back the green and white checked curtain and saw the KTNR-TV news van go by. She had already decided she wasn't going to talk to the media, no matter what.

"You nervous about the memorial service?" Elam Griffith said.

Ivy nodded. "Yeah, I just want it over with."

"It's nice they're remembering Joe Hadley, too. Poor kid never really had a decent burial."

Ivy's eyes welled as her mind flashed back to the old cottonwood tree and the pile of dirt and snow Pete, Reg, and Denny were shoveling into the hole where they had dumped Joe's body as if it were a sack of potatoes.

"This must be so hard, honey." Carolyn Griffith squeezed Ivy's hand. "Especially right after Lu's death. It's good Ian's mother offered to pick up Montana from school. That'll give you time to let your emotions settle down before you have to go get him."

The front door opened, and Bill Ziwicki walked in, dressed in tan trousers, a yellow shirt, and a navy sport coat. He smiled at Ivy and walked over to the table. "I thought I saw you folks sitting there in the window." He held out his hand to Elam. "Good to see you, Mr. Griffith. Mrs. Griffith."

"You here for lunch?" Ivy said.

"Yeah, but looks like I should've come earlier. This place is bustin' at the seams."

"Well, you're welcome to join us," Carolyn said. "We haven't placed our order yet."

Bill glanced at Elam and then at Carolyn. "Thanks. I appreciate that. Every restaurant in town is packed. Guess a lot of people are here for the memorial service."

"I assume you're going," Elam said.

"Yes, sir. I rearranged my schedule." Bill picked up the menu and opened it. "Pretty neat they're includin' Joe Hadley's folks."

Elam nodded. "Yeah, very nice. I was just telling the girls the same thing. I understand you and Ivy are driving down to Durango to see a movie tonight."

Bill laid the menu on the table and looked over at Ivy. "Yes, I'm lookin' forward to it."

"I suppose she told you I don't want her out of the house by herself till Flint Carter gets whoever did the shooting off the street?"

"Yes, sir. Not to worry. I'll take good care of her."

"I know you will. Can't hurt for the two of you to get out of Dodge and unwind a bit after the past week."

Ivy bit her lip and wondered if her father was ever going to trust her to do anything for herself.

Flint Carter stood in the doorway to his office, looking over the list of deputies, marshals, and special agents assigned to security detail for the memorial service.

"Suppose the new theatre will hold everybody?" Flint said to Bobby Knolls. "Could be standing room only."

"Well, the feds insisted on runnin' the show," Bobby said. "It's their problem. KTNR advised people to get there early if they want a seat."

"I hope we don't end up having to turn people away."

"We'll figure out somethin'. You headin' over there now?"

Flint nodded. "Yeah, Mrs. Barton asked me to say something. I sure hope it doesn't end up sounding like a press conference. I mean, what am I supposed to say to the families of four young men who've been murdered when I don't have one solid lead?"

Bobby shrugged. "That you're real sorry? And you share their pain?"

"Yeah, something like that. Okay, Bobby. See you over there."

Flint locked the door to his office and walked out of the court-house and over to his squad car. The afternoon sun hung high in the bluebird sky and seemed to have taken the chill out of the breeze.

Flint climbed in the front seat of the Explorer, then took out his copy of the shooter's profile and reread it. He put the paper back in his pocket, wondering if the guy would show up at the memorial service to revel in the attention being paid to his dirty deed. He started the car and drove toward the civic theatre, think-ing he'd never seen this much traffic in town in the off-season.

He finally pulled onto a side street and took the back way to the civic theatre, then drove around to the side entrance and parked behind Bobby Knolls's squad car. He spotted Bobby stand-ing next to the building with Special Agent Nick Sanchez and Investigator Buck Lowry.

Flint got out of his car and walked over to them, concerned about the scowl on Bobby's face. "Fill me in."

Sanchez nodded. "I was just telling Knolls and Lowry that people need to feel a strong FBI presence here, and I'm position-ing my agents in key locations inside the theatre and at the entrance and exits."

"Which means the rest of us get traffic and parking detail," Bobby said.

Flint shot Bobby a just-force-yourself-to-be-cooperative look. "Okay, Nick. I'll make sure my deputies keep things moving out-side. From the looks of the traffic, we're going to have a lot more people than places to sit."

Nick dropped his cigarette on the cement and stepped on it.

"We've worked that out with the families. They want a chance to greet people afterwards, so as soon as the service is over, they're going to form a receiving line. At that point, all those who couldn't get in will be allowed to line up and pay their respects."

Flint nodded. "Sounds like you thought of everything. We'll make sure the crowd outside is informed and stays orderly. With any luck at all, this thing will go off without a hitch."

"Just remember the shooter may try to avoid suspicion by coming to pay his respects. So make eye contact with people. Pay attention to details. Make a note of anyone who acts suspicious or whose mood strikes you as out of place for the occasion, especially classmates. And if Unger shows up, nab him first and ask questions later. We'll meet again when this thing's over and compare notes."

"You think Ivy Griffith's in any danger?"

"I doubt it," Nick said. "If the shooter wanted to take her out, he could've done it before now. I doubt he's going to do anything in a crowd and risk getting caught."

Ivy walked away from reporters without answering questions, her hand clinging tightly to Bill Ziwicki's, and followed her parents up the steps to the glass doors of the civic theatre. She was prepared for the stares she would get from classmates who would be shocked to see Bill and her together, especially at a memorial service for Pete.

They walked into the lobby where men in dark suits stood handing out programs. Ivy took a program, then peeked in the theatre and saw the front half was already filled. She followed her parents up the stairs to the balcony and down the center aisle to the front row, where she nestled in the crushed velvet seat between Bill and her mother. The unmistakable new-building smells permeated the facility.

She looked down on the stage, which was lavished with flower arrangements, wreaths, and plants. "I wonder where they're going to put the caskets," she whispered to her mother.

"I don't think they're planning to have them brought here for the memorial service."

Ivy turned her gaze to the seats below and the somber attendees dressed in varying shades of black. In the stillness, the truth
pressed so heavily on her that she could hardly breathe. If only she
hadn't gotten high that January afternoon ten years ago, maybe
these four young men would still be alive. Unexpected tears
clouded her eyes and trickled down her cheeks. She opened her
purse and fumbled to find a tissue.

Bill handed her a handkerchief, then leaned over and put his
lips to her ear. "It's gonna be okay. We just need to get through
this part."

We. Ivy clung to the word as if it were intended to be some sort
of vow. She glanced at her watch and saw that it was 1:47. She
tried not to think about why she was there, and was only vaguely
aware of a piano playing until a door opened to the right of the
stage and brought her back to the moment. People started filing
out of a room and toward the empty seats in front of the stage.

She focused on the faces and was able to pick out Pete's mom
and the other three sets of parents before her eyes homed in on a
young pregnant woman, clutching tightly to the arm of another
woman, both about Ivy's age.

Reg and Denny's widows.

She closed her eyes when Father McGregor opened in prayer
and let her thoughts wander back to when she was a kid and the
worst thing she'd been guilty of was sassing her mother.

She remembered Rusty and herself galloping across Phantom
Hollow on their horses, the wind tickling their faces and the
sense that at any moment they might sprout wings and take
flight. She remembered warm summer afternoons running
through the lawn sprinkler, Zeke yelping playfully and Rusty
pelting her with water balloons. She saw herself clomping on the
wood floor in her mother's high heels and dressing her cat in doll
clothes.

She recalled the day she and Rusty took off riding their bikes
on old Tanner Highway and went all the way to Mt. Bryon and
back, and then rewarded themselves by cutting up Toll House
cookie dough and putting it in vanilla ice cream.

Happy memories came one after another, her mind racing with snippets of her life, and then all of a sudden she was fourteen again, sitting at her vanity table, dressed for her first dance...

Ivy had just finished putting on her makeup when she saw her father's reflection in the mirror.

"Okay if I come in?" Elam said from the doorway.

"Sure." Ivy spun around on the stool, then stood and turned three hundred and sixty degrees and stopped, her hands on her hips. "Well, what do you think, Daddy?"

Elam smiled, his eyes glistening, his nose red. "I think you're going to be the prettiest belle at the ball."

"So you like my dress?"

"It's perfect. I love you in blue with that pretty blond hair of yours. So what time are your date and his parents picking you up?"

"Seven."

"Ah, then we still have time." Elam walked over and stood in front of her and took a bow. "May I have the first dance, mademoiselle?"

Ivy giggled. "Oui, monsieur."

He held out his hands. "After tonight, I may be chopped liver. But for the next twenty minutes, you're still my little princess, and I'm your daddy." Elam started humming some famous waltz Ivy recognized but couldn't name.

She put one hand on his shoulder and the other hand in his and followed his lead around the room, smiling and giggling all the while, and wondering why he thought things between them would ever change...

The sound of someone sneezing jolted Ivy back to the moment. She glanced over at her father, flooded with an incredible longing to feel like his little girl again, yet knowing the things she'd done made it impossible for him to see her that way now.

She looked at her watch, shocked that almost an hour had passed. She looked at the podium and realized Pastor Myers was giving the benediction!

"And, Father, how grateful we are for the positive comments shared by family and friends in honor of these young men who have impacted each of us in different ways. We ask that happy memories fill the void left behind by their absence—and that You fill us with the peace that passes understanding.

"Almighty God, we thank You that in all things, even the tragedies that confound us, You are working for the good of those who love You and have been called according to Your purpose. We pray that our momentary troubles will not overwhelm us, but will cause us to look to Your Son Jesus Christ, who alone is our hope of everlasting life. For it is in His holy name we pray. Amen."

Pastor Myers kept his head bowed for several more seconds, and then looked up and said, "Thank you for coming. The families will be forming a single reception line right here below the stage in just a few minutes. They will stay until every person who would like to speak to them has had that chance. God bless you all."

"That wasn't so bad," Bill said.

Only because I missed the whole thing.

"We probably should say something to the parents, don't you think?" Bill said.

Ivy nodded, and then turned to her mom and dad. "Are you going through the receiving line?"

"I'd like to." Carolyn looked questioningly at Elam.

"Okay," Elam said. "Let's go get in line so we don't wind up at the end of it."

Ivy sidestepped out of the front row of the balcony, linked arms with Bill, and walked up the steps and out the exit. What could she possibly say to her friends' widows or their parents that wouldn't sound like platitudes? Ivy decided it would be better to just say whatever was on her heart than to rehearse something that might sound rote—and that she would pay special attention to how Mr. Hadley reacted to her.

Ivy moved forward another foot or so. She and Bill had been in the receiving line twenty minutes, but it didn't look as though it would be much longer before they were next up. She noticed

Brandon and Kelsey Jones had gone through the line and were cir-
cling around to exit.

"Hi, guys," Ivy said.

Kelsey came over and gave her a hug. "Wasn't that an incredible service?"

Yes, it was lovely." *Or so I hear.* Ivy turned to Bill and Brandon,
who were already talking. "I see you guys introduced yourselves."

"Oh, we know each other," Bill said. "We've talked a few times
at the camp when I was cleanin' the offices."

Ivy listened and nodded politely as Brandon and Kelsey discussed what they considered highlights of the service. She could
hardly believe that she had spaced out the entire thing.

"Come on, honey," Brandon said to Kelsey. "We need to let
them go or they're going to hold up the line."

Kelsey kept talking as she walked away. "I'm serious about
wanting to get together with you for cake and coffee."

"Me, too," Ivy said, aware of Bill gently prodding her forward.

"You go first," he said. "Just be calm."

Ivy walked up to Pete's mother and started to cry before she
ever got a word out of her mouth. "I'm so sorry, Mrs. Barton…"

"It's okay, honey," Evelyn Barton said. "It's been an emotional
time for both of us. Thanks for coming. I know this was hard."

Ivy moved to Denny's parents and shook their hands. "You
may not remember me. I'm Ivy Griffith."

"Oh, Ivy. Of course we remember you," Mrs. Richards said.

"I can't tell you how sorry I am about Denny."

Mr. Richards nodded. "Thank you. We're so sorry you and your
friend had to see him like that…" the man's voice broke. He put his
hand on Ivy's shoulder and squeezed. "Hope you can put that out of
your mind and remember Denny the way he was before."

Ivy moved down one and said something comforting to
Denny's wife and decided that, had circumstances been different,
they might have been friends.

She greeted Reg's parents, hoping her words weren't starting to
sound rehearsed, then moved over and stood facing Reg's pregnant
wife, wishing she were anywhere but there.

She struggled to find her voice and finally said. "I—I'm Ivy Griffith. We've never met, but I went to school with Reg."

The woman shook her hand. "Becca Morrison. And I feel as if I know you. Reg told me all about what good friends the four of you were in high school."

"We really were." Ivy blinked rapidly to clear her eyes. "Reg was a great guy. I'm going to miss him."

"Yeah, he was—*oooh*!" She placed her palms on her round tummy. "I swear this kid's gonna be a kicker for the Broncos…" Becca's voice cracked and she struggled to gather her composure. "Sorry. It's so hard knowing Reg won't be here to see Zack grow up." She wiped the tears off her cheeks and managed a weak smile, her chin quivering. "I'm glad I finally got to meet you, Ivy. Sorry it had to be under these circumstances."

Ivy wanted to say something encouraging but couldn't think of anything that wouldn't cause them both to lose it. She took Becca's hand and squeezed it and moved over to the Hadleys, her pulse racing in protest.

Bill put his lips to her ear. "Just be yourself. I'll be watching him closely."

"Mr. and Mrs. Hadley, I'm Ivy Griffith. I dated Pete Barton in high school and knew Joe from the basketball team. I've agonized about Joe ever since he disappeared…" Ivy felt as if the words were caught in her throat. *Come on, you can do this.* "I can't even imagine what it's been like for you all these years."

Mr. Hadley's dark eyes locked on to hers. "No, you can't. It took a lot of courage for you to come here."

What was that supposed to mean? Ivy thought.

Mrs. Hadley extended her hand. "We could hardly believe that the other parents would think to include us when they're so distraught themselves. I'm sure we'll all rest better when we know why these young men were killed."

Ivy nodded and tried to hear what Bill was saying to Mr. Hadley.

"Well, sir…I'm really sorry about what happened to Joe. I

hope someday the sheriff'll solve the case. People here'll never forget him."

"I don't know about that," Mr. Hadley put his hand on Bill's shoulder and shook his hand with the other, "but I believe *you* never will."

25

Ivy Griffith sat out on the front steps, a north breeze nipping at her face, the mountains appearing dark and mysterious against the crimson sky. In the distance, she heard Sasha barking playfully and wondered if she had found a rabbit to chase.

Down the hill at the camp, there seemed to be an unusual amount of activity, and she remembered a writer's conference was scheduled to start this weekend. She heard the front door open behind her.

"Mom, can I come out?" Montana Griffith said.

"Sure, sweetie. Put your coat on and come sit with me."

Half a minute later, Montana flopped down next to her, wearing the new ski jacket Carolyn had bought him, a white sucker stick protruding from his mouth. "Whatcha doing?"

"Just thinking."

"About the dead guys?"

"Partly."

"Ian said they were shot and all bloody. Is that true?"

Ivy sighed. "How about we don't put those images in your mind?"

"I've seen shot people before on TV."

"Then you already know the answer."

There was a short stretch of silence, and then Montana moved closer to her and put one of his hands in her coat pocket and the other in his own. "Do you miss Gramma Lu?"

"Very, very much. How about you?"

Montana nodded. "But *someday* I get to see her again in heaven. Grandma said someday can be real short or real long because it's never the same. But it always comes."

"Grandma's pretty smart." Ivy put her arm around Montana and savored the moment.

"Mom, when are you gonna tell me about Jesus? Gramma Lu said He knows the way to heaven and to ask you."

"Well, not tonight. Bill's picking me up any minute."

Montana covered a grin with his hand. "You gonna let him kiss you?"

"I might."

"You ever had a boyfriend before?"

"Of course I have."

Montana looked up at her, his dark eyes wide and questioning. "Was my dad your boyfriend?"

"Kind of. Well, not exactly. But I had boyfriends in high school."

"Did they call you *darling* and act all lovey dovey mushy gushy?" Montana let out a husky laugh and flashed her an impish grin.

"Listen, mister. You ask too many questions." Ivy reached down and tickled his knee until he squealed and cherry saliva dripped out of his mouth and down the front of his jacket.

Montana pulled the sucker out and surveyed the sticky mess. "Oh-oh."

"That's okay, it'll come out." Ivy took a Kleenex out of her pocket and wiped off the excess, just as Bill Ziwicki's van pulled into the circle drive in front of the house.

"I'll go tell them he's here!" Montana ran up the steps and in the front door.

Ivy stood and waited for Bill to walk over to her, and then said, "Hi."

"Hi, yourself." His voice was flirtatious. "You look terrific."

"Thanks. So do you."

After taking Bill inside to greet her parents, Ivy got up in the passenger seat of Bill's van and thought how strange it was to be on an official date with the guy who used to buy her drugs and had been considered the biggest loser in the class by her old boyfriend.

Bill got in and sat for a moment, the corners of his mouth twitching. "I can't believe this is really happenin'. You have no idea how I used to dream about this moment when we were in high school."

"I guess not," Ivy said. "But I'm not sure I'd have made a very good date back then. I was pretty messed up."

"Well, same here. There's a lot to be said for growin' up."

Bill drove down the driveway and turned right on Three Peaks Road and headed for the highway. "Okay, let's hear your impression of Mr. Hadley. He acted weird, right?"

Ivy nodded. "It was like his comments had double meanings. I mean, why'd he emphasize that it took courage for *me* to go to the memorial service—just because I found Pete, Reg, and Denny dead or because I was with them when they killed Joe?"

"Maybe both, but he definitely wanted us to read between the lines. When I told him people here will never forget Joe, did you hear what he said?"

"He said he believes *you* never will. Sounded almost like he was confirming that he knows you know that I know what happened to Joe."

Bill smiled. "I actually understood that. Yeah, sounded like his way of lettin' me know without admittin' anything that he's the one who left the envelope on my porch."

"So what're we supposed to do about it? I've thought about this a lot, and I think you're right that I shouldn't go to the sheriff. Like you said, I had nothing to do with killing Joe, so why should I have to pay the price?"

"Exactly. Why should you be the one to go to jail?"

"But if Mr. Hadley is trying to manipulate me into telling the sheriff what really happened to Joe, what's to stop him from slipping the sheriff an index card like the ones we got?"

Bill shrugged. "Nothin'. But I don't think he's goin' to if he hasn't already."

"I find the whole thing puzzling."

"Me, too. But I'm convinced he's the shooter." Bill paused and seemed to be thinking, and then went on. "In fact, I'm thinkin' seriously about confrontin' him with it."

"You can't do that! If he knows you've figured out he did it, he might kill you, too."

Bill shook his head. "Not if I tell him he did us all a favor by takin' out the guys who killed Joe. Like I said before, he doesn't have the heart of a murderer. He just knew there wasn't any evidence to convict the guys for killin' his son, so he took them down. And once he knows I'm on to him, he'll have to back off tryin' to pressure you into tellin' the sheriff."

Ivy leaned her head back on the seat and shook it from side to side. "I don't feel good about this. You can't be sure Mr. Hadley did the shooting."

"Sure enough to confront him."

"But what if you're wrong, and he goes straight to the sheriff and tells him everything you said?"

"Come on, Ivy, Mr. Hadley's guilty. If anything, he'll be relieved to think somebody actually understands the reason he did what he did."

"How can you even think of telling him you *understand* why he shot three people to death?"

"I'd say anything to get him to back away and leave you alone."

"But Mr. Hadley's note never actually said I should go to the sheriff. You're just making an assumption."

Bill exhaled. "Ivy…that's what he wants. I've studied criminal behavior. My instincts are really good. I need to go confront him so he'll—"

"Please don't! I couldn't stand it if anything to happened to you."

She was stunned for a moment by her own words and the realization behind them.

Bill glanced over at her. "I think that's the nicest thing anyone's ever said to me."

"Well, it's true. I'm starting to have feelings for you." Ivy looked at her hands. "I've spent my entire adult life paying the consequences for making that pact with Pete, Reg, and Denny. Now that they're gone, there's really no reason for me to tell what I know and end up in jail. I've got a son to raise. I'm ready to start living again. For the first time in ten years, I'm starting to feel good about getting up in the morning. And it's because of you."

"I—I don't know what to say. Does this mean I might have a shot at a long-term relationship with you?"

"Well, I'd sure like to give it a chance. You've treated me with more respect than any man ever has." Ivy turned to him just as he turned to her. "Please promise me you won't confront Mr. Hadley."

Bill picked up her hand and kissed it. "Okay. I just wanted you to feel safe. Let's wait and see if he backs off."

Flint Carter sat in the conference room at the sheriff's department, comparing notes from today's memorial service with Special Agent Nick Sanchez and Lieutenant Bobby Knolls.

"So, what it boils down to," Flint said, "is the only suspects we have so far are the elusive Unger and some nutcase Bobby discovered out stopping traffic and claiming he'd done the shootings?"

Nick rolled his eyes. "Melvin Lloyd Archer. The guy shows up on the FBI's radar at least once a year. He's a real loon, but he's harmless. He wouldn't know how to pull a trigger if it wrapped itself around his finger."

"Is that a yes?" Bobby blew a pink bubble and sucked it into his mouth.

"For now, Lieutenant," Nick said. "If the APB on Unger doesn't yield anything, we'll stake out his apartment this weekend and pick him up there or at his workplace on Monday morning when he gets back from his alleged vacation. In the meantime, I want my team to take a closer look at the people who were working in the lodge the night of the shooting. I want to dissect their alibis, know every move they made—when they timed in or out, took a break, went to the john, made a phone call. I want to know what part of the building they were in and at what time and what they were doing. Somebody had to have seen something suspicious."

"My investigators have already done that," Bobby said.

Nick jotted something on the back of his business card. "Well, mine are going to do it again—just to be sure nothing got missed. Also, my team will continue going through all the statements and background checks on the classmates and compare what we have on each person to the perp's profile. We've got a ways to go till we've narrowed down the field."

"Bobby's investigators could assist," Flint said.

Nick shook his head. "It'll go faster if we just do it ourselves. We have our system down pat."

Bobby pushed back his chair and jumped to his feet. "Knock yourselves out. I'm outta here."

"Good night, Bobby." Flint waited until Bobby's footsteps grew faint down the hallway, and then said, "You know, Nick, it's not easy for Lieutenant Knolls having you stomp all over his turf. A little sensitivity would go a long way in diffusing the resentment that's obviously building."

"I haven't got time to coddle the lieutenant's wounded ego. He needs to toughen his hide and pay attention. He just might learn something. And for the record, it'd be a whole lot easier taking him seriously if he'd spit out the bubble gum."

"Bubble gum keeps him away from cigarettes. He used to smoke three packs a day till his son was born. Look, Bobby's smart, and he's got a good team of investigators. Whatever your personal opinion of him, you can't argue with his record. The lieutenant knows his stuff, and he's well connected in the region. You need him as much as he needs you."

Nick folded his arms, a smirk on his face. "I do believe I've just been scolded by the sheriff of Tanner County."

"With all due respect, Special Agent Sanchez, this isn't Mayberry. I asked you to help us because the bureau has more experience and resources than we do. Treating us like the professionals we are would only serve to strengthen your efforts. Seems to me you have a choice to make: Either we can spend our energy solving the case or waste it antagonizing each other. Either way, the taxpayers are footing the bill. It's your call."

Nick stood and didn't make eye contact. "Think I'll step outside and have a cigarette. I'll call you on your cell if we discover anything. You have a nice evening, Sheriff."

Ivy sat across from Bill at a cozy table for two at the Sherwood Forest Inn, anticipating the rack of lamb she had ordered and studying Bill's features by candlelight. The only time she could remember a date taking her out for a fine meal was prom night when she and Pete had tripled dated with Denny, Reg, and their dates and gone to the Tanner House. It was the first and last time she had ever tasted quail.

"You have the most intriguing eyes," Bill said.

"I always wished they were blue."

"Why, when they're so dreamy-lookin'?"

"They're gray, Bill—like metal, rainy days, and smoke. Doesn't seem very feminine."

"You kiddin'? Look at yourself. A guy could get lost in those eyes. I thought so the first time I ever met you. Bet you don't even remember when that was."

Ivy smiled sheepishly. "Not offhand. Remind me."

"We were both in Mrs. Pierce's third-period English class our junior year. I sat behind you and over a couple rows. Could hardly keep my eyes off you from day one."

"I don't remember you saying anything to me."

Bill shrugged. "My acne was so bad then that I hardly spoke to anyone."

"I wish I could go back and change all that for you," Ivy said. "Kids are so mean. I doubt if most of those students even realized how devastating their teasing was."

"Probably not. We were all just a bunch of clueless kids tryin' to figure out where we fit in. I was kinda surprised when a few of them spoke to me at the reunion. But I don't get why Pete, Reg, and Denny gave me the cold shoulder. The four of you were the only friends I had in high school."

Ivy put her hand on Bill's. "Just so you know, I was hoping Pete would come back and see us dancing. I wanted everyone to. It felt great breaking out of the mold and just being myself."

Bill's smile stole his face. "Just *dancin'* with you was more than I ever dreamed possible…but in front of the whole class? Well, I'll never forget it."

"Me either. It's like the real Ivy Griffith came out of the closet. Suddenly, I didn't care what anybody else thought. I did what *I* wanted."

"That's exactly what you should've done." Bill kissed her hand. "Same with this Joe Hadley situation. I'm glad you decided not to take the rap."

"I'm still struggling with the fact that I'm not entirely innocent."

"We've already been over this. There's no way you could've broken up a fight between those four guys, even if you'd tried."

"Maybe not, but I'll always wonder if Joe would be alive if I had. And I was wrong to make the pact and cover for them."

"What were you supposed to do—sell your friends down the river? You did what anyone would do. But that's all behind you now."

"I know." Ivy sighed. "But Lu always said only the truth will set me free. What if I can't be free unless I confess what really happened?"

"You did confess—to me."

"But Lu said I need to be honest with myself and God, and with the sheriff—that I can never go wrong if I do what's right."

"With all due respect to your friend Lu, you couldn't decide what was right until you had all the facts. And now that the killers are out of the picture, everything's changed."

"Except the truth. And the pain I caused Mr. and Mrs. Hadley because I didn't speak up."

"For cryin' out loud, Ivy, Mr. Hadley *knows* the truth and

decided to settle the score himself. What's left to feel guilty about?"

Ivy sat for a moment and let Bill's words sink in. "I hadn't really thought of it that way."

"Well, you should. How about you stop blamin' yourself for other people's choices and let yourself experience some long-overdue happiness?"

"I want to, but I'm not sure I remember how."

Bill smiled with his eyes. "Oh, I think it'll come back to you."

Ivy stood on the front porch, feeling nervous as a teenager coming home from her first date.

"I had such a great time tonight," Bill finally said. "I'd like to go out again sometime soon."

Ivy smiled. "Me, too. Thanks for everything. Dinner was incredible. I can't remember when I've enjoyed a meal more."

"I was pretty sure you'd like it. Why don't we plan to go back for your birthday? It's two weeks from today, right?"

"How in the world did you remember that?"

Bill shrugged. "I don't know. I guess I remember what's important to me. Of course, that doesn't mean I can stand to wait two weeks before askin' you out again." There was an awkward pause, then he cupped Ivy's face in his hands and let his lips melt into hers. Time seemed to stand still, and then she was aware of Bill's voice. "I'll call you tomorrow. Good night."

"Good night. Thanks again for such a nice evening."

Ivy went in the house, then stood leaning with her back against the door, amazed that any man would pay for such a fine dinner, spend hours listening to her as she worked through her feelings, and then seek nothing in return except a good-night kiss.

Ivy tiptoed up the stairs, thinking how wonderful she felt tonight compared to those nights long ago when she had come home from her dates with Pete, laden with guilt for having slept with him.

Bill made her feel clean and innocent, and life was starting to look promising.

26

At ten till six the next morning, Ivy Griffith got out of her father's Suburban at the back door of Jewel's Café, trying not to resent being chauffeured.

"I'll bring your mom and the boy back for breakfast later," Elam Griffith said. "He'd probably enjoy seeing you at work."

"Okay, Dad. Thanks. Montana's been wanting to try the cinnamon apple pancakes."

"Maybe when you get off work, we'll go look at that Jeep Liberty I was telling you about. You might as well be set up to start driving when Flint cracks this case. Can't imagine it's going to take long."

Are you kidding? He'll never suspect Mr. Hadley. "Okay. I don't have anything planned."

Ivy shut the car door, then went in the back door of the café and was hit with the aroma of bacon frying.

"Mornin', doll," Jewel Sadler said. "Glad to see you made it through the memorial service okay."

"Yeah, but I'm glad it's over. Did you go?"

Jewel nodded. "I shut the café down and slipped into the back row, but I didn't go through the receiving line. Had to get back here and prepare for the Friday-night crowd."

"Was it busy?"

"Very. But that's the way I like it."

"Yeah, me too. I'd better go make sure we're ready for customers." Ivy put on her name tag and went out front and plugged in the coffeepot. She looked around the dining room and made sure all the tables had been set, then poked her head in the restrooms to be sure they had been restocked.

She plugged in the Open sign and unlocked the door, and a few seconds later, Flint Carter walked in.

"Good morning, Sheriff," Ivy said. "I didn't expect to see you on a Saturday."

"I can't take weekends off right now. We're working with the FBI 24/7 to solve this triple homicide. How're you holding up?"

"Okay, I guess—as long as I don't close my eyes. I still see their faces."

"I know what you mean. I spent some time at the murder scene myself." Flint went over and sat at his usual table.

"Have you got any suspects yet?" Ivy said.

"I'm not really free to comment on that while the case is under investigation. But if you have any thoughts on the matter, I'm all ears."

Ivy shook her head. "Not really."

"We may need to ask you more questions as we get deeper into the investigation."

"Okay." Ivy thought about Bill, knowing that would put a pleasant look on her face. "I'll answer any questions you want me to."

"Good. By the way, what'd you think of the memorial service?"

"I'm sure it was very nice, but I spaced a lot of it out. Just too depressing, especially seeing Reg's pregnant wife."

"Yeah, that was tough."

Ivy took her green pad out of her pocket. "You want your usual?"

"Why don't you substitute the orange juice with grapefruit juice?" He winked. "I feel like living dangerously."

"I'll bring your coffee in just a minute," Ivy said. "Oh, be sure to tell your wife again how much I appreciated her picking up Montana from school yesterday. He loves playing with Ian."

Flint walked in his office and saw Special Agent Nick Sanchez working at the table, files stacked at both ends.

"Any big revelations overnight?" Flint said.

"Yeah." Nick blew a huge pink bubble and sucked it back into his mouth. "The bubble gum did the trick. I haven't had a cigarette since midnight."

Flint smiled to himself and wondered if Nick was serious or if it was just his way of saying he'd been a real jerk. "So what's the status this morning?"

"My team didn't find any suspects among the lodge personnel, so we finished narrowing down our list of classmates. We eliminated those who didn't fit any aspect of the profile and came up with five guys who fit at least part of it."

"What are their names?"

Nick picked up a piece of paper and handed it to Flint. "Carlos Ortega, Blake Summerfield. William Ziwicki. Spencer Mansfield, and *Ronald Unger*. All experienced with either handguns or rifles. All introverted. All with a history of failed relationships. Also some negative social interaction in high school, though Ziwicki's the only one of the five who actually spent time with the victims. I think it's pushing the envelope to think he wanted them dead since the three victims were actually nicer to him than the other classmates were. And except for Unger, whom we haven't talked to yet, each of these guys claims to have been in the Aspen Room all evening except to go to the john, and they have witnesses who can verify they were there at least part of the time."

Flint pulled out a chair and sat at the table. "So what now?"

"We nab Unger the minute he shows up at his apartment. In the meantime, we go back through the thousands of photographs the classmates turned over and concentrate on picking out just these five guys. Maybe that'll tell us something."

Flint folded his arms across his chest and sat back in his chair, his weight balancing on the balls of his feet. "I'm beginning to lose confidence in the word *maybe*. Just because these guys fit a few points on the profile doesn't prove they're guilty of anything."

"Yeah, well, I'm chomping at the bit to get at Unger. Too bad we couldn't have tested him for gunpowder residue and blood. Seems a little too convenient that he came to the reunion with plans to leave for vacation in the middle of the night. And since the darned security camera was on the fritz, we don't even have tapes of who entered the lodge and who left or at what time."

Brandon Jones walked into Jewel's Café right behind Kelsey, and saw Elam and Carolyn Griffith sitting at a table with Montana, menus in their hands.

Kelsey went right up to them. "Hey, how're you guys this morning?"

"I get to try the apple cim…cimm-a-mon pancakes." Montana flashed her an impish grin. "With lots and lots of maple syrup."

"Mmm, that's sounds good," Kelsey said. "My favorite is cheese blintzes with lots of strawberry sauce."

Brandon glanced around the room. "Is Ivy working?"

Carolyn nodded. "This is the first time Montana has gotten to see his mother in action."

"So did she wait on you?" Kelsey said.

Montana's head bobbed and he wagged his finger. "I said, 'Ma'am, you bring my order right away. I'm starved,' and my mom laughed."

"Why don't you join us?" Elam said. "Plenty of room at our table."

Kelsey looked over at Brandon, yes in her eyes.

"Great, we'd love to." Brandon seated Kelsey and then himself. "You guys have hardly had a chance to catch your breath. I hope things are calming down."

"My mom has a boyfriend," Montana announced.

Brandon chuckled. "She does, huh?"

"His name is Bill Bazicki."

"It's Ziwicki, sweetie," Carolyn said. "And Brandon knows him. Bill cleans the offices at the camp."

Ivy came over to the table. "You two want your usual?"

"Sure," Brandon said.

Kelsey smiled. "We are so boring."

Ivy scribbled something on her green pad. "I'll be right back with another pot of coffee."

Montana reached over and patted Kelsey's back. "You're not boring. You're fun. When are you gonna come over and play checkers with me? You said you would."

"I did, didn't I?" Kelsey put her finger to her mouth. "Well, let's see…Brandon's going rafting tomorrow. If you're not busy, maybe we could play checkers after church."

Montana folded his arms across his chest. "I don't go to church."

"Well, starting tomorrow, you do," Carolyn said. "If your mother's working, you'll need to be with me and your grandfather."

"We'll be home all afternoon," Elam said. "Feel free to stop in any time. Carolyn just made some cherry cobbler that'll knock your socks off."

Ivy walked out the back door of Jewel's at five after two, surprised and pleased to see Bill Ziwicki leaning against his van, his arms folded, his face aglow.

"Hi, beautiful." He went over and kissed her on the cheek. "I know I said I'd call, but I could hardly wait to see you again."

"My dad's picking me up in a minute," Ivy said. "He wants to show me a Jeep Liberty he's thinking of buying me."

"That's cool. So he's changed his mind about you going out alone?"

"No, but he doesn't think it's going to take long to solve this case." Ivy rolled her eyes. "The sheriff will never in a million years suspect Mr. Hadley. They're never going to solve it."

"You're probably right."

"I wish I could convince my dad that I'm not at risk. But I don't know how to do that without revealing too much."

Bill nodded. "Maybe you just need to play along for now. If it would help, I could pick you up from work and take you home. That would save your folks one trip into town four days a week."

"But that'd cut into your workday."

"I can pack a sandwich and not take a lunch hour. That'd give me time—unless, of course, you'd rather ride home with your mother."

Ivy smiled without meaning to. "Hardly."

"I was wonderin'…you wanna go out again tonight?"

"Sure, but I have to be at work at six in the morning. I'm not sure I can handle two late nights in a row. What'd you have in mind?"

"I was thinkin' we could drive over to Mt. Bryon and hang out at the Blue Moon. It's a quaint old tavern that has an exceptional jazz band on Saturday night."

"Sounds like fun, but I don't drink. I stay away from everything that could be addictive."

He smiled and pulled her into his arms. "What about me? Could I be addictive?"

Ivy giggled. "Yes, but that's different."

"Well, the bartender makes some pretty fancy booze-free specialty drinks. The band's really worth hearin', and I'd love to dance with you. If we go early, I can have you home by ten."

"Okay. I'll have to check with my mom first and see if she's open to watching Montana again. I've been out a lot lately."

"What if we do somethin' with him tomorrow—take him to the park or let him play video games down at Clicker's?"

"Uh, I don't let him play video games. I'm putting that off as long as I possibly can. And remember, I don't get off till two, so it'll be a short afternoon."

"We could hike up to Tanner Falls. It only takes forty minutes, and it's not a hard climb. Phantom Creek is bustin' at the seams, and it oughta be pretty spectacular. The weather's supposed to be nice."

"I think he'd like that. We can always bribe him with the promise of a Happy Meal for dinner."

"Or you could come over to my place and I'll cook us hamburgers."

Ivy leaned back, her arms around Bill's neck, and looked into his eyes. "That's really sweet of you. But for now, I'd be more comfortable if we met in public."

"Okay, then. MacDonald's it is. We can talk about what time when we're out tonight. How about I pick you up at five o'clock, and we'll eat somethin' when we get to the Blue Moon? Their food's good."

"All right. If there's a problem with my mom watching Montana, I'll call you. Otherwise, I'll see you then."

27

IVY GRIFFITH WENT UP the front steps, the afternoon sun warm on her shoulders, and followed her father into the house and flopped on the couch next to her mother.

"I *love* it! It's perfect!" Ivy felt a grin stretch her cheeks. "I can't believe you and dad bought me a car."

Carolyn Griffith laughed. "So tell me what you *really* think of the little white Jeep?"

"I'll go nuts not being able to drive it till the sheriff solves the case. What if it goes on for months? Or years?"

"It won't," Elam said. "Flint's going to get this guy."

"Ivy has a point." Carolyn set her magazine on the coffee table. "It could be a long time before Flint makes an arrest. From what I'm hearing on the news, they aren't even close."

"Law enforcement isn't going to release every bit of information they have." Elam handed the mail to Carolyn. "I went ahead and wrote a check for the car. I'll get on the computer tonight and transfer the funds from savings to checking. Ivy liked the deluxe floor mats and snazzier hubcaps, so they're getting those from another dealership. Car'll be ready Monday at noon."

Ivy rarely thought of her parents as wealthy people, though she knew they must be worth millions. They never flaunted what they had and rarely even spoke of it. After all the years she had struggled just to keep food on the table, it was hard to fathom that they could just write out a check and pay cash for a car. Then again, her parents had probably forked over even more than the price of the car to pay for her drug rehab and the lawyer they hired to keep her out of jail. It occurred to her that she had never sincerely thanked them.

"Maybe I could break in the car out here on the property," Ivy said. "There are some really neat off-road trails. Montana and I could have a ball using the four-wheel drive."

Elam nodded. "There you go."

"By the way, Bill offered to bring me home the days I work, which would save Mom four trips into town every week."

"Wasn't that nice of him?" Carolyn said. "But he's working. I couldn't ask him to do that."

"He says he can pack a sandwich and use that time as his lunch hour."

Carolyn smiled. "I imagine you'd love it if I'd take him up on his offer."

"I'm enjoying his company a lot more than I ever thought I would," Ivy said. "He wants me to go out again tonight, and tomorrow wants to take Montana and me hiking up to Tanner Falls."

"Moving a little fast, aren't you?" Elam said.

"I don't think so." Ivy hated that she sounded defensive. "We went to a movie and out to dinner. What's so fast about that?"

"Where's he want to take you tonight?"

Ivy bit her lip. *I'm not a teenager, Dad!* "To the Blue Moon over in Mt. Byron to hear a jazz band he thinks is exceptional. And since I have work tomorrow, he promised to have me home by ten. Assuming, of course, I can leave Montana with Mom. I don't want to take advantage of your generosity."

"I don't mind watching Montana," Carolyn said. "But you haven't seen much of him lately."

Ivy nodded. "I know. That's why we want to take him hiking tomorrow afternoon."

"Well, you should've asked first, honey. Montana invited Kelsey Jones to come over and play checkers with him tomorrow after church. Brandon's going rafting, and she said she'd love to come."

"Okay. I'll stay home with him."

"Well, only two can play checkers," Carolyn said. "Why don't you and Bill go ahead and do something together and plan an outing with Montana next weekend?"

Ivy left the dance floor, her hand holding Bill's, and went back to their table at the Blue Moon Tavern.

"That was nice," Bill said. "I love the bluesy quality of this band, especially the saxophone."

"Tell me their name again."

"Blowhards."

Ivy smiled. "Clever. Great sound."

"How's that chocolate whatever-it's-called?"

"Really good." Ivy took a sip through the straw. "I don't miss the rum."

The band started to play again, and Ivy just listened and enjoyed the great music while she studied the audience. All of a sudden her eyes stopped on a familiar face. What was he doing here?

"What are you staring at?" Bill whispered.

"I know that guy in the red shirt. His name's Buzz Easton. He and his wife come in for breakfast on Saturdays."

"Why do you look mad?"

"Because the lady with him isn't his wife."

"Maybe she's a relative."

"I doubt it. Look at the way their arms are touching. And his eyes keep wandering down to her cleavage. It's really disgusting. I just saw him with his wife this morning. What a creep."

Bill turned and fixed his eyes on Buzz. "If I were married, I'd never cheat on my wife, and I sure as shootin' wouldn't put up with her cheatin' on me. I'm not into sharing."

"Neither am I." Ivy took a sip of her drink and wondered if Bill's ex-wife had been unfaithful. "Well, there's no point in letting his indiscretion infringe on our evening."

Bill put his hand on hers. "As far as I'm concerned, nothin' could spoil this evening. So what time tomorrow should I pick up you and Montana?"

"Oh, sorry. I forgot to tell you he sweet-talked Brandon's wife Kelsey into coming over to play checkers with him tomorrow afternoon. Mom thinks he has some sort of little-boy crush on her and that you and I should go ahead and do whatever we want and make plans to take Montana some place next weekend."

"Okay. You still wanna take that hike? Or is there somethin' else you'd rather do?"

"I'd love to hike up to Tanner Falls. I haven't been there since I was in high school."

Ivy glanced over at Buzz and noticed he was nuzzling his companion's neck, and she was belly laughing as if she were drunk. How angry and humiliated would Maggie be if she knew what he was up to?

Ivy's mind flashed back to an incident from her own past when she had agreed to have sex with a guy for drug money and remembered seeing a gold band on his left hand.

"Are you there?" Bill said. "You seem miles away all of a sudden."

"Sorry. I was just thinking about Buzz and wondering why people do such awful things." *And what you'd think of the dark secrets in my past.*

Bill shrugged. "I suppose people have different ideas of what's awful."

"Anyone can deceive himself, but it's pretty hard to misinterpret 'Thou shalt not commit adultery.'"

"Yeah, if you accept moral absolutes."

"And you don't?" Ivy asked.

"Not really. I believe we should all decide for ourselves."

"Well, if you don't believe committing adultery is a sin, then why would you even care if your wife cheated on you?"

"Because I don't *wanna* share. It's a personal preference, not a moral issue."

"I see. So, if her preference was to sleep around, which of you would be right?"

Bill took a gulp of beer. "I'll never allow myself to be in that position. Whoever I marry will have to agree with me on stuff like that before I'll ever tie the knot."

"Isn't that what wedding vows are for?"

"Yeah, but instead of payin' lip service to a bunch of do's and don'ts, we'd decide ahead of time what *we* think is right, and that's what we'd promise to do."

"You'd custom-make your marriage parameters?"

"Yeah, that's a good way to put it."

"Do you do that with everything?" Ivy said.

"Pretty much. I think right and wrong is relative to circumstances. No one has the right to decide for someone else what they should do."

Ivy sat for a moment, her eyes focused on her hands, trying to process the implications of what Bill had just said. Finally she lifted her eyes and leaned closer to him and spoke just loud enough for him to hear. "If you think right and wrong is relative, then you think Mr. Hadley was justified in shooting Pete, Reg, and Denny, right?"

"Well...look at what the guys put him through all those years."

"So everyone who gets wronged is free to exact revenge outside the law?"

"I didn't say that. But we both know that the sheriff's never gonna solve that case, and it wasn't fair for those guys to get away with it."

"Then why was it fair for me to get away with it?"

Bill's face softened. "You didn't do anything."

"Let's just change the subject. You're never going to understand."

"Come on, don't shut down."

Ivy made a tent with her fingers. "I've never doubted the Bible is true and moral absolutes are nonnegotiable, though I certainly haven't lived it. That's why I have so much guilt. I *know* I've sinned and haven't repented. I just haven't been ready to face God with it."

"You're not some terrible sinner. You were the victim of circumstances."

Ivy put her fingers to her temples as if that would stop the throbbing. "How can you say that? It was my choice to get high and do nothing while the guys beat Joe till he couldn't fight back. And it was my choice to conspire with them to cover up the murder and let the Hadleys live with it all those years."

"Even if you'd told the sheriff what happened, Joe would still be dead. And the Hadleys would still be devastated. And Pete, Reg, and Denny would still be guilty. So tell me how your decidin' to keep quiet made *you* the bad guy?"

"I don't know! I can't think anymore." Ivy sat back in her chair, Bill's words seeming like missiles intercepting her own thoughts.

"What's it gonna take for me to convince you to ditch this pointless guilt and stop beatin' yourself up over the notion that you've committed some horrible sin?"

The first Bible verse Ivy had ever memorized rang in her mind. *If we claim to be without sin, we deceive ourselves and the truth is not in us. If we confess our sins, he is faithful and just and will forgive us our sins and purify us from all unrighteousness.*

"Bill, if right and wrong is relative and there's no such thing as sin, then why did God send Jesus to die on the cross so we can be forgiven?"

"I don't believe He did. As far as I can tell, Jesus was no different than dozens of other cult leaders who've professed to have secret knowledge that you have to follow or go to hell. They're all religious fanatics. And they all end up dead."

"But Jesus rose from the dead."

Bill lifted his eyes, his gaze cold as steel. "According to a handful of his followers who needed to believe it to keep from feelin' betrayed. I can't believe you really buy all that."

"Well, I sure can't buy the idea that there are no moral absolutes. Everything I was ever taught tells me differently."

"And what good's it done you? You nearly destroyed your life with drugs—all to escape this giant guilt trip from on high. Who needs that? Can't you see the whole God, sin, heaven, and hell thing is a myth? You have to let go of it if you want to move forward."

"It's not a myth!" Ivy said, louder than she meant to.

"Okay. Okay. This doesn't need to be an issue with us. I just want you to stop sabotagin' your happiness. The power to change all that is right there in your heart. But you've gotta stop buyin' the whole sin and guilt trip. There's no proof any of it's true, and it's just gonna destroy you."

The piercing look in Bill's eyes caused her to shudder and look away.

"You cold?" he said.

"All of a sudden."

"Why don't we dance and get your blood movin' again?"

Ivy got up, relieved to end the conversation. She walked out to the dance floor, her pulse pounding in her ears, the soprano sax suddenly grating on her like fingernails on a chalkboard. She placed one hand on Bill's shoulder and the other hand in his and willed her feet to move to the music, not really sure which of them was leading.

28

No stars were visible through the thick shroud that clothed the night sky as Ivy Griffith got out of Bill Ziwicki's van and hurried up the steps to her parents' front porch.

She didn't see any lights on inside and assumed her mom and dad had gone to bed already. "Thanks for everything, Bill. I enjoyed the band. Good night." She turned and grabbed the doorknob, aware of Bill taking her gently by the arm.

"You wanna tell me what's wrong?" Bill turned her around and pulled her into his arms.

Ivy stiffened. "I don't see the point. We're never going to agree."

"Just because we don't see eye to eye on religious stuff, you give me the silent treatment all the way home, and now you can't stand for me to touch you? What am I missin'?"

"It's not you. I'm just more confused right now than I realized. I think it might be good if we don't see each other for a while."

"What?" Bill dropped his hands to his side.

"I have a lot to work through," Ivy said. "My life has changed dramatically in the past month, and I don't think I'm ready to pursue a relationship. I just don't have the emotional energy."

Bill threw up his hands. "Since when? Five hours ago you couldn't wait to see me. Why don't you just admit you're mad about the sin and guilt issue?"

"I'm not mad, Bill. I'm scared. There, I said it. Are you happy?"

"Scared of what?"

"You'll never understand so there's no point in getting into it."

"I'm not stupid, Ivy."

She looked into his eyes and saw that same icy look he got when Pete, Reg, and Denny had denied knowing him. "Of course you're not."

"So what's the problem?"

"You're never going to accept it."

"Try me."

"I'd rather not tonight. I need to go." She tried to wiggle out of his arms and couldn't.

"Ivy, please. Just say it. I doubt if either of us is gonna sleep tonight unless we clear the air. What'd I say wrong?"

"It's not what you said. It's what I *did.* No matter how I try to pass off the responsibility for Joe's death, I made choices that played into it. No matter how much I want to clean up the truth, the guilt won't go away."

"So I'll help you overcome it."

"I can't *overcome* it! I have to deal with it! There's a difference."

"The last thing you need right now is to try to handle this by yourself."

"I think I have to. It's obvious we're coming from two entirely different perspectives. I'm just not comfortable with yours." Ivy looked away. "I wouldn't hurt you for anything. But I don't think we're going to see eye to eye on this—ever."

Bill stood silent for what seemed an eternity, and then said: "So this is it? We're done? Just like that?"

"I'm sorry."

"Sorry? You're *sorry?* Do you have any idea how I feel about you? I hardly think of anything else. You're everything to me. I can't believe you're walkin' away just because I wanna rid you of this absurd guilt that's practically destroyed your life."

"You can't *rid* me of it! Nobody can. I have to face it. Wrestle with it. And make my own decision about what to do."

Bill shook his head from side to side and let out a loud sigh. "This is insane."

"No, what's insane was thinking I could be free any other way than God's way."

"Ivy, wake up and smell the coffee! You've been deceived! There's nothin' anybody can do to help you as long as you wallow in guilt that's self-inflicted and cling to a God who doesn't exist."

Once-familiar words resounded in her head. *Come near to God and he will come near to you.*

Ivy's eyes locked on to Bill's, and she shuddered again, the way she had at the Blue Moon. "I need to go in now."

"Wait, we can work this out—"

Ivy pushed open the door and hurried inside, relieved that Bill didn't try to stop her. She fumbled to set the dead bolt, then ran up the stairs to her room, fell on the bed, and hugged her pillow.

She heard Bill's van drive away, but the fear did not leave her and seemed even more intense. She clutched her pillow tighter, her heart hammering wildly, her eyes searching the darkness for glistening eyes or a sinister grin or some evidence of this evil presence that didn't have a voice but seemed to have breath.

She flipped over on her stomach and buried her face in the pillow, too afraid to move. Why wasn't it leaving?

Come near to God and he will come near to you.

The words of her youth rang true and promising in Ivy's mind, and she forced her trembling body off the bed and onto her knees, her eyes clamped shut, her hands folded.

"Okay, I'm here, God," she whispered. "Please make it go away!"

The pounding of her heart filled the room and seemed to bounce off the walls, and every fear she had ever known seemed less terrifying than whatever it was she had brought home with her.

Brandon Jones opened his eyes, sensing that Kelsey's side of the bed was empty. He glanced at the clock and saw it was only 10:40.

He threw off the covers and slipped into his bathrobe, then went out to the living room where Kelsey lay on the couch, her eyes closed, her Bible set on the floor beside her.

He went over and shook her gently. "Honey, you need to come to bed."

"I'm not asleep," Kelsey Jones said. "I can't get Ivy off my mind. I've been praying for her for the past twenty minutes."

"How weird. That's the second time this has happened."

"Yes, but this time there's an urgency to it. I'm half tempted to call the house and see if everything's all right."

Brandon sat on the edge of the couch. "What do you suppose this is all about?"

"I don't know. But the kinds of prayers I'm feeling led to pray make me think there's some serious spiritual warfare going on. I'm thinking I should invite Ivy to come over sooner rather than later. I know she's not working Monday. I think I'll see if she'll come then."

"You think you're equipped to deal with Ivy's problems?"

Kelsey's hazel eyes drooped with sleepiness. "I must be since the Lord's opened that door. There's no way I would do it otherwise."

"I'm kind of surprised about this," Brandon said. "Ivy seems so much happier. I got the impression that she and Bill were hitting it off pretty good."

"Yeah, I know. I don't understand it either, but I promise you, the Lord's prodding me to pray was unmistakable."

Ivy was suddenly aware of how hard the wood floor felt beneath her knees—and that she was shaking, not from fear, but because she was cold. She slowly opened her eyes, relieved that whatever had been there—real or imagined—was gone now.

She got up, kicked off her shoes, and crawled under the covers, hoping that she would stop shivering soon and wondering what it was that had scared her so. She thought back over the events of the evening and tried to remember when she started to feel afraid. The memory of it made her skin crawl.

"Come on, Ivy," Bill had said. *"Can't you see the whole God, sin,*

heaven, and hell thing is a myth? You have to let go of it if you want to move forward."

Ivy tucked the covers around her neck. Bill had no idea how deceived he was. God was real, all right. And so was sin—and hell.

What she feared more than anything was that she could never be forgiven for her indifference that contributed to the murders of four people. Or for destroying her body with drugs. Or for prostituting herself. Or for neglecting her son while she lived in a drug-induced stupor and trying to forget what an awful person she really was.

And what about the lying? Stealing? The agony she had put her parents through? Ivy cringed at the thought of admitting to her mom and dad—or worse yet, Montana—that she had sat in the car and done nothing while her best friends murdered Joe Hadley.

On the other hand, if Mr. Hadley had exacted his revenge on Pete, Reg, and Denny, would Ivy's dumping her guilt in the sheriff's office benefit anyone, least of all poor Mrs. Hadley, who would have to face the future without her son *and* her husband?

It was hard to believe how repulsive Bill seemed now, when just hours ago her heart was aflutter with the hope that she might be falling in love with him. Was it hypocritical to reject him because he didn't accept moral absolutes when she, despite her upbringing, had lived a more sinful life than he had?

If she was so sure that God was real and moral absolutes essential, then why couldn't she bring herself to tell Montana about Jesus? About salvation? About heaven? Or even about the Ten Commandments?

Ivy felt a tear run down the side of her face. Lu had been gone barely two weeks, and already Ivy was back in the old pattern of confusion, doubt, and indecision. Why was it so hard to just go forward with the plan she and Lu had discussed many times? Why was she less sure than ever that confessing the truth to the sheriff was the right thing to do? Or that God would be with her if she did?

Ivy picked up the extra pillow and clutched it to her chest. One thing she *was* sure of: Bill Ziwicki wasn't the man of her dreams.

29

THE NEXT MORNING, Ivy Griffith slid out of her father's Suburban at exactly 5:50, then mumbled a weak thank-you and walked in the back door of Jewel's Café.

Jewel Sadler was sitting at her desk, reading the Sunday paper. "Morning, doll."

"Good morning."

Ivy walked over and timed in, then picked up her name tag and put it on.

"You don't look like you're awake yet," Jewel said. "Maybe you'd better have a cup of coffee. I made a pot for myself, and there's still some over there."

"Okay, thanks. That sounds good."

"Everything okay?"

Other than my whole world is spiraling out of control? "I just haven't gotten cranked up yet. Nothing a little caffeine won't fix."

"Did you see the front page of the *Courier*?"

Ivy poured herself a cup of coffee. "No, what's up?"

"Joe Hadley's parents are upset their son's murder is taking a backseat to the triple homicide. They told reporters that they believe his murder and the shooting of those guys at the reunion are related—maybe even done by the same person. And they don't think the sheriff and the feds are doing enough."

What a smoke screen! Ivy thought. *Mr. Hadley is just trying to throw off the investigation to cover his tail.*

Jewel took off her reading glasses, then folded the newspaper and pushed it aside. "You knew all four of these guys. What's your take on it?"

"Joe's death happened so long ago that I don't see how the killings could be related." Ivy blew on her coffee, chagrined that she had just lied to Jewel. "But the shooter must've been one of the classmates who was there that night. I don't see why any employee of the lodge would have it in for three strangers."

"Darned if I know. Sheriff Carter told the press that they're considering the idea that the killer might've been targeting just one of those young men, and the others got in the way."

Oh, brother. Mr. Hadley must be eating this up.

Jewel rose to her feet. "Well, I'll tell you one thing—Sheriff Carter and the feds sure do have their work cut out for them. Couldn't pay me enough to do their job…You sure you're all right? You look a little down."

"I'm fine. I just didn't sleep very well, that's all. I'll go check everything out front and get the door open. Once this place fills up, my adrenaline will kick in."

Jewel smiled. "Okay, doll. By the way, if I haven't said so before, I'm really pleased with your work, and I'm getting positive comments from our customers."

"Thanks," Ivy said. "I enjoy what I'm doing." *And it's about the only thing in my life that feels normal.*

Brandon Jones bent down and kissed Kelsey on the forehead, then turned and started to tiptoe out of the bedroom.

"Be careful on the river," Kelsey Jones said sleepily.

Brandon went back and sat on the side of the bed. "I didn't mean to wake you. I'm about to head out for my rafting trip. Buzz insisted on picking me up so you wouldn't be stranded without a car."

"Thoughtful of him."

"Honey, look. I know how uncomfortable you are about me

being with Buzz, but you have nothing to worry about. We're just a couple of crazy outdoorsmen who want to take advantage of every opportunity nature throws our way. The Phantom River is running full from the spring runoff, and it's going to be a blast shooting the rapids."

"Well, have a blast with your *quiet time* on the way to Durango. I'm sure it'll be a wonderful opportunity for prayer and worship, what with Buzz being so spiritual and all. The way he uses the Lord's name should evoke all sorts of spiritual thoughts."

"The Lord and I will do fine today, Kel. I'll see you this evening. Have a great time at the Griffiths' with Montana. I'm really glad he's warmed up to you. He's such a cute kid."

Kelsey smiled. "He really is. One of these days I'll have him over and make *cimmamon* pancakes."

"Or maybe some *spasketti* and meatballs." Brandon held her gaze and felt his heart lighten.

"Be safe, okay?" Kelsey slipped her hand into his. "I worry more about you and Mother Nature than I do you and Buzz. Just don't forget she's a powerful lady. Treat her with respect."

Brandon stroked her cheek. "Always. See you tonight."

Flint Carter sat in the conference room with Special Agent Nick Sanchez and Lieutenant Bobby Knolls, comparing notes.

"All right, then," Nick said. "If we're going to pursue the angle that the shooting was intended for just one of the victims, we need to dig into their backgrounds and put everything under a microscope. I want to know where they bought their clothes, what they had for breakfast, what brand of dental floss they used, and if they had a conflict with *anyone*—even the paperboy."

Bobby blew a pink bubble that quickly disappeared into his mouth. "We've already done that. It didn't reveal anything."

"Well, it's time to go deeper, Lieutenant. This Pete Barton was a piece of work. He was arrogant. A gambler. And a rounder. Maybe one of the ladies he jumped in the sack with had a jealous husband or boyfriend. Didn't the Griffith girl used to date him in high school?"

Flint nodded. "Yeah, but I don't see what that has to do with anything. Ivy moved away and didn't see him for ten years."

"I saw her background check," Nick said. "This girl's no stranger to trouble, and she just moved back here. And you know what they say: 'Birds of a feather flock together.' Maybe she knows something about Barton she's not telling us."

Flint combed his fingers through his hair. "I think you're way off on this one. Ivy got mixed up in drugs, yes, but that was years ago. She wasn't convicted of anything. And she's been clean for three years. She's just trying to raise her young son. According to her and her parents, any association with Pete Barton ended when they went off to college."

"She sat with him at the reunion," Nick said. "She must've felt some bond with him."

"Reunions are for old times' sake. What are you driving at?"

Nick smirked. "Her *old times' sake* friends are all dead—and she isn't. Maybe Griffith hired the shooter. Maybe she had a bone to pick with Pete. She could've hired the hit—told the shooter not to leave witnesses behind."

"That's unlikely," Flint said. "For one thing, she's working as a waitress and doesn't have a nickel to her name. For another she's not the type."

"They never are. Think about it: She just happened to wander onto the murder scene just minutes after the shooting?" Nick looked at Bobby and then at Flint. "Could've been staged to make her look innocent."

"We considered that," Flint said. "But Ivy seemed genuinely traumatized."

"Ziwicki didn't. And his alibi isn't airtight."

"Pretty darned close. And he tested negative for blood or gunpowder residue. Come on, Nick, you're grasping at straws."

"Hey, that's how I solve cases. Let no straw go ungrasped."

Flint looked out the window at the sun peeking over the top of Jacob's Peak. "So what do you want us to do?"

"Bring Griffith and Ziwicki back in for questioning. I want to explore this angle some more."

Ivy walked out the back door of Jewel's Café at five after two, neither surprised nor pleased when she saw Bill Ziwicki's van parked in the alley. She pretended not to notice and walked around the side of the building. A few seconds later, she heard footsteps running in her direction. She stopped and turned around, her hand on her hip.

"Bill, I told you I need space to deal with things. I don't want to see you right now."

"I was hopin' you'd come to your senses," he said. "It's nuts to throw away what we've got goin' just because you're confused about guilt."

"I'm not confused about *guilt*. I'm guilty. What I'm confused about is the right course of action."

"Let me help you decide, Ivy. There's just too much at stake."

"I told you, we're coming from two different perspectives."

"Did you ever think that maybe you need to hear both sides of the issue before you do somethin' you'll be sorry for?"

Ivy shook her head. "I'm guilty, Bill. You're going to have to accept that."

"So does that mean you're gonna kick yourself for the rest of your life over somethin' you never meant to happen and can't change?"

Ivy put her hands to her temples. "I can't do this. I need time to think. If only Lu were still here. She could get me back on track."

"Maybe Lu isn't what you need at all. Maybe Lu's the one who fed you all this religious junk in the first place."

"How dare you say that when you don't know anything about her!"

"All I know is what I see: a beautiful young woman with a ton of love to give who's about to make a crazy decision that's gonna rob her of a future. If you go to the sheriff, your life's over. You know that?"

"Maybe not. The judge might go easy on me."

"And what if he doesn't? What if he agrees that your silence contributed to all four murders? Is that the legacy you wanna leave Montana? Or your folks? Are you really willin' to take the rap for Joe's death when Mr. Hadley already settled the score?"

Ivy put her hands to her ears. "Stop. I can't listen to this right now."

Bill looked over her shoulder, and then pulled one of her hands away from her ear. "Your mother just pulled up out front. I'm beggin' you, don't go to the sheriff and admit anything. Take some time and think it through. You've held on to this secret for ten years. A few more days or weeks isn't gonna matter."

Ivy felt her mind shut down, and she just wanted to run.

"Okay?" Bill said.

"Okay, but I need you to give me space to think. Please…don't come around anymore. I'll let you know when I've decided what to do."

Ivy walked briskly toward the front of Jewel's Café and saw her mother parked there. She walked over and got in the passenger side.

"Did you have a bad day?" Carolyn Griffith said.

"Not really. I'm just tired."

"I heard you come in. It wasn't late."

Ivy nodded. "I know. I couldn't sleep."

"Did you make plans to go out with Bill this afternoon?"

"Actually, I didn't. I thought I'd spend it with Montana and Kelsey."

Carolyn sighed and glanced over at her. "Unfortunately, Flint called a few minutes ago. He wants you to go down to the sheriff's office and answer a few more questions."

"About what?"

"I don't know, honey. He said it was routine, that every possible angle they explore evokes more questions. I told him I'd drive you there after work."

Ivy sat in the interrogation room across from Lieutenant Bobby Knolls, her hands folded on the table, and hoped she was the only one who could hear her heart pounding.

"Thanks for agreein' to talk with us," Bobby said. "I'd like to ask you some questions about Pete Barton. Some of them are personal, and I apologize ahead of time for havin' to ask. But every detail's important, so I need you to answer honestly, even if you think it's none of my business."

Ivy nodded.

"What was your relationship with Pete Barton?"

"We dated our senior year of high school, and I wore his ring."

"So you dated each other exclusively?"

"Yes."

"So as far as you know, Pete wasn't seein' anybody else?"

"That's right."

"Was your relationship physically intimate?"

Ivy felt the color flood her face. "Eventually. Why do you need to know that?"

"Just bear with me. So you probably knew Pete as well as anybody did. Is that accurate?"

"Yes."

"Did he ever mention havin' a conflict with anyone?"

"Pete got along with everybody."

"Even Bill Ziwicki?"

"Pete, Reg, and Denny all teased Bill, but they also let him eat lunch with us. That's more than anyone else did."

"Is that yes or a no?"

"Yes."

"Why do you suppose popular jocks like Pete, Reg, and Denny would bother to include an outcast like Bill?"

Ivy shrugged. "We all felt sorry for Bill. His acne was really bad." *Please don't ask about the drugs.*

"Were all of you on good terms with Bill when you graduated?"

"Sure."

"What about the 'fab four'—were you guys on good terms with each other?"

"The best. Going off to separate colleges was hard."

"Is that why you and Pete broke up?"

"Neither of us wanted a long-distance relationship. Why are you asking me this?"

Bobby held up his palm. "Just answer the questions, please. Had you had any contact with Pete Barton, Reg Morrison, Denny Richards, or Bill Ziwicki from the time you moved away from Jacob's Ear until you returned home?"

"No."

"Did you contact any of those people when you returned home?"

"No. Pete came to see me when he heard I was back. Reg and Denny were in town the weekend before the reunion and asked me to have coffee with them."

"What about Bill? Did you contact him?"

"No, we bumped into each other the Saturday before my friend Lu's burial. My son and I were walking back to the parking lot from the cemetery at Woodlands Community Church when Bill's cleaning van pulled up."

"To the cemetery?"

"No, the church. He cleans there on Saturdays. He recognized me and we talked for a few minutes. He reminded me about the class reunion and wanted me to go."

"As his date?"

"No, I told him I was meeting the guys there."

"Did you have any contact with him again before the reunion?"

"Well, he sent me flowers when Lu died," Ivy said. "That was really touching. He called me a couple times after that, and we got sort of reacquainted. Bill's really changed a lot. We all have."

"What did Pete think of you and Bill seeing each other?"

"We weren't seeing each other. Bill called a couple times."

"So Bill and Pete weren't fighting over you?"

Ivy rolled her eyes. "Absolutely not. Like I told you, Pete and I weren't the least bit interested in each other."

"Yet you sat with him at the reunion."

"I sat with Pete, Reg, and Denny at the reunion. And two other guys from the basketball team—and their wives."

"Were you angry with Pete for not asking you to go as his date?"

Ivy breathed in slowly and exhaled. "No. Pete and I weren't attracted to each other that way anymore."

"Whose idea was it for the four of you to sit together at the reunion?"

"Pete's. He wanted the fab four to be together again."

"Why'd he pick the other two couples to join you? Why not Bill Ziwicki?"

Ivy shrugged. "I didn't ask him. It didn't really matter to me who we sat with. He had already filled the table before I got there."

"So you came alone?"

"Yes."

"Kendra Clawson recalled that you arrived with Bill Ziwicki."

"Not on purpose. We rode up the elevator at the same time."

"You came in separate vehicles."

What are you implying? "Yes."

Bobby Knolls wrote something on the legal pad in front of him and then leaned forward on his elbows. "Okay, let's go back to Pete Barton. Did you know he was gamblin'?"

"I heard it from my dad. I never asked Pete about it. Like I said, I really wasn't interested in him anymore."

"Did you know he had a reputation for sleepin' around?"

"My dad mentioned it."

"Did that make you mad?"

Ivy blew the hair off her forehead. "I thought it was pathetic. But like I said, I had zero interest in Pete."

"So you wouldn't have had any reason to want to get even with him?"

Ivy stared blankly at Bobby. "Even for what?"

"Say…for rejectin' you when you came back?"

"I told you, I wasn't interested in him."

Bobby's eyes narrowed. "Come on, Ivy. A big hunk like Barton? You're tellin' me you weren't attracted to him?"

"I wasn't."

"Or maybe it was Pete who wasn't interested. You haven't exactly aged gracefully now, have you? Your cocaine habit put a few extra years on you. And took twenty-five or thirty pounds off that schoolgirl figure you used to have."

Ivy's face felt hot. "It wouldn't have mattered whether Pete was interested in me or not. I wasn't interested in him."

"You're expectin' me to believe you went off to college after bein' lovers, had no contact for ten years, then reconnected with zero interest in each other? No chemistry? Not even a little curiosity?"

"That's the truth."

"Then I have to ask myself what turned you off."

Ivy's pulse raced. "We both changed a lot. And since you read my rap sheet, you know I was arrested for solicitation and possession of a controlled substance, and the charges were dropped. Some of the stuff I did to pay for my drug habit didn't exactly leave me feeling good about myself—or make me want to get hooked up with a man."

"But you hooked up with Bill Ziwicki. You must see somethin' in him. You've been datin' him, right?"

"He's a sweet guy who treats me with respect. But I'm not that interested in him either."

"So your relationship isn't romantic?"

Ivy glared at the lieutenant. "It's not going that direction. We're friends."

"Judgin' by the way you and Bill danced together at the reunion, some of your classmates thought you were an item."

"Well, we're not. I only danced with him once."

"So you didn't conspire with Bill to get rid of Pete Barton so the two of you'd be free to pursue a relationship?"

Ivy's jaw dropped. "What? I was free to pursue any relationship

I pleased, Lieutenant. I didn't have to conspire with anybody to do anything."

"Is that a no?"

"An emphatic no."

"Sorry if the implication insulted you, Miss Griffith. But we gotta get to the bottom of what happened. Some of the questions may be tough, but they've gotta be asked."

Ivy sat through another round of being asked the same questions phrased differently. Did Bobby Knolls think she was too dumb to get what he was doing?

Finally, Bobby got up and walked over to the wall and leaned on it, hands in his pockets. "There's still somethin' botherin' me. Whoever did the triple homicide meant it to be personal. He was a good shot and made it look pretty much like an execution. Since these three guys hadn't really hung out together since high school, I'm inclined to think someone had it in for them for somethin' that happened back in high school. Now, since you were thick with those guys, I have to believe you would've picked up some bad vibes along the way."

Bill's words echoed in Ivy's mind. *Are you really willin' to take the rap for Joe's death when Mr. Hadley already settled the score?* "The guys didn't tell me everything. Maybe they didn't even know someone had it in for them."

"Someone like Icky Ziwicki, who got tired of being picked on?"

No, someone like Mr. Hadley, who's smarter than you are! "Bill wouldn't hurt a flea. You're wasting your time if you think he had anything to do with the shooting. Besides, the only time he left the Aspen Room was to go to the men's room."

"We haven't been able to prove that."

"You can't prove otherwise either because it's the truth."

Bobby came over and sat across the table from her and leaned forward on his elbows. "Well, here's why I'm not buyin' it. You admitted that *you* asked Pete to take Reg and Denny to their room. And we can't find anything to confirm that Ziwicki was in the Aspen Room from the time you saw him at the bar at 1:20 until 1:45 when he asked you to dance. And then less than thirty minutes later, you and Ziwicki just happened to go lookin' for Pete and wandered onto the murder scene. A reasonable person could conclude that you conspired with Bill Ziwicki to kill Pete Barton."

Ivy's eyes burned and she blinked away the tears. "This is so unfair. I would never do such a thing—and neither would Bill. You're looking at the wrong people!"

"Then suppose you tell me who I should be lookin' at. Because right now, you and Ziwicki are lookin' good for this."

30

Sheriff Flint Carter pushed open the door of the Tanner County Courthouse and felt a nip in the air and noticed the sun had already dropped behind the peaks in the western sky. He spotted Elam Griffith down on the sidewalk, pacing in front of a park bench.

Flint jogged down the steps and took Elam by the arm. "Okay. What's so important you had to call my cell and pull me out of a meeting?"

Elam put his face directly in front of Flint's. "You told Carolyn and me you had a few questions you wanted to run by Ivy. You never said anything about an interrogation! Ivy said Bobby Knolls grilled her for two hours—and not once did anybody suggest she might want to call a lawyer."

"Didn't think she needed one."

"Don't give me that!" Elam threw up his hands. "You want to tell me what's going on?"

"We're working to solve a triple homicide is what's going on. And you might want to change your tone, friend. I don't appreciate you getting up in my face."

Elam's arms hung at his side, his hands turned to fists. "Friends don't trick friends. There's no way I would've allowed her to be interrogated without an attorney present."

"The questioning got more intense than we planned," Flint

said. "She's a grown woman. If she would've asked for a lawyer, we'd have let her call one. She didn't ask."

"Is Ivy a suspect?"

"No. Her alibi's airtight. We're pulling out all the stops looking for a motive. I mean, the victims hardly saw each other in a decade. If someone had a beef with all three, then it had to be related back to something that happened when they were hanging around together—probably in high school."

"Or the shooter wasn't after all three of them," Elam said, "but didn't want to leave any witnesses."

"Right. So you can see why Ivy's important to us. She might have the key to unlocking the motive to this whole thing and not even realize it."

Elam tugged at his mustache. "She's just going to close off if you keep throwing questions at her."

"Well, she didn't. She answered every question. You'd have been proud."

"So are you done with her?" Elam said.

"For now. We've got teams taking a close look at different aspects of the case. We may need to question her further on down the line."

Elam's eyes narrowed and he seemed to be studying the mountains. "Okay. But I don't want you talking to her anymore without her attorney present."

"So you're hiring someone?"

"Seems like the smart thing to do."

"Why, since she's got nothing to hide?"

"Come on, Flint. Ivy's background doesn't look good, and I don't want this girl's character misread because she had a drug problem. Besides, she's fragile. She's lost three friends right on top of Lu's death. I'd feel better if she had a legal professional looking out for her best interests."

"Suit yourself. I need to get back to my meeting."

Ivy slipped on her ski jacket and went out and sat on the front steps, her hands in her pockets, her eyes focused on one stubborn patch of snow under the tallest blue spruce that graced the property.

She heard the door open, and then Kelsey Jones came out and sat on the step beside her.

"You mind if I sit with you a minute before I walk down the hill?" Kelsey said.

"No, not at all. Thanks for spending time with Montana this afternoon." Ivy smiled. "Better look out. He has a crush on you. Actually, it's a toss-up between you and his teacher, Mrs. Shepard."

"He's a joy to be around. I hope Brandon and I have a son like him someday."

Ivy hugged her knees. "Thanks. But the credit should go to Lu. She spent a lot more time with him than I did."

"Because you were working."

"Yeah, the past three years. Before that I was high much of the time. If it hadn't been for Lu, it's hard to say where Montana would be. Probably in foster care." *Or dead.*

"I know you must miss her very much."

Ivy sighed. "I think about her all the time. She's the one I always went to when I needed advice. Sometimes it's hard to believe she's really gone. I keep expecting her to walk through the door."

"I'm sorry you have to go through this."

There was a long stretch of silence, and then Kelsey said, "On a lighter note, how's it going with Bill?"

"It's really not. He's nice and everything, but I don't see the relationship going anywhere. We just think too differently."

"Well, I guess it's good you recognize that now."

Ivy nodded.

"I guess I should scoot down the hill. Buzz should be bringing my weary adventurer home pretty soon."

"Buzz Easton?"

Kelsey nodded. "He's the one I told you about who has the white-water rafting business. Do you know him?"

"Not well. He and his wife come in the café on Saturday mornings. But I saw him with a woman who wasn't his wife at the Blue Moon Tavern last night. It was probably nothing."

"Listen, I'm off tomorrow. Would you like to come over in the morning? I made that chocolate cream cheese Bundt cake I told you about and would love an excuse to pig out." Kelsey chuckled. "And I'd like to get to know you better. I hardly have anyone my age to talk to."

"Okay. What time?"

"Oh, I don't know. How about nine, or is that too early?"

"No, it's fine. See you then."

Ivy watched Kelsey walk down the hill toward the camp, wondering what Kelsey would really think of her if she knew the things she had done.

Brandon Jones pushed open the front door, pulled off his shoes, and dropped his backpack on the couch.

"How was it?" Kelsey said. "I didn't think you'd be this late."

"Awesome. I've never been on white water that rough. What a ride! But I'll tell you one thing: I'm starting to feel my age. I need to get into shape before camp starts."

Kelsey pinched his middle. "Nothing there."

"Yeah, well, my stamina isn't what it was. I need to start running in the mornings now that I don't have to contend with snow."

"You could've used the workout room."

Brandon kissed her on the cheek. "I know. There's just something exhilarating about running in the outdoors."

"So why are you so late? Surely you weren't on the water after dark?"

"Oh, the guys wanted to sit around awhile and relive the day, so we went to some little place called Rogue's and had great T-bone steaks. Have you eaten dinner?"

"Yeah, I had leftover chili. Actually, I missed cooking for you." She put her arms around his neck. "In fact, I missed you all day."

Brandon's lips met hers. "Yeah, same here. So how were your checker games with Montana?"

"Fun. He's good. I didn't have to let him win even once.

And Ivy's coming over in the morning."

"You're a good sport," Brandon said. "I wish your day had been as exciting as mine."

Kelsey's eyes danced, her finger tracing his ear. "Well, it's not over yet. We could go sit in the Jacuzzi and light some candles, put on some soft music…"

Brandon thought about the photograph Buzz had passed around the dinner table. When the guys started laughing at the look of surprise on Brandon's face, he knew they were all in on it. It was all he could do not to punch Buzz in the mouth. Instead he laughed to cover his embarrassment and couldn't find the courage to stand up for what he really thought.

"Truthfully, honey, I'm kind of beat up," Brandon said. "I don't think I would live up to your expectations tonight." *And I don't want porn in my mind when I'm with you.*

Kelsey brushed the hair out of his eyes. "You do look a little washed out—no pun intended. Why don't you go take a hot shower and I'll make you some hot herbal tea. That'll relax those tired muscles."

Brandon went in the bedroom and undressed, then stepped into the shower and let the water wash over him, bothered that he hadn't told the guys he wasn't into porn. What's the worst that could've happened: They would've razzed him for being a Christian? Tried to convince him he was missing out? Tried to make him feel like a prude—or less than a man? He knew better. Why hadn't he just told them where he stood?

Brandon grabbed the shampoo and lathered his scalp, almost as if to cleanse his mind. He would be on guard for Buzz's crude antics in the future. With just a few weeks left to shoot the rapids before he was immersed in summer camp, why should he let Buzz's worldly ways get in the way of good, clean fun?

Carolyn Griffith sat next to Elam on the couch, her arm linked in his, and watched the embers in the fireplace. "Who do you think we should hire to represent Ivy?"

"I'm thinking Brett Hewitt. He's not intimidated by the DA."

"You can't believe it'll go that far! Ivy didn't kill those boys and has no idea who did."

"I'm just covering all bases. Flint pulled one over on us, and I'm ticked. It's hard to say how much of what he's doing is coming from the feds. I just want him to know Ivy's got a big gun on her side."

"She didn't act as though she wanted an attorney."

"Well, she's going to get one anyway. She'll thank me later."

"Did she tell you Kelsey invited her over for coffee and cake in the morning?"

"No. But I sure like Kelsey. She'd be a good Christian influence. God knows, Ivy needs all the help she can get. It's hard for me to accept that she's turned her back on everything we taught her."

"Well, maybe she just shoved it onto a back burner for a while."

"Yeah, *way* back. I was glad to see the boy didn't seem to mind going to church with us this morning."

"Montana told me he enjoyed Sunday school. He's asking all sorts of questions about Jesus. He wants to know the way to heaven so he can see Lu again."

"You'd think Ivy would at least give us the green light to talk to him about it," Elam said.

"Did you ask her?"

"No. Didn't you?"

Carolyn shook her head. "I suppose we should. But right now I hate to do anything that might pull Ivy and Montana apart—or cause Ivy to pull away from us. It's a difficult adjustment for both of them, living without Lu. If Montana takes to church the way Ivy did as a kid, it could get very uncomfortable for them."

"Might do her good if the boy hounded her for answers. Never could understand why she grew cold in her beliefs."

"I think she blamed God for Joe Hadley's disappearance."

Elam shook his head. "Seemed to happen before that—when she started dating Pete. I know the creep got her into bed and got her hooked on pot. I think she turned her back on God out of guilt."

Carolyn squeezed his arm. "Well, we need to pull her back gently. I have to believe she loves Montana too much to deny him the truth she knows in her heart of hearts is right, even if she won't claim it for herself."

"Well, let's pray that Kelsey has some impact there. I'll tell you one thing—nice as Bill is, it's no good for Ivy to get involved with an unbeliever or we'll never get her back into church."

Flint Carter sat in his office with Nick Sanchez and Bobby Knolls, discussing everything they knew so far about the triple homicide.

"It's late," Flint said. "Why don't we call it a night and pick it up in the morning?"

Nick captured a yawn with his hand. "All right. I want Ziwicki in here for questioning first thing in the morning. And I want the lieutenant to have first crack at him. I want you to ride him hard about how Pete treated him in high school. Rattle his chain. Get him to react. He had plenty of reasons to want to get back at Pete and might've jumped at the chance to take him out. Maybe Griffith and Ziwicki really were in this together. Push him to the edge and get him to talk."

"My pleasure," Bobby said. "I've never trusted the guy. I think he knows somethin'."

Nick put his hand on the back of his neck and rubbed. "Unger ought to be back from vacation tonight. My agents are waiting at his apartment. Also, I've got a team dissecting Pete Barton's life. If there was someone besides a classmate with a personal grudge against him, we're going to find it. We're doing the same thing with the other victims. But I have bad vibes about Barton. I think he's the most likely of the three to have been the target of somebody's wrath."

31

IVY GRIFFITH WALKED up onto the front porch of the Jones's log home and rang the doorbell. She heard footsteps and then Kelsey Jones opened the door and invited her in.

"Wow, this is cozy," Ivy said. "My mom said you like to make drapes and pillows and quilts. This looks really nice."

Kelsey smiled. "Thanks. I love to sew. Brandon says I'm going to be out of control when I get pregnant with our first child. I have all these fun ideas for the nursery. Would you like to see the rest of the house?"

"Yeah, thanks. I would."

Ivy followed Kelsey from room to room, taken with the coordinating colors and fabrics she had used for drapes, quilts, pillows, curtains, and afghans.

"I'm so impressed," Ivy said as they walked out to the kitchen. "I'm lucky to get a needle threaded and a button sewn on. You have an amazing talent."

"It's nice of you to say that. I've been making quilts and taking them to a gift shop in Silverton on consignment. I can hardly keep up with the demand." Kelsey chuckled. "Brandon's started calling me the Quilt Queen of Jacob's Ear. Now that's a title for you."

"Well, you should be proud of your work. It's really good."

"Enough about me. Why don't you make yourself comfortable

there at the table and let me get us a piece of this Bundt cake and some coffee. So what do *you* enjoy doing?"

Ivy sat at the table, which had been set with china cups and saucers and dessert plates. "Truthfully, I've never really thought about developing anything that was just mine—I mean, like a talent or something."

"What about when you were younger? What'd you enjoy doing?"

"Riding horses. I loved it. My brother Rusty and I used to ride out on the open range. I pretended my horse was a purple unicorn and could fly." Ivy smiled without meaning to. "I'd love to go back to that time and feel the freedom of being a kid without a care in the world."

Kelsey poured Ivy a cup of coffee and one for herself and set the Bundt cake on the table. "Sounds like you had a happy childhood."

"Very. Of course, our house was the only thing out here in those days. We lived in our own little world and everything was safe. I don't remember being afraid of anything."

"The innocence of childhood is so wonderful and so fleeting. It seems like today's kids have to grow up a lot faster than we did."

Ivy blew on her coffee. "Well, I kind of did when my baby sister died. Actually she was stillborn. Her name was Amy. I was only ten, but I still remember how sad my parents were. I guess it was my first taste of how hard life can be."

"It's surprising how traumas like that stay with us. My cousin drowned at the lake when we were both eight. To this day, I can still hear the sound of my aunt screaming while my grandfather tried to revive him."

"Well, some traumas are accidents. Some we bring on ourselves. Like I'm sure you know I got into drugs after I left home. I know the staff at the camp had been praying for me."

"I'm aware you've been in and out of rehab. Must've been hard."

"The worst part is how it hurt my parents and my son. I started out smoking killer joints—that's marijuana mixed with angel dust. But when that didn't do enough, I started shooting up with cocaine. When that got too expensive, I switched to meth. It was never hard to find, especially near the campus."

"You started this in college?"

"Stupid, huh? If only I'd gotten my degree instead of wasting my life getting high, I'd be able to provide for Montana and give him the things he deserves."

"Is his father able to help out?"

Ivy felt the blood rush to her cheeks. "I don't know where he is." She looked up at Kelsey and saw only compassion. "The truth is, I don't even know *who* he is. I dread the day when Montana starts asking me about him. How pathetic is that?"

"Well, you can't go back. Today's a new day, and things are starting to look up. And Montana's a great kid who seems to be doing really well despite the hurdles you've both had to face."

Ivy was surprised that Kelsey's tone didn't sound judgmental and wondered if someone like her could really understand how high the hurdles had been. "I'll bet you never experimented with drugs."

"I'm not sure why, but I stayed away from drugs." Kelsey slowly stirred her coffee. "The kids I hung around with were from families that shared the same values I was taught. We pretty much avoided the pushers and the kids who were using. Our parents wanted to know where we were every minute, and I resented it. But I thank them now. I could've easily experimented with drugs. I certainly had plenty of spending money, and I knew where to go to get them. I just never did."

"You were smart. I got pressured into smoking killer joints when I was a senior in high school. My parents trusted me and never had any idea what I was doing. They would've died."

Kelsey picked up the knife and cut two pieces of Bundt cake and put them on the dessert plates. "I have a real sweet tooth. But I can't eat this stuff like I used to without blimping out."

"Give the pounds to me," Ivy said. "I lost a ton of weight when I was doing meth. Seems like I went days at a time without eating. I loved the way it made me feel, but it didn't last long enough. I was always looking for another fix." Ivy took a bite of the Bundt cake. "Yum. This is great."

"I got this recipe from my mother-in-law." Kelsey took a bite and seemed to be pondering something. Finally she said, "Montana told me he loved going to Sunday school yesterday. He made two new friends."

Ivy nodded. "He told me."

"Think you'll ever get Sundays off so you can come to church with him?"

"I doubt it. I think my willingness to work weekends is what made Jewel hire me so quickly. Most people don't want to work every weekend." Ivy wiped her mouth with a napkin. "Truthfully, I don't have any real desire to go back to church."

"Did you get hurt?"

"Not really. It's complicated."

Kelsey seemed to be deep in thought, almost as if she were arguing with herself about something. Finally she said, "Would it surprise you to know that God has laid you on my heart and asked me to pray for you?"

Ivy stopped chewing. "Actually, yes. God and I haven't been on speaking terms in a long, long time. I doubt if He ever thinks much about me. I'm pretty much a lost cause."

"No child of His is a lost cause."

Ivy pressed her fork into the moist cake crumbs. "And what makes you think I'm His child?"

"You gave Him your heart, didn't you?"

"A long time ago. I took it back."

Kelsey set down her fork and lifted her eyes. "But did you ever consider that maybe He never let go of it?"

Carolyn Griffith picked up the sack containing her purchase and walked out of the drugstore just as Evelyn Barton was walking in.

"Oops, sorry." Carolyn said. "I should've been watching where I was going."

"Actually, I'm glad I ran into you." Evelyn reached into her purse and took out what appeared to be an envelope of photographs. "I went by Jewel's to give these reunion pictures to Ivy, but apparently she's off today. One of Pete's classmates sent them to me, but I thought Ivy might like to keep them. I've got plenty of pictures of Pete. I don't want anything to remind me of that night."

Carolyn took the pictures and quickly looked through them. "Ivy might feel the same way you do, but I'll give them to her. Though I understand the authorities want copies of every picture taken."

"They have them. These are duplicates. There's a nice one in there of Ivy dancing with that young man she came to the memorial service with. I'm sorry, I can't recall his name."

"Bill Ziwicki."

"If Ivy doesn't want the pictures, tell her to give them to someone else or just pitch them. I didn't have the heart to do it."

Carolyn gently took Evelyn's hand. "I understand. I thought the memorial service was very nice. And it was quite generous of you, the Morrisons, and the Richardses to include the Hadleys. I know it meant a great deal to them…and to all of us."

Evelyn eyes brimmed with tears. "Well, they're suffering, too. I can't imagine their pain is any less intense than ours, having gone ten years hoping their son might be alive, and then finding out he was murdered."

"I'm sure you're right."

"I'm going to put the deli on the market as soon as I can think straight enough to deal with the details. I'm thinking seriously of moving to Idaho to live near my sister's family. I don't think I can handle being in Jacob's Ear after this."

"Well, I can certainly understand that. Promise you'll call Elam if he can help you with any of the business aspects. I know he'd be glad to. He might even know someone who'd be interested in buying the deli."

Ivy listened for several minutes to Kelsey's attempt to reassure her that God still cared about her. Would still forgive her. Wanted a relationship with her. But how would Kelsey feel if she knew that the woman sitting across the table from her was partly responsible for four murders? Had withheld invaluable information from the authorities? Had been a liar? A thief? A prostitute? Could someone as wholesome as Kelsey really handle the truth about her?

"What are you thinking?" Kelsey said.

Ivy shrugged. "I don't know. Like I said, it's complicated."

"*Sin* is complicated. And since we all sin, I guess that makes us all complicated."

"Not you. You're every parent's dream: talented, smart, pretty, happily married, the perfect homemaker. And someday you'll be the perfect mother. Montana adores you."

Kelsey pushed her plate aside and folded her arms on the table. "It's nice of you to mention my better traits, but I assure you my sin is very complicated. God and I are working on it all the time."

"Well, you've never been a drug addict."

"No. But I have a terrible problem with money and possessions."

"You don't come across as stuck-up."

Kelsey smiled. "Thanks. But I used to be. When Brandon and I were first engaged, he was a vice president of Mavis and Stein, this upscale women's clothing chain in Raleigh. I was *so* full of myself—more concerned with my social status than how Brandon was struggling with his job. I knew he hated it, but I kept encouraging him to stay there because I wanted to marry a vice president. I wanted the prestige. The fat salary. The classy clothes. The stately house. The Jaguar. The country club. The whole ball of wax."

"What happened?"

"Brandon burned out and quit. I was so upset with him that I broke off the engagement. I couldn't accept that we'd never have the life I had envisioned. I'd let my shallow, social-climbing friends convince me that I was the center of my own universe. I mean, how dare Brandon change the plan? *I deserved* better." Kelsey shook her head. "Hard to believe that I broke up with him over that."

"Couldn't he get a different job that made a lot of money?"

Kelsey's eyes widened. "That's what I said. But he wanted out of the corporate world and was looking for a job with *significance*—something that made him feel like he was making a positive difference. All I saw was all my hopes and dreams being shattered."

"How'd you get back together?"

"It's a really long story, but he went to Seaport, Florida, and moved in with his parents for a while. The Lord had some work to do in his heart, too. And a few months later, we were engaged again—only this time we both had our priorities straight. Now Brandon's doing what he loves and feels God's called him to, and I fully support him in it. We've learned to live on a lot less. But we're right where we need to be."

"Well, this log house is pretty nice."

Kelsey's face lit up. "It really is. But a year ago, I would've stuck my nose in the air at the idea of living at a Christian camp."

"But that doesn't seem like such an awful sin to me. Not compared to drug abuse."

Kelsey refilled Ivy's cup, and then her own. "Well, that's the amazing thing about God—He doesn't compare sins. None is acceptable. That's what grace is all about. But you know that."

"Yeah, but don't you think some sins are beyond forgiveness?"

"Not if a person has trusted Jesus as his or her Savior."

"What about a rapist or a child molester or a murderer?"

"Anyone who truly repents and asks for God's forgiveness is forgiven."

"What if it's someone who knows better, like someone who used to be a believer?"

"Ivy, repentance is repentance. That's the only requirement for forgiveness. Pretty amazing trade, considering Jesus gave His own life to make that possible."

Ivy traced the lip of her cup with her finger. "What do you mean by repent?"

"I mean that a person is remorseful for whatever he's confessing and really wants to change."

"What if he can't change?"

"Then I'd say he's not trusting God. Because there's nothing God can't do—no heart He can't change."

"Well, what if he hasn't told someone the truth about something? Does he have to go and tell that person the truth if he wants God to forgive him for lying?"

Kelsey paused and seemed to be thinking. Finally she said, "What I believe is that a truly repentant heart wants to make things right—whatever it takes."

The phone rang.

"Excuse me just a minute," Kelsey said. "I'm expecting a call from the gift shop that's selling my quilts."

Ivy pinched the last of the cake crumbs with her thumb and forefinger and put them in her mouth, thinking that, for now, doing "whatever it takes" sounded harder to cope with than living with the secret.

32

SHERIFF FLINT CARTER stood outside the interrogation room, his arms folded, and observed Lieutenant Bobby Knolls question Bill Ziwicki. He glanced at his watch. Bobby had already been at it forty-five minutes, and Ziwicki hadn't given up anything useful.

"Sure I remember you told me Monday's your busy day," Bobby said. "But you wanna help us make an arrest in this case, don't you, Bill? I mean, you don't have anything to hide, right?"

"Of course not. But I've told you everything I know at least half a dozen times."

"Okay, let me recap what you've said." Bobby sat at the table, his hands folded, his gaze intent. "You went to the reunion alone. Ran into Ivy Griffith in the elevator and rode up to the second floor where the registration was set up in the hallway. You registered and got your name tag, and then you and Ivy went separate ways. You mingled some. Had a few beers. And spent the rest of the evening people watchin'. At approximately 1:45, you got up the nerve to ask Ivy to dance. After that you sat at the table with her, and she expressed concern that Pete hadn't come back from takin' Reg and Denny to their room and thought he might be passed out somewhere. Is that accurate so far?"

"Yeah."

"Okay." Bobby leaned back in his chair, his hands clasped

behind his head. "Around 2:00 a.m., the band started packin' up, and you offered to help Ivy find Pete. You followed her to the front desk, where the clerk gave her Morrison and Richards's room number, which she called and got no answer. Then the two of you went up to Room 312 and found the door unlocked. You went inside and discovered the three victims shot to death. Is that accurate?"

"Yeah. And I've already told you that over and over. What are you tryin' to get me to say?"

"You feel pushed, Bill?"

"Well, kind of. Seems like you're harassin' me, for some reason."

"Why would you feel that way if you don't have anything to hide?"

"I guess you'd have to be sittin' in my shoes to know how it feels."

Bobby flashed a phony smile. "And I thought we were becomin' friends."

"Look, I lost three friends in a really horrible shooting. Just ask me what you need to so I can put this thing behind me."

Bobby got up and started pacing. "All right. You didn't really need to ask for the room number, did you, Bill? That was all staged because you already knew Reg Morrison and Denny Richards's room number. See, I'm thinkin' maybe you and Ivy conspired to get rid of Pete."

"What? This is nuts. Do I need a lawyer?"

"Not if you're innocent."

"Of course I'm innocent. Man, what're you gettin' at?"

Bobby put his palms on the table and leaned forward, his face close to Bill's. "It seems a little too convenient that you and Ivy claim you weren't seein' each other prior to the shooting. And then immediately after, you went to the memorial service together and started datin' without any grievin' period. Did she hire you to kill Pete Barton?"

"You can't be serious."

"Oh, I'm dead serious."

Bill raked his hands through his hair. "Why would you think either of us had anything to do with this?"

"Did you?" Bobby said.

"Absolutely not! We were horrified when we found those guys dead. Why would we kill our friends?"

"I'm thinkin' you had this thing for Ivy. And Pete was in the way."

"Ivy wasn't attracted to Pete anymore."

"Or Pete didn't find her attractive anymore. You know what they say, 'Hell knows no fury like a woman scorned.'"

Bill shook his head. "You're so wrong. Besides, do you think if we'd had anything to do with it, we'd be dumb enough to go anywhere near the murder scene?"

"Maybe you thought it would help you avoid suspicion if you acted like you stumbled into it."

"You're way off, man. Whoever killed those guys is out there somewhere, not in here! I passed all those tests you did on me. I didn't shoot anybody!"

Bobby sat at the table again, his tone less offensive. "Okay, Bill. Let's go back to when you first met Ivy. High school, right?"

"Yeah. Junior year. She was a knockout."

"So would you say you've had a thing for her all this time?"

"I did in high school. I didn't see her for ten years after that. I guess the chemistry's still there."

"Were you jealous of Pete?"

"Sure. Who wasn't? He had it all: looks, build, smarts. He was a jock. And the girls drooled over him."

"Did girls drool over you, Bill?"

Bill's face turned red. "Are you gonna put me through this again?"

"Just answer the question."

"No. I wasn't popular. I had acne, and I was kinda shy back then."

"Why do you suppose Pete, Reg, and Denny would let a social outcast sit with them at lunch?"

"I don't know. I was just glad they did. It was always somethin' I could be proud of."

Bobby blew a pink bubble. "I'd like to explore that a little more.

I keep askin' myself why three jocks would bend over backwards for a shy kid with acne that everyone called Icky Ziwicki." Bobby leaned forward on his elbows. "I just don't see Pete Barton bein' tender-hearted."

Ivy Griffith walked in the front door of her parents' house and went out to the kitchen where her mother was putting away groceries.

"Hi, honey," Carolyn Griffith said. "How was your visit with Kelsey?"

Ivy smiled. "Good. She's really nice."

"What did you two talk about?"

"Oh, lots of stuff. Girl talk mostly. Her house is really decorated nicely. Have you seen it?"

Carolyn put the milk in the fridge. "Uh-huh. She's got more talent in her little finger than most of us have in our entire body."

"No kidding. She's like this young Martha Stewart." Ivy picked up some canned goods and started putting them in the pantry.

"Oh, I almost forgot." Caroline walked over to her purse and handed Ivy an envelope. "I ran into Evelyn Barton at the drugstore. She wanted you to have these pictures from the reunion. She couldn't bear to keep them. Said she has plenty of pictures of Pete and doesn't want to remember the reunion. She said if you don't want them, either give them away or throw them out."

"Sheriff Carter said we had to give him copies of all the pictures," Ivy said.

"He has these. They're duplicates."

Ivy quickly thumbed through the photos and noticed a number of pictures of her at the table with Pete, Reg, and Denny. "Who took these?"

"She just said one of the classmates sent them to her."

"Some of these pictures are really good. But I don't know if I want them either."

"Did you see the one of you dancing with Bill?"

"No, I missed that." Ivy thumbed through the stack again until she found it. They almost looked as though they belonged together. "I don't think my relationship with Bill is going anywhere."

"Really? I thought you two were hitting it off."

"He's really sweet, but I don't think he's my type."

"Maybe you should consider getting involved with the singles group at church. We draw young people from several churches in the region. I think someone said we have almost sixty singles now."

Of which zero want to date a recovering drug addict, Ivy thought.

"You want some lunch?"

"Thanks, Mom, but I'm not hungry. Kelsey made this awesome chocolate cream cheese cake, and I had two big pieces. I think I'll go upstairs and read or something and just take it easy till Montana gets out of school—unless you need me to do something."

"No. You go ahead."

Ivy walked through the living room and grabbed a magazine and started to go upstairs, then went back and pulled her old Student Bible out of the bookshelf and went up to her room and closed the door.

She sat in the rocker hugging the Bible, remembering a time when she felt happy and filled with hope—the same hope that had been so evident in Kelsey Jones this morning. Sometimes she almost believed that God might take her back, forgive her past, and give her another chance at a normal life. But when she thought about how her silence had contributed to the murders of Joe, Pete, Reg, and Denny, it seemed too much to hope for.

How different things would have been had she never started compromising all those years ago. Never traded her virginity for Pete's attention. Never let him talk her into taking the first drag of a joint. Never agreed to keep the pact. Her mind raced back through the excuses she had used to justify her lying and stealing and the drug habit she needed to silence the guilt. And all the degrading acts she had done for drug money.

Ivy opened the Bible and her eyes fell on a highlighted passage in 1 John:

> If we claim to be without sin, we deceive ourselves and the truth is not in us. If we confess our sins, he is faithful and just and will forgive us our sins and purify us from all unrighteousness.

Her eyes stung and welled with tears, hope and fear pulling her in opposite directions. How she wanted to believe that promise for herself.

She wiped the tears off her cheeks and closed the Bible, then picked up the stack of photos and began looking at them, one by one. A heavy sadness fell over her as she saw the faces of her murdered friends—faces that haunted her almost every time she closed her eyes. She wondered if Mr. Hadley had trouble sleeping at night. Or if he felt so satisfied at having exacted his revenge that he hardly gave it a second thought.

Ivy held up the picture of Bill and her slow dancing and remembered how freeing it had felt to dance with him in front of her classmates and not care what any of them thought. She still marveled at how tender Bill had been with her, and already she missed it.

Had she been too impulsive in deciding to back off from her relationship with him? What if he possessed the exact qualities she needed in a husband? What if she were passing up a chance for a loving relationship and a crack at a "normal" future? Montana liked him. Her parents seemed to like him. Maybe she was way off base. Maybe she was just afraid of commitment. Afraid of being hurt. What difference did it make if they had different ideas about God? It wasn't as though she were living it anyway.

Ivy's heart was suddenly a kettledrum in her chest, and she felt as though she wanted to run, though she didn't know what from. She tossed the pictures on the bed and hurried down the stairs and out to the front porch, then sat on the steps, hugging her knees.

God, why am I so confused? Should I listen to Kelsey or Bill—or neither? I don't want to make any more bad decisions. Please help me figure this out!

Bill Ziwicki threw up his hands. "Why are you askin' me all these questions about Pete? I hadn't seen the guy for an entire decade. All I really know about him is he was nice to me sometimes when we were in high school."

Bobby pushed back his chair and stood, his palms flat on the table. "He was also mean to you sometimes! Why don't you just admit it? Pete Barton made up the nickname Icky Ziwicki. He laughed at you. Isn't that right?"

"Everyone did. I learned to let it roll off my back."

Bobby blew a pink bubble and popped it. "Ivy never called you Icky Ziwicki, did she?"

"No. She was nice to everyone."

Bobby started pacing. "And you didn't think Pete deserved this sweet, gorgeous creature that was every guy's fantasy."

"She wore his ring. It was her choice."

"You wanted her in the worst way. But you didn't stand a chance with her, did you, Bill?"

"I didn't take it personal. She could only belong to one guy."

"*Belong?* Interesting choice of words."

"You know what I mean."

"Did you know she and Pete were sleeping together?"

"I figured. Pete always got what he wanted."

"And that made you crazy. Jealous. *Angry.*"

"More like sad for her. Pete didn't appreciate what he had."

"And you would've?"

"Not only would I have, I *do.* I've never disrespected Ivy the way Pete did."

"And just how did Pete disrespect her?"

"I don't know if I can explain it. He just didn't treat her like a lady. She was there for his convenience and pleasure."

"And you knew this how?"

Bill stared at his hands. "I just knew. I could see it in her eyes."

"And you wanted to rescue her?"

"I guess. But I couldn't."

"So Ivy goes away for ten years, then comes back completely different—underweight, dried out, and lookin' much older than her age. Pete doesn't want her anymore, and you finally get the leftovers, is that it?"

"Ivy wasn't interested in Pete!" Bill glared at Bobby. "I'm the one who looks inside her heart. Her physical beauty will come back after she gets over…"

"Gets over what?"

Bill shrugged. "The effects of the drugs."

"Ah, that's right. She went off the deep end for a while. Any idea why?"

"You'd have to ask her that."

Bobby walked over and sat again at the table. "I'm asking you. Since you're smitten with this woman and seem to be lookin' beyond the surface, you must've either discussed her past with her or wondered about it."

"Sure. But I'd never violate her privacy by askin'."

"So she hasn't talked to you about her drug problem?"

"Former drug problem. And not much."

"I have to wonder what would cause a popular, seemingly well-adjusted beauty like Ivy to become addicted to drugs. She had an intact family. Was an honor student in high school. By all indications, she had a bright future."

"Beats me."

"Ever think there might be a lot about Ivy you don't know? Maybe somethin' in her background with Pete?"

"I'm willin' to invest however long it takes to get to know her. But I'm not gonna push her too hard to talk about painful things till she's ready."

"Funny you think you've got somethin' goin' with Ivy. She told me she's not interested in you."

"She wouldn't say that."

"She sure did. Yesterday afternoon. I had her in here for

questioning, just like I'm doin' with you. You mean she didn't tell you?"

"I don't believe she said she wasn't interested in me. You must've misunderstood."

"That'd be a slap in the face, wouldn't it? Especially if she came on to you and hired you to get rid of Pete Barton so the two of you could be together—and then dumped you and left you to take the rap."

Bill jumped to his feet. "That's a lie!"

"Sit down. Now!"

Bill sank into his chair. "I can't stand to hear you talk about Ivy that way. She'd never do anything like that."

"Like what? Dump you?"

"Or pay someone to get rid of Pete."

Bobby cocked his head. "Well, we're beginnin' to think the same guy who shot your three buddies also strangled Joe Hadley. The only connection between these four guys is high school. What do you say to that?"

"I say lots of people are thinkin' the same thing. But what does that have to do with me or Ivy?"

A slow grin spread across Bobby's face. "That's what I intend to find out."

"Am I under arrest?"

"Not yet."

"Then I don't have to listen to this garbage." Bill pushed back his chair. "I've got a business to run. I'm not sittin' through this harassment again without a lawyer."

Flint moved away from the glass that separated him from the interrogation room and noticed Nick Sanchez walking toward him.

"So how'd it go with Ziwicki?" Nick said.

"He didn't give up anything, and now he's about to lawyer up. Ivy, too. So did your agents finish talking to Ronnie Unger?"

"Oh, yeah." A slow grin spread across Nick's face.

"What?"

"Seems Unger's old lady neglected to tell us that she was sleeping with Pete Barton."

"Well, for crying out loud. There's our motive!"

"Except Unger swears he didn't even know about the shooting until he got home and found my agents waiting for him."

"You believe him?"

Nick folded his arms across his chest. "I might if he didn't have a motive. His story is that he planned to corner Pete at the reunion and rake him over the coals for breaking up his marriage, then decided it wasn't worth it. Says he left around 11:40 and drove up to Telluride to meet a couple of buddies for a week, which was already in the works before the reunion. Swears he never even knew about the shooting, that he never turned on a TV the whole week. His buddies backed up his story, and his employer confirms that he was scheduled to be out for a week's vacation. Unger surrendered the clothes he wore at the reunion, but they'd already been laundered. No trace of blood in the car or on his shoes."

Flint shook his head. "So why didn't Unger's wife tell us she'd been involved with Pete Barton? And why'd she lie and tell us her husband had never mentioned the names of any of the victims? Clearly he knew about her affair with Pete."

"She claims that since she never suspected Ronnie of the shooting, she saw no reason to tell us her private business."

"You believe *her*?"

"I don't know yet. But if she's got any more secrets—or if she's covering for Ronnie—we're going to find out."

Ivy sat out on the porch steps, going over in her mind the discussions she'd had with Lu about her coming forward with the truth about Joe's death. She heard the door open behind her.

"Honey, Bill's on the phone. Why don't you take it out here?" Carolyn Griffith handed her the cordless phone and then went back inside.

"Hello."

"I can't believe you told that bubble gum-chewin' lieutenant you weren't interested in me," Bill said.

"What I *told* him is you're a sweet guy who treats me with respect, but that our relationship wasn't romantic. He grilled me over and over yesterday afternoon. My dad was furious and said I can't talk to them again without an attorney present."

"And you didn't bother to call and give me a heads-up? I was just interrogated by the lieutenant, who implied maybe I killed Pete so I could have you all to myself. I don't know where they're comin' up with this stuff. They must be desperate."

"I know. They asked me all about my relationship with Pete, and if I had conspired with you to get rid of him so the two of us could be free to pursue a relationship."

"Then it was probably smart you played down the romance. Good thinkin'."

I played it down because it's never going to happen! Ivy sighed. "Don't you get it? We're going to have to tell them Mr. Hadley shot the guys."

"Not if it means implicatin' you in Joe's death!"

"Bill, they're looking at you as a suspect in the shooting, and you're innocent! We've got to tell the truth or we're both going to get pulled into this."

"Let's don't get ahead of ourselves. They can't prove somethin' that never happened. Why don't we meet and talk this through— make sure we're on the same page?"

"No. We can say whatever we need to over the phone."

"That's not smart. Isn't there a way you could get away for an hour?"

"Sorry, I can't."

"Why not?"

"Look, I already told you I need time away from you to think."

"We don't *have* time, Ivy! That's the point. We need to com- pare notes and make sure we're sayin' the same thing so we don't slip up. Let me pick you up so we can talk this out. I promise not to pressure you about our relationship."

Ivy saw a white Jeep Liberty coming up the drive. "Bill, my dad's home. He's got my new car. I need to get off the phone."

"Call me later on my cell and tell me when and where to pick you up."

"I don't know…"

"Come on, Ivy. I'm not askin' for the moon. Just one hour."

33

THREE HOURS LATER, Ivy Griffith sat behind the wheel of her new Jeep Liberty in the driveway of her parents' home, Montana nestled in the passenger seat.

"This is so cool, Mom!" Montana said. "We've never had our own car before. Tell me again why Grandfather Griffith won't let you drive it yet."

"Oh, sweetie, it's kind of hard to explain. But for a while, I'll probably drive it out here on the property. There are miles of unpaved roads, and I'll bet you and I could find some really neat trails to explore."

Montana grinned, exposing four holes where his teeth were missing. "Will you teach *me* to drive?"

"I think for now one of us behind the wheel is enough. You can be the lookout when we go exploring, though. I'll need a good lookout."

"Okay."

Elam Griffith walked over to the driver's side window. "So what do you think, Ivy?"

"I think it's great, Dad. Just saying thank you doesn't seem like enough. I can hardly believe you and Mom did this for me."

Elam patted her arm. "I know it's going to be hard just parking it for a while, but the shooter will be arrested soon, and you'll be driving before you know it."

Montana leaned over and looked up at his grandfather. "Mom said we can drive out here on the property and maybe find some cool trails to explore—and I can be the lookout."

Elam bent down and looked in the window. "The lookout, huh? That'll work." He winked at Ivy. "You wanna take it for another spin?"

"No, I'd better go help Mom get dinner on the table. Maybe later."

"Can I sit in the driver's seat?" Montana's eyes pleaded. "I promise not to touch anything. I just like the way it smells."

Ivy reached over and tugged at his stocking cap. "Okay. But I'm taking the keys."

Ivy put the last of the dinner dishes in the dishwasher. She looked outside and saw Montana and her father walking around the car, talking and looking at the tires, and seeming to hit it off. The thought was at the same time satisfying and terrifying. Once Montana became secure with both her parents, she would have to decide whether to go through with her original plan to tell the sheriff how Joe had died, or let Mr. Hadley's revenge close the chapter on it.

She went upstairs to her room and saw the photos she had tossed on the bed. She put them in a stack, then sat in the rocker and began looking at them one by one till she came across the best one of Pete, Reg, Denny, and her posing together at the table. She wanted a closer look at their faces, and went in the bathroom and got the magnifying glass out of the drawer.

She picked up the picture and held the magnifying glass over Pete's face and felt a pang of sorrow. He had spent all his years on himself, and she wondered how many other people he had used. How she had loved him once—or thought she did. It was always about Pete. Everything was. Had she refused him, he would have found some other pretty girl to wear his ring.

Ivy placed the magnifying glass over Denny's face, and then Reg's, remembering the sound of their laughter. She blinked quickly to clear her eyes and wondered if they had suffered before they died. The ATF agents said that death was instantaneous. But how could anyone know what happened in those final seconds?

She thought of Becca Morrison and of baby Zack growing up without a father and how different things might have been had Ivy refused to make the pact all those years ago and just told the truth. The court might have gone easy on Reg and Denny. Maybe they would have paid their debt to society by now and gotten on with their lives instead of falling victim to Mr. Hadley's vengeance.

Ivy dabbed her eyes, then thumbed through the stack of photos until she found the one of her dancing with Bill. Whoever took the photo had captured a full-length shot, giving the impression the pair were the only two people on the dance floor.

She studied Bill's face, his eyes closed, his expression sweet. She wondered if anyone really knew how much he had suffered in high school when no girl would have been caught dead with him, including her.

How sharp he had looked in his brown leather jacket, yellow shirt, and khakis—certainly a step up from the threadbare jeans and wrinkled shirts he had always worn to school. She smiled, remembering how surprised and impressed she had been that he was a good dancer—much better than Pete.

Ivy started to move on to the next photo, then did a double take. She held the magnifying glass over the picture. "Brown *oxfords?* That's odd."

Her mind flashed back to those first awkward moments when they had ridden the elevator up to the second floor. She'd noted his brown leather loafers because they matched his jacket perfectly. Maybe he had changed shoes because he had been standing much of the evening and his feet hurt. That was probably it.

The kettledrum in her chest started pounding again. Bill had been adamant that he never left the dance except to go to the men's room. Why didn't he just say he had gone out to the car to change his shoes? It was no big deal—or was it?

Ivy got up and jogged down the steps to the kitchen, glad that no one else was in there. She stuck the photo in her purse, then picked up the phone and dialed.

"Hello."

"Bill, it's me."

"What took you so long to call me back?"

"I had a lot to do. Listen, why don't you pick me up at eight o'clock? I agree we need to talk."

Brandon Jones sat in Jake Compton's office, wishing he were home eating dinner and feeling a bit like a schoolboy in trouble with the principal.

"Frankly," Brandon said, "I resent having to justify what I do on my own time to you or anybody else."

Jake folded his hands on his desk. "I didn't ask about it to make you defensive. Suzanne and I ran into Kelsey at church and wondered where you were. She told us you went rafting with Buzz and some of his friends."

"So?"

"Just seemed odd that you went on Sunday morning instead of Saturday."

"Buzz wasn't free on Saturday. Look, Jake, I don't mean to be rude, but what I do in my personal time is my business. I'm not doing anything that reflects poorly on the camp."

Jake looked out the window. "Did you ever tell Kelsey about the pornography Buzz sent you on your computer?"

"I already told you I didn't. I couldn't see the advantage in making her dislike Buzz any more than she already does."

"There's safety in being accountable to her."

Brandon sighed. "Why don't you let me decide who to be accountable to, okay? I know you mean well, but I can handle myself just fine."

There was an extended pause, and the lines on Jake's forehead deepened. "The few times you've been with Buzz, has he ever made an unscheduled stop at someone's house?" Jake looked up, his gaze holding Brandon's.

"He stopped at a condo once. I waited in the car. Why?"

"Did he tell you why he was there?"

"He said he had to take care of some business."

Jake took off his glasses and laid them on the desk. "And what did he tell you when he came back out?"

"Nothing." The lie pricked Brandon's conscience.

"And you didn't ask what took him so long?"

"I never said he was gone long. Jake, what are you driving at? What's with all the mystery?"

Jake started to answer and then appeared to change his mind. Finally he said, "Just don't go in, okay?"

"What?"

"No matter what, don't go in."

"I've had about all the innuendos I can handle regarding Buzz. Either tell me outright what your problem with him is, or drop it!"

"I've already said too much. Just keep up your guard. Buzz's sense of right and wrong differs from ours, and he can't be trusted."

"How do you know?"

"I just do." Jake's face turned a bright shade of pink. "Just remember it's easier to get sucked into the darkness than to walk in the light. And that if you ever need to talk about anything, I'm here."

Brandon got up and walked out of Jake's office, feeling the way he used to when his father acted as if he didn't have good sense. What right did Jake have to instruct him on private matters? And what was it that had him so concerned that he was willing to risk antagonizing Brandon to make his point?

"Bill's here." Ivy poked her head in the living room where her parents were seated on the couch watching TV. "Montana should be down for the night, but I won't be late. I have to go to work in the morning."

"We'll leave the porch light on," Carolyn Griffith said.

"Isn't Bill coming to the door to get you?" Elam said.

"Not this time. I'll see you later."

Ivy went out the door before they could ask her any more questions. She skipped down the steps and opened the door to Bill's van and climbed in the passenger seat. She didn't say a word until Bill stopped at the bottom of the long driveway and turned onto Three Peaks Road.

"I need to be home in an hour," Ivy said.

"Okay, let's go someplace quiet where we can eyeball each other."

"How about Grinder's?"

Bill shook his head. "Too public. How about the church?"

"It's not open this time of night."

"I have the key. I clean the place, remember? There won't be anybody there."

"All right." Ivy looked out the window, trying to think of how she could make Bill understand that she didn't want to see him again—ever.

"Where are you?" he said. "You seem a hundred miles away."

"I've got a lot on my mind."

"Just don't overreact to Lieutenant Bubble Gum. Remember the sheriff and the feds can't prove we conspired to kill the guys when we didn't."

Bill drove past the cemetery and pulled into the church parking lot.

Ivy looked out at the headstones, her heart suddenly aching. "I'm going to walk down to Lu's grave for a few minutes."

"Okay. I'll go with you."

"No, I'd rather go alone."

"Whatever. I'll open the church and wait for you in the sanctuary."

Ivy hopped out of the van. Off to the west, the last vestiges of daylight looked like a pale pink canvas stretched behind the jagged peaks.

She ambled across the churchyard, past the wrought iron gate, and into the cemetery. She walked beyond the marble angel that kept watch over baby Amy and went to the back row, surprised that the cross headstone was already in place at Lu's grave. She stood in front of it, ashamed that she hadn't been out there even once since the burial.

The cross was polished white stone that bore a simple statement of faith, just the way Lu wanted it:

LUCIA GUADALUPE MARIA RAMIREZ
Born January 5, 1937 – Died April 14, 2007
Forever at Peace with Her Lord

Ivy's eyes burned and then clouded over. "I miss you so much, Lu. Are you happy? Do you even know what's going on down here? I wish you could tell me what to do. You always seemed to know what's right." Ivy wiped the tears off her face. "Montana's doing well in school, and he and Dad are finally hitting it off. I guess you know Pete, Reg, and Denny are dead now, and that I don't know *what* I should do about telling the sheriff—"

"What you should do is *not* tell him."

Ivy jumped, her hand over her heart, then looked up and saw Bill standing there. "Don't sneak up on me like that!"

"Sorry."

"I wanted a few minutes alone with Lu."

"Yeah, well, I promised your dad I wouldn't leave you alone."

"Come on, we both know Mr. Hadley isn't out to get me." Ivy watched to see if he reacted to her comment, but he didn't.

"A promise is a promise. You done here?"

Ivy bit her lip. "I guess I am. Though that wasn't exactly my idea of a few moments alone with Lu."

"I brought you out here to talk. We've only got an hour."

34

SHERIFF FLINT CARTER hung up the phone and glanced at his watch, thinking he should be home tucking Ian into bed for the night instead of spending every waking moment on this case.

He walked over to the table in his office where Special Agent Nick Sanchez sat eating the last slice of sausage pizza and looking through a stack of files.

"Is your wife understanding when you have to be away on a case?" Flint said.

Nick glanced up at him. "Not always, especially when I'm not there to see my son's soccer games. Or attend my daughter's dance recitals. But she knows what I do is important. Somebody's got to do it. Why not me? I've certainly got the temperament for it."

"Do any of the cases keep you up at night?"

Nick smirked. "My wife says I turn into an owl when I'm working the tough cases—kidnappings, serial killings, drug busts. I learned to detach myself from the victims a long time ago, but my mind almost always goes into overtime when I'm getting close to nailing the perp. I take it your wife isn't thrilled you're working late again?"

Flint sat at the table and sighed. "Betty's about had it with my obsession over the Joe Hadley case all these years. And this case gets more complex by the minute. We've torn the Ungers' personal lives apart, and there's just nothing that points to this guy being capable of killing Pete for messing with his wife—much less killing two innocent guys. I know you think this case and the Hadley case are related somehow, but I just don't see it."

"I think you're about to." Nick seemed to be mulling something over. Finally, he looked up from the file, his eyebrow arched, that unmistakable *aha* expression on his face. "Remind me when the coroner confirmed that the bones found at that construction site were Joe Hadley's."

"Let me look." Flint went over to his computer and pulled up the date. "April 4."

"And the three lodge victims were shot on April 23, just nineteen days later."

"Yeah. Where are you going with this, Nick?"

"I know Barton, Morrison, and Richards were on the basketball team with Hadley. But I'm wondering if they have an alibi for the afternoon he went missing?"

"They were with Ivy Griffith down at Louie's Drive-in."

Nick popped the last bite of pizza into his mouth, then leaned back in his chair, his hands folded across his chest. "Any eyewitnesses that confirm they were there?"

"No. But the four of them vouched for each other when we reopened the case as a murder investigation last month."

"What about immediately after Hadley disappeared?"

"Back then we questioned each of the players on the basketball team, but had no reason to single out any of them as suspects. What are you thinking?"

"I'm thinking we've been looking for one perp who looks good for all four murders. But what if Barton, Morrison, and Richards murdered Joe Hadley and buried him out on that ranch? Could explain why somebody went after *them*."

Flint stared at Nick, the implications screaming like a siren in his mind. "I never even considered it. What would be their motive for killing Joe? As far as we could tell, those guys didn't have a conflict with him. Besides, Ivy said she was with them the afternoon Joe disappeared."

"So?"

"She's not a murderer, Nick."

Nick flashed a phony smile. "Did you ever ask her?"

"No, but—"

"Maybe it's time we did."

Flint took off his glasses and rubbed his eyes, his mind racing faster than his pulse. "But even if Barton, Morrison, and Richards did kill Hadley, which I'm not ready to seriously consider, then who shot them? And if Ivy was in on Hadley's killing, why wasn't she shot, too?"

Ivy Griffith sat in the back row of Woodlands Community Church, her eyes focused on the stained glass that had no beauty without the light shining through it. She thought that's how God must see her, too. How many times had she sat in this church as a young believer, unable to pray and consumed with guilt because she was sleeping with Pete and experimenting with drugs? She let her eyes wander around the quaint old church. Except for the banners hanging behind the pulpit, nothing had changed. Including the darkness she concealed in her heart.

"Okay, the door's locked." Bill said. "Nobody's gonna walk in on us."

Ivy thought Bill's face looked hard as stone. "Are you mad?"

"No, I'm concerned you're gettin' freaked with all the questions the authorities are askin'."

"Of course I'm freaked. They're implying that I hired you to kill Pete."

Bill smirked. "Which they can't prove because it's not true. So why are you worried?"

"I don't want my family subjected to this! Everybody knows my parents, and I've already shamed them once. I don't want to do it again."

"How can you shame them if you're innocent?"

"But I'm not innocent in *Joe's* death. And I'm tired of living in fear. It almost seems easier just to tell the truth and get it over with."

Bill sat next to her, closer than she would have liked. "Which is why you need me to talk some sense into you. Nothin' is gonna be easier if you go public about Joe's death. All you're gonna get out of it is jail time."

"For a while. But I'll have peace of mind."

"You really think you're gonna find peace in the slammer? You're gonna worry about your kid the whole time. You're gonna miss watchin' him grow up. Then when you get out, no one will hire you. It'll be too late to find a husband and have a family. You'll be doomed to a life of misery—and for what? Mr. Hadley already got justice for Joe's death. And the feds can't find any evidence to charge you with the shooting because you had nothin' to do with it."

Ivy sat quietly, thinking Bill was in a bad mood and this wasn't the right time to confront him with the photograph. Then again, she didn't want to see him again.

"Mrs. Barton gave me some pictures that somebody took at the reunion. She doesn't want them and said I should either keep them or throw them out. There was one of you and me dancing, and I brought it with me." Ivy reached in her purse and took out the photo and handed it to him.

Bill's stony expression softened, the corners of his mouth twitching. "This was one of the greatest moments of my life. Notice how relaxed you seem in my arms—just the way I always imagined."

"That's a really great-looking leather jacket," Ivy said. "I thought so the minute we ran into each other at the elevator."

"Thanks. I spent a lot of time decidin' what to wear. I almost chickened out and didn't come. But I couldn't stay home, knowin' you'd be there."

Ivy glanced at him out of the corner of her eye, her heart pounding. "What happened to those cool brown loafers you were wearing?"

"What do you mean?"

"You had on brown loafers when you got in the elevator."

"Loafers? Nah. I don't wear loafers." Bill kept his eyes fixed on the photo. "You must have me mixed up with someone else."

"I'm positive because I remember they matched your leather jacket perfectly—right down to the smooth texture. Reminded me of a Hershey bar."

Bill turned, his eyes locking on to hers. "I'm tellin' you I've never owned a pair of brown loafers. You're obviously mistaken."

Or I've been duped.

Suddenly, the room seemed to pulsate with the same terrifying presence that had followed her home after her last date with Bill.

Ivy sucked in a breath and forgot to exhale, her heart hammering, her behind feeling as though it were welded to the church pew.

"What's the matter with you?" Bill said. "You look like you've seen a ghost or somethin'."

She struggled to find her voice but couldn't make a sound.

"Ivy, what the—?"

She shoved him with all her might, then jumped up and raced to the back door and pushed it with her shoulder again and again, but it wouldn't budge.

"Will you settle down?" Bill's hands closed around her upper arms like a vice.

"Take me home right now!"

"Will you please just tell me what's wrong?"

Ivy looked down at her belt and realized her cell phone was in her purse on the pew. "I want to go home!"

"Why have you gone postal on me? What'd I do?"

"You lied to me!" she shouted. "You absolutely *were* wearing brown loafers. I don't trust you anymore."

"You're being irrational!"

"No, I'm not. You wouldn't lie unless you had something to hide."

"Like what?"

Ivy thought her heart would pound out of her chest.

"Come on," Bill prodded. "If you're accusin' me of somethin', let's hear it."

"Just take me home."

"Not till we clear this up. Just talk to me straight and say what you're thinkin'."

"All right. I think you're the one who put the note in my pocket and tried to make me think Mr. Hadley shot Pete and Reg and Denny!"

"Why would I do that?"

"So I wouldn't suspect that you did it! *You* killed them!"

Bill spun her around and grabbed her wrists. "Ivy, listen to me. You're not thinkin' clearly."

"Oh, yes, I am. For the first time in a long time! You deceived me!"

"It's not what you think! I love you. I've always loved you. I just wanted us to have a chance to be together. I had to break Pete's hold on you."

"I told you I had no interest whatsoever in Pete!"

Bill tightened his grip. "Come on. Even after ten years you wouldn't go to the reunion with me because you were afraid of what he'd think! It was always gonna be like that. I couldn't compete with Pete, and you needed to be free. Don't you see? It was the only way."

Ivy started to cry. "That's not true! And why would you kill Reg and Denny? Reg's wife is eight months pregnant. Did you even think of that?"

"I didn't have a choice. They saw me." Bill's eyes blazed. "But they shouldn't have dissed me at Grinder's either. How dare they treat me like I was nothin' more than a cockroach? And how dare they dump Joe Hadley's body in a hole, throw dirt on him, and just walk away like nothin' ever happened? They got what they deserved. What difference does it make if it was me or Mr. Hadley who evened the score?"

"Don't hand me that! You didn't know they killed Joe until I told you!"

"Yeah, I did. I saw you guys drive off with Joe the afternoon he disappeared." Bill let go of her wrists. "I never said anything to the sheriff because hangin' out with you guys was all I really had. Plus if I'd blown the whistle, the guys would've turned me in for buyin' drugs. I never knew for sure how they killed Joe till his bones were found, but I knew they did."

"How'd you know I wasn't in on it?"

"Because I know you—better than anyone."

Ivy raked her hands through her hair. "So you just left the Aspen Room, followed the guys to their room and shot them, then came back and asked me to dance? How cold can you get?"

"Look, I didn't plan to kill Reg and Denny, but when I saw the three of them leave together, I knew it was the opportunity I'd been waitin' for, and I took it. I had an exact change of clothes out in the car, except the shoes were different. I didn't think anyone would notice."

"Bill, you're in so much trouble."

"Not unless you tell. The feds can't prove anything. I tested negative for gunpowder residue because I wore gloves. I tested negative for blood because I changed clothes. I was only out of the Aspen Room for maybe twenty minutes max. I've burned all the evidence. They'll never catch me."

Brandon Jones sat at the dinner table picking at his mashed potatoes, thinking back on his earlier conversation with Jake Compton.

"Are you okay?" Kelsey Jones said. "You finally come home after a late meeting with Jake, never even asked me how my day was, and you've hardly touched your dinner."

Brandon glanced over at her and took a bite of meatloaf. "Dinner's great, honey. I'm just a little preoccupied. How *was* your day?"

"I really enjoyed having Ivy over this morning. We can talk about that later, though. Tell me what's bothering you."

"Oh, Jake really ticked me off just before I left the office, and I'm not sure how I should respond to it. I know one thing, if he doesn't stop butting into my personal business, my job is going to get old really fast."

"How can you say that?" Kelsey put down her fork. "We spent weeks praying about this job. You're right where the Lord wants you."

"I'm beginning to wonder."

"Tell me what happened."

Brandon lifted his eyes and looked into Kelsey's. "Jake's got some personal grudge against Buzz and resents me hanging out with him, that's all."

"What grudge?"

Brandon shrugged. "Don't know. He's being really weird about it, but he won't talk straight to me."

"Did you ask him point-blank?"

"Yeah, but he never said. I told him either to tell me outright why he has a problem with Buzz or drop it. He's got a lot of nerve ragging on the guy without giving specifics."

Kelsey snickered. "Well, we can all guess the gist of his concern. Buzz's crude talk is probably just a preview of what's in his heart."

"I admit Buzz is rough around the edges, but he totally respects the fact that I'm a Christian. He's different around me than he is other guys." *I can't believe I just lied to my wife to protect Buzz.*

"Ivy mentioned something when she was here that really has me bothered now," Kelsey said. "She was out with Bill Saturday night and saw Buzz with a woman at some tavern in Mt. Byron. She said the woman wasn't his wife. And Ivy knows who Maggie is because the Eastons go to Jewel's every Saturday morning for breakfast. Do you know if Buzz is cheating on Maggie?"

Brandon picked up his iced tea and took a sip. "How would I know a thing like that?"

"Well, has he ever flirted with other women when he's with you?"

Why flirt when he can stop in any time and have sex with his girlfriend? "Not that I've noticed."

"What, no wolf whistles? Crude remarks? Off-color jokes?"

"Honey, Buzz is who he is. I blow off most of what he says and does. As long as he respects where I'm coming from, we get along fine."

"I think you should press Jake to tell you specifics. What if there's something you need to know so you don't end up in a compromising situation?"

"Like what?"

"Well, for one thing, if Buzz is cheating on Maggie, I don't want her to think you're covering for him."

Brandon buttered his dinner roll. "Do you really think I would do that?"

"Absolutely not. I trust that you've got the spiritual backbone to stand up for what's right."

Ivy felt as if she were going to throw up. "Will you please just take me home?"

"I can't do that," Bill said.

"I promise not to say anything about this."

"I can't take that chance."

"Meaning what? You going to kill me, too?"

Bill's face fell. "After all I've done so we can be together, and you still don't believe I love you?" He stroked her cheek, then took hold of her arm and unlocked the door. "Come on. I know where we can go till I figure out what to do."

Bill pulled her close, his hand over her mouth, and forced her out to the van, then pushed her up in the back. He put a gag in her mouth and tied her wrists and ankles.

"I hate doin' this, Ivy. But until you get your thinkin' straightened out, I don't want you doin' anything that'll mess up what we've got goin'."

"We haven't got anything going!" Ivy shouted, her words muffled and indistinguishable.

"I'll take the gag off when we get to the cabin," Bill said.

Cabin? Her mind raced with the horrible implications of being holed up with a guy obsessed with possessing her. The thought that he might force himself on her was revolting enough. But she knew he could never let her go now that she knew the truth.

God, please help me get out of this. I promise I'll tell the truth about Joe's death. Don't let Montana lose his mother. Not now. Not after all he's been through.

"Okay, sweetheart. Just try to relax and enjoy the ride." Bill lifted her head and gently slipped something soft under it. "After all these years, my dream's finally comin' true."

Ivy winced when the back doors slammed shut. Seconds later the van started and turned right onto Three Peaks Road.

35

Ivy Griffith, her wrists tied behind her, walked up four wooden steps covered in pine needles to the front porch of what appeared to be a small log cabin. She'd almost made a run for it when Bill Ziwicki untied her ankles, then realized that, even if she could manage to escape, she might not survive in the crisp Colorado night dressed in only jeans and a sweater.

Bill unlocked the door, pushed it open, and flipped the light switch, then prodded her inside to a large room reeking with an unpleasant fishy odor and the distinctive smell of charred firewood. She saw an iron skillet on the stove and considered that she might be able to use it as a weapon if she ever got her wrists untied. She noticed Bill had left the van keys in the ignition.

She walked across the creaky wood floor and a grimy oval rug that looked as though it had never been vacuumed and decided the place looked at least fifty years old. The furnishings were basic: a knotty pine table and chairs. A dilapidated brown sofa and two gold chairs that would have been stylish in the seventies. Maple end tables with spindly legs, and a matching coffee table marred with deep scratches and coffee rings. The curtains on the windows had probably been white once, but were now a dingy yellow.

This is hideous—just like him! Ivy thought.

"I'll take off your gag if you promise not to scream," Bill said. "No one will hear you anyway, so you'd be wastin' your time."

Ivy nodded, and Bill removed the gag.

She took a couple of slow, deep breaths, thinking the air in the room was so stale it must have been years since the windows had been opened.

"Where are we?" she said, stealing a glance at her watch and noting it had been thirty-seven minutes since they left the church.

"Does it really matter? We're finally together the way I always dreamed." Bill brushed the hair off her face and a chill shot up her spine.

"You cold?"

"Freezing."

"Okay, let me get a fire goin'. There's absolutely no place to run so forget tryin' to run off. You might as well settle in and get comfortable."

"How am I supposed to feel comfortable when you're holding me here against my will?"

"You'll change your mind when you realize we were meant for each other. You just need to reconcile Pete's death, that's all. He had to die for you to be free. Eventually you'll understand that. It's all that garbage about God and sin and guilt that's messin' with your mind."

"Bill, I'm supposed to be at work in the morning. I can't afford to miss. I need the money."

"Yeah, well, you're not goin' back to Jewel's. I'll be takin' care of you now."

"But I need to get home to Montana. He needs me."

"I know." Bill struck a match and lit the kindling, then used the bellows until the logs were ignited and flames danced in the fireplace. "We'll worry about Montana as soon as we get settled. We need time to get used to each other first."

Ivy looked around and saw only one bedroom, and dread covered her like a heavy, dark mantle.

Father, help me get out of here!

———

Flint Carter paced in his office, his hands in his pockets, his mind alive with the one possibility he had never considered in a decade of wondering what had happened to Joe Hadley.

"Don't be so hard on yourself," Nick Sanchez said. "Why *would* you suspect Barton, Morrison, and Richards? Even the feds working the case thought the Hadley boy had been kidnapped."

Flint sighed. "Yeah, I know. But it makes perfect sense when we put all the facts together."

"Which is exactly what we did. But we need to pull Ivy Griffith back in here ASAP and pursue this angle."

"Tonight?" Flint glanced at his watch. "It's already nine-thirty. She goes to work at the crack of dawn."

"Tough. We can't afford to work on her schedule. Let's get her down here."

"Okay, I'll call the house. If it's okay with you, I'd like to swing by and pick her up myself. You realize her father isn't going to let her talk to us without an attorney present?"

"Whatever. Just get her here where I can see her reactions. I'll put on a pot of coffee."

Flint went over to his desk and dialed the Griffiths' number, then popped two Tums into his mouth, thinking there was no way he was ready to break it to Elam that his daughter was a murder suspect.

"Hello."

"Elam, it's Flint. Sorry to call so late, but I need to talk to Ivy. Would you put her on the phone, please?"

"She's not here. She's out with Bill."

"Any idea where we can find her?"

"Not really. She said she wouldn't be late. What's so important you need to talk to her tonight?"

"We've had a breakthrough on the case and need to ask her some more questions."

"I'm not letting you grill that girl again without Brett Hewitt there."

Flint exhaled into the receiver. "You hired *Hewitt?*"

"You better believe it. I know the DA can't stand him, but Hewitt's the best. If you think I'm going to sit back and let Ivy get railroaded, think again. She had nothing to do with the shooting, and this is starting to border on harassment."

Flint paused, his eyes closed, and then said, "This isn't about the shooting, Elam."

"Then what?"

"This is regarding the Hadley case."

"Hadley? What about it?"

"Just have Ivy call my cell number when she gets in. I don't care what time it is. I'll swing by and pick her up."

"This is crazy!"

"Sorry, Elam. But that's the way it is. Call Hewitt and give him a heads-up if you need to, but the feds want Ivy down here tonight."

Ivy sat in one of the ugly gold chairs, her nose itching and her hands tied behind her, and watched as Bill took a wet towel and attempted to remove a thick layer of dust that seemed to cover everything in sight. At least he had untied her long enough for her to use the bathroom.

"This place could use a woman's touch," Bill said. "Too bad it's not ours so you could fix it up the way you like. I'll get my cleaning supplies in here when I can work in the daylight. I'll have it immaculate in no time."

"How long are we staying here?"

Bill turned to her and smiled. "The owners aren't coming for summer vacation until July."

July? Ivy tried to get her hands free, but to no avail. "How do you think we're going to survive if you can't work? You can't go back to Jacob's Ear or you'll be arrested."

"I've got plenty of money saved."

"When they figure out you've taken me, they'll freeze your bank accounts."

"I have cash for whatever we need."

"And where are we supposed to go when July comes?"

"You ask too many questions, sweetheart. Let's just enjoy the time we have together. I suppose I should go get us some groceries."

"Please, just take me home," she pleaded.

Bill squatted next to her chair, his hand on her knee. "But you are home. You're with me."

Ivy tried not to show her revulsion. "You're right. You should probably go get groceries so we can have breakfast in the morning."

"Okay, but I'll have to tie your ankles while I'm gone. I'll leave the gag off this time. There's no one out here to hear you, even if you wig out again. Just relax, sweetheart. Everything's gonna work out fine. You'll see."

Bill tied her ankles, then pressed his lips to her cheek. He put on his jacket, a pair of horned-rimmed glasses, and pulled a stocking cap down over his ears. "Wouldn't want anybody recognizing me now, would we? Okay, I'll see you in a while. Try to get some rest."

Ivy watched him walk out the door and heard him lock it. Seconds later, the van started, and then she heard the tires crunching on gravel. She wondered how far Bill would have to drive to find a grocery store up here—and how much time she had to come up with an escape plan.

Carolyn Griffith stood at the front window, aware of the grandfather clock striking eleven. "It's not like Ivy to stay out this late when she has to get up at four-thirty to get ready for work."

"She and Bill seem to like each other," Elam said.

Carolyn went over and sat on the couch next to him. "That's just it. She told me earlier today the relationship wasn't going anywhere—that Bill was sweet but not her type."

"I doubt if Ivy even knows what her type is. I just hope she's not sleeping with him."

"She's a grown woman, Elam. We can't control her behavior."

"Could we ever?"

Carolyn sighed, her mind flashing back to Ivy's life before Pete Barton. "She's trying really hard to make a fresh start. She loves Montana and really wants to be a good mother."

"I know." Elam took her hand in his. "That's why I'm so upset about this totally unnecessary harassment coming from Flint's office. They know darned good and well she wasn't involved in that shooting. So why are they pulling her into the Joe Hadley investigation—because of her drug history? I mean the girl hardly knew Joe. What could she possibly offer them toward solving his murder?"

The phone rang.

"I'll get it." Carolyn walked out to the kitchen and picked up the phone. "Hello."

"Carolyn, it's Flint. Has Ivy come home yet?"

"No. We told you we'd call when she did. Why can't you talk to her tomorrow?"

"The feds have waited around to talk to her tonight."

"Well, she's not here. What can I say?" Carolyn hated the sarcasm in her voice. "I'm sorry, Flint. I don't mean to be rude. I'm just confused about why Ivy is under the gun. The poor thing's been through the mill in the past month. She really can't handle much more."

"Let's give it till midnight. I'll check back."

"Elam told you we'd call the minute she gets in."

"Okay, thanks. I'll wait to hear from you."

Carolyn hung up the phone. *Lord, what's going on that's so urgent the FBI is waiting around for Ivy?* She walked back in the living room. "That was Flint."

"Yeah, I gathered."

"He was just checking to see if Ivy's home."

"Makes me mad he won't tell me what he wants to talk to her about—other than it pertains to the Joe Hadley case."

"Well, Ivy's over twenty-one. From a legal standpoint, I guess it's really her business and not ours."

Ivy opened her eyes when she heard a car motor outside. She had no idea how long Bill had been gone, but it had taken her only a few minutes of hopping around the house with her wrists and ankles bound to realize how helpless she was.

After she spotted a box of candles in the bedroom, she went back in the living room and flopped in the gold chair, committed to spending the night in the dilapidated old thing, even if she had to fake an episode of hysteria to keep Bill away from her. Maybe in the morning she could sweet-talk him into letting her cook for him so he would untie her.

She heard a key in the lock, and then the front door opened. Bill came in carrying multiple plastic bags in both hands.

"How's my girl?"

"Completely miserable. What time is it?"

Bill set the bags on the table and glanced at his watch. "Five after twelve. Sorry I took so long, but there wasn't much open. Anyhow, I got lots of stuff. We should be good for a few days if this old fridge doesn't give out."

I'm not staying here that long! "Could you please untie me? I'm getting stiff sitting in the same position."

"I'll untie your ankles, but I think we'd better leave the wrists tied till I'm sure you're done bein' mad."

"Leaving them tied just makes me madder! I'm not an animal! You have no right to keep me here!"

He untied her ankles, then reached up and brushed the hair off her forehead. "You'll thank me after your thinkin' gets straightened out."

"You keep saying that. There's nothing wrong with my thinking, Bill. What woman in her right mind wants to be held prisoner?"

"The only thing in prison is your mind, sweetheart. I just have to break you of all that useless guilt you're carrying around so we can have a future together."

Elam jumped up off the couch and started pacing. "It's two-thirty in the morning. The bars are closed. So where's Ivy?"

"Honey, calm down," Carolyn said.

"I don't want to calm down. I want to wring her fool neck. What is she thinking? She has to leave for work in three hours."

"She's not missed a day yet."

Elam's eyes turned to slits. "She obviously doesn't want us to know what she's doing or she would've called. I have half a mind to go over to Bill's place and see if she's there. Maybe he's just not answering the phone."

"I just don't see Ivy spending the night with Bill. She didn't seem at all enthused about him earlier today or even tonight when she left." Carolyn sighed. "If she *is* at Bill's, what are you going to do—grab her by the ear and lead her out to your car? It's not as though we can dictate her behavior at this stage of her life."

"Well, you can bet I'm going to try! I should've put my foot down when she was dating Pete." Elam stroked his mustache for several seconds, and then said, "Actually, I doubt she's at Bill's or Flint would've found her by now."

Carolyn caught her husband's gaze, her worst fear mirrored in his eyes. "What if they've been in a car wreck? Or have gone off the road somewhere and are hurt? I'm not even sure Ivy's got our address on her."

Elam opened the closet door and took out his parka. "I'll head into town and start looking for her. Call my cell if she shows up."

36

BRANDON JONES OPENED his eyes and realized Kelsey wasn't in the bed, nor was the bathroom light on. He glanced at the clock: 2:45. He swung his legs over the side of the bed and put on his bathrobe and slippers, then went out to the living room, where Kelsey sat on the couch, her Bible in her lap.

"Honey, what are you doing up?" he said. "You're not going to be worth a hoot at work."

Kelsey looked up at him, seemingly wide-awake. "I can't get Ivy Griffith off my mind. I have this really powerful urgency to pray for her."

"I wonder why that keeps happening?"

Kelsey shrugged. "I don't know, but there's no way I can sleep."

"We got sidetracked earlier tonight, and you never did tell me about your conversation with her."

Kelsey closed her Bible and recounted her conversation with Ivy—and how guilt ridden she had seemed.

"I'm not surprised," Brandon said, "considering her past and all she's put her parents through."

"But I just hate that she feels like a lost cause. And I'm not sure I was able to convince her otherwise."

"Sounds like you said all the right things, honey. It's up to God to change her heart."

Kelsey tucked her hair behind her ear and seemed to be thinking. "Ivy did say something I thought was odd. She wanted to know if a person hadn't told the truth about something, would he have to go back and tell the truth if he wanted God to forgive him."

"That is odd. How'd you answer?"

"I said a truly repentant heart that wants to make things right will do whatever it takes. Someone called after that, and then we got on a whole nother subject."

The phone rang and Kelsey jumped, her hand over her heart.

Brandon went into the kitchen and grabbed the receiver on the wall phone. "Hello."

"Brandon, it's Carolyn. I'm sorry to call you at this hour, but Ivy's missing, and we need you and Kelsey to pray."

"That's so strange because Kelsey's already been up for a while, feeling led to pray for Ivy. What's going on?"

"Ivy and Bill went out around eight o'clock, and she said she wouldn't be late. It's totally out of character for her not to call. And to make matters worse, Sheriff Carter and the FBI have been waiting all night to talk to her—something about the Joe Hadley case they want to ask her about." Carolyn's voice was shaking. "Elam is out looking for her, and she's not at Bill's. I'm really worried."

"We're coming over there," Brandon said. "You don't need to be alone right now."

Ivy sat in the ugly gold chair, shivering from the cold and feeling too vulnerable to allow herself to fall asleep. She wondered how Bill would treat her in the morning. Would he be angry she had insisted on sleeping in the broken-down chair when he had offered her the bed all to herself? He hadn't acted as though he intended to take advantage of her, but she was determined to stay out of the bed. Period.

She heard footsteps on the creaky floor and opened her eyes. Bill's dark form stood over her.

"You still okay out here?" he said softly.

"I was asleep. Why'd you wake me up?"

Bill draped another blanket over her. "Sorry. It seems cold in here to me, and I didn't think one blanket was enough to keep you warm."

How can you be so sweet and be a monster at the same time? "Thanks." *Now go away!*

"I just don't feel right takin' the bed with you sleepin' in the chair."

"But I'm fine. Really."

Bill reached in the bathroom and turned on the light, then left the door cracked and flopped on the couch. "Go back to sleep. I'll be right here if you need anything."

Ivy closed her eyes for half a minute and then opened them. "I can't sleep with you staring at me."

"I love to watch you sleep. I do it all the time in my mind—only you're lyin' next to me."

Ivy shuddered at the creepy, almost hypnotic look in his eyes. She cringed to think what else Bill had imagined in his mind and blinked away the images that popped into her own. How much longer would she be able to evade whatever sick fantasies he hoped to fulfill?

All at once, a familiar presence permeated the room and seemed almost as if it were slithering across the floor toward her—laughing, taunting, threatening. Her tears seemed frozen and unable to escape, and her pulse raced wildly as the evil seemed to wrap itself around her throat. She wanted to scream, but couldn't catch her breath. Wanted to fight but her wrists were tied.

Ivy clamped her eyes shut, the presence so sinister, so terrifying, that she wondered if hell could be any worse.

She wanted to fall on her knees, but couldn't move, so she pictured herself kneeling, her hands lifted in total surrender, knowing there was only one way out of this pit of despair—and she should have taken it a long time ago.

Jesus, I need You! I want to come back! I'm sorry for all the ways I've sinned against You. If You'll get me out of here, I promise I'll go to the sheriff immediately and tell the truth. I promise to teach Montana

about You. I promise never to run from You again! I'm not just saying
that so You'll help me. I really mean it!

Ivy pictured herself clinging to the foot of the cross and whispered the name of Jesus over and over. The evil presence vanished.

Sheriff Flint Carter bounded up the front steps of the Griffiths'
home, Lieutenant Bobby Knolls, Investigator Buck Lowry, and
two of Nick Sanchez's agents behind him, and rang the doorbell.
Sasha started barking, and he heard footsteps coming closer.

Elam Griffith opened door and held it open. "Thanks for
coming. I started to look for Ivy myself, but realized I don't have a
clue where she could be. She's not at Bill's."

Flint stepped inside just as the grandfather clock struck four
and noticed a young couple sitting in the living room with
Carolyn. He introduced his entourage to Carolyn and Elam, and
was introduced to the couple, Brandon and Kelsey Jones.

"Okay," Flint said, "let's cut to the chase. I've got my men
searching in town and along the main highways. We'd like to look
through Ivy's room, if that's okay. You want her attorney present?"

"That's not necessary," Elam said. "Do whatever you need to.
Please, just find her."

Flint followed Carolyn up the stairs and into Ivy's bedroom.
He moved his eyes slowly around the room.

"Carolyn, I'd like to search through her dresser drawers, under
the mattress, in the closet—everything. Do we have your permission for that?"

Carolyn nodded, her lips pressed together tightly, her eyes
brimming with tears. "I'll wait downstairs."

"Actually, it might be helpful if you'd stay." Flint eyed the photographs on the bed. "What are these?"

"Class reunion pictures that Evelyn Barton didn't want and
gave to Ivy. Your department has copies."

"Did Ivy comment on them?" Flint said, noting the magnifying glass next to the photos.

Carolyn put her fingers to her temples. "Uh, she liked them.

Said there were a few really good ones. Oh, there was one of her and Bill dancing that Evelyn thought she might like. It was very nice."

"Could you point it out for me?"

Carolyn gathered up the pictures and thumbed through them. "Hmm…it's not here. Maybe I missed it." She thumbed through the stack a second time, then shook her head. "I don't see it."

"Okay." Flint folded his arms across his chest. "Any idea why Ivy would look at the photos with a magnifying glass? Is that usual for her?"

Carolyn shrugged. "I don't know, but she didn't do that when we looked at them earlier."

Flint, Bobby, Buck, and Nick's agents searched every inch of Ivy's room, and then went back downstairs.

"We didn't find anything helpful," Flint said. "No diary. Notes. Phone numbers. Ticket stubs. Receipts. Nothing." He turned to Kelsey. "Carolyn mentioned you had Ivy over for coffee yesterday. Did she say anything strange—anything out of the ordinary?"

Kelsey linked her arm in Brandon's. "I don't know Ivy very well, so I'm not sure what's out of the ordinary for her. We talked a lot about spiritual things. She seemed burdened by guilt for hurting her parents and Montana when she was involved in drugs. I did think it was odd that she asked me if a person hadn't told the truth about something, would he have to go tell the truth if he wanted God to forgive him."

Flint shot Bobby a knowing look. "Ivy didn't indicate whether *she* was that person who hadn't told the truth?"

"No, and I didn't ask. But she seemed really bothered by it."

"Okay," Flint said. "I want to take a look at the missing photograph and would like Carolyn and Elam to come down to the station and pick it out of our copies. It may not mean anything, but it's worth checking out."

"Okay," Carolyn said. "But one of us needs to stay with Montana."

"Kelsey and I will stay," Brandon said. "You go. We'll call if Ivy comes home."

Ivy sat in the chair, her hands still bound, and Bill snoring on the couch. But the crushing weight in her heart was gone and so was the fear.

She felt as though she were wrapped in a blanket of peace and tried to comprehend the magnitude of what had just happened.

She thought for a moment about how difficult it was going to be for her parents and Montana to accept the truth about Joe Hadley's death—and how she had been a party to the cover-up. As hard as it would be to admit her guilt, she knew she could go through with it now that God had forgiven her. No punishment she would face could compare with the horrible feeling of being separated from Him—something she never again wanted to experience.

Bill exhaled and smacked his lips, then turned on his side and continued to snore.

Ivy closed her eyes and pictured Jesus sitting on the arm of the chair. She was determined to stay focused on that image, no matter what Bill decided to do with her.

Flint Carter, Nick Sanchez, and Bobby Knolls gathered around the computer monitor where thumbnail prints of each reunion photo were displayed, including duplicates of the pictures they had found on Ivy's bed.

"Okay," Nick said to the special agent who sat at the computer, "bring up the picture Mrs. Griffith pointed out of her daughter and Ziwicki dancing and blow it up. All right. Now let's look through the photos in time sequence and enlarge each one where Ziwicki's pictured, then crop him out of it. I want to see every detail—if he has so much as a gravy stain on his shirt."

Flint watched as the special agent at the computer cropped Bill Ziwicki's image out of several photographs and enlarged them. "Some of these aren't very clear."

"Yeah, but some are," Nick said. "Keep going. There's nothing in these photos that proves Ziwicki was in the Aspen Room at the time of the murder."

Flint took a sip of coffee. "Ivy said she saw him at the bar at 1:20 when Barton, Morrison, and Richards left."

"Could be she's coverin' for him," Bobby said. "Maybe that's why she got rid of the photo."

Flint shook his head. "We don't know that she got rid of it. Maybe she wanted to show it to Bill when they went out. It's a nice picture of the two of them."

"If Griffith isn't with Ziwicki at his house, where are they?" Nick said. "There's no reason to go to a motel. And they're a little old to be fooling around in the back of the van. Something's not right."

"Stop!" Bobby said. "Go back to the first photo taken of Ziwicki, the one where the clock shows 7:40. Yeah, that's it. Look at the shoes. Now go to the one of him dancin' with Griffith."

"Well, ain't that sweet?" A slow grin spread across Nick's face. "Ziwicki changed his shoes—and probably everything else. Good spot, Lieutenant. Add a silencer and a pair of gloves to the scenario, and we might just have our shooter. He and Griffith were probably in on it together and fled when they knew we were on to them. Let's get an APB out on his van."

"I'm not convinced Ivy knew anything about this," Flint said.

"Well, you keep defending her." Nick stood to his feet. "But I'm going to nail her and Ziwicki. My guess is they conspired together in the shooting."

"You might be right about Ziwicki being the shooter, Nick. But what would be Ivy's motive? I just don't see that girl sending those three guys up to the room so Ziwicki could blow them away."

"She sure didn't have any problem being a party to Joe Hadley's murder."

"Come on," Flint said. "We don't know what happened to Joe Hadley. It's speculation at this point."

Nick smiled. "Not for long. Let's get a warrant to search Ziwicki's place."

37

SHERIFF FLINT CARTER, search warrant in hand, entered the home of Bill Ziwicki just before dawn, followed by a whole team of deputies and FBI agents, including Bobby Knolls and Nick Sanchez.

"This is the neatest bachelor pad I've ever seen," Nick said. "My wife should be this organized."

Flint ran his finger along the top of a picture frame and found no dust. "Don't forget, Ziwicki's in the cleaning business."

Nick went in the kitchen and started opening cabinets and drawers. "You ought to see the way he's lined up the glasses according to size, every knife and fork neatly stacked. Even the pot holders are arranged by color. This guy has way too much time on his hands."

"Hey, sheriff!" Bobby appeared in a doorway. "You'll wanna see this!"

Flint followed Bobby into what appeared to be a bedroom. "What the…?"

One wall was covered with a symmetrical arrangement of photographs—all of Ivy Griffith—some from high school, others from the class reunion, a few from old newspapers. Flint recognized the poster-sized photo in the center as Ivy's homecoming queen portrait. A vase of roses and two candles had been set on a small table in front of the photo wall.

Flint studied the collage of photos with his arms folded, his mind racing with the implications. "The profile indicated our perp lives in his own fantasy world where he can turn off the emotional pain, but this is really sick."

Bobby blew a pink bubble and popped it. "Yep."

"The profile also indicated that the perp might've felt rejected by a parent early in life," Nick added. "Ziwicki's mother died when he was ten."

"Is that the same thing?" Flint turned to Nick.

"Could seem that way to a kid."

"You think he'll hurt Ivy?"

"Well, we know he's a killer." Nick arched one eyebrow. "But for all we know, Griffith's in this thing with him and left willingly. I don't think he'd hurt her unless he thinks he's going to lose her or thinks he's going to get caught."

"Which he is," Flint said. "So where does that leave us?"

"For starters, we need to tear this place apart and see if we can figure out where they might've gone."

"Well, the dresser's full and so's his closet," Bobby said. "Everything's arranged neatly by size and color, no less. If he decided to flee, it doesn't look like he planned it."

Sheriff Carter looked in the window of Jewel's Café at 6:45 a.m. and didn't see any sign of Ivy. He walked inside and noticed about a dozen customers, and also Jewel Sadler standing next to Deke and Roscoe's table, filling their coffee cups.

Flint walked over to her. "Has Ivy come in for work this morning?"

"Not yet." Jewel said, glancing up at the clock. "It's not like that girl to be late either."

"I was hoping she was here."

"Is something wrong, Sheriff?"

Flint lowered his voice. "Ivy went out with Bill at eight last night and said she wouldn't be late. No one's heard from her since, and she's not at Bill's. It was a long shot, but I was hoping she might show up for work."

"Well, she hasn't. It's hard for me to believe that girl wouldn't call. She's been extremely responsible."

"Has she seemed worried about anything lately?" Flint said. "Or acted out of character?"

"It's hard to say. Ivy's been dealing with sad things since she started working for me, what with Lu's death and all, and then the shooting. But one thing I do know: She's responsible. Never been late. Never left early. Never been anything but reliable. For her not to be here without calling is definitely out of the ordinary."

Flint sighed. "Yeah, I was afraid of that."

"Is there anything I can do?"

"Thanks, Jewel, but I don't think so. My department and the feds are all over it."

"Do you think something's happened to her?"

"I think it's best if we just stick to what we know. If you hear from her, would you call me right away?"

"Of course I will."

Flint was just about to leave when Deke motioned him with his finger. "I seen Ziwicki's service van last night just before nine. I remember 'cause I was headin' for the bed when it went by, right under the streetlight."

"Could you tell if Ivy Griffith was with him?"

"Wasn't nobody in the passenger seat."

"Say what?" Roscoe put his hand to his ear.

"Hold yer horses," Deke hollered. "I'm not talkin' to you!"

"You sure, Deke?" Flint said. "This is really important."

"Sure as anybody can be."

"Which way was the van going?"

"Up the mountain."

Flint nodded. "Okay, thanks."

Brandon Jones sat at his computer, his eyelids heavy, when Jake Compton came in his office and shut the door.

"You're here early," Jake said.

"I couldn't sleep. Figured I might as well get something done."

"Elam just called and told me what's been going on," Jake said. "I can't believe Ivy's missing."

"It's weird, all right."

"Well, don't feel as if you have to work all day. I'm sure you're exhausted."

"I'm fine." Brandon stared at the keyboard, wishing Jake would leave. "I'll have this report you wanted before lunch."

"Actually, I have something much more pressing on my mind."

Brandon exhaled audibly. "Jake, I hope this isn't about Buzz because I'm done talking to you about my private business."

"I came to apologize," Jake said. "I was wrong not to give you an explanation, and I'd like to do that now if you'll give me your attention for a few minutes."

Brandon looked up at him and saw his face was flushed.

Jake folded his hands between his knees. "This is a difficult conversation I'm about to have with you. I've never had it with anyone else—not even Suzanne."

Brandon turned and faced Jake, surprised at the change in his tone.

"When I started as camp administrator, Buzz was a private ski instructor looking to earn extra money to start his own white-water operation. Elam hired him part-time to help with maintenance projects at the camp. Suzanne couldn't stand Buzz, but I overlooked his character flaws because he was my free pass to the slopes on my day off."

"Then why fault me for doing the same thing?" Brandon said.

Jake held up his palms. "Just hear me out. One day I got an e-mail from Buzz with the filthiest porn you can imagine. I was shocked, but instead of deleting it the way you did, I got curious and explored the website. Long story short, I got hooked and found myself looking at porn almost every day—and on numerous websites. Not only did it become an obsession, but it affected my relationship with Suzanne. After a while, she wasn't enough for me..."

Jake's voice cracked, and it was several seconds before he could talk again. Finally he said, "Seeing all that stuff made me hungry for more. I entertained sexual fantasies about other women, but I never acted on any of it.

"Then one day on our way to the slopes, Buzz pulled in the driveway of a chalet-style house and told me there was someone he wanted me to meet. I had no idea what was coming, but the minute the door opened, a gorgeous redhead was all over me. I didn't even try to resist. She was everything I had imagined and more."

"Jake, you don't have to tell me all this. I—"

"Just hear me out." Jake held up his palm and continued. "Buzz disappeared with some scantily clad brunette, and I went upstairs with the redhead. When Buzz and I finally left, he suggested that the four of us could enjoy some fun *together*. I was already so guilt ridden about what I had done that I told Buzz I wasn't going to see him *or* her anymore. He laughed and tried to tell me that it was just all that churchy guilt that was holding me back—that this kind of thing was good for my marriage. I didn't care what he said. All I could think about was how I was going to look Suzanne in the eyes. I knew my secret was safe as long as I didn't tell Buzz's wife what was going on. But I've lived in fear every day since."

Brandon shook his head. "How could you let it go that far?"

"I never intended to. I figured as long as the porn stayed in my head, I could control it. But my first mistake was taking that first look. Next thing I knew I was addicted, and when I had a chance to act on it, I did. So instead of my Christian values rubbing off on Buzz, I ended up in *his* filthy pit." Jake put his face in his hands.

"No wonder you were worried about me."

Jake nodded. "I just know what a stronghold it is. I didn't want you to fall into the same trap, but I was ashamed to admit to you what I'd done. By the grace of God, I've never looked at porn since. Any time I'm tempted, all I have to do is remember how awful I felt when I left that house, knowing I'd betrayed Suzanne. But I've never had the courage to tell her what happened. I'm so afraid she'll leave me..."

Jake broke down and wept.

Brandon got up and pulled his chair over next to Jake's. "It took guts to come clean with me. You're a good man, Jake. Yes, you made a big mistake, but it's not who you are. It's something you did."

"How can you separate the two?"

"Well, God does. If our sin defined us, we'd have no hope. Isn't that what Jesus came to fix?"

Jake wiped his eyes and looked at Brandon. "Then why am I not fixed?"

"One of my Bible teachers used to say, 'To fall down is not dead.' What you did isn't unforgivable. Take that sin to the cross, leave it there, and stop carrying the guilt."

"I realize I'll never be free of it unless I confess what I've done to Suzanne. I've been putting it off for two years. I guess it's time."

"You two have a strong marriage."

"I can only hope it's strong enough."

Flint Carter stood talking with Nick Sanchez in Bill Ziwicki's living room as the team continued to search the house. One of the FBI agents came and stood next to Nick, a stack of yellow papers in his hand.

"Sir, I found something interesting—receipts for the shooting range over in Mt. Bryon. Looks like Ziwicki's been frequenting the place for quite a while."

Nick smiled. "Well, well, well. Seems Mr. Ziwicki handles more than rifles after all. Find out what."

"Yes, sir. I'm on it."

"Hey, looky what I found," Bobby said. "A list of Ziwicki's clients. There's an asterisk beside two of them—both mountain cabins that need to be cleaned just before the owners come for the summer. One's empty till June 15 and the other till July 1, and we can assume Ziwicki has the keys."

"Let me see that." Nick took the folder from Bobby and perused it. "Good work, Lieutenant. This could be where they're hiding. At least it's a start. Can you tell from the addresses where these cabins are?"

"Not really, other than somewhere on Tanner Ridge," Bobby said. "We'll have to get a map and figure out exactly where. Some of the mountain roads are tricky."

"Well, what are we waitin' for?" Flint glanced at Bobby and then at Nick. "Let's go check it out."

Ivy Griffith sat at the pine table, her hands tied behind her, and let Bill Ziwicki spoon-feed her scrambled eggs, bacon, and toast. She had tried resisting, insisting she wasn't hungry, but that seemed to anger him.

"Here you go," Bill said. "One more bite."

Ivy opened her mouth, wishing she could pick up the iron skillet, whack him with it, and steal the van.

"I'll get the cabin all cleaned up for you today," he said. "Then I'll get you moved into the bedroom."

Ivy shook her head and spoke with her mouth full. "I don't want the bedroom."

"Sweetheart, you can't sleep in that old chair till July. And we need to start thinking about where we want to make our home. What do you think about Albuquerque?"

"I want to live with my son at my parents' home. That's where I belong."

Bill smiled and tilted her chin toward him. "Wrong. You belong with me."

No way, sicko!

"I'm going to make you so happy," Bill said. "Of course we won't be able to get married legally under the circumstances. But I've got a beautiful white dress picked out for you for when the time is right."

"Bill, I'm not ready to get married!"

"You will be."

"Not like this."

He smiled. "Relax. I just need to get your thinkin' straightened out. I've hardly thought of anything else since the first time I kissed you. It's so obvious we were meant to be together."

"I need to be with Montana."

"I'll figure out a way to get him later. We need to adjust to each other first." Bill took a sip of coffee. "You realize this wouldn't have been possible until I got rid of Pete? It was obvious you were attracted to me but couldn't break the hold he had on you. That just wasn't fair. I had to free you."

Ivy wondered why he kept explaining over and over his reason for killing Pete. "If you care so much about me, why didn't you ask me what *I* wanted?"

"Because you were confused. Pete was controllin' your mind. You couldn't see it, but I did. Some day you'll thank me."

"Don't you ever feel bad that you took three lives?"

"Not if I get to spend the rest of my life with you. That's all I'm livin' for."

38

BRANDON JONES WALKED in the front door of his house just before ten and found Kelsey sitting at her sewing machine, making a new shower curtain for the bathroom.

"Any news about Ivy?" he said.

Kelsey nodded. "Carolyn called a few minutes ago and said she and Elam were going over to the church to pray with Pastor Myers, that the authorities are beginning to think Ivy was somehow involved with Bill in the shooting. She didn't go into detail, and she asked me to tell you but to keep it between us for now."

"That's a horrible thought. I wonder if that's why you've felt led to pray for her?"

Kelsey shook her head. "I don't know. But Ivy doesn't strike me as bad enough or bold enough to be involved in something like that."

Brandon's conscience seemed to throb in the silence that followed, and he knew he had to say what was on his heart.

"Honey, can we change the subject for a few minutes? There's something I need to talk to you about."

Kelsey turned and looked up at him. "Sure. What's up?"

"Why don't we go sit at the kitchen table?"

Brandon followed Kelsey out to the kitchen and sat across from her at the table, his hands folded in front of him. "First of all, you'll be happy to know I'm not going to be hanging out with Buzz anymore."

"Good. Did he make you mad?"

"I'm afraid it's worse than that. He's into pornography, and he's cheating on Maggie." Brandon breathed in slowly and exhaled. "And I lied to you. He doesn't respect my Christian values and isn't any less crass around me than he is with the other guys."

Brandon told her that Buzz had sent him an e-mail with a porn link, and how funny Buzz thought it was—and how upset Jake was when he discovered it in Brandon's delete box.

"I can't believe you didn't tell me!"

"I was mad at Jake for reading my mail and trying to pressure me into telling you. He felt that if I was hanging out with Buzz, I should be accountable to you. I knew he was right, but I didn't want to fight with you about it. I thought it was going to be a one-time thing. Unfortunately, it wasn't."

Brandon felt the blood rush to his face as he told Kelsey about his having waited in the truck at the condo, unaware of what Buzz and his girlfriend were doing inside.

"I can't believe you would even speak to him after he tricked you like that!" Kelsey said. "Much less go rafting with him!"

"I told him in no uncertain terms never to put me in that situation again. I guess I thought he would back off, but after the last time I was with him, it's obvious he's going to keep pushing the envelope." Brandon told her about Buzz passing the porn picture around the dinner table at Rogue's, just waiting for his reaction. "The guy's a complete sleaze."

"Then it's true. Ivy did see Buzz at that tavern with another woman?"

Brandon shrugged. "I don't know about that. But I know he's into some really dark stuff. Jake's known about it a long time because he had a similar experience with Buzz, but he didn't actually spell it out until this morning. I knew I had to talk to you and tell you everything. I can't be around Buzz anymore."

"And Maggie knows nothing about this?"

"Supposedly not. But I don't see how she can be that naïve.

Buzz is hardly subtle about anything. I just don't think it's my place to run to Maggie with this."

"Well, someone should." Kelsey's eyes welled. "I can't believe you kept this from me. I thought we shared everything, and it makes me wonder what else you aren't telling me."

"Nothing. I promise." Brandon put his hand on hers. "I'm sorry, honey. If I had seen where it was going, I would've put a stop to it much sooner."

"I told you Buzz was trouble."

"I know you did, and I should've listened." Brandon thought back on Jake's confession, grateful that he wasn't facing Kelsey with something as awful as that. "Honey, I just need to know we're okay and that you forgive me. I promise that from now on I won't keep secrets from you. I realize that one of the best safeguards for me is to be open with you about everything so I won't cross the line."

Ivy Griffith sat on the front steps of the cabin, her eyes closed and her wrists and ankles bound, and tried to imagine Jesus sitting there with her. She was aware of Bill running the vacuum cleaner inside, the noonday sun warming her head, and pine trees scenting the chilly breeze.

She wondered if her parents thought she and Bill had run off together—or if the authorities had convinced them that she and Bill had planned the shooting and were on the run.

Lord, don't let my parents give up on me. Ivy had the most awful feeling that they might be so disappointed and angry that they wouldn't even bother looking.

She heard the vacuum go off and felt the muscles in her neck tighten. A minute later Bill came outside and sat on the step next to her, much too close for her liking.

"All done," he said. "The bedroom's clean as a whistle, and it's all yours."

I'm not going in there! "Why don't you untie me so I can make us soup and grilled cheese sandwiches for lunch? That's a good way for me to start feeling at home."

"I'm not sure your mind's thinkin' right yet."

"I'd really like to cook for you." Ivy turned to him. "Come on, Bill. We've got to start trusting each other."

"It would be nice to have you enjoyin' the kitchen. Can I trust you to behave?"

Bill stroked her arm, and her skin turned to gooseflesh. She forced herself not to recoil.

"Of course," she said. "I don't want to be tied up anymore. What kind of a partnership is that? You don't want me to feel inferior, do you?"

"I never said you were inferior. I don't think that."

"Well, that's what it feels like when you're holding me here like a prisoner. If we're ever going to start living like a couple, I need to be free."

"You won't run away?"

"No. Cross my heart. I just want to start feeling like the other half of this partnership. Let me start by fixing lunch for you."

Bill studied her face for several seconds. "Okay, but if you try to run, I'll have to tie you to the bed. I'm not losin' you now—not after all I've done so we can be together." Bill took his pocketknife and cut the ropes from her ankles and then her wrists.

"Thanks, that's so much better." Ivy looked out at the dense forest of pines and aspens and fought the impulse to make a run for it.

Carolyn Griffith looked up at the hawk soaring high above Woodlands Community Church as Elam pulled the Suburban into the parking lot. The bright blue sky was dotted with cloud puffs, and the gold cross on the steeple looked like a fireball in the morning sun.

"What are we supposed to tell Montana if Ivy's not home by the time he gets out of school?" she said.

Elam reached over and took her hand. "The truth, honey. We don't know why Ivy left, but we know she's with Bill. All he needs is to feel abandoned by his mother. I'm committed to not letting that happen."

Carolyn shook her head. "I'll never believe Ivy and Bill conspired to kill Pete, Reg, and Denny. I don't care what that arrogant FBI agent said."

"I'm not buying it either. Ivy's no killer. And she sure didn't prance back in here after ten years away and pull off a flawless triple homicide with less than a month to plan it. It's total bunk. And I don't believe she knows anything about Joe Hadley's death either."

Carolyn wiped a tear off her cheek. "I just wanted her to have a second chance to get her life together. I sure don't believe she would abandon her child and run off with a guy she hardly knows."

"I might've believed it five years ago, but not today. That girl is really trying. And Montana's a great kid." Elam smiled sheepishly as his gaze caught Carolyn's. "Okay, so I said I wasn't calling the boy by name till I was sure he was here to stay. What can I say? I'm fond of Montana. I like having a grandson, and I can't imagine life without him now."

"If Ivy's run off, we're the only relatives he's got."

"Ivy didn't run off," Elam said. "There has to be another explanation. Come on, let's go inside and wait for Pastor Myers."

Carolyn slid out of the SUV and walked up to the church entrance and pulled open the heavy wood door. She looked up at the familiar wall of stained glass behind the pulpit and wished she were here for the Sunday service instead of to beg God to bring Ivy back.

She stepped to the back pew and started to slide in when she spotted something. "Elam, look, that's Ivy ski jacket! And her purse!"

Carolyn grabbed the jacket and went through the pockets and found nothing but a pair of gloves. She picked up the purse and found the missing photograph, and then dumped the contents and started sifting through it. "There's nothing here to tell us where she went!"

Elam tugged at his mustache the way he always did when he was thinking intently about something. "Ivy must've gone out with Bill to confront him with the photograph. If she suspected him of being the shooter, there's no way she left with him voluntarily."

"What if he hurts her?" Carolyn started to cry. "How'd they even get in here on a Monday night?"

"Bill has the key to the church, honey. He has the cleaning contract, remember? My guess is they came here so they could talk privately. And it appears Bill didn't like what he heard. Let's pray he took Ivy to one of those cabins on his client list, so we might actually stand a chance of finding her before they leave the state. I'd better call Flint." Elam took his cell phone off his belt clip and keyed in the numbers.

"This is Sheriff Carter."

"Flint, it's Elam. You'll never guess what Carolyn and I just found."

Ivy picked up the iron skillet and decided it was too heavy and bulky for her to hit Bill in the head with it. She rubbed the inside of the skillet with margarine, sensing he was watching her every move.

"It's wonderful to be in the kitchen again." She turned and flashed him a phony smile and began to slice the Velveeta for grilled cheese sandwiches.

A few seconds later, Bill came up behind her and put his arms around her, his chin resting on her shoulder. "I still can't believe you're mine, and we're really going to be together. Sounds like you're finally startin' to think that way too."

Ivy's heart pounded so hard she could hardly catch her breath. She was all too aware of the risk she was taking by leading him to think she was ready to step into his sick make-believe world. What if she couldn't figure out a way to escape? What if he determined it was time for her to put on that white dress he had told her about?

"Bill, while I'm getting lunch ready, why don't you go see if you can get some music on that radio on the bookshelf?"

"Okay, good idea."

As soon as he walked across the creaky floor to the other side of the room, she searched around the stove, not surprised that all sharp objects were missing but desperate to find something she could use as a weapon.

Flint Carter held the phone away from his ear and let Elam holler for a minute, and then put the phone to his ear again. "I know how upsetting this must be. But you don't have any business being there if we find Ivy and Bill, whether she left willingly or was coerced. It could be dangerous."

"I'm willing to take that risk," Elam said.

"Well, I'm not. The best thing you and Carolyn can do now is go home and wait to hear from me. I'll call you as soon as I know something. We have teams headed to both cabins, but we have no way of knowing whether they went to either of them. It's just a hunch."

"I never thought you'd turn on Ivy this way."

Flint sighed. "Elam, I'm not turning on her. I'm just trying to get at the truth."

"You can't possibly believe Ivy conspired with Bill to kill Pete and those other boys."

"For crying out loud, Elam. I want Ivy to be innocent as much as you do. But we still need to talk to her about the Joe Hadley case. We have every reason to believe that these two cases are related—and that Ivy knows who did the killing in both instances."

"Don't you think she would have told you if she knew anything?"

"This is not the time to get into this. I need to go find her. Stay put and I'll call you when…Elam, you there?…Hello?…" Flint rolled his eyes and put his phone on his belt clip.

"I take it Mr. Griffith is steamed?" Nick Sanchez said.

"He's pretty hot, all right. I suppose any father would be if he thought his daughter was getting railroaded."

"And what do you think?"

Flint sighed. "I think I don't really like my job at the moment."

Ivy reached up to the spice rack and snatched two bottles and removed the dusty lids.

"What're you doin' over there?" Bill said.

"Oh, just adding some basil to the tomato soup."

She quickly pulled off the inside plastic lid on the second bottle and loosened the contents with the stem of a spoon, then carefully tucked the open bottle into the waistband of her jeans and pulled her sweater down over it.

The radio came on with loud static, and Bill fooled with the dial until a news station came in with clarity.

"Tanner County Sheriff Flint Carter refused to comment on whether William Ziwicki and Ivy Griffith are under investigation for the murder of Peter Barton, Reginald Morrison, and Dennis Richards in last month's shooting at the Phantom Hollow Lodge, but a source inside the sheriff's department told KTNR News that due to the couple's unexplained disappearance, they are now at the top of the suspect list.

"Officials are asking that anyone with information on the whereabouts of William Ziwicki or Ivy Griffith immediately contact the Tanner County Sheriff's Department or the FBI..."

Ivy glanced over her shoulder to make sure the keys to the van were still on the table by the door. She put the lid on the soup and turned the flame down to low. *Okay, Lord, here goes.*

She carefully removed the open spice bottle from her waistband and concealed it in her fist, then walked over and stood facing Bill, her heart pounding so loudly she was afraid he could hear it above the radio.

"Lunch is almost ready," she said.

Bill smiled and stroked her cheek. "Great. Guess you heard the feds are lookin' for us. They're wastin' their time. Nobody knows about this place."

Ivy held his gaze and tried to look pleasant. She would get only one chance to do this and couldn't afford to miss. She silently counted to three, then flung ground cayenne pepper into Bill's face.

He let out a shriek and started clawing at his eyes.

Ivy darted for the door, grabbed the keys off the table, and raced toward the van.

"What have you done to me?" Bill shouted as he stumbled after her. "Come back here! How could you betray me like this?"

Just as she got the van door open, Bill grabbed her arm and spun her around, his eyes inflamed and tearing. He tried to pry the keys from her fist. Ivy bit his finger with the ferocity of a pit bull, and he let go of her and shouted a string of curse words.

She climbed in the van and quickly locked the doors.

"I'll find you, Ivy!" he shouted as he banged on the driver's side window. "You belong to me! I love you! I've always loved you! We're meant to be together! I'll never let go of you! You're mine!"

Ivy turned the key, and the van made an awful grinding noise. She pressed the accelerator and turned the key again and again, and then stopped when she smelled gasoline, afraid she had flooded it.

Lord, please help me! I don't know what else to do.

Bill slammed his fist against the window, his face red and blotchy and his eyes nearly swollen shut.

"Open the door, Ivy! Or I swear I'm going to break this window and drag you out of there!"

She took her foot off the accelerator and again turned the key. The van started. She backed it up and stopped abruptly, then shifted into drive and eased onto the gravel driveway.

Bill clutched the door handle and ranted like a madman.

"Let go of the door! I'm leaving!" she shouted.

"I'll find you, Ivy! You can't escape me! We were meant to be together!"

Ivy pressed the accelerator harder than she meant to, kicking up a shower of gravel and leaving Bill in a heap about thirty yards back.

His desperate, mournful pleadings could be heard all the way to the paved road, and then faded to silence as Ivy turned and raced down the mountain toward freedom.

39

CAROLYN GRIFFITH STOOD at the picture window in the living room, her eyes fixed on nothing, her heart praying without ceasing. She was suddenly aware of someone's hand on her shoulder.

"Honey, you should come sit with us," Elam said. "It might be a long time before Flint calls back."

"That's okay. I just feel better watching and waiting. I'm sure Kelsey and Brandon will understand."

Elam gently massaged her shoulders. "I don't know that I can handle losing that girl again. Nearly killed me the first time. I keep wishing I'd told her how glad I was that she came home. And what a great kid Montana is."

Carolyn turned around, her eyes searching his. "You're talking as if you never expect to see her again."

"Now don't go putting words in my mouth. I just regret I didn't warm up to her faster, that's all. I've been doing a lot of soul-searching today. And I promised the Lord that when I see Ivy, I'm going to stop holding the past against her."

Carolyn's eyes welled. "I'm so glad, Elam. Ivy really needs you to accept her just as she is."

"I realize that now. I think my biggest problem is that I've always blamed myself for Ivy walking away from her faith. I should've put my foot down the minute she came home wearing

Pete Barton's ring. It was my job to protect her, and I feel as if I threw her to the wolves."

"You're being too hard on yourself. If you'll remember right, *I'm* the one who insisted she was mature enough to handle a steady boyfriend."

"But you left the final decision up to me. I didn't want to jeopardize my relationship with you and Ivy, so I allowed her to get involved with Pete. That set her up for a conflict of values that I know that creep took full advantage of."

"She was seventeen, Elam. She knew right from wrong."

He nodded. "Maybe so. But she wasn't strong enough to handle that kind of pressure. Just think how different her life might've been if she'd dated some nice kid from the youth group instead."

"Well, we'll never know. But Ivy desperately needs to know you love and accept her right now, regardless of her mistakes."

Elam's chin quivered, and he looked away. "I just want to tell her how much I love her. I want to be there for her."

Carolyn noticed his eyes had narrowed and seemed intent on something outside. "What are you looking at?"

"A car just turned into the drive. Probably Flint coming to give us an update." Elam moved closer to the window and watched as the vehicle moved closer and closer to the house. "Carolyn, that's not Flint's Explorer. It's Bill's van!"

Elam darted out the front door and down the porch steps, Carolyn close behind, and stood in the driveway, his neck craned, his gaze fixed on the van.

"Ivy's driving," Carolyn said. "I don't even see Bill."

"Me either." Elam took off running toward the van.

Carolyn resisted the urge to follow him, hoping that Ivy would see his concern as an indicator his heart was softening.

Suddenly, the van came to a stop and the driver's side door flung wide open. Ivy jumped out and ran wailing to her father's arms.

Flint Carter stood next to his squad car with Nick Sanchez while the FBI SWAT team surrounded a log cabin, which was visible through the pines about fifty yards down a gravel drive. Nick had just received word from the SWAT team that had gone to the other cabin that Bill and Ivy were not there, and it didn't appear they had been.

"From the looks of the rubber on the pavement," Nick said, "someone recently hightailed it out of here. Let's hope we're not too late." Nick put his walkie-talkie to his ear. "This is Sanchez, over…Copy that, Eagle Scout. Are you saying Ziwicki appears to be alone?…Yeah, copy that. Go in and get him. Out."

Nick looked over at Flint. "Ziwicki's in there, all right—bent over at the kitchen sink pouring water into his eyes. No sign of the Griffith girl."

Flint put his binoculars to his eyes and watched the SWAT team swarm the cabin and kick in the front door, and then heard shouts coming from inside. A minute later, a handcuffed Bill Ziwicki stumbled out the front door, his hair soaked and parts of his face looking red and blistered. His eyes appeared to be swollen shut. Two of Nick's agents escorted him down the gravel drive and put him into the backseat of an FBI vehicle.

Nick went over and talked to the leader of the SWAT team and then came back and stood next to Flint.

"Did he say anything?" Flint said.

"Just that he wants a lawyer. And that Griffith bit him and threw something in his eyes and stole his van."

Ivy Griffith sat between her parents at the kitchen table and recounted for her attorney, Brett Hewitt, the details of her relationship with Bill Ziwicki, beginning with the incident at Grinder's until she confronted Bill with the photograph and got him to admit that he had shot Pete, Reg, and Denny—and why. She also told Brett how obsessed Bill was with her, how he had kidnapped her and held her against her will, and how she had managed to escape.

Brett made a tent with his fingers. "You're innocent of any wrongdoing. I don't see you being charged with anything."

"I know," Ivy said. "But there's something else—something

I've needed to confess for a long, long time."

Ivy held her father's hand and told Brett what she had told her parents earlier: the truth about what had happened the afternoon Joe Hadley was killed. When she had finished, she exhaled a sigh of relief. *Thank You, Lord.*

"You can see why Carolyn and I called you," Elam said. "This thing is complicated."

Brett pursed his lips. "Not really. The murders are unrelated. Ziwicki shot the three guys because they trashed him and because he was obsessed with Ivy—certainly not to get even for Joe's murder. So let's get that straight from the get-go. Ziwicki's going down for the shooting. I don't want Ivy's name even mentioned in the same sentence with that scumbag. She has no responsibility whatsoever."

"But I do share some of the blame for Joe's murder." Ivy wiped the tears off her face. "I should've tried to stop it, and if I hadn't been high, I probably would've. Everything happened so fast, and I was in shock when I agreed not to tell. But when I realized later how much trouble we were in, I was too scared of going to jail to say anything. Pete kept reminding me that I was an accessory and that telling the sheriff would make my parents hate me, and then I'd have no one…" Ivy let out a sob and then stifled it, aware that her father had put his arm around her.

"Ivy, listen to me," Brett said. "I don't want you telling the authorities you were partly responsible for Joe Hadley's death."

"But I was."

"Technically, you had nothing to do with it."

Ivy shook her head. "Mr. Hewitt, I promised God if I got away from Bill, I would tell the truth about Joe's death—the whole truth. If I have to go to jail, then I will. But I'm not going to pretend I was innocent. Just think about what I put the Hadleys through because I didn't speak up."

Brett lifted his eyebrows and looked at Elam. "Maybe you and Carolyn can talk some sense into her."

"I don't think so. Ivy talked to us about this before we called you. She wants to pay her debt to society. I think it's up to her."

"And I want whatever's just," Ivy said. "I owe the Hadleys that much."

Brett threw up his hands and sat back in his chair. "It's a little hard to defend you if you're determined to be punished."

Ivy looked up at her father. "The only thing I'm determined to do is never *ever* again let anybody talk me into compromising what I know is right." Ivy looked over at Brett. "Not even you, Mr. Hewitt."

Elam shrugged. "Like I said, it's her call."

Brett exhaled loudly, then seemed to be thinking. "All right. I'll talk to the DA. Maybe we can arrive at some kind of plea agreement that will cleanse your conscience without making you pay for the murder you *didn't* commit but feel inordinately responsible for. The statute of limitations has expired on your failure to report a felony, so that's out. There's no statute of limitations on murder, but you really aren't guilty of murder. And there's no one to corroborate your story, one way or the other. Maybe the DA will let you plea out to a Class A misdemeanor instead." Brett pushed his glasses up higher on his nose. "Then again, I suppose we could waive the statute of limitations and plead you to the Failure to Report a Felony, even if it is too old to prosecute. But that's probably going to get you jail time."

"Well, that's what I deserve," Ivy said. "I'm not going to water down what I did just because I got away with it for ten years."

Carolyn turned and looked out the window. "Looks like the cavalry's arrived. I see three vehicles headed this way. One of them is Flint's."

Brett looked at Ivy, his gaze penetrating. "I'm not going to try to talk you out of your conviction. But for now, let me answer any questions. I want to talk to the district attorney's office before you give any statements to the authorities. I'll meet you at the jail and make bond for you, and you won't have to go beyond the booking room. If you'll just do as I say, I'll make sure you get to unburden yourself."

Brandon Jones helped Kelsey clear the dinner table, then went in the living room and sat in front of the fire just as the phone rang. A few minutes later Kelsey came and sat next to him on the couch.

"That was Carolyn on the phone," she said. "She wanted to thank us again for keeping Montana after school and to let us know that Bill Ziwicki confessed to the shooting and Ivy's kidnapping."

"The creep."

"He's a scary guy, all right. Carolyn also said Ivy's out on bail in the Hadley case, but won't let her attorney plea her out so she doesn't get jail time."

"Are you kidding? Why not?"

Kelsey tucked her hair behind her ear. "She really wants justice to be done—*and* she's recommitted her life to Christ."

Brandon smiled and threw back his head. "Amazing! Then your talk with her was totally a God thing. He really used you."

Kelsey nodded, her eyes brimming with tears. "Pretty humbling."

"If Ivy's walking with the Lord again, I wonder why she's hung up on paying for what she did."

"Carolyn said this isn't about guilt as much as Ivy's accepting responsibility for having done nothing to stop Joe's murder or to report it to the sheriff. Ivy wants the statute of limitations waived so she can be charged with failure to report a felony. She could get up to a year in jail."

Brandon sighed. "What a mess. Don't you wonder how people get themselves into such trouble?"

"After what you told me today, I'm surprised you have to ask."

"Touché." Brandon ran his thumb over the cross on his wedding band. "I've been thinking a lot about how risky it was to allow myself to be exposed to the stuff Buzz was into."

Kelsey rolled her eyes. "Do you think?"

"Jake tried to warn me when he first realized I was hanging out with Buzz. He said it's easier to get sucked into the darkness than to walk in the light. I didn't know exactly what he meant at the time, but I do now."

Kelsey put her arm around him. "I'm glad. I don't ever want us to have another conversation like the one we had this morning."

"Don't worry. I learned my lesson. The best way to avoid getting pulled into something we know is wrong is never to cross the line."

Kelsey poked him in the ribs. "Or do anything we'd be ashamed to tell our spouse."

Ivy knocked on Montana's door and then opened it. "May I come in?"

"Okay."

Ivy went over and sat on the side of the bed next to him, her hands folded in her lap. "It's been a very hard day, hasn't it? How are you doing?"

Montana shrugged, his lower lip quivering.

"Can you tell me what's bothering you the most?"

A tear trickled down Montana's cheek. He looked up at her, his puppy eyes brimming with tears. "If you go to jail, will I be an orphan?"

Ivy pulled him into her arms and choked back her own tears. "Oh, sweetie, no. I'll still be your mother. And you'll still be the most important person in my life. And you can stay right here with your grandparents and go to school. You can play with Ian and have adventures with Sasha and go do things with Brandon and Kelsey."

"How long will you be gone?"

"The judge will decide that. I know this is so hard for you, and I don't blame you if you're disappointed in me for keeping such an awful secret all those years. I'm certainly disappointed in myself. Mommy made a very bad decision that caused her to make lots of other bad decisions. You see, holding all that guilt inside caused me to get hooked on drugs to try to forget. And I couldn't take care of you when I was high."

Montana hugged her tighter. "That's okay. God sent Gramma Lu."

"Yes, He did. And she knew that the only way I would ever get over the guilt was to turn back to God. But I'd convinced myself that the wrong things I'd done were too bad to ever be forgiven. Of course, that's not true. Gramma Lu knew that and convinced me to come back here and tell the truth so I could get right with God again."

Montana drew back and cupped his hands around her face. "Do you think she knows you did?"

"I really do." Ivy's voice cracked, and she paused to regain her composure, determined to say what was on her heart. "I'll understand if you're angry with me. But I want you to remember something, so put on your big boy ears and listen carefully." Ivy looked into her son's eyes, which looked so much like Rusty's she almost smiled. "I would rather you be mad at Mommy for telling the truth than be proud of Mommy for living a lie. Do you understand?"

"Yeah, I get it. I think."

Ivy wet her thumb and wiped the tear streaks off Montana's cheeks.

"What's gonna happen to Bill?"

"He's going to prison for the rest of his life."

"Grandpa says his mind is sick. That he killed those three guys at your school thing you went to. And that he took you away last night and wouldn't let you come home."

"I'll tell you what—why don't we not think about all the unhappy things and just enjoy each other as long as we can?"

"Okay, you wanna hear me read?"

"Sure." Ivy reached over and tousled his hair, thinking there was nothing on earth she would rather do. "So what do you want to read to me?"

"*Green Eggs and Ham*," they said at the same time.

40

ON THURSDAY AFTERNOON, Ivy Griffith pulled her Jeep
Liberty into the parking lot of Woodlands Community Church,
her mind flashing back to Monday night's confrontation with Bill.
She wondered how he was handling being locked up—and if he
even realized how sick he was.

Ivy got out of the car and ambled across the courtyard and
through the wrought iron gate to the cemetery. She walked past
the guardian angel that marked baby Amy's grave and stopped in
front of the white cross in the back row. She stood for a moment,
sobered again by the sight of Lu's name engraved on the headstone.

"I finally did it, Lu. I asked God to forgive me and told the
sheriff the truth. But I guess you already know that." Just then a
slight breeze tickled Ivy's cheek, and she smiled. "I thought so."

She sat cross-legged on the ground and brushed her hands
across the soft blades of green grass that had shot up through the
brown crunch.

"Did I ever thank you for saving my life? God used you so
powerfully, and I didn't even realize how much until I recommitted my life to Him. I'm so grateful to you, especially for being
everything to Montana that I couldn't…" The words seemed
caught in her throat, and she paused for a moment and considered
what a blessing her son had turned out to be. "He's doing really

well. You'd be so proud of him. He gave his heart to Jesus, and now we both know we'll see you again. That'll make missing you so much easier.

"I never understood what it was you saw in me that made you care so much. You said when you looked at me, you saw light under the door, and that when I figured out what that meant I'd feel you smiling in heaven."

Ivy leaned back on her hands, her gaze fixed on a gold-rimmed cloud that had hidden the sun. "Well, you must be smiling because I think I get it. You saw the light of Jesus in me, even when I thought I had pushed God out. You knew He was in my heart and would never let go of me—not ever. And that someday I would realize that and let Him love me again."

Ivy blinked away the tears, then sat in the stillness of the spring afternoon and drank in the magnificence of the San Juan Mountains, mighty and steadfast, like the God who made them. She thought about how dramatically the course of her life had been changed in the past couple days—and tried not to worry about tomorrow morning when she would stand before the judge.

41

AT ELEVEN O'CLOCK Friday morning, Ivy Griffith stood before Judge Wilbert Stanton, her legs wobbly, her heart doing flip-flops—and the peace of God buffering her from the blow she was about to receive. She answered each question the judge asked her, just as she had practiced with Brett Hewitt, and then pleaded guilty to the misdemeanor charge of Failure to Report a Felony.

Judge Stanton folded his hands and seemed to study her. "Miss Griffith, do you have anything to say before I pronounce sentence?"

"Just that I'm very sorry I didn't tell the truth about Joe Hadley's death right after it happened. My silence has caused his parents a great deal of grief, and I'd give anything to go back and do things differently. But I'm ready to accept responsibility and the punishment I deserve."

"Very well, then. I hereby sentence you to twelve months in the Tanner County Jail, your sentence to commence immediately."

The judge took off his glasses, the look in his eyes holding her captive. "Miss Griffith, it is highly unusual for a defendant not to accept a lesser plea when the DA's office has offered probation, a fine, and community service in lieu of incarceration. And even more so since the statute of limitations has run out, and you were advised you couldn't be prosecuted anyway. I must say I find your desire to pay your debt to society commendable, albeit uncommon, considering you will have a criminal record from this day forward.

"I truly hope that after you've served your sentence, you'll reenter society with a clean slate and make something of yourself. Any young woman as determined as you are to set things right has enough grit to turn her life around. I hereby order you into the custody of the sheriff. Case adjourned."

A female jail deputy came over and escorted Ivy out of the courtroom and into a hallway and patted her down.

Just as the deputy took the handcuffs off her belt, Ivy spotted her parents and Montana standing just a few yards away. "Before you cuff me, would it be okay if I said good-bye to my family—or at least my little boy?"

The deputy smiled. "Sure. It's not the normal procedure, but I've done it before. Come on." The deputy stepped across the hall and opened the door to an empty room. "Wait here."

Ivy stood with her arms around her mother and held her tightly, not wanting to let go. "I love you, Mom. I don't know how I can ever thank you for everything you've done—and for not making me feel like a failure."

"Oh, honey," Carolyn Griffith said, "I've never thought that. You just took a wrong turn and lost your way. You're back on track. And once you get this behind you, life is just going to get better and better."

"Take good care of Montana..." Ivy's voice trailed off and her vision went blurry.

Carolyn nodded, then let go of her and stepped back.

Ivy took in a slow, deep breath and let it out. *Lord, give me the right words. This is so hard.*

She sat in a chair and pulled Montana into her lap, determined not to upset him by getting emotional. "Promise me you'll never ever forget how much I love you."

"I won't," he said. "I'll already be eight when you get out, right?"

"Well, here's the deal. Prisoners who do everything they're supposed to can get two days credit for each day served. That means I could be out twice as fast—in just *six* months."

"How long is that?"

Ivy took his fingers and counted out each month. "May, June, July, August, September, October. Grandma will show you on the calendar, and you can mark off the days. But you can come visit me every week." She wet her finger and wiped a smudge off his chin. "Grandma and Grandpa will take good care of you. And if you ask Jesus to help you get through each day, He will. That's what Mommy's going to do."

Montana played with the zipper on his ski jacket. "Grandpa's taking me to Vacation Bible School. And fishing. He said Brandon knows how to catch trout at this really cool stream he's taking us to."

Ivy hugged him tighter, as if that would stop the tears that threatened to spill down her cheeks. "Grandpa told me how much he's looking forward to spending time with you. You're going to have a really fun summer."

Ivy rested her cheek against her son's and held him for a few moments, whispering a prayer of protection. She helped him off her lap, and then rose to her feet, her gaze catching her father's.

Elam Griffith glanced over at Montana. "Would you take Grandma outside and let me have a minute alone with your mom?"

Montana took Carolyn's hand and walked over to the door, then turned around. "Grandma said I can sleep in your bed while you're gone, and then I won't get so lonesome." Montana stood for a moment, his puppy eyes brimming with tears, then ran back to Ivy and threw his arms around her. "I love you, Mom!"

"I love you, too. So much."

Ivy felt her throat and chest tighten and held back the tears until Montana left the room with her mother. Then she broke down in her father's arms.

A minute passed before either of them said anything.

"I'm so sorry, Dad. It seems like all I've ever done is shame this family."

Elam drew back and brushed away the hair that stuck to her wet cheeks. "I'm not ashamed of you, Ivy. I'm proud. This is probably the most courageous thing you've ever done, and I know it cost you a lot. Most people would've taken the easy way out. But you refused to make excuses for yourself, even though it meant jail time. That tells me a lot about what you're made of."

"I don't have any doubt that God's forgiven me. And I hope the Hadleys will eventually. I just knew I couldn't downplay what I did. It was important to tell the whole truth. I spent ten years doing the exact opposite. Never again."

"Well, if what Brett told us holds true, you'll be back home and settled before Thanksgiving." He took his thumbs and wiped the tears off her cheeks. "Maybe the time will go faster than you think."

There was a knock at the door, and the jail deputy poked her head in the room. "Are you about ready, Miss Griffith?"

"Could we have just a couple more minutes?" Elam said.

The deputy nodded and gently closed the door.

"Whew!" Elam pretended to wipe the sweat off his brow. "I thought I'd blown my big chance."

"For what?"

"To do something I haven't done since you were fourteen." He cleared the chairs from the front of the room, then stepped back, a twinkle in his eye, and took a bow. "May I have this dance, mademoiselle?"

Ivy stood dumbfounded, the corners of her mouth twitching. "This is kind of weird, Dad. Are you serious?"

"Absolutely." Elam held out his hands, as if to beckon her. "There's only been one princess in my life. You didn't think I'd waltz with just anybody, did you?"

Ivy put one hand on his shoulder and the other hand in his, and for a few awkward moments they stood looking at each other.

"Let's don't ever lose each other again, Ivy. When you're in that jail, serving your sentence, don't ever doubt my love for you—not for a second."

"Not even when you see me in that awful orange jumpsuit? Or

when everyone in town is talking about me?"

"Especially not then." Elam's chin quivered and his eyes glistened. "I love you, sweetheart—just the way you love Montana. And I can honestly say I've never been prouder to be your father. Now…would you grant your old dad this one request before that lady deputy comes back in here and ruins everything?"

"She's going to think we're nuts."

"Too bad." His eyes smiled as he began humming that familiar waltz Ivy remembered from years ago but still didn't know the name of. "Come on, honey. Hum the tune with me. I know you remember it."

Ivy listened for a moment and then began to hum along, at first softly and then louder and louder, as she whirled in perfect step with her father. She gave no thought to past or future, but rather entered wholly into the present, experiencing for a second time that week the cleansing, liberating, inexplicable power of grace.

AFTERWORD

"Be self-controlled and alert. Your enemy the
devil prowls around like a roaring lion
looking for someone to devour."

1 PETER 5:8

Dear friends,

In today's culture where moral absolutes are rapidly disintegrating, it isn't easy for believers to keep both feet planted on a biblical foundation, especially when we're continually exposed to people and situations in direct conflict with God's Word. It's so important that we remain keenly aware of the ever-present danger of compromise, because the enemy of our souls knows only too well where each of us is most vulnerable.

Compromises can start out small and escalate into tragedies with heartbreaking repercussions. At the very least, they weaken our spiritual defenses and our witness. And there seems to be no end to the excuses we invent to justify the unbiblical choices we make:

"So what if I took a few pens and office supplies from work? Everybody does it. They don't pay us enough anyway."

"Abstinence isn't realistic for my generation since we have to wait a lot longer to get married than our parents did."

"I know soap operas can be raunchy, but I need a harmless escape from my boring life."

"Looking at pornography isn't the same as cheating on my wife. I've never laid a hand on another woman."

"So I sold that couple more than they needed. Okay, a lot more. But they can afford it, and I needed the commission to pay bills."

"I called in sick so I can catch up on things at home. Big deal. I have more sick leave than I'll ever use, and I needed a mental break."

Friends, compromises can seem perfectly legitimate to our carnal minds. That's why it's so important for believers to "put on the mind of Christ." Our best defense against compromising is to be grounded in the Word so our conscience stays tender and to be in fellowship with trusted believers who will hold us accountable.

Just as bad company corrupts good character, good company can help to grow it. The time to decide we're going to stand firm is before we're faced with moral decisions, not in the heat of the moment. And not in the company of people whose values conflict with ours. Staying faithful to God's Word doesn't just happen. It takes forethought and resolve—and ever-present vigilance.

I enjoyed writing this first book in the Phantom Hollow Series and hope you'll join me in book two, *Never Look Back,* where we will meet up again with the Griffiths and the Joneses and also some interesting new characters who will take us through a maze of twists and turns. As always, it promises to be a page-turner!

I love hearing from my readers. You can write to me through my website at www.kathyherman.com. I read and respond to every e-mail and greatly value your input.

In His love,

Kathy Herman

DISCUSSION GUIDE

1. Do you agree that the propensity to compromise biblical principles is an ever-present danger for believers of all ages? In American culture today, what are some popular beliefs and behaviors that conflict with God's Word? Do you think many Christians have compromised on these beliefs and behaviors? If so, in what ways?

2. Do you agree with Jake Compton's comment, "It's easier to get sucked into the darkness than to walk in the light"? Do you think this can apply even to mature Christians? Can you think of examples of Christian leaders who compromised their values and lost their witness? Do you think they might have avoided the compromise had they remained in close fellowship with other believers who held them accountable?

3. Do you agree that bad company corrupts good character? Do you think a believer can be bad company for another believer? Do you think peer pressure is something only children and teens face, or do you think adults are equally vulnerable? Which generation of Christians do you think is most vulnerable to peer pressure? Do you think males and females are affected differently by peer pressure? If so, explain.

4. How might things have been different for Ivy Griffith if she had made the decision to stand by her Christian convictions *before* she entered into a close relationship with Pete? Do you think Pete was responsible for Ivy's bad choices? If you think compromising often leads to even more compromising, why do you think that is so?

5. Do you think Elam Griffith compromised 2 Corinthians 6:14 ("Do not be yoked together with unbelievers. For what do righteousness and wickedness have in common? Or what fellowship can light have with darkness?") when he gave in to Ivy and allowed her to pursue a steady relationship with an unbeliever? If you had been Ivy's father or mother, how would you have handled the situation? Do you think parents should ever compromise a scriptural principle to keep from angering or disappointing their children?

6. Have you ever known a believer who acted as Brandon Jones did and used the ideal of winning someone to Christ to justify a relationship he or she knew was unacceptable? Do you think Christians are ever called to go along with someone's sinful lifestyle in order to win that person to Christ?

7. Have you ever compromised what you knew was right and found a way to justify your wrong behavior? If so, did you feel guilty at the time? Or did the conviction come later?

8. Can you identify some of the subtle moral compromises believers routinely make? Can you identify the more serious compromises? Do you think a lesser compromise is any less offensive to God?

9. In which situations do you find it most difficult to stand firm in your convictions? In these situations, is the difficulty you experience self-inflicted or is it brought on by the conflicting values of someone else? If you could see Jesus standing next to you, would you have the same response?

10. Based on 2 Timothy 3:16–17 ("All Scripture is God-breathed and is useful for teaching, rebuking, correcting and training in righteousness, so that the man of God may be thoroughly equipped for every good work"), would you say that having a thorough knowledge of God's Word is a valuable weapon for

not succumbing to the lure of compromise? Do you think if Ivy, Elam, Brandon, and Jake had daily put on the full armor of God as outlined in Ephesians 6, they might have been equipped to respond differently in their precarious circumstances? Would you? If your answer is yes, explain why.

11. Since every believer's commission is to take the Good News to unbelievers, and God clearly does not want us to live our lives isolated from them, can you think of some boundaries that believers should set before they go out into the "world"? In other words, how can we be in the world and yet keep ourselves "unspotted from the world"?

12. Who was your favorite character in this story? If you could meet that person, what would you like to say to him or her?

13. Has what you think and feel been affected by this story? What will you take away from this story?

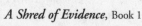

A Quiet Little Seaport Town...
So You Think!

A Shred of Evidence, Book 1

Ellen Jones stumbles onto information too alarming to keep to herself. Will she become enmeshed in speculation and gossip—or can she become a catalyst for truth and healing?

Eye of the Beholder, Book 2

Guy Jones becomes enamored with his newfound status in a prestigious law firm and grows increasingly embarrassed by Ellen's needy friends. Their marriage is on the rocks, and Guy's integrity on the line!

All Things Hidden, Book 3

How do you let go of a past that won't let go of you? That's what Ellen Jones would like to know. The consequences of past mistakes don't just disappear...

Not by Chance, Book 4

Thirty-year-old Brandon Jones arrives at his parents' house burned out, jobless, and now fiancée-less. As he struggles to find his life's purpose, he discovers the pieces of his life are not by chance.

The Seaport Suspense series
by KATHY HERMAN

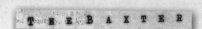 

ANOTHER ONE OF

KATHY HERMAN'S

PAGE-TURNING NOVELS!

Poor Mrs. Rigsby

Nursing Assistant Sally Cox is about as happy to be at Walnut Hills Nursing Center as the patients are. But it's work or starve now that her husband has found a younger companion. Sally's new crowd skews toward the elderly—ninety-year-old Elsie Rigsby, for instance, whose dementia comes and goes with her gold-digging son and grandson's visits. Elsie's not going to tell those vultures where she stashed her money. Still, she's not getting any younger, and someone besides her needs to know. Three deaths later, is anyone watching Sally?

Available NOW!